THE INCENSE GAME

ALSO BY LAURA JOH ROWLAND

THE INCENSE GAME

Laura Joh Rowland

MINOTAUR BOOKS
NEW YORK

THE INCENSE GAME. Copyright © 2012 by Laura Joh Rowland. All rights reserved. Printed in the United States of America. For information, address St. Martin's Press, 175 Fifth Avenue, New York, N.Y. 10010.

www.minotaurbooks.com

The Library of Congress has cataloged the hardcover edition as follows:

Rowland, Laura Joh.
    The incense game : a novel of feudal Japan / Laura Joh Rowland.—1st ed.
        p. cm.
    ISBN 978-0-312-65853-3 (hardcover)
    ISBN 978-1-250-01528-0 (e-book)
    1. Murder—Investigation—Fiction.   2. Sano, Ichirō (Fictitious character)—Fiction.
3. Police—Japan—Fiction.   4. Police spouses—Fiction.   5. Earthquakes—Fiction.
6. Tokyo (Japan)—Fiction.   7. Japan—History—Genroku period, 1688–1704—
Fiction.   I. Title.
    PS3568.O934153 2012
    813'.54—dc23

                                                                    2012024300

ISBN 978-1-250-03111-2 (trade paperback)

Minotaur books may be purchased for educational, business, or promotional use. For information on bulk purchases, please contact Macmillan Corporate and Premium Sales Department at 1-800-221-7945, extension 5442, or write specialmarkets@macmillan.com.

First Minotaur Books Paperback Edition: August 2013

10 9 8 7 6 5 4 3 2 1

To my fellow survivors of natural disasters,
and in memory of those who lost their lives

Historical Note

ON DECEMBER 31, 1703, a powerful earthquake struck a vast area of Japan that included Edo. The castle, the city, and many towns in outlying provinces sustained catastrophic damage. The death toll is difficult to quantify, due in part to the fact that the Tokugawa regime kept secret the number of its people who were killed. Sources estimate that several thousand people died in Edo and more than 100,000 in the entire earthquake zone. Casualties were concentrated along the coast, where a giant tsunami washed villages out to sea, flooded rivers, and drowned inland towns. The earthquake was one of the worst natural disasters in world history.

The Incense Game is my story of what could have happened before, during, and after the earthquake.

Real, historical characters in the novel include the shogun, his friend Yanagisawa Yoshiyasu, his nephew Ienobu, his mother Lady Keisho-in, and Lord Hosokawa. Yanagisawa did have a son named Yoshisato. Ienobu actually was a hunchback and the shogun's heir apparent. Lady Keisho-in did have a close relationship with a priest named Ryuko, who was a spiritual advisor to her and the shogun. Lord Hosokawa, the *daimyo* of Higo Province, played a role in the famous tale of the forty-seven *rōnin*, the subject of my previous book (*The Rōnin's Mistress*). Everyone else is fictional.

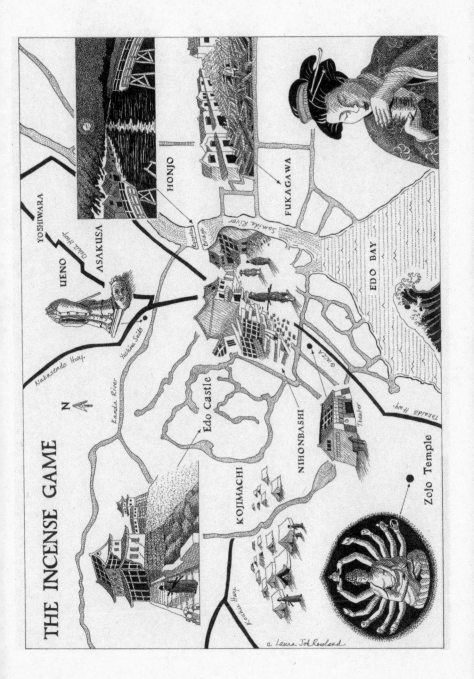

THE INCENSE GAME

Prologue

*Edo, Month 11, Genroku Year 16
(Tokyo, December 1703)*

THE EARTH TREMBLED as if a massive, restless dragon were uncoiling beneath the city. On the black expanse of the Sumida River, the moon's reflection shivered. Thousands of houses shifted, groaning and creaking. Wind chimes tinkled in the icy air. At two hours before midnight, the few soldiers patrolling the streets reined in their skittish horses. Sleepers tossed, troubled by bad dreams.

In a small house in the Nihonbashi merchant district, three women looked up as the tatami floor where they knelt shook under them and ceramic vessels on shelves rattled. The square white lantern above them swayed, casting eerie patterns of light and shadow across their anxious faces, made up with white rice-powder and red rouge. Breath held, the women didn't speak.

The shaking stopped.

They released their breath.

Earth tremors were common. Everyone lived with the fear of the great quakes that devastated Japan at unpredictable intervals and went about their business in the meantime.

The oldest woman turned her attention to the items arranged on a mat before her. Her name was Usugumo. In her forties, she had the sleekness of a cat, her face molded from triangular planes. Silver streaks gleamed in her upswept hair. She picked up metal chopsticks, removed a white-hot coal from a brazier, and dropped it in a celadon ceramic bowl filled with ash. While she mounded the ash over the charcoal, pierced a hole in the mound, and drew a pattern of lines on it, she flicked her narrow-eyed glance at the other women.

They were sisters, in their twenties. The younger was prettier, the elder more expensively dressed. Usugumo could feel hostility between them. She used tweezers to place a mica plate above the hole in the ash, then picked up three origami packets made of pale green, gold-flecked paper. She shuffled the packets, opened one, and removed a little ball of incense, which she set on the mica plate. Smoke tinged with the aromas of fruit, wood, musk, and spices arose from the bowl as the incense burned. Usugumo sensed anticipation in the air and a tension at odds with the serene ritual. The other women gazed down at the paper, brushes, ink, and inkstones arranged before them, their expressions stony.

"The incense game begins," Usugumo said. The sisters sat up straighter, like warriors preparing for battle. "Listen to the incense. Let its voice tell you who it is."

She set the celadon bowl on the floor between her and the elder sister and bowed. The elder sister picked up the bowl, holding it on her left palm. She curled her right hand on top of the bowl, forming a small hole between her thumb and forefinger. Her sister watched closely, leaning forward, as if impatient for her turn.

The earth shuddered again.

The elder sister lifted the bowl to her face, placed her nose against the hole, closed her eyes, and slowly, deeply, inhaled.

SANO ICHIRŌ, CHAMBERLAIN and second-in-command to the shogun, the military dictator of Japan, was alone in a small boat on a turbulent sea. Thunder boomed in the stormy sky. He clung to the sides of his boat as it rocked and pitched. High up to the crest of an enormous wave he soared; then he came down with a jarring crash.

He awakened, a yell caught in his throat.

He was lying in his dark bedchamber. His fingers gripped the heavy quilts that covered him. The rocking and thunder continued. His wife Reiko, beside him, said in a sleepy, worried voice, "Why are you shaking?"

"It's not me," Sano said.

Their twelve-year-old son Masahiro ran into the room, shouting, "Earthquake!"

The room heaved and rocked with an erratic, accelerating rhythm and terrible force. Sano and Reiko sat up while doors slid open; cabinets spewed their contents. They heard the rasp of the house twisting, its joints wrenching. Cracking, shattering noises came from above as roof tiles loosened and fell. Crashes reverberated throughout the compound inside Edo Castle, where Sano and his family lived. From her room down the hall his five-year-old daughter screamed.

"Akiko!" Clad only in her night robe, Reiko ran out the door, her long braid of hair flying.

Sano was up now, too, shivering in the winter air. He said to Masahiro, "Help me get everybody outside before the buildings come down."

They raced through corridors, where they met guards and maids already fleeing. They leaped over gaps that opened between sections of the mansion. "Be careful!" Sano shouted. "Hurry!"

Ceiling beams crashed behind them. Lattice-and-paper partitions collapsed. Sano and Masahiro herded people between leaning walls and down tilted floors. The crowd stumbled free of the mansion into the icy night.

"Reiko!" Sano called, looking frantically around.

"I'm here!" Reiko trudged toward him, carrying Akiko on her back.

The family huddled together in the courtyard with Sano's retainers and the servants. The barracks that enclosed the compound shuddered as the earth rocked harder and faster. Roof tiles flew like missiles. Cracks zigzagged across plaster façades. Buildings began to crumble.

"Go out!" Sano yelled. "It's not safe here!"

The crowd surged through the gate to the stone-paved avenue. Across from this, estates belonging to other government officials occupied a lower level of the hill on which Edo Castle stood. Buildings collapsed like strips of silk curling in a breeze. Screams of terror and agony came from people trapped and injured. Sano looked up to see trees, walls topped with covered corridors, and guard towers sliding down the hill. Groans swept the crowd.

"Merciful gods," Reiko exclaimed.

Sitting astride Reiko's back, Akiko cried, "Look!"

Sano turned in the direction she was pointing. With the estates across the avenue gone, a new, clear view of the city below had opened up. Sano, his family, and his household gazed down in stricken fascination, clinging to one another as the world bucked with thunderous jolts. In the dim moonlight Sano could see that Edo's skyline had flattened. Faint, distant screams rose amid scintillating dust clouds. Orange lights flared like torches across the landscape. Fires inevitably followed earthquakes, when lamps, braziers, and stoves were knocked over and ignited the houses.

"The city is burning," Akiko said, her voice hushed with awe, her eyes round and solemn.

Sano and Reiko looked at each other in horror: The world as they knew it was ending.

1

A MONTH AFTER the earthquake, Edo was a landscape from hell. Entire neighborhoods were leveled. The few intact areas stood like islands amid a sea of wreckage. Edo Castle resembled a beehive after a monster has shaken and mauled it to steal the honey. Up and down the hill, laborers swarmed, cleaning up timbers, plaster, and roof tiles from fallen buildings. The cold air rang with their shouts, the din from their shovels and hammers, and the rattle of the oxcarts that carried the debris downhill. Dust hazed a wintry blue sky darkened by smoke that rose from bonfires as Edo's million people—the majority now homeless—tried to keep warm.

Accompanied by troops, officials, and secretaries, Sano inspected the palace. His chief bodyguard, Detective Marume, walked ahead of him, clearing a path through crowds of porters hauling planks. Sano strode through gardens once beautifully landscaped, now awash in mud and manure, while men sawed boards, mixed plaster, and lugged supplies. Much of the huge complex had collapsed during the earthquake. Although the wreckage had been cleared away, new framework for only one section—the shogun's private chambers—had been erected. Other sections were nothing but bare foundations. Sections that hadn't collapsed leaned precariously.

"When can you finish?" Sano asked the chief architect.

"I wish I knew." One of thousands of samurai officials in the *bakufu*—Japan's military government—the architect had the grimy, haggard appearance of them all, including Sano. They'd been working day and night to rebuild the castle and the city and help the survivors of the earthquake. "We haven't enough skilled carpenters, or building materials, or food for the workers. Can you get us some more?"

"I'll try." Sano was in charge of the rebuilding and disaster relief. People came to him for everything. "But I can't make any promises. The other carpenters are busy fixing the bridges." Most of the bridges that spanned Edo's rivers and canals were down; movement through the city was severely limited. "I've ordered building materials from the provinces, but they'll be slow getting here because the bridges along the highways are down. Food shipments are delayed, too." Would that they arrived before a famine started! Much of Edo's food supply had been destroyed by the fires, and what remained was quickly dwindling.

A clerk carrying a scroll hurried up to Sano. "Excuse me, Honorable Chamberlain, here is an urgent communication."

Sano unfurled the scroll and read it. His spirits sank lower. "The death toll in Edo is now at three thousand," he said to Marume.

Every new count was higher than the last. This was the worst disaster Sano had ever seen. He still couldn't believe it had happened.

Sano continued reading. "There's more bad news. The treasury is already seriously depleted by earthquake relief and repairs." The Tokugawa regime, which had endured for a century, was nearing insolvency.

Marume didn't answer. Once Sano could have counted on him to make humorous remarks that lightened the direst occasions. But Marume's partner, Fukida, was among the casualties, killed when the barracks at Sano's estate collapsed. Sano thought back to that terrible night, when he'd led the search for victims in the ruins of Edo Castle. He remembered Marume sobbing over Fukida's broken body. The two men had been like brothers. Marume seemed a ghost of himself. His eyes were darkly shadowed. He never smiled anymore.

Sano felt guilty that his own wife and children were alive and well, when Marume and so many others had suffered such grievous losses. And he missed Detective Fukida, who'd been one of his favorite, most trusted retainers. Although he customarily had two bodyguards, Sano hadn't assigned Marume a new partner. He didn't have the heart. Now he felt a wave of exhaustion so powerful that he swayed. He hadn't had a full night's sleep in a month. Closing his eyes, he took a moment's nap on his feet. He couldn't keep up this pace for much longer.

He was forty-six years old, and he felt like a hundred.

Edo had risen from disasters in the past, most notably the Great Fire almost five decades ago. Would Edo rise again? If only Sano could pull it up from the ruins with the strength of his own hands and will!

Another messenger came running toward Sano. "Excuse me, Honorable Chamberlain, His Excellency the Shogun wants to see you, right now!"

THE SHOGUN'S TEMPORARY quarters were in a minimally damaged guesthouse. A few cracks in its plaster façade had been patched, a few broken roof tiles replaced. Pine trees and a stone wall screened it from the disorder everywhere else in the castle. Sano entered the small reception room, which was stifling hot from the lanterns and charcoal braziers that surrounded the two men seated on the dais. Both men were bundled in quilts up to the chin. The shogun, Tokugawa Tsunayoshi, wore a silk scarf around his head under the cylindrical black cap that proclaimed his rank. An angry pink spot on each withered cheek brightened the pallor of his weak, pouting face.

"I've been waiting for, ahh, more than an hour," he said as Sano knelt on the tatami floor and bowed. Intolerant of disruption under the best circumstances, the shogun had been thoroughly unhinged by the earthquake. He viewed it as a personal affront, and he had more complaints every time Sano saw him. "Why does it always take so long for you to be fetched?"

He hadn't seen the devastation created by the earthquake, or how much work there was to do, because he never left his quarters. He vaguely knew that many of his subjects had died and many more had lost their homes, but all he really cared about was his own convenience. A mere month after the disaster, he thought everything should snap back to normal and everyone be restored to his beck and call.

"My apologies, Your Excellency," Sano said. A samurai must serve his lord respectfully and unstintingly, no matter how thin his patience was stretched. That was Bushido, the warrior code of honor that Sano lived by. He turned to the other man on the dais, the shogun's nephew. "Greetings, Honorable Lord Ienobu."

"Greetings," Ienobu said, his voice a tight rasp that sounded squeezed out of his stunted, humpbacked body. He had an abnormally small lower jaw, which made his upper teeth protrude. At age forty-two he looked a decade older. Rumor said he had a hereditary, degenerative bone condition that caused him chronic pain. No one knew for sure except his physician, a blind acupuncturist. No one spoke openly about his condition because he was a Tokugawa clan member—the only son of the shogun's deceased older brother Tsunashige—albeit one of dubious status.

His father's birth and death had been shrouded in mystery. His mother had been a chambermaid, who'd borne Ienobu when his father was quite young. His parentage was kept secret lest it jeopardize his father's betrothal to a noblewoman. Ienobu had been brought up by a family retainer and given the retainer's surname. Not until Ienobu was eight years old, and his father's noble wife died, was he recognized as Tsunashige's son and heir and a true member of the Tokugawa ruling clan. Not until this past year had Ienobu emerged from his luxurious villa to renew his slight childhood acquaintance with the shogun, who was sixteen years his senior.

The shogun said to Ienobu, "Chamberlain Sano leaves me here all by myself. But at least I have you, Nephew."

"Yes." Ienobu smiled; his lips stretched around his protruding teeth. "I'm glad to help you through this difficult time."

Sano thought Ienobu had taken advantage of the earthquake to get close to the shogun. With all the court officials busy at work, there was less competition for the shogun's favor than usual. And Sano doubted it was a coincidence that Ienobu had appeared on the scene ten months ago, after the shogun's then-favorite male lover, Yoritomo, had died suddenly. That was when Yanagisawa Yoshiyasu—father of Yoritomo, former chamberlain, and long-standing chief advisor to the shogun—had relinquished his control over the government and gone into seclusion. Sano wondered what Yanagisawa, his longtime enemy, was doing, but felt thankful not to have to worry about him. Yanagisawa's absence had left a political vacuum that Ienobu had filled. Sano suspected that Ienobu had designs on the succession. Ienobu's pedigree made him a logical candidate to become the next dictator, since the shogun had failed to produce a direct blood heir.

But today Sano didn't have time for speculation about Ienobu. "What can I do for you, Your Excellency?" he said, hoping to get it out of the way fast.

"You can answer a question," the shogun said. "Where is everybody?"

It was the question that everyone had been hoping the shogun wouldn't ask. "Whom do you mean, Your Excellency?" Sano said, buying himself time to think how to defuse a dangerous situation.

"My usual attendants and servants," the shogun said. "They've been, ahh, very scarce lately. Some of my boys are missing, too." An enthusiastic practitioner of manly love, he had numerous young male concubines. "And I don't recall seeing some of my, ahh, most important officials in a while. I'm aware that their offices in the palace were damaged and they have to, ahh, work from wherever they're living, but I should think they would come and see me every so often. Where have they gone?"

No one wanted to tell the shogun how many casualties his regime had sustained during the earthquake. Soon after it, he'd greeted the news of each death with attacks of hysteria that made him so ill, everyone feared he would die. The Council of Elders, Japan's chief governing body, had ordered that he wasn't to be apprised of any more deaths. He'd calmed down and been satisfied to believe that the people he missed were simply busy elsewhere.

Until now.

Ienobu hunched forward. He reminded Sano of a vulture. Sano gave up on deception, partly because he didn't like lying, partly because he was tired of cosseting the shogun. "They're dead, Your Excellency."

A strange look came over the shogun's face, a mixture of horror and chagrin. Sano saw that he'd known all along but hoped it wasn't true. "How many people in the government died?" the shogun asked in a small voice.

"Three hundred and fifty-one, so far," Sano said. "Some are still unaccounted for." He recited the names of dead ministers, functionaries, and army officers, onetime pillars of the regime.

"Merciful Buddha," the shogun whispered, his complexion ashen. "This is a terrible, terrible blow for me!" Stress and fatigue undermined Sano's tendency to hope for compassion from the shogun. He'd expected the shogun to care less about the deaths than their consequences for him. "Who is running my government?"

"The rest of us who are still alive," Sano said, thinking, *with no help from you*. He quashed that thought as unbecoming to himself as well as disrespectful to his lord. "There's no need to worry, Your Excellency."

"But the government has been reduced to a skeleton," Ienobu said.

Panic filled the shogun's eyes. "Who is protecting me? How many troops did I lose?"

"Over a thousand," Sano said, "but your army is still huge."

"The army is spread very thin," Ienobu said, "trying to maintain order in the city."

Sano narrowed his eyes at Ienobu. Was Ienobu deliberately trying to frighten the shogun so that he would become even more dependent on his nephew?

"Is the castle fixed yet?" the shogun asked.

"Unfortunately, no," Sano said.

"The castle wasn't built in a day. It can't be rebuilt in a day." Ienobu's soothing manner didn't soften the truth of his words.

Maybe Ienobu was trying to tip the shogun into his grave. Sano was so tired he could barely think straight.

"I'm so afraid!" The shogun cowered. "What if I should be attacked?"

"Nobody is going to attack you," Sano said, although an insurrection was a possibility that the government feared. "Nobody knows exactly how vulnerable you are. The number of deaths within the regime is being kept secret."

Even as the shogun looked relieved, he lamented, "The court astronomer just told me that the cosmos is displeased about something. He read it in the constellations. He says they say the earthquake was sent as a message." His eyes were round and shiny with terror. "There will be more trouble, I just know it!" He toppled onto the dais, writhed in his quilt like a silkworm in its cocoon, and groaned. "I'm so miserable, I feel a sick spell coming on!"

Astrology was serious business. A dictator must look to the stars for explanations for natural disasters and other calamities. He must heed their warnings, which were interpreted by his astronomer, that his regime was out of harmony with the cosmos. Sano knew this and felt alarmed himself, but his patience snapped like a stretched rope frayed down to its last thread. After fifteen years of listening to the shogun whine, of catering to him, of enduring insults and death threats, the shogun's reaction was too much. After seeing the devastation wrought by the earthquake, after toiling to pick up the pieces, Sano felt ready to explode. He opened his mouth to tell the shogun to stop acting like a baby and take responsibility for leading his country through this crisis.

The shogun pointed a shaky finger at Sano and cried, "You always bring me bad news! I'm sick of bad news! Go and fetch me some that's good!"

"You'd better go." Ienobu was watching Sano with interest, as if he could read Sano's thoughts. "Why not take a tour of inspection around the city?"

"Yes!" The shogun latched onto the idea with frantic zeal. "Begin at once!"

Sano came to his senses. The heat of his anger faded into cold realization of what he'd almost done—cast aside honor, offended the shogun beyond reparation, and doomed himself, his family, and all his close associates to death. Shaken by his close call, Sano went.

2

DRESSED IN ARMOR tunics and padded coats, Sano and his troops rode on horseback out of Edo Castle's main gate. Logs supported the guardhouse above it. A temporary bridge made of planks spanned the moat, whose embankment was riddled with cracks as wide as a man's hand. Laborers used ropes, pulleys, and muscle to haul up stones from the crumbled walls and guard towers that had fallen into the water. Sano inhaled freedom along with the dust and smoke in the air. Even though he didn't have time for a tour of inspection, he was glad to leave the castle for the first time in days. Maybe it would do his spirits good.

Then again, maybe not.

The avenue outside the castle was crowded with people who held out their hands and pleaded for alms. They weren't only the usual beggars, monks, and nuns; they were artisans and other workers who'd lost their livelihoods when the earthquake had shut down businesses and destroyed the houses where many among the lower classes had been employed as servants. Sano's attendants tossed coins, but the ranks of the poor had swelled so much; Sano couldn't help everyone. He entered the district where the *daimyo*—feudal lords who governed the provinces—owned huge estates. Long sections of the walls decorated with black-and-white geometric tile patterns had fallen. Barracks and mansions were reduced to debris piles and cracked foundations. Some estates had burned down. Tents made of oiled paper and cloth, hung on bamboo poles or wooden beams, served as quarters for the *daimyo*. Not even their enormous wealth could restore their homes anytime soon. Their troops cleared away wreckage. Scraping noises and crashes deafened Sano. The amount of work it would take to restore the city, Sano's mind could barely fathom.

A lone samurai came riding toward Sano. It was Hirata, his chief retainer, who'd taken over Sano's former post as top investigator for the shogun. He wore a simple cloak, kimono, and trousers. His hair was shaved at the crown and pulled back in a topknot, the customary style for samurai, the same as Sano and his other men. Hirata's two swords, mark of the warrior class, jutted at his waist, but he never wore armor. Sano marveled at how much Hirata, in his late thirties, had changed from the boyish, awkward fellow he'd been when he'd first entered Sano's service. Hirata was all lean, sinewy muscle and unnatural grace. That and his confident, keen-eyed aspect were a result of his years spent studying the mystic martial arts. He was the top fighter in Edo.

"Where have you been?" Sano asked.

"Searching for people trapped inside collapsed houses." Hirata turned his mount and rode beside Sano.

Sano looked askance at Hirata. Hirata had frequently been absent, without permission, during the past year, since he'd met three fellow disciples of the man who'd taught him the mystic martial arts. Instead of investigating crimes himself, Hirata often had his detectives cover for him. He spent so little time with Sano that he was Sano's chief retainer in title only. Hirata always had good excuses, but Sano had the distinct, uneasy feeling that they weren't true.

Sano didn't know what was going on with Hirata, but he didn't like it. "Have you found anyone alive?"

"Not in the past few days. Just bodies," Hirata said.

Although Sano had every right to demand a true account of Hirata's actions and order Hirata to attend to his duties and punish him if he neglected them, Sano didn't. They were more than master and retainer; they were old, close friends, and Sano owed Hirata his life. Hirata had once taken a blade meant for Sano and almost died. Sano wasn't the kind of master who would take that for granted. He would have to confront Hirata eventually, but now, when there were so many more important problems to address, wasn't the time.

"Where are you going?" Hirata asked.

"On a tour of inspection. The shogun wants me to bring him some good news."

Sano and Hirata looked around at the ruins. Expressionless, they looked at each other. Then they burst out laughing. Finding good news for the shogun seemed so ludicrously impossible, it was funny. Sano's men laughed, too, except for Detective Marume.

Humor quickly fled as they rode through the townspeople's quarters. Survivors picked through leveled neighborhoods, looking for anything salvageable. Water-sellers roved, their buckets suspended from poles on their shoulders. The prices they called out were exorbitant, but people paid. Sewage and debris clogged the canals, wells had been blocked by shifts in the rock underground, and the system of wooden pipes that channeled water from the hills had been damaged. Clean water was at a premium.

In the intact areas, a few shops and market stalls had reopened. Long lines of people waited at each. Merchants lucky enough to have goods left to sell demanded prices ten times higher than usual, making fortunes off the earthquake. Crowds gathered on the Nihonbashi River banks as a lone fishing boat docked. Many other boats had sunken or burned. Fights over the catch broke out. Army troops tried to keep order. Sano and his men rode through areas that had burned into deserts of black timbers. Soot drifted; the air reeked of smoke.

Along the banks of the Sumida River floated remains from warehouses and docks. Soldiers stood around the few existent warehouses, guarding the rice that the regime paid out as stipends to its retainers. The rice normally fed thousands of samurai and their households, and the surplus was sold to merchants for cash that funded the government; the townspeople consumed the surplus rice. But much of it had been swept into the river during the earthquake or burned up in the fires. Hungry citizens clamored outside the warehouses. Food riots were becoming frequent.

Where the Ryōgoku Bridge's high wooden arch had once connected the city with the opposite shore, only a few pilings jutted up from the water. This was the site of one of the earthquake's worst disasters. Fleeing crowds had massed so tightly on the bridge that they were stuck. The bridge had collapsed under their weight. Hundreds of people had drowned in the river, which had been heated almost to a boil by burning debris.

"We've seen enough for now," Sano said quietly.

They headed back to the castle, through an area crisscrossed by huge cracks that had swallowed entire houses. Townspeople who wore cloths over their faces, thick cotton gloves, and leather boots climbed down into the cracks, searching for victims. Decayed, stinking corpses lay on the street. Sano felt nausea turn his stomach. He doubted that anyone could still be alive underground, but he couldn't help hoping so. He jumped off his horse and said, "Let's help."

He and Hirata and their troops joined the townsmen in lifting heavy roof beams off a wide chasm. The townsmen removed their cloth masks to cool their perspiring faces. A sweet odor wafted up from the darkness underground.

"Is that incense?" Sano asked.

"Yes." Hirata's nostrils flared as he employed his keen sense of smell. "There are people down there, but they don't smell dead."

The hope of rescuing survivors spurred the group to work faster. They cleared a hole above a room in which three women lay curled on their sides. Diarrhea stained their vividly colored robes and the tatami around them. One woman's hair was streaked with gray, the others' glossy black. Vomit crusted their mouths. But the skin on their faces, and their outstretched hands, was unmarked by decay. Their eyes were open.

"They're alive!" exclaimed a young townsman with bristly hair. He squeezed through the hole feetfirst, without putting on his mask. He jumped down to the room, calling to the women, "Hey, we're here to save you!"

They neither answered nor moved. Sano and Hirata frowned in puzzlement.

The townsman touched the women's bodies. Recoiling, he cried, "They're all dead! And their eyes! What is this?" He thrust his hands up and yelled, "Get me out of here!"

His comrades pulled him up. He sat on the ground, panted, and babbled. Sano and Hirata flung away more beams until the entire room was exposed. Now they saw what had frightened the young man. The dead women were eerily, disturbingly well preserved, their eyes a bright, gleaming red. The other townsmen exclaimed in shock.

Concern, curiosity, and the instincts honed by fifteen years of detective work compelled Sano to say to Hirata, "We'd better investigate this."

The townsmen inserted a ladder into the hole. Sano and Hirata descended. Seen up close, the women's condition was even more unnerving. Their eyes looked as if fresh blood filmed the irises and whites. Their skin was as fresh as life, their makeup smooth.

"Something prevented them from rotting," Hirata said.

Sano bent to examine each woman. "They don't seem to have been injured."

"What killed them, then? Underground gases?"

"I don't know." Sano turned his attention to items on the floor—writing brushes and paper, inkstones and cakes of black ink, small jars for water. The gray-haired woman had a charcoal brazier, green paper packets, metal chopsticks, and silver tweezers by her. A celadon ceramic bowl of ashes lay tipped on its side.

"They were playing an incense game," Sano said.

Incense games originated from a tradition called *kodo*, the art of incense, that had begun more than a thousand years ago. A great industry for formulating and manufacturing incense had grown up in Nara and Kyoto. Incense-makers procured ingredients from around the world—Japanese camphor, pine, and magnolia wood; frankincense from Arabia; clove and nutmeg from Java; patchouli, sandalwood, and cinnamon from India; cedarwood and star anise from China; ambergris from sperm whales; musk from Himalayan deer. They ground the ingredients, blended them with honey and oil, and shaped the mixture into sticks or pellets. The emperor's court ladies perfumed their hair and their kimonos with incense, which also became an important element of religion.

At Buddhist temples priests lit incense sticks that symbolized the Buddha. Shinto priests offered incense to the spirits at every shrine. The sweet smoke rose from earth to heaven, summoned the deities to hear prayers, facilitated meditation and trances, led the souls of the dead to the netherworld. Incense had practical applications, too. Some incense blends were stimulants, sleep aids, or aphrodisiacs. It was also used to fumigate diseased places, mask body odor, and sweeten the smell of cremation.

The samurai class had embraced *kodo*. During the civil war era that had ended a century ago, samurai going into battle carried pouches of incense around their necks, to help their spirits find their way to heaven if they died. Today, *kodo* was a fashionable hobby. Cultured folk from all classes employed incense experts to teach them how to blend and appreciate incense. Games were an important aspect of *kodo*. They had elaborate rules by which players burned incense samples, smelled the smoke, and attempted to guess what type they were. The games weren't really competitions; winning mattered less than sharing the enjoyment of the incense.

"It looks like the women didn't finish the first round," Sano said. "Only one packet is open, and all the score sheets are blank."

"This is one of the strangest things I've ever seen, and I've seen a lot of strange things since the earthquake," Hirata said. "What happened? And who are these women?"

3

A VAST CAMP occupied the Nihonbashi merchant district. Where shops and houses had stood there were now rows upon rows of tents made from anything available—oiled paper and cloth, quilts and tatami mats, costly silk brocade and rags, bamboo poles and scrap wood. Inside the tents huddled thousands of homeless people—mostly women, children, the elderly, wounded, and sick. Able-bodied men and boys had been sent to clean up debris or help rebuild Edo Castle. A few old men played cards outside the tents; blind musicians tootled on flutes; children danced in mud and laughed. But the general atmosphere reeked of misery and sewage. The outcasts who usually collected human waste couldn't haul their carts out to the fields to dispose of it because the roads were blocked. Night soil removal was suspended indefinitely.

A gong boomed. People trudged, bowls in hand, toward a large tent in which Lady Reiko and four other women stood behind a table laden with pots of rice, tureens of stew made from miso, tofu, vegetables, and fish, and barrels of pickled radish and turnips. Soldiers prevented pushing, taking cuts and fights while the ladies served the food. Many people didn't have chopsticks; they ate with their hands. Many didn't have bowls; they shared with others or used roof tiles. They all took turns drinking from a common cup tied to a water barrel. Some, injured during the earthquake and fires, had bandaged heads or broken limbs tied to wooden splints. People carried food to those who couldn't walk because they were too badly wounded or too sick from the diseases that ravaged the camp.

Reiko saw samurai whose masters didn't have enough food for them. Shamed, they bowed their heads. Their suicides numbered among the deaths that occurred daily in the camp, the earthquake's never-ending casualties. Reiko saw two men carry away a corpse. She felt a terrible pity for her people. Although women of her class didn't usually work or mix with the public, she came here every day because she wanted to help.

"Make the portions smaller," she told the other women, her friends from Edo Castle. "We need to stretch the food as far as possible."

The stores of grains and seeds, pickled vegetables and fruit, salted and dried fish that usually tided the population over the winter were running low. Jars had broken during the earthquake; food had burned in the fires or spoiled in the rain that leaked into damaged houses. Spring crops hadn't been planted yet. Harvests were months away. Food requisitioned from the provinces had yet to arrive. Reiko had heard of people catching and cooking rats and birds, in defiance of the Buddhist prohibition against killing animals and eating meat.

"The food is going to run out anyway," grumbled the wife of the finance superintendent.

"There are too many people," her daughter complained. "We can't feed them all."

They didn't want to be here. Neither did the other two women. After the earthquake they'd begged Reiko to ask Sano for favors—the return of their servants who'd been commandeered for the rebuilding effort, carpenters to fix their homes. Instead of helping them, Reiko had roped them into working with her. They couldn't refuse the wife of the chamberlain, but they muttered about her under their breath:

"Some people don't know their place. They investigate crimes for their husbands." Reiko had been doing that since she'd married Sano thirteen years ago. "They don't know how to be proper wives." Reiko and Sano had an unconventional marriage in this society where most wives were confined to domestic duties. Reiko's exploits had furnished much grist for the high-society gossip mill. "So unfeminine. So scandalous." Most ladies of her class thought that about Reiko. They deplored her father for educating her like a son instead of a daughter. "She even forces well-bred ladies to slave for the peasants."

Accustomed to criticism, Reiko just worked harder. Every morning she rose before dawn to chop vegetables and clean fish. She rode to town on an oxcart that carried food to the tent camps. After serving the meal, she assisted the doctors who ministered to the inhabitants. She didn't get home until after dark. She was exhausted, and she missed her daughter Akiko, but she couldn't bear to sit at home while the townspeople were suffering. Idleness would give her too much time to think about her friends, relatives, and acquaintances who'd died in the earthquake or fires, and to miss those from whom the disaster had separated her. She rarely saw Sano; he was too busy. Masahiro, a page for the shogun, was always on duty. Reiko never saw her father, one of Edo's two magistrates and a leader in the relief effort. And her best friend Chiyo was nursing her father, who'd broken his leg during the earthquake. Work alleviated Reiko's grief and loneliness and her horror at what had happened to Edo. Without work to distract her, she might start crying and not be able to stop.

Now, as Reiko scraped the last rice out of the pot, a sudden wave of dizziness swept over her. Her vision swam, then went dark around the edges. She fainted.

SANO AND HIRATA climbed the ladder out of the hole. "Bring the women up," he told the townsmen. Their bodies needed to be identified, if possible, then disposed of at Zōjō Temple, where the remains of earthquake victims were burned in the crematoriums every night.

Four townsmen went into the hole, while four above ground threw down ropes. They hauled up the bodies and laid them in a row on the street. Sano and Hirata stood over the bodies, paying their silent respects to the dead. Smoke veiled the sun. The din of hammers, shovels, and picks resounded. Sano mentally increased the death toll in Edo to three thousand and three.

One of the rescuers joined Sano. He was in his forties, with sad features, his eyes red from the dust, his jaws covered with beard stubble. He pointed at the gray-haired woman. "I know her."

"Who is she?" Sano tried to see past the weird red eyes and the white makeup. Her face reminded him of a cat's—triangular and feral. She'd been attractive. Her dark green kimono patterned with pinecones was made of cotton; she was a commoner. The sumptuary laws permitted only the samurai class to wear silk. Sano thought of how little these distinctions seemed to matter nowadays.

"Madam Usugumo. She was an incense teacher. That's her house." The man said, "I lived down the block. My name is Jiro. I'm the neighborhood headman." He cast a rueful glance around. "Or at least I was when there was a neighborhood."

Headmen kept a register of the people on their block. They normally acted as liaison between their residents and the higher authorities. That system had broken down after the earthquake—one reason it was difficult to get an accurate count of the dead.

Sano introduced himself and Hirata and Detective Marume. The headman bowed, awed to meet such important personages.

"What about the other women?" Hirata said. "Do you know them?"

"I've never seen them before. They're probably pupils of Madam Usugumo." Jiro added, "She was very private. She didn't mix with the neighbors."

Sano studied the two other women. Their robes had the luster of expensive silk; they were from the samurai class. They had youthful, rounded features and a family resemblance. "Sisters," Sano deduced.

One's lavish brocade kimono was a deep rose color; she was the elder sister, probably married. The other's was a brighter pink, appropriate for a maiden. Their hair was elaborately coiffed, studded with jade beads on lacquered spikes. A motif in the patterns of their sashes caught Sano's attention. It was a large dot circled by eight smaller dots.

"I know who their family is." Sano pointed to the symbol. "That's the Hosokawa clan crest."

Dismay mixed with his satisfaction at finding a clue to the women's identities. Lord Hosokawa was one of Sano's top political allies, who headed an ancient family that controlled the fief of Higo Province. Higo was a top rice-producing domain and the Hosokawa clan one of Japan's largest, wealthiest landholders.

"I'll have to inform Lord Hosokawa," Sano said, even though he had a million other urgent things to do. This was too sensitive a matter to delegate to a subordinate. "I'd better take some of their personal effects to show him." Sano gingerly untied the women's sashes and tucked them in his horse's saddlebag.

A loud groan came from the bristly haired young townsman. He staggered as if he were drunk; he held his head in both hands. "Ow, my head aches!" Wheezing, he cried, "I can't breathe!" and then he fell to the ground.

His friends hurried to his aid. He vomited violently.

"What's the matter, Okura?" the headman asked.

A stench arose as Okura's bowels moved and diarrhea gushed down his legs. "I don't know," he said between retches and gasps. "My stomach hurts. I hurt all over." Dazed, he looked around at the ruins as if seeing them for the first time. "What happened? Where am I?"

Sano started to say, "Fetch a doctor," then remembered that since the earthquake doctors were too few and too far between.

Detective Marume said, "Vomiting, diarrhea—the women had those symptoms, too."

"You're right," Sano said. "I think they were poisoned."

"Okura must have breathed the poison when he went down in the hole," Hirata said.

Okura went into shuddering convulsions while the other townsmen tried to soothe him. The headman said, "But we all went down. Why is he the only one who's sick?"

"The rest of us didn't go down until the hole was opened up and the fresh air got in," Sano recalled. "And he didn't wear his mask."

"Is he going to die?" the headman asked anxiously.

"I don't know." But if Sano was right about the poison, it had already killed three people. "He's young and strong. Maybe he got only a small dose of the poison and he'll recover."

Sano did know that the likelihood of poison complicated the matter of the dead Hosokawa women. He said to Hirata and Marume, "This looks like murder to me."

4

"I'M HUNGRY," THE shogun announced to the boys crowded into his chamber. Lounging on cushions on the dais, wrapped in quilts, he stroked the heads of his two favorite boy concubines. They were twins, thirteen years old, with rosy, pretty faces and sweetly bland smiles. "Where's lunch? It must be, ahh, at least an hour overdue."

Chamberlain Sano's son Masahiro opened the door to let in three elderly servants. They staggered up to the dais, carrying trays laden with covered dishes. All the younger servants were out helping to fix the castle. Only two of Masahiro's fellow pages and a lone, middle-aged bodyguard were on duty. The old servants set the trays before the shogun and bowed.

"Ahh, at last." The shogun took the lids off dishes, revealing rice, pickled vegetables, and a soup made with dried shrimp, tofu, and seaweed. The boys leaned forward hungrily. Masahiro's stomach growled. The shogun frowned. "This is the same lunch I had yesterday! I want something else."

One of the servants said, "A thousand apologies, Your Excellency, but—but I'm afraid . . . there isn't anything else."

Food had been scarce and limited in variety since the earthquake, even in the castle, Masahiro knew. But the shogun either didn't know or didn't care.

"There has to be something else for me to eat! I'm the shogun!" He picked up a bowl and hurled it. The servant ducked. Soup sprayed from the bowl as it flew. It hit the wall, then broke on the floor. The boys gasped. Masahiro couldn't help thinking that if he'd acted like that when he was little, his nurse would have spanked him.

The shogun flapped his hand at the servants. "Take this slop away and bring something new, or I'll, ahh, have you and the cooks put to death!"

Lugging the trays, the servants hurried off. Masahiro and the other boys gazed longingly after the food. The shogun said to them, "Clean up the mess!"

The two other pages jumped to obey. They, like Masahiro, were sons of government officials. They were in competition to show who could best serve the shogun. If they impressed him favorably, they would get high positions when they grew up. They raced each other to pick up the broken bowl.

"Pour me some tea—I'm thirsty," the shogun said. One of the twins lifted the teapot from a table. He poured tea into a cup held by his brother, who handed it to the shogun. The shogun drank, and grunted. "This is cold!"

The twins set the pot on a brazier, then discovered that the fire inside had gone out. The pages stepped on the spilled soup and tracked it across the tatami.

"You're making things worse!" the shogun cried. Other concubines removed the grate from the brazier and fanned the coals. Ash billowed into the air. "Stop, stop!" He waved his hand and coughed. The pages rushed to open the window. "No! I'll freeze to death!"

Masahiro had witnessed many scenes like this since the earthquake, since the shogun's concubines and youngest retainers had been given charge of the private chambers. Incompetence and chaos reigned. Masahiro slipped quietly from the chamber and fetched a broom and dustpan. Unlike other samurai boys, he'd learned from his family's servants how to make fires, clean house, and even cook simple foods when he was little; he'd thought it was fun. Every day he resisted the urge to put his skills to use lest he attract too much attention from the shogun. His parents had warned him against that, when he'd first become a page last year.

"This is a great opportunity," Sano had said. "Do well, and you'll bring honor to the family as well as secure yourself a good place in the regime. But it's also dangerous, because the shogun likes boys."

As his father awkwardly explained what the shogun did with them, Masahiro wasn't surprised. He'd happened upon similar goings-on among the retainers in his own household. Manly love was considered normal, acceptable. And Masahiro had heard the gossip about the shogun and the boys at the palace.

"Your mother and I don't want that for you," Sano said. "We'd rather you get a lesser post than become the shogun's plaything."

Masahiro had learned that their attitude was unusual. Most parents in their position would willingly, if not happily, sacrifice their children to advance the family.

"We can't keep you away from the shogun, and even if we could, we wouldn't deny you the opportunity to make good for yourself." Regret showed on Sano's face. "All we can do is tell you to be careful."

"How?" Masahiro asked. Even though he felt no disapproval toward people who practiced manly love, he didn't have any urge to do it himself—especially not with the shogun, who was a cranky old man.

"Be obedient, but don't volunteer for anything," Sano said. "Do the best work you can, but quietly. Only speak if you're spoken to." His conflicted expression said he knew his advice ran counter to what a courtier should do if he wanted to succeed. "Don't stand out."

"Yes, Father," Masahiro said.

At the time he couldn't have foreseen the earthquake or how hard it would be to sit by and watch other people do badly what he could do well. Now he handed the broom and dustpan to the other pages. He surreptitiously wiped the floor mats with a cloth while they made a show of sweeping up the china fragments. He stood in a corner instead of taking over for the two boys who were poking at the coals in the brazier, trying to restart the fire.

"I'm bored," the shogun announced. "Somebody read to me."

The twins took turns reading aloud from a book of poems. They faltered and made mistakes. Masahiro winced.

"Enough!" the shogun cried. "I can't bear to listen to you mangle fine literature!" The twins fell silent. "Why am I surrounded by idiots?"

Everyone looked at the floor while he began ranting. No one dared say a word. Into the room shuffled Lord Ienobu, the shogun's nephew. He climbed onto the dais, knelt, took the book from the twins, and said, "Please allow me, Honorable Uncle."

His voice was raspy, but he read every word perfectly. The shogun nodded, appeased. The sight of the hunchback with the ugly, toothy face gave Masahiro the same creepy feeling he got when he saw a toad. Ienobu flicked his gaze around the room, as if looking for prey to eat. Masahiro sat still and quiet among the other boys. He reminded himself of his father's advice. He must avoid standing out, even if it killed him.

"I'LL PAY MY call on Lord Hosokawa," Sano said to Hirata as they stood by the bodies on the ground by the sunken house. "You take the women to Edo Morgue."

Hirata understood that Sano wanted the bodies examined by his friend Dr. Ito, the morgue custodian. Dr. Ito would use his scientific expertise to determine the cause of death. But Sano couldn't say that in public. Nor could he personally seek Dr. Ito's advice.

An empty oxcart rolled by. Hirata beckoned the driver, a tough peasant youth. The townsmen left their sick comrade and wrapped the bodies in hemp sacking, then loaded them into the open cart. Hirata mounted his horse. As he rode off leading the oxcart, he saw Sano watching him and felt a stab of guilt. He remembered how often he'd shirked his duties during the past year. He guessed that Sano didn't believe the excuses he made; he understood that Sano was making allowances for him that other masters wouldn't. He knew he should tell Sano the truth about what he was up to and face the consequences, but the time never seemed right.

While he traveled through the city, Hirata noticed soldiers patrolling on foot rather than horseback. Hundreds of horses had been killed by the earthquake or injured so badly they'd had to be put down, their carcasses cremated. Hirata saw an ash heap littered with their blackened skeletons; he smelled rotting and burned flesh. He also observed things that were beyond ordinary human perception.

His training in the mystic martial arts had sharpened his senses until he could see the cracks in the walls of Edo Castle as if they were as close as his hand, smell the green life dormant in winter mountain forests, and hear a man across town coaxing another man to invest in a scheme for buying liquor in Osaka and selling it for a huge profit in Edo. He could taste salt from the ocean far down past the mouth of the Sumida River, and feel against his cheeks the minute, invisible dust particles in the air.

He could also sense the auras of living things, the energy that their bodies emitted. Each human had a unique aura that signaled his personality, health, and emotions. The landscape of Hirata's mind hummed, blazed, and crackled with the auras from the city's million people. He could pick out those that belonged to people he knew, and the misery-laced, fading energy of victims trapped in earthquake rubble. That plus his supernatural strength had made him useful in search and rescue. A part of him always remained on alert for one particular aura—the conjoined energy from the three fellow disciples of Ozuno, his teacher. Hirata never knew when they would show up, and he was always on his guard in case they did.

He followed a dirty track through the slums of Odenmacho, which were carpeted with the remains of flimsy hovels once occupied by Edo's poorest citizens. Emaciated men, women, and children crowded around fires. Haunted eyes gazed at Hirata from grimy faces. Suddenly Hirata felt the aura, a mighty, booming pulsation that countered the rhythm of his heart and tingled along every nerve. Its force made the air ring and shimmer like shattered crystal. His hand flew to the sword at his waist at the same time he fought instinctive terror and the urge to run. He reined in his horse, jumped down from the saddle. The cart driver halted his two oxen and beheld Hirata with puzzlement.

Three men appeared, some fifty paces away, as if they'd materialized out of the bonfire smoke. Side by side, they moved toward Hirata. Although they strolled at a leisurely pace, they covered the distance so fast that they arrived in an instant. Their aura dissipated as if sucked inside them by a vacuum. They, unlike other people, could turn it on and off. They stood before him, two samurai and a priest.

"Surprise," the samurai in the middle said. With his athletic physique and strong, regular features, he looked the perfect samurai. His flowing dark gray coat and trousers swirled around him in a wind of his own creation. A twinkle in his deep black eyes, and a left eyebrow that was higher than the right, gave him a rakish charm.

"Greetings, Tahara-*san*," Hirata said.

Tahara was the trio's leader, the one Hirata feared most, although he was almost as afraid of the others. They were the only men in Japan capable of defeating him in combat. His friendship with them felt as hazardous as holding a wasp in his mouth.

"Fancy running into you," Hirata said. "I haven't seen you in, what, seven days?"

"Eight." Tahara's eyes twinkled brighter: He knew that Hirata knew the exact length of the time since their last meeting. "Sorry to make myself so scarce." His voice had a curious quality that was at once smooth and rough, that brought to mind a stream flowing over jagged rocks. "I've been busy guarding the Tokugawa rice warehouses." His clan were retainers to the *daimyo* of Iga Province, known for its tradition of mystic martial arts practiced by the *ninja*, a cult of peasant warriors adept at stealth. The *daimyo* had loaned Tahara to the government for security work.

"Pity the poor thief who tries to get past you," Hirata said.

Tahara, who could kill a man as quickly and effortlessly as look at him, shrugged with a modest smile.

Hirata turned to the other samurai. "What have you been up to, Kitano-*san*?"

"Leading Lord Satake's fire brigade." Kitano Shigemasa was a retainer to Lord Satake. He wore the iron helmet and armor tunic of a soldier. Although he was in his fifties and gray-haired, his figure was robust. His eyes crinkled as if in a smile, but the rest of his face, a mesh of scars, remained immobile. As a youth, he'd been wounded in a drunken brawl, his face badly cut. The cuts had damaged his facial nerves. "Can't let the rest of Edo burn down."

The government delegated the responsibility for fighting fires to the *daimyo*, whose efforts had proved woefully inadequate during the earthquake. Since then, they'd much increased their manpower and vigilance.

"And you, Deguchi-*san*?" Hirata turned to the third man.

Deguchi was a Buddhist priest from the Zōjō Temple district. His maroon cloak covered a saffron-dyed robe. His shaved head was bare. Thirty years old, he could pass for twenty or forty. Although his long, oval face was plain—the eyes heavily lidded, the nose flat, and mouth pursed—he had a haunting, luminescent beauty. His eyes glowed as they met Hirata's.

"He's been giving charity to the earthquake victims," Kitano said. Deguchi never spoke; he was mute. Tahara had explained to Hirata that Deguchi was an orphan who'd lived on the streets, working as a prostitute. A customer had strangled him and damaged his throat.

And Hirata had been wounded in the leg and crippled when he'd taken a blade for Sano. He and Deguchi and Kitano had something in common—a life-changing injury. Ozuno had helped them overcome their handicaps. Hirata couldn't tell what, if any, injury Tahara had sustained.

Tahara glanced at the bodies in the oxcart. "Taking earthquake victims to Edo Morgue? Isn't that a bit menial for a fellow of your rank? What are you up to?"

"It's confidential." Hirata couldn't tell anyone what was in store at the morgue, and he didn't like sharing his business with these men. "What do you want?"

Kitano wagged his finger at Hirata. "There's no need to be so abrupt with your friends."

Tahara sidled off, drawing Kitano, Deguchi, and Hirata out of the oxcart driver's earshot, then said, "It's time for a ritual."

Irritation jabbed Hirata. "Not again."

"Why not?" Kitano said, a hint of pique beneath his amusement. "The rituals are the purpose of our secret society. That was explained to you before you joined."

"When I joined your secret society, you explained that the purpose was to influence the course of fate and transform the world according to a cosmic plan for its destiny," Hirata reminded Kitano. "You said you had an ancient book of magic spells that you inherited from Ozuno when he died. You told me that the spells are activated by the rituals you do. But that's starting to sound like nonsense. Because you won't show me this book. And because I've done five rituals with you and nothing has happened. We sat in the woods at night. We burned incense and chanted some gibberish. All we accomplished was to get stung by mosquitoes in the summer and freeze our behinds in the winter. So excuse me if I'm not eager for another ritual."

Kitano's eyes narrowed. Deguchi brooded. Tahara looked a little abashed as he said, "We also told you that we don't control whether, or when, the rituals produce the magic. That's up to the spirits that the rituals are designed to invoke."

"That's how it works," Kitano said.

"How it doesn't work, you mean," Hirata retorted.

"Oh, it works," Tahara said with an edge to his voice. "You saw for yourself, the day Yoritomo died."

What Hirata had seen was the reason he'd believed the three men could do everything they claimed, the reason he'd joined their secret society. But his awe had faded. "You said the magic reveals actions for you to take, that might seem trivial but will change the course of fate. Yes, I believed you brought about Yoritomo's death. But now I think it was just a lucky fluke."

Temper ignited in the men's eyes. Tahara said, "It was no fluke." Their aura pulsed faintly, ominously.

"I'm not doing another ritual," Hirata said, despite his fear. "I'm already in trouble with my master, for taking time off work and lying about what I've been doing. Count me out."

"When you joined us, you swore to put the secret society ahead of all other things," Tahara reminded Hirata. "You also swore that you wouldn't reveal its business to outsiders."

"Those are terms I never should have agreed to." Hirata had wanted to acquire the supernatural powers the men had, but he'd also wanted to gain some control over them and protect Sano. Now he regretted that he'd let the society come between him and Sano, him and the Way of the Warrior. "Why do you need me, anyway? The three of you have so much power—aren't you enough?"

They didn't answer. Was that uncertainty Hirata sensed in them? He started to walk back to his horse and the oxcart. The three men moved so swiftly that their images blurred. As they blocked his path, their aura strengthened.

"You agreed nonetheless," Tahara said. "And now that you're in the society, you must participate in the rituals. If you don't—"

Suddenly Hirata couldn't speak or move. His body was stone, his breath caught. Tahara's, Deguchi's, and Kitano's mental powers paralyzed him. Nearby, the oxcart driver napped and people huddled around the bonfires, unaware that anything unusual was afoot.

"We'll give you a little time to think about what you want," Kitano said.

Hirata's heart pounded in his ears; his lungs struggled to suck air. Blackness rimmed his vision. His mind filled with the terrible knowledge of his helplessness, his mortality.

"Then we'll talk about the ritual," Tahara said.

A moment before Hirata lost consciousness, the men relaxed their power. His paralysis broke. He gulped huge, wheezing breaths, like a fish freed from a net and tossed back in water. The blackness receded. Flexing his muscles, he glared at his companions.

Tahara smiled. Mirth crinkled Kitano's eyes. Deguchi's eyes glinted with satisfaction.

"If you ever do that again, you'll be sorry." But Hirata knew he had no way to make them sorry. Three against one, they were too strong; even singly, they could each best him. "And I'm not doing any more rituals."

He stomped past them, brushing his hands against his sleeve. But his bravado was false. While he rode away, the skin on his back flinched under their gazes. Inside he trembled with fear that joining the society was the worst mistake he'd ever made, that he'd gotten himself into something far beyond his ability to handle.

5

THE WAY TO Lord Hosokawa's house led Sano and his troops along the Daiichi Keihin, the main highway to points south. Fewer scenes of destruction met them as they left the outskirts of the city. Sano felt as if an iron clamp around his chest had loosened. Inhaling air that wasn't tainted with dust or the smell of decay, he rested his tired eyes on the forests, whose bare trees laced the rim of a blue, clear sky. He was surprised that beauty still existed in the world. But even here there were reminders of the disaster. Trees leaned where the earth had shifted. Sano and his men jumped their horses across cracks that split the road. At last they neared a group of samurai estates, private towns enclosed by barracks. The damage was slight here. If Sano squinted, he couldn't see the cracks in the long walls of the barracks or the few broken roofs. Soldiers milled around outside. The illusion of normality was jarring.

The Hosokawa estate was the grandest in the area, with a gate made of wide, iron-studded planks. As Sano dismounted and approached the gate, two sentries scrambled out of an ornate guardhouse. They recognized Sano, greeted him, and bowed.

"Are any women in Lord Hosokawa's clan missing?" Sano asked.

"Yes," said a sentry. "Lord Hosokawa's two daughters."

Resigned to being the bearer of bad news, Sano said, "Then I must speak with Lord Hosokawa."

He left his troops outside the estate while one servant escorted him into the mansion and another fetched Lord Hosokawa. Sano had barely entered the reception chamber when Lord Hosokawa rushed in. Lord Hosokawa was in his sixties, gray-haired and slight of build. He wore modest robes patterned in neutral colors instead of the opulent, fashionable garb that *daimyo* of his wealth usually affected. The lines in his face bespoke intelligence and constant worry. Two women, both in their late forties, followed.

Lord Hosokawa rushed through the polite ritual of greeting. "My wife," he said, introducing the woman with gray hair, sallow skin, and drab brown clothes. He gestured toward the other, who was done up with dyed-black hair and full makeup, her robes in brighter shades of maroon and teal. "Tama, my concubine." The women leaned toward Sano, their faces anxious, their hands wringing. "Honorable Chamberlain, have you news of my daughters?"

"I'm afraid so," Sano said somberly. "We've found the bodies of two young women."

"Why do you think they're my daughters?" Lord Hosokawa looked torn between the hope that the missing had been located and the wish that the dead weren't his kin.

"They were wearing these." Sano displayed the sashes he'd brought.

Lady Hosokawa snatched the magenta sash with the crests worked in gold thread. "That's Myobu's! I embroidered it for her myself!" She pressed the sash to her face and wept.

The concubine grabbed the green, plainer sash. Cradling it, she fell to her knees, sobbed, and rocked back and forth. "Kumoi! No! No!"

Pained by their grief, Sano averted his eyes. He'd witnessed similar scenes too many times since the earthquake. No family was untouched by loss.

The lines on Lord Hosokawa's face knitted his features into a mask of agony. He sagged to his knees. "Myobu. Kumoi." He sounded as if he'd aged ten years. "My only two girls, my treasures. I prayed that they were alive, but I knew that after all this time, they couldn't be."

Sano crouched opposite Lord Hosokawa. "I'm sorry to bring you such bad news."

"There's no need to apologize. Thank you for coming. I know how busy you must be." Lord Hosokawa swallowed tears. "It's better to know that my children are dead than to spend the rest of my life wondering what had become of them."

Tama the concubine crawled up to Sano. "I want to see Kumoi!" The sash was twisted in the clasped hands that she raised to him. "Where is she?"

"And Myobu?" Lady Hosokawa lifted her face. "May I see her?"

Sano hesitated. He couldn't tell the parents that the bodies were on the way to the morgue for an illegal examination.

"You mustn't," Lord Hosokawa told the women. "Not after this long." He obviously thought the bodies were too decomposed for the mothers to bear viewing.

The women wept harder but accepted his pronouncement. Sano felt guilty about letting them keep a false impression.

"After our daughters are cremated, may we have the ashes to bury in our family tomb?" Lord Hosokawa asked.

"Certainly." Sano couldn't help feeling relieved that the family wouldn't see the signs of the examination.

Lord Hosokawa seemed to draw on the strength of will that had made him one of the most capable provincial rulers in Japan. "Where were they found?"

"In a house in Nihonbashi that sank underground during the earthquake," Sano said.

Surprise momentarily distracted Lady Hosokawa from her grief. "Whose house?"

"What were they doing there?" Tama asked between sobs.

"The house belonged to an incense teacher named Usugumo," Sano said. "She and your daughters were playing an incense game when the earthquake struck. They all died."

Lord Hosokawa shook his head, puzzled. "We didn't know Myobu and Kumoi had left the estate that night. We didn't realize they were missing until after the earthquake." He turned to the women. "Did you know they were taking incense lessons in town?"

"No," Lady Hosokawa said.

"Kumoi never told me," Tama said.

"I taught Myobu not to mix with commoners unless they're people we know well, who work for our family or do business with us," Lady Hosokawa said. "She never would have gone there on her own." She angrily turned on Tama. "It must have been your daughter's idea. She liked new fads. She liked slumming with the lower classes."

"That's not true!" The fury in her eyes and the makeup running down her face made Tama look like a demon in a Kabuki play. "Your daughter was the big sister. Kumoi would follow her wherever she went. It's Myobu's fault that my daughter died in that house!"

"Don't you speak to me like that!" Lady Hosokawa slapped Tama's face.

Tama threw herself on Lady Hosokawa. The women became a clawing, sobbing, thrashing tangle of silk robes and disheveled hair. Lord Hosokawa grabbed his wife. Sano grabbed the concubine. They tore the women from each other. Ladies-in-waiting ran into the room. Two groups formed—one with Lady Hosokawa at the center, the other around Tama. They exchanged glares, like rival armies. Lady Hosokawa's pack swept out of the room, followed by Tama's.

"Please forgive our bad manners," Lord Hosokawa said, shamefaced, to Sano. "My wife and my concubine don't get along."

Many men's wives and concubines didn't. That was one reason Sano would never bring another woman into his home. If he did that to Reiko, he would never have a moment of peace. The other reason was that he loved Reiko so much that he couldn't imagine wanting anyone else. He was sorry that the death of Lord Hosokawa's daughters had increased the strife between their mothers, who couldn't even comfort each other.

"How did my daughters die?" Lord Hosokawa asked. "Was it quick and merciful?"

Here came the part of his mission that Sano had been dreading the most. He wished he could assure Lord Hosokawa that his daughters hadn't suffered, but he couldn't withhold the truth. Were he in Lord Hosokawa's position, he would want to know.

"It looks as if they weren't killed by the earthquake." Sano described their red eyes and the rescuer's illness but omitted mentioning their eerily preserved corpses. "They appeared to have been poisoned. There may have been foul play."

"Do you mean murder?" Lord Hosokawa's grief yielded to bewilderment and horror. "By whom?"

"I don't know."

"Whoever killed my daughters will pay," Lord Hosokawa said, angry now. "But I have no expertise in hunting criminals. Will you do it for me?"

Sano could have said that it wasn't his job anymore; but he would make an exception for his friend and ally. "I would be glad to, as soon as I've finished dealing with the problems caused by the earthquake."

A visible jolt of dismay ran through Lord Hosokawa. "When will that be? Years from now, when Edo is back to normal?" He made a slicing motion with his hand. "No. The killer's trail will be cold by then."

"The trail is already cold," Sano gently pointed out. "It's been a month."

Lord Hosokawa seemed not to hear. "I can't wait that long for justice. The hunt for the killer must begin now." His eyes met Sano's. Gone was their usual cautious, worried expression. They glittered with lust for revenge. He jabbed his finger at Sano and spoke as if addressing a subordinate instead of a representative of his lord. "You will help me at once!"

"I'm sorry," Sano said, disconcerted. "The shogun wouldn't want me to take time off from rebuilding his capital to investigate two deaths."

Lord Hosokawa set his jaw against the implication that his daughters' deaths were but a drop in the pail of casualties that the earthquake had begotten. "A few days or a month to find the killer—what difference will it make if Edo is rebuilt that much sooner or later?"

Pitying the man, Sano sought a compromise. "I'll send my people to investigate." He thought of Hirata, then decided that Detective Marume would be more reliable, and perhaps the challenge would distract him from his grief.

"No," Lord Hosokawa said, obstinate. "I want the best for my daughters. I'll have no one but you." His unnaturally bright gaze revealed the wits he'd used to make his domain among the best managed and most profitable. "I'll make it worth your while. The government is desperately in need of money, isn't it? The treasury is almost drained?"

Sano was too surprised to control his expression. The regime's finances weren't supposed to be public knowledge.

"Just as I thought," Lord Hosokawa said with a smug smile. "But Higo Province had the best rice harvest in a decade this past year. I'll make you a proposition." His clan must have merchants in its family tree; he sounded like one now. "Investigate my daughters' murders, and I'll give you a million *koban.*"

The huge sum astounded Sano. Here was his chance to kill two birds with one arrow—serve justice and fund the regime. Although tempted, he said, "I can't accept. The shogun won't approve of his chamberlain having to earn the money by working for you. You're obligated to let him have it for free."

"I'll give you an incentive to accept," Lord Hosokawa replied promptly. "Many of the most powerful *daimyo* are tired of being ruled by the Tokugawa. It's been a hundred years of paying tribute and swallowing their pride. But now the regime's capital is in ruins, its castle is as full of holes as a sieve, its army is minuscule. Three hundred and fifty-one officials are dead. For the first time in a century, the Tokugawa is vulnerable."

The secret of the death toll had leaked out, too, Sano realized with alarm.

"In contrast, we *daimyo* are in good shape," Lord Hosokawa went on. "Granted, many of us lost estates in Edo and quite a few men, but most of our wealth and property and armies is safe in our provinces. The earthquake has given us a once-in-a-lifetime opportunity. If we band together, we can conquer the Tokugawa and rule Japan."

Sano stared in shock at Lord Hosokawa, a friend suddenly turned potential enemy, the regime's worst fear embodied. "Are you one of the *daimyo* who want to strike at the Tokugawa regime while it's down?"

"Of course not," Lord Hosokawa said. "You know me better than that." But an unfamiliar brazenness in his eyes told Sano that he didn't know this man at all. Deranged by his daughters' death, Lord Hosokawa had absorbed the evil that had pervaded the air since the earthquake, that led people to do things they never would under normal circumstances. "Mine is the voice that's urging the hotheads to keep the peace. My clan is a barricade between them and the shogun. But that will change unless you do as I ask. Catch my daughters' killer, or I'll join forces with the others, fight alongside them in a civil war, and ensure their victory."

Flabbergasted, Sano stood. "That's blackmail." He had a nightmarish feeling that had plagued him since the earthquake, that the world had become a place of madness.

Lord Hosokawa rose, meeting Sano's gaze. "It's the length I'll go to to secure your cooperation."

"It's treason to even talk about a revolt, let alone conspire to start one! It's punishable by death!"

"It's only punishable if the revolt fails. If it succeeds, the shogun will be in no position to deprive us of our heads."

Sano grabbed Lord Hosokawa by the shoulders. "Stop this!"

Lord Hosokawa emitted a sound that was half moan, half chuckle, and all awareness that he'd put himself in grave danger. He resembled a man who is crossing a river that gets deeper with his every step. He gazed at Sano as if Sano had thrown him a rope while the current swept him down a waterfall. "It's too late. I've already said too much."

"I'll have to report it to the shogun," Sano said with regret. This was a double tragedy—first his daughters murdered; now Lord Hosokawa would go down for treason, his clan dissolved, its wealth confiscated. There seemed no end to the evils following the earthquake.

"No, I don't think you'll report me," Lord Hosokawa said, suddenly crafty.

Sano tightened his face so it wouldn't show the fear that trickled through him. "Why not? Because you're going to kill me before I can leave this house?" He was alone here, his few troops outside no match for the Hosokawa army.

"Certainly not. Remember, I need you to investigate my daughters' murders. You will decide for yourself that it's better not to tell the shogun what has passed between us."

As Sano frowned in disbelief, Lord Hosokawa said, "Think about what will happen if you tell. The *bakufu* will send what's left of the Tokugawa army to arrest me and the other *daimyo*. Then we'll have no choice but to fight. What would we have to lose?"

"You won't win," Sano said, trying to convince himself as well as Lord Hosokawa. "The Tokugawa branch clans and hereditary allies will support the regime."

"You know they're as weakened as the government," Lord Hosokawa said. "Their domains are located near Edo, in the earthquake zone. Before they can get their troops provisioned and their rear ends on horseback, we'll have our armies on the march from all over Japan, fully supplied with food, equipment, and ammunition."

Appalled by this all-too-realistic scenario, Sano said, "It won't work. You can't coerce me into doing what you want."

"If you bring my daughters' killer to justice, I'll hold off the rebels. They can't win without me. I'll hand over the money to you and persuade them that it's better to donate money to rebuild Edo and shore up the Tokugawa regime than to gamble on coming out on top after a civil war. But if you don't, you'll be to blame for the end of the Tokugawa reign because you wouldn't give up a few days of your precious time. Neither you nor your family will survive the wrath of the shogun, who will see *you* as the traitor." Mournful yet triumphant, Lord Hosokawa said, "So, Chamberlain Sano: Which will it be?"

Sano felt the sting of betrayal, the burn of outrage. Never had he been subjected to such a devious form of pressure to solve a crime, and from a friend, yet! Never had the price of refusal or failure been greater. He was as trapped as the earthquake victims who'd been buried inside their collapsed houses.

Nodding in defeat, he said, "May the gods damn you to hell!"

6

BEARERS CARRIED A palanquin into Sano's estate, whose outer wall was cracked in some places, entirely crumbled in others. Within the wall, sections of the barracks had collapsed. Once, these two-story structures had formed a continuous inner wall around the mansion and the estate's other buildings. Now the few barracks that still stood resembled teeth in a mouth punched by a fist. Followed by four guards on horseback, the bearers plodded through the courtyard, where tents served as quarters for Sano's homeless troops. They set the palanquin down by the mansion, also badly damaged. The front of the half-timbered building listed on its granite foundations. Timbers propped up the eaves that overhung the verandas. The guards dismounted, opened the palanquin's door, and lifted Reiko out.

"I'm all right now, Lieutenant Tanuma," Reiko told her chief body-guard, who held her shoulders. She'd regained consciousness a few moments after fainting in the tent city, but he'd insisted on bringing her home even though she'd wanted to stay. "I can walk."

The guards insisted on carrying her into the mansion. Because the private quarters had collapsed, Sano and Reiko had moved with their children into the mansion's relatively intact front section, which contained offices and reception chambers. They lived in one reception chamber; Sano's principal retainers slept in the others. The guards brought Reiko to her family's chamber, which was crammed with tables, chests, charcoal braziers, other furniture, clothes, and personal belongings salvaged from the ruins. The maids who hurried to assist Reiko had barely enough floor space to spread the futon. Akiko ran in, calling, "Mama, Mama!"

Mother and daughter didn't have the easiest relationship. They often fought, but Akiko didn't like Reiko to go out and leave her. Usually when Reiko returned, Akiko sulked and refused to speak to her. But now she seemed upset by the unusual sight of her mother being carried home like an invalid.

"Don't worry, Akiko, I'm fine." Reiko touched the little girl's hand as the soldiers carefully set her on her feet. But she still felt weak and shaky as she crawled into bed. When Tanuma sent for a doctor, she hadn't the strength to object.

The physician was a nice old man who treated her children's colds and fevers. As he felt the pulse points on Reiko's body, Akiko watched anxiously. He made comical faces at Akiko; she giggled. Reiko heard Sano's officials and secretaries talking and their footsteps in the corridors. There was little privacy or peace since the earthquake. Noise from the construction in Edo Castle started at sunrise and didn't stop until dark. Reiko listened to cooks working in their makeshift kitchen, a flat wooden roof supported by posts in what had once been the garden. The kitchen buildings had burned down. Cooks and other servants slept under the roof at night because their quarters had collapsed.

"How have you been feeling lately?" the doctor asked Reiko.

"A little tired." Reiko explained about her work.

"Are your monthly courses regular?"

Reiko started to say yes, but her mouth stayed open in abrupt, silent surprise. She remembered that shortly before the earthquake, her courses had been a few days late. After the earthquake, with all the turmoil, she'd forgotten. Now she realized that another month had come and gone. "I've missed two courses."

"Ah." The doctor palpated her abdomen with his fingers. "Your little girl will be getting a new baby brother or sister."

Reiko had thought that Akiko and Masahiro were to be her only children. Although she was thankful to have them, she yearned to reexperience the joy of holding a new baby in her arms. She envied women who had big families, and she felt as if she'd let Sano down by giving him only two children, even though he never complained. Now she clasped her belly, which suddenly felt full and swollen. Her eyes welled with happiness.

"Don't exert yourself," the doctor warned. "How many years has it been since your daughter was born? And how many between her and your son? You aren't particularly fertile. You should be careful not to lose this child."

He prescribed herbal concoctions, to foster a healthy pregnancy, and a meat stew—normally prohibited by Buddhist dietary laws but allowed for medicinal purposes—to build up Reiko's strength. After he left, Akiko crept under the quilt and snuggled against Reiko in a rare moment of closeness. Reiko hugged her daughter. But even as she lay smiling with pleasure, she thought of the many women whose children had been killed by the earthquake and fires, and she felt ashamed of her good fortune. She already missed her work in the tent camp. And now she looked forward to months of confinement, idleness, and boredom.

Reiko could hardly wait for the baby's birth and her return to action.

EDO JAIL WAS missing several watchtowers. Those, and much of the surrounding wall, had crumbled into the moat. The dungeon inside stood exposed, minus half its roof and walls. Prisoners were housed in a makeshift jail elsewhere. The bridge was gone. Hirata and the driver had to carry the bodies one by one across a new, flimsy plank bridge that couldn't bear the weight of horses, oxen, or carts. The sentries waved Hirata through the gate with barely a glance at the wrapped corpses; they'd seen many earthquake victims brought in, and assumed these were more of the usual.

Inside, Hirata and the driver set the bodies in a courtyard by a row of corpses covered with blankets. The morgue was a dumping ground for bodies unidentified and unclaimed. The stench of death was powerful. Hirata dismissed the driver, then looked around. Tarps draped the morgue where one of its scabby plaster walls and part of its shaggy thatched roof had fallen. The custodian shuffled out the door, a white-haired old man with a stern face, dressed in the traditional dark blue coat of a physician.

"Hirata-*san*," he said. His bushy brows rose in surprise; he smiled.

"Greetings, Dr. Ito," Hirata said.

Once an esteemed physician to the emperor's court in Miyako, Dr. Ito had been arrested for practicing science learned from Dutch traders. Convicted and sentenced to lifetime servitude in the morgue, he could conduct his experiments without fear of punishment. No one assigned to enforce the law against foreign science ever came to check on him; repugnance and the fear of spiritual pollution and physical disease kept most people away.

Now Dr. Ito was well past eighty. Although his figure had shrunken and his shoulders curved, his eyes had lost none of their keen, bright intelligence. "What have you brought me? More victims of the earthquake?"

"Perhaps they aren't," Hirata said.

Dr. Ito nodded. He understood that Hirata had come at Sano's behest and knew the reason why. "We'd better bring them inside. We'll talk there."

Officialdom didn't care what Dr. Ito did, but it was a different matter for Sano and Hirata. If the authorities got wind of their association with Dr. Ito's science, they would be exiled. Not even men of their high position could break the strict law against foreign science and escape the consequences. Hirata took the risk for Sano, who sought Dr. Ito's assistance only in rare, special cases.

Dr. Ito called to his assistant. Mura came out of the morgue, a thin but sturdy figure clad in unbleached muslin coat, kimono, and trousers. Silver hair gave his square, clever face a distinguished appearance at odds with his social position. Mura was an *eta,* a member of the hereditary outcast class that was linked to occupations such as butchering and leather-tanning, which bore the physical and spiritual taint of death. Shunned by other citizens, the *eta* did dirty work, like collecting garbage and night soil. They also served in Edo Jail as wardens, corpse handlers, torturers, and executioners. Dr. Ito and Mura had become friends across class lines, and Mura did the physical work associated with Dr. Ito's studies.

Mura helped Hirata carry the bodies into the morgue and lay them on the tables. The morgue was cluttered and crowded; the cabinets, the stone troughs for washing the dead, and sundry equipment had been pushed away from the damaged section. The tarp flapped in the wind. Dr. Ito lit lanterns whose flames wavered in the cold drafts.

"Who are they?" Dr. Ito moved toward the bodies.

"An incense teacher named Usugumo. And her two pupils." Hirata described how and where the women had been found. "The pupils appear to be members of the Hosokawa clan. Sano-*san* has gone to the Hosokawa estate to break the news to the family."

"He believes that these women were murdered?"

"Yes. Poisoned."

Mura unwrapped the bodies. In their contorted poses, the women looked even more bizarrely lifelike than before. Their hair stirred in the draft. The lanterns lit sparkles in their terrible red eyes. Hirata almost expected them to stretch their stiff limbs and sit up.

"Ah." As Dr. Ito beheld the women, his eyebrows flew up in astonishment, then slanted downward in an expression of concern. "I shall have to perform an internal examination. On which one would you prefer?"

"The teacher." Hirata figured it was wise not to mutilate the bodies of persons from such an important clan as the Hosokawa.

Mura fetched a long knife with a sharp steel blade. He cut the stained, dusty, dark green kimono and white under-robe off Usugumo, then positioned her on her back. She lay naked, arms bent upward, knees flexed. Her skin was white, smooth for a woman her age, her breasts and stomach firm. Her open mouth in her triangular cat's face made her look as if she were hissing. Her red eyes glared as if she took offense at this rude treatment. Hirata shivered.

Directed by Dr. Ito, Mura made a cut that went straight down the middle of Usugumo's chest then branched in two diagonal cuts across her stomach. He peeled back the flesh. When he opened her abdominal cavity, the strong, pungent odor of garlic arose.

"That's one sign," Dr. Ito said.

"Of what?" Hirata asked.

"Arsenic. It's a mineral that's been used in Chinese medicine for thousands of years, in small doses. In larger doses, it kills. It also delays putrefaction. The Koreans blend it into a drink that's given to criminals of high political status who've been sentenced to death. More commonly, it's a poison for rats." Dr. Ito leaned over Usugumo's body, his eyes agleam with fascination, and pointed. "Observe the other signs."

Her abdominal cavity was as bright yellow as if coated with yellow paint. Hirata stared, amazed. He'd seen plenty of bodies eviscerated during combat, but nothing like this.

"The color is caused by the mixing of arsenic and bodily substances." Dr. Ito added, "Arsenic is used by artists, as a pigment. Some have accidentally poisoned themselves by breathing the powder or licking their paintbrushes. Mura, please cut open the lungs and the stomach."

Mura obeyed. The lungs were congested with lumps of clotted blood, the tissue covered with purple spots. The inside of the stomach was as red as a boiled lobster.

"Note the residue of the stomach contents. Perfectly preserved," Dr. Ito said. "My diagnosis is confirmed."

Hirata looked at the chewed-up rice, greens, and tofu in brown liquid. His own stomach felt queasy. "How was the arsenic administered?"

Dr. Ito examined Usugumo's nose, mouth, and throat. Her tongue was thickened, the membranes red and enflamed. "She inhaled it, I would surmise. Although her digestive tract would look the same if it were taken in food or drink. Did you find any clues at the scene?"

Hirata removed the green paper packets from the pouch at his waist. "Incense samples from the game."

Dr. Ito picked up the open packet and shook the small, round, dark brown pellets onto the table. "Let's try a test."

He went to a cabinet and fetched a pair of fine tweezers and a knife with a wide, flat blade. He lifted down a lantern from its hook on the wall. He held the knife over its flame until the blade glowed red-hot. Then he used the tweezers to pick up an incense pellet and drop it onto the hot blade. The pellet burned and smoked. There came the sweet incense odor, then the stench of garlic. Dr. Ito quickly carried the knife to the open window to disperse the fumes.

"The test is positive. Iron and heat plus arsenic produces a garlic smell. The arsenic was administered by way of this incense sample." Dr. Ito added, "The women may have inhaled only a little poisoned smoke, but it went straight into their lungs and was enough to kill them. The incense probably continued burning after they were dead. The fumes accumulated inside the house and preserved their bodies."

"So we know that the women were poisoned and how," Hirata said, gratified yet disturbed. "If only we knew who did it."

7

THE TOP OFFICIALS of the Tokugawa regime had once lived in fine estates within Edo Castle, in mansions surrounded by gardens and walls. Now their quarter was reduced to a few intact sections of buildings amid rubble heaps. Most of the residents had evacuated. Only one estate was still occupied. Here, sentries guarded the private chambers, a square building with rooms arranged around an inner courtyard. Its covered corridors were attached to nothing—the wings once connected to the chambers lay in pieces. The site was as still as a tomb.

Inside the chamber, he lay in bed beneath heavy quilts. The only light came from a barred window slightly open to vent the smoke from the sunken charcoal braziers. His muscles and bones ached. Pain throbbed in his head behind his sore, closed eyes. Suspended between wakefulness and nightmare, he breathed shallow sips of air. But his physical pain was nothing compared to the agony in his spirit, which wracked him every moment of every day. Emptiness yawned in his heart like a black cavern so deep that all the tears he cried could never fill it. The distant noise of shovels and pickaxes barely impinged on him while he mourned.

The floorboards squeaked as footsteps paused outside his room. The door slid open a crack. The cautious voice of his manservant said, "Master Yanagisawa-*san*? Are you awake?"

Yanagisawa lay still, his eyes closed.

"You have a visitor," the servant persisted.

"I don't want to see anyone." Yanagisawa's voice was rusty from disuse.

"It's Kato Kinhide. From the Council of Elders."

Kato was an old ally of Yanagisawa's, from the days when Yanagisawa had still cared about politics. "Tell him to get lost."

"I will not get lost," said a man's irate voice. "Not until I've talked to you."

The door scraped all the way open. Yanagisawa screwed his eyes shut tighter. Kato entered the room, made a sound of disgust, and said, "It smells like a wild animal den in here! Don't you ever wash?" He tripped over trays of food that Yanagisawa had barely touched. "And when was the last time you ate a good meal? Not since Yoritomo died, I'll wager."

Yanagisawa had forbidden everyone to speak Yoritomo's name or mention his death. That his beautiful, beloved son was gone was unbearable enough. Hearing the fact spoken made it even worse. Anger at Kato's insensitivity shook him out of his torpor. His eyelids, crusted with dried tears, peeled open. Kato moved across his bleary vision, a thin figure with wide shoulders exaggerated by the epaulets of his surcoat, the topknot protruding from his narrow head. As Kato flung open windows, cold, fresh air blew into the room.

"Don't." Yanagisawa pulled his hand from under the quilts and raised it to shield his eyes from the light.

Kato stood by the bed, staring down at him. "Merciful gods." Kato had a flat face with leathery skin, its features so minimal that they looked like slits cut for eyes, nostrils, and mouth. He studied Yanagisawa's long, scraggly hair, mustache, and beard, sallow skin, sunken eyes, and the fingernails as long and curved as talons. "You're even worse than I expected."

Yanagisawa didn't care what Kato thought; nor did he care that he'd lost the beauty in which he'd once taken great pride. "You've talked to me. Now you can go."

"I'm not finished." Urgency did away with the respect that Kato owed to Yanagisawa. "I came to tell you it's time to stop playing dead and pull yourself together. It's been almost a year."

A stab of offense pierced the barrier that Yanagisawa had built between himself and his fellow humans. "That's easy for you to say. You don't know what it's like."

"I know that Yoritomo had his throat cut. I know he died a horrible, premature death," Kato said with brutal frankness. "I also know that letting yourself go to hell won't bring him back." He noticed the tears welling in Yanagisawa's eyes. "Unless you snap out of it, you'll have a lot more to cry about besides Yoritomo."

"Leave me alone," Yanagisawa whispered.

Kato went on, relentless: "Your political faction is in shambles. Allies have been deserting you like water leaking from a punctured bladder. Pretty soon you can forget about regaining the status and power you lost when the shogun blamed you for that fiasco at the palace last year. You can say good-bye to your hope of ruling Japan."

"I don't care about that anymore." Yanagisawa pulled the quilt over his head.

Kato tore it off. The slits of his eyes blazed with anger. "Well, I care! So do the others who've stood by you and fought for you all these months. We're not going to let you destroy us as well as yourself!"

That was all they really cared about—their own fate. Yanagisawa said, "Thank you for your loyalty. I'm sorry I've disappointed you."

"You'll have to do more than apologize." Desperation roughened Kato's voice. "Get out of bed, man! Before it's too late!"

"I'm not moving."

"You will move whether you want to or not." Kato unfurled a scroll in front of Yanagisawa's face, displaying elegant black calligraphy and the red official seal. "This is a decree from the shogun. It contains orders for you to vacate your home and travel to Tosa Province."

Shock hit Yanagisawa so hard that he stirred in spite of himself. "What for?"

"To take up a new post, as administrator of the local government office."

The *daimyo* ruled the provinces, but the Tokugawa regime had officials stationed in each, to look out for its interests. Tosa was located in southwest Japan, some two months' journey from Edo. Yanagisawa couldn't believe what he was hearing. "I'm being banished."

"That's the gist of it," Kato said, triumphant because he finally had Yanagisawa's attention. "You're to leave Edo in ten days."

For the first time in almost a year Yanagisawa's thoughts turned to matters other than Yoritomo. His mind, dulled by too much sleeping and crying and not enough nourishment and exercise, cranked into motion. A roil of anger encroached on his grief. "This is Sano's doing."

Sano was his longtime rival for the shogun's favor, for control of the regime. Sano had set off a chain of events that had cost Yoritomo his life. On top of all the other blows Sano had dealt him, Yanagisawa had Sano to thank for the loss of his son, the only person he'd loved and who'd loved him. Hatred burned away the fog of mourning that engulfed Yanagisawa.

"He's not satisfied to have brought me so low," Yanagisawa said bitterly. "He convinced the shogun to run me out of town."

"I do believe I see a spark of life returning." Kato's sardonic smile was tinged with relief. "But I must correct you. Sano isn't behind the shogun's orders. It's Ienobu."

"Ienobu? The shogun's nephew?" Fresh surprise jolted Yanagisawa upright too fast. He winced at the pain in his muscles. "But we've always been on good terms. In fact, we discussed the possibility of a marriage between his daughter and . . ." He couldn't say Yoritomo's name. "It would have sealed our alliance." An alliance that would have defeated Sano.

"Water under the bridge. While you've been gone, Ienobu and the shogun have become very close. Ienobu thinks he doesn't need you anymore, with good reason. You seem about as useful as a dead dog."

"If I'm a dead dog, why doesn't he just leave me in peace?"

"Ienobu is a smart, cautious rascal. He's not about to gamble that just because you're down now, it means you'll stay down. He won't take the chance that you'll interfere with his becoming the next shogun. No—he's sweeping you out of the way as if you were burning cinders in a gunpowder arsenal."

Yanagisawa flopped back on the bed. Accustomed to quiet and solitude, he felt exhausted by the conversation, unable to cope with threats. Grief immobilized him like iron shackles. "Go away."

Kato regarded Yanagisawa with contempt that didn't hide his hope that Yanagisawa would rise to the occasion or his fear that Yanagisawa couldn't. Then he stood. "Farewell, for now. But hear this: Don't think you can just ignore the shogun's orders. When ten days are up and you're still here, the army will come and pry you out. You'd better do something."

8

SANO AND HIS troops rode back to Edo Castle through deserted streets as the last rays of daylight faded. Since the earthquake the city had been eerily quiet at night. The only sounds were the horses' hoofbeats and the howling of dogs. Sano fancied that the darkness brought out the evil spirits that had erupted from hell when the earth split open. They owned the night, while humans hid in their tents and ruined homes. Sano looked up at Edo Castle, looming against a sky that was the dull red color of a wound. A black hulk with jagged outlines where broken towers and walls rose, it seemed a haunt for demons.

Hirata rode up beside Sano on the avenue outside the castle and said, "You were right. It was poison." In a low voice, in case of spies, Hirata described Dr. Ito's examination.

"Just as I thought," Sano said without satisfaction. "I've been hoping I could tell Lord Hosokawa I made a mistake and his daughters weren't murdered. Because he's put me in a bad position." He told Hirata about the bargain that Lord Hosokawa had forced him to make.

Hirata let his breath out in a whistle. "That is bad. I suppose we'd better not waste any time. Where do we start the investigation?"

"Meet me at my house and we'll talk about it. Right now I have to report to the shogun." As they neared the castle gate, Sano said, "Have you anything else to tell me?"

He noticed that Hirata paused for an instant before replying, "No. Nothing."

* * *

SANO FOUND THE shogun right where he'd left him, in the guesthouse with Ienobu. The pair sat on the dais in the same positions. The same lanterns burned; the air in the room was just as stale. Sano had the strange sensation that time had stood still for them, whereas a lifetime had passed for him since morning, when all he'd had to worry about was building a new Edo up from the ruins.

"Well, ahh, it's about time you came back," the shogun said.

"We've already finished dinner." Ienobu scrubbed his protruding teeth with a napkin.

Their tray tables held the remains of an abundant meal—fish with plenty of meat left on the bones, rice bowls half full, vegetables and dumplings picked over. Sano thought of all the hungry people in Edo. He tried not to think ill of the shogun for wasting food. His own stomach growled. He hadn't eaten since breakfast.

"What took you so long?" the shogun demanded.

"I did an extensive inspection of the city, so I could bring you an accurate report." Sano couldn't breathe a word about how he'd really spent the day. Lord Hosokawa's warning shackled his tongue. "The *daimyo* have started to rebuild their estates. The townspeople are clearing out their neighborhoods. Everyone is hard at work." Sano downplayed Edo's miserable state, lest he upset the shogun. "Things are progressing."

"No, they are not!" the shogun exclaimed. "I went up in a guard tower today and had a look at the city. And what did I see? Ruins everywhere! And all those tents." His face puckered with disgust. "Everyone has reverted to, ahh, savagery!"

Sano felt his temper slipping even faster than it had that morning. He wanted to say, *Where else do you expect the homeless people to live?* And, *Why did you send me on a tour of inspection when all you had to do was climb a few steps and see for yourself?* If he hadn't gone on the tour, he wouldn't have found the bodies and he wouldn't be in this impossible position.

"Fixing Edo is going to take time," he managed to say instead. "What you saw was the preliminary stage. Things will improve rapidly from now on."

He saw Ienobu smirk: The man was enjoying his struggle to control his tongue. Sano suspected that the shogun's idea to view Edo from the guard tower had come from Ienobu.

"You'd better be right," the shogun said. "Because you're always using work as an excuse for why you're too busy to be with me. And since you, ahh, have so little to show for all the time you've been gone, I'm beginning to wonder what you're really up to."

If he only knew, Sano thought. But the shogun would never know everything Sano did on his behalf. That now included hiding the fact that the *daimyo* were close to rising up against his regime. Sano realized that his conspiracy of silence with Lord Hosokawa was tantamount to treason. The irony of it astounded him. That his samurai loyalty required him to commit treason in order to protect his lord!

"I'll have more to show soon," Sano said. It would be a civil war if he didn't catch whoever had killed Lord Hosokawa's daughters. That would give the shogun something to complain about.

"In the meantime, you have me," Ienobu told the shogun.

The shogun turned his pique on Ienobu. "You can't do the things that need to be done! You just, ahh, hang around and live off me! That's why I need Sano-*san*."

Ienobu sat up straighter than Sano had thought his hunched back would allow. Offense and humiliation showed on his ugly features. He turned to Sano, who felt a sudden change in the atmosphere between Ienobu and himself. They weren't just cautiously watching each other anymore. Ienobu now resented how much the shogun depended on Sano, and his caution toward Sano had changed to active dislike.

"Your nephew performs a valuable service by providing counsel to you, Your Excellency," Sano said in an attempt to help Ienobu regain face. The last thing he needed was another enemy.

Ienobu tightened his lips until they almost covered his teeth.

"Well, ahh, you had better think about improving your service to me," the shogun told Sano. "I want some real progress in the city, and I want it tomorrow!"

Sano's fortitude strained toward the breaking point. Mutinous ideas came unbidden to his mind. Maybe the shogun deserved to be overthrown. It would be a fitting punishment for his selfishness and stupidity. What if Sano deliberately failed to satisfy Lord Hosokawa's demands and let matters run their course? He could then join the rebels. They would surely welcome him, his troops, and the allies he could bring to their side. The shogun would never threaten him, abuse him, or make impossible demands on him ever again. These ideas tempted and horrified Sano. He was infected with the same madness as Lord Hosokawa; the earthquake had eroded his own sanity. The honor he'd served all his life was a dam cracking under the strain.

The dam held, shored up by forty-six years of following the Way of the Warrior. "Yes, Your Excellency." Sano promised, "I'll do better." Leaving the room, he glanced at Ienobu.

Ienobu gazed back as if he'd sensed Sano's thoughts and wondered how best to use them to his own advantage.

NOISES IN THE corridor awakened Reiko from a sound sleep. She stretched under the quilts, drowsy and relaxed. Akiko was gone. The room was dim, the lamps in the corridor lit. It was evening; she'd slept the whole afternoon. She heard Sano's voice.

Then she remembered.

Fully awake now, Reiko clambered out of bed and quickly dressed. She must tell Sano about the baby. But when he came into the room, Hirata and Masahiro were with him. She decided to wait until she and Sano were alone. She wasn't yet ready to spread the news outside their family, and she and Sano would want to tell Masahiro privately together, as they'd done when she became pregnant with Akiko.

"You're home early," she said to Sano. This was the first time since the earthquake that he'd come home before midnight. He looked even more careworn than usual. "Did something bad happen today?"

Sano exchanged glances with Hirata. "That would be an understatement."

"What is it?" Masahiro said, full of eager curiosity.

"We'd better sit down," Sano said. The family took places around the *kosatsu*—a table built over a sunken charcoal brazier. Their feet and legs were warm in the space around the fire. A quilt covered the table and their laps. The clutter of their belongings surrounded them. A maid served them tea and departed. "Before I tell you, you must swear to keep it secret."

Apprehension crept through Reiko. "I swear," she and Masahiro said in unison.

"Hirata-*san*, will you make sure nobody eavesdrops?" Sano asked.

There were spies everywhere, Reiko knew; even in their own household. Hirata went to stand outside the door. Sano told Reiko and Masahiro about the dead women in the sunken house, his visit to the Hosokawa estate, and Lord Hosokawa's blackmail.

"If you solve the crime, Lord Hosokawa will hand over a million *koban* to pay for rebuilding Edo? And if you don't, he and the other *daimyo* will overthrow the Tokugawa regime?" Reiko was so shocked that she forgot about her own news. "Did I hear you correctly?" When Sano nodded, her disbelief gave way to horror. "Doesn't Lord Hosokawa know that's treason?"

"Yes. I told him," Sano said. "But he's not thinking about anything except his own grief and revenge for his daughters."

"So you agreed to do what he wants?" Masahiro asked.

"I didn't see any other choice." Sano explained why he couldn't just report Lord Hosokawa to the shogun. "The best thing to do is solve the case quickly."

"But how can you fit a murder investigation in with all the work you have to do?" It seemed impossible to Reiko.

"I'll need some help, even if I handle it personally. The problem is, it needs to be kept secret. I can't send my retainers out to interview people and dig up clues. My enemies would surely notice that I was diverting effort away from the earthquake repairs to investigate the murders. They would wonder what sort of hold Lord Hosokawa has on me."

Reiko knew that Sano had many enemies, including a large faction loyal to Yanagisawa. The secret deal between Sano and Lord Hosokawa, and their conspiracy of silence, made Sano a party to treason. This information would be just the weapon his enemies needed to destroy Sano.

"If people start prying, your deal with Lord Hosokawa could come out," Reiko said.

"The Tokugawa regime would have to take action against Lord Hosokawa and the *daimyo*. The war would start." Masahiro's clever mind quickly grasped the implications.

"Which means I can only use assistants I can absolutely trust to be discreet," Sano said. "That means Hirata, Detective Marume, and the two of you."

Reiko decided to put off telling Sano she was pregnant. If he knew, he would refuse to let her join in the investigation, for fear it would tax her health and endanger the baby. But he needed her help. Unless he caught the killer, Lord Hosokawa would make good on his threats. The civil war would start. Sano would be blamed and executed as a traitor. His family would be put to death as well. If Reiko didn't live long enough to give birth, the baby would die with her. Although Sano had never failed to solve a case, this might be the first time. Reiko couldn't allow that to happen. Furthermore, she'd carried and given birth to Masahiro and Akiko without any trouble, and she felt fine now. As long as she restricted herself to visiting and talking with a few people, what harm could a little detective work do?

"You can count on me," she said.

Sano smiled; the tension in his face relaxed. "I know I can."

Reiko saw more reason to help Sano. He couldn't count on Hirata or Marume for much. Marume was so grief-stricken; the investigation might be beyond his capabilities. And Sano had confided to her that something was amiss with Hirata, who often disappeared for lengthy, unexplained periods. That left her and Masahiro.

"You can count on me, too," Masahiro said.

But he was only a child, Reiko thought. No matter how clever and mature he was, he couldn't do everything that a murder investigation required. And he had other duties.

"You'll have to stay with the shogun," Sano said. "Both of us deserting him at the same time would be asking for trouble."

Disappointed, Masahiro said, "Isn't there any way I can help?"

"Watch Ienobu," Sano said. "Let me know what he does. I may find other things for you to do later."

Masahiro nodded happily. But Reiko knew he couldn't do the things she could. Sano needed her. She couldn't bow out of the investigation.

"What have you learned so far?" she asked.

"The cause of death." Sano described the results of Dr. Ito's examination.

"Arsenic in the incense," Reiko mused. "It suggests that someone who was present at the game is the poisoner. Perhaps Madam Usugumo, the teacher."

"But why would she poison her students?" Masahiro asked. "Weren't they paying her money?"

Reiko smiled, proud of his astuteness. "Usugumo had the best opportunity to poison the incense, although she must have taught her pupils to blend incense. One of them could have mixed in the arsenic."

"That would have been stupid," Masahiro said. "I think somebody else killed them all."

"We'd better pray that you're right, or that Usugumo is guilty," Sano said.

"Why?" Masahiro asked.

"Picture me telling Lord Hosokawa that the killer is one of his daughters," Sano said.

"Oh," Reiko said. "He would be furious."

"Maybe furious enough to renege on our deal and lead the *daimyo* into war."

"Surely he wouldn't be so vindictive or so rash!" Reiko exclaimed.

"I wouldn't like to find out the hard way," Sano said.

Reiko and Masahiro pondered the implications of what they'd heard. Reiko said, "I was about to offer to go to the Hosokawa estate and talk to the women who live there." That was her strength as a detective—she could go places where a man wouldn't be welcome and question people who would hide information from Sano. "But if I do, I might turn up evidence against the daughters. Maybe I shouldn't go?"

"No, you should," Sano said. "We need to get to the truth about the murders."

He wanted the truth even if it wasn't what Lord Hosokawa wanted to hear. Reiko loved him for his honor. "I don't suppose you would consider blaming the murders on Madam Usugumo or someone else who's dead and won't suffer any consequences?"

"I can't say I haven't thought of it." Sano spoke with chagrin. "If one of the daughters is the killer, I'd much rather say it was Usugumo. But I promised Lord Hosokawa justice. That's what I'll give him if I can. And if I frame a scapegoat, the real killer would go free, possibly to kill again."

"You're right," Reiko said. Masahiro nodded. "I'll go to the Hosokawa estate tomorrow. What will you do?"

"Hirata-*san* and I will go back to the incense teacher's house and look for what we would have looked for today if we'd known we would be investigating the murders."

"It's dinnertime," Masahiro said. "Is there anything to eat?"

The household food supply was running low. "I'll go and see," Reiko said. As she left the room, her conscience pricked her, but she told herself that keeping her pregnancy a secret from Sano was for the best.

9

THE NEXT MORNING was warmer but cloudy. As Sano rode through the ruined city with Hirata, Detective Marume, and his troops, it looked like a painting done in ink. Black crows flew from crumbling gray earthen walls into a gray sky. A gray dog detached itself from a gray pile of debris. Sano felt as if his eyes had lost their ability to see color. He had to glance at the red medallion design on his coat sleeve to reassure himself that they hadn't.

He and his group arrived in the incense teacher's neighborhood. The same townsmen they'd met yesterday were still searching for earthquake victims. Sano was glad to see the young, bristly haired Okura among them, apparently recovered. The headman named Jiro came to greet Sano.

Sano explained that he was curious about the murders; he didn't mention that he was investigating them. "Are any of Madam Usugumo's neighbors around? They might have seen or heard something that could indicate who poisoned her and her pupils."

Jiro's face saddened. "Most of the people from our block were killed. Others are missing. We'll probably find them eventually." He nodded toward the sunken houses. "I know of only three people besides myself who are alive. A papermaker and his wife, and a little girl from next door. They're in a camp somewhere."

Sano was disturbed to learn that so few potential witnesses existed, yet he'd expected that. "Do you know of anyone who might have wanted to harm Usugumo?"

"As a matter of fact, I thought of someone after you left yesterday." Jiro brightened. "A man named Mizutani."

"Who is he?"

"An incense master. Not just a teacher, but a big expert. He came to visit Usugumo a few times. They got into arguments. He would yell so loud, you could hear him all the way down the block. Once, he dragged Usugumo out of her house by her hair and started beating her up. I had to call the police. He wasn't arrested, they just told him not to come back."

"But maybe he did come back," Hirata said.

"One more time, to slip poison into Usugumo's incense." Sano asked the headman, "Do you know if Mizutani is still alive?"

"Yes. He is. He came by a few days after the earthquake. When he saw what had happened to Usugumo's house, he laughed."

"Can you tell me where he is?"

"He's probably at his house in Asakusa district. It's still standing."

"I'll talk to Mizutani and the neighbors," Sano told Hirata. "You take another look inside Usugumo's house and see if you can find any clues."

"All right," Hirata said.

Sano hoped Hirata would prove to be more reliable than usual.

ACCOMPANIED BY GUARDS on horseback, Reiko traveled in her palanquin along the southern highway, toward Lord Hosokawa's estate. Mixed emotions beset her. She felt ecstatic about her pregnancy but guilty because she hadn't told Sano. She was anxious about bringing a new child into the shambles that she saw through the windows of her palanquin, and frightened by the thought of what would happen if she and Sano couldn't find out who had killed the Hosokawa daughters.

But even as she worried, Reiko had faith in Sano and her marriage, a faith that burned within her like a flame that never went out. They'd always prevailed in the past. Surely they would again. And she was invigorated by the sense of a mission they always shared during an investigation. She felt better than she had since the earthquake, and the new life growing inside her fueled her determination to succeed.

When she reached the samurai estates, she saw that they were hardly damaged at all. She couldn't help envying people whose houses were in better condition than hers, but she knew the earthquake had touched everyone in some way, even if it didn't show. Then Reiko saw the black cloth—the symbol of death—that draped Lord Hosokawa's gate. The portals of almost every house in Edo that still stood had worn a black drape during the past month.

The sentries stepped out of a guardhouse to meet her party. Lieutenant Tanuma, her guard captain, told them, "This is Lady Reiko, wife of Chamberlain Sano. She's here to offer her condolences to the Hosokawa clan."

The gate opened. Her bearers carried Reiko into the courtyard. A maid came out on the veranda and bowed. She was an older woman, her face round, friendly, and creased with smile lines despite the tears that trickled down her cheeks. She ushered Reiko into the mansion. From down the corridor wafted a strong smell of incense. Reiko thought of the three women poisoned during an incense game, lying dead underground. She shuddered.

Drumbeats resonated, male voices chanted prayers, and women wept—sounds that were too familiar since the earthquake. Reiko followed the maid into a large chamber divided in half by sliding wooden doors. In the half that Reiko entered, people knelt near a table which held a wooden tablet that bore the name "Myobu," a portrait of a young woman, lit candles, smoking incense burners, and offerings of rice, fruit, and sake. A priest in a saffron robe beat a gourd-shaped wooden drum as he chanted. A woman with gray hair, dressed in white—the color of mourning— knelt amid other women who dabbed their eyes with handkerchiefs. Reiko supposed this was Lady Hosokawa. She had well proportioned features that must once have made her attractive although not beautiful. Her skin was sallow, her expression stoic, but when she looked up at Reiko, her eyes were so full of pain that Reiko shied away from her gaze.

The maid introduced Reiko. Reiko knelt and bowed, ill at ease. "Lady Hosokawa, my husband told me about your daughter." She'd come under false pretenses, to take advantage of a grieving mother. "Please accept my sympathy."

"Thank you." Lady Hosokawa's voice was hoarse from weeping. "You're very kind."

Even if solving the murder case would lead to justice for the Hosokawa clan, that didn't assuage Reiko's guilt. She looked away, through the open doors. In the other half of the chamber were another funeral altar, another chanting priest, another group of female mourners. The woman at that group's center lay prostrated before the altar. She must be Tama, Lord Hosokawa's concubine. Her companions tried to soothe her as she wailed.

Reiko remembered Sano mentioning that Lord Hosokawa's wife and concubine didn't get along. They must hate each other so much that they'd chosen to hold separate funerals for their daughters. Reiko was thankful that Sano had never taken a concubine. She would hate any woman who shared her husband.

Lady Hosokawa and her companions sat in silence while her priest chanted and drummed. Reiko ventured, "It's so terrible, what happened."

"Yes." Lady Hosokawa seemed disinclined for conversation.

"Who would do such a thing?" Reiko asked, pretending mere curiosity.

"I don't know."

Forced to be bolder, Reiko said, "Is there anyone who was angry with your daughter or her sister and might have wanted to hurt them?"

Lady Hosokawa contemplated the portrait on the altar. Her daughter Myobu had been an ordinary-looking girl, her forehead low and her chin weak. "No." She turned to Reiko, and her dry eyes narrowed. "Why do you ask?"

Reiko flushed. She decided she owed the woman the truth rather than continue her subterfuge. "My husband is investigating the murders," she began.

"I am aware of that," Lady Hosokawa said crisply. "I am also aware that you often assist him with that sort of business. I assume that is what you are doing now." She clearly disapproved of Reiko's behavior. "If you and your husband expect to find out who killed my daughter, you should not be wasting your time here."

Chagrined because she'd been so quickly dismissed, Reiko said, "My apologies for bothering you." She bowed, then stood. "I'll just pay my respects to Tama-*san* before I leave." She felt Lady Hosokawa's gaze on her as she walked to the other side of the room.

Tama sat up. Her face was a wet, shiny mess of tears, her dyed-black coiffure lopsided from her tearing at it, her white brocade kimono wrinkled. Even so, Reiko could see that she was prettier, and younger, than Lady Hosokawa. Reiko knelt, bowed, introduced herself, and offered condolences.

"I heard what *she* said to you." Tama shot a bitter glance at Lady Hosokawa. "That mean, stiff-necked old crow!" she muttered, too quietly for Lady Hosokawa to hear. Her companions nodded. They were women her age, similarly overdressed. "I could have told you it's no use talking to *her*. *She* doesn't care about avenging our girls. All that matters to *her* is being proper and discreet."

Reiko saw a chance to take advantage of the enmity between Lord Hosokawa's concubine and wife. "Maybe you can help me find out who killed your daughter."

Tama's tearful gaze moved to her daughter's portrait. Either the painter had flattered his subject or Kumoi had possessed the beauty that her older sister had lacked. Kumoi's eyes were large and tilted in her oval face, their expression alluring, her lips delicate and sensuous.

"I'll do whatever I can," Tama said. "Ask me anything you want."

"Thank you," Reiko said. "Who would have wanted to kill Kumoi?"

"Oh, that's an easy question!" Tama glared at Lady Hosokawa.

"Tama." Lady Hosokawa didn't raise her voice, but its ominous force carried it across the room.

Tama choked on whatever words she'd planned to say. Fear hunched her shoulders. Her anger faded into sullenness. Her companions cringed. The maid walked over from Lady Hosokawa's half of the chamber and said to Reiko, "Lady Hosokawa wants me to take you to the other room for refreshments."

Reiko looked through the doors. Lady Hosokawa stared back. Reiko had no choice but to say "Many thanks," and rise. She glanced at Tama as she left the chamber. The concubine wouldn't meet her gaze.

Following the maid down the corridor, Reiko realized that what little she'd managed to learn was worse than nothing. Tama had seemed about to accuse Lady Hosokawa or her daughter. Here was the clue Reiko had dreaded finding, evidence which implicated a Hosokawa clan member in the crime. Fear brought on morning sickness as Reiko sat in a chamber where the maid poured tea and set food on a tray table before her. The smell of the sweet rice cakes was nauseating. She breathed deeply and sipped the bitter green tea; her stomach settled.

The maid knelt nearby. Her friendly smile broadened, revealing gaps between childlike teeth. She leaned toward Reiko, obviously bursting to talk. Here, perhaps, was the witness who would reveal the things that Reiko had failed to learn from Tama and Lady Hosokawa.

LYING IN BED, Yanagisawa watched gray daylight brighten the open slit of his window. He turned restlessly, trying to find a comfortable position. Sleep was a quarry he'd been chasing all night and failed to catch. The order from the shogun had jarred him out of his lethargy. Anger at Ienobu rekindled the fire in him that Yoritomo's death had extinguished. His blood raced, stimulating muscles and nerves, flushing the rust out of his brain, which teemed with thoughts and plans.

He was reviving in spite of himself. The threat had awakened some primitive, animal instinct that said he'd mourned enough. And there was a spark in him that had never gone out, his hatred toward Sano, who had brought about Yoritomo's death. He couldn't let Sano get away with it. Yanagisawa threw off the covers and stood up.

Queasiness and sore joints almost toppled him. Only fury and pride kept him vertical. He called his servants: "I want a bath."

They scrubbed and poured water over him three times to remove the filth from his emaciated body. By the time he climbed into the tub, he was exhausted. He lay in the hot, steaming water and closed his eyes. This was the first pleasure he'd experienced since Yoritomo's death. He steeled himself against it because Yoritomo would never feel pleasure again. His servants dried him and put a robe on him. His valet filed his nails and shaved off his scraggly beard and mustache. The mirror showed gaunt cheeks and pallid skin. But his large, liquid eyes still gleamed. Miraculously, he was still handsome.

His reflection smiled a ghost of his old, sardonic smile.

The valet shaved his crown, then trimmed his hair, oiled it with wintergreen oil, and tied it into a topknot. Dressed in opulent crimson and black silk robes, Yanagisawa ate his breakfast, rice gruel with dried fish and pickled vegetables. It tasted wonderful; he was actually hungry.

Kato returned while Yanagisawa was finishing his tea, and said, "Well, well, somebody's feeling better. When I saw you yesterday, I was afraid you were done for."

"Never underestimate me," Yanagisawa said. "And you would be wise to address me with a little more respect from now on."

"Yes, of course." Kato hastily knelt opposite Yanagisawa and bowed. The slits of his eyes glinted with the fear that Yanagisawa had always inspired in friends and foes alike, but his narrow mouth smiled; he was glad Yanagisawa had risen from the dead. "I take it you're not leaving Edo?"

"That's correct."

"What are you going to do?"

"Reclaim my rightful place at court. Take up my business where I left off." Yanagisawa didn't say that his business was to gain absolute domination over Japan. That would be treason, punishable by death. Spies still lurked in Edo, despite the earthquake. And he didn't have to say it; Kato understood.

Skepticism wrinkled Kato's brow. "There's not much room for you at court these days. Not with Sano leading the government and Ienobu sucking up to the shogun."

Sano and Ienobu, the two adversaries he had to battle. "I don't need much room." Yanagisawa held up his thumb and forefinger, a hairsbreadth apart. "Just enough to slip my secret weapon in."

"What secret weapon?"

"An ally to plant close to the shogun, to influence him and help me regain control over him," Yanagisawa whispered.

Kato reacted with confusion and disbelief. "That's what you did before. You mean to do it again?"

"It worked, didn't it?" Yanagisawa wouldn't admit that he wasn't exactly flush with new ideas; his mind still hadn't quite regained its usual speed or originality.

"But how are you going to——?" Kato said with startled enlightenment, "You're going to replace Yoritomo."

Pain twisted through Yanagisawa like a skewer studded with barbs. "Don't say that! Yoritomo can't be replaced! Not ever!"

"Forgive me." Kato raised his hands, patted the air. "Let me rephrase that: You intend to find a young man to perform the duties that you need performed. Correct?"

Yanagisawa nodded, regretting his outburst. He would have to keep a tighter control over his emotions, which made him vulnerable.

"Who's the lucky pawn?" Kato asked.

The word *pawn* rankled. Yanagisawa had made a pawn of Yoritomo, who'd become the shogun's favorite male concubine, the sole, dubious achievement of his short life. "I have four candidates."

"Oh, I see. Your other sons."

Yanagisawa had fathered five sons on five different women. He also had a wife and a daughter, stashed away in the country, whom he seldom saw. His four remaining sons ranged in age from pubescent to late teens, just right to appeal to the shogun's taste. It couldn't have worked out better if he'd planned it. Yoritomo had been his favorite, and he didn't know the others, whom he monitored from a distance, like a merchant keeps track of business interests in faraway provinces. But that was about to change.

Kato regarded Yanagisawa with admiration and repugnance. "First you share the shogun's bed, then Yoritomo does, and now you're going to put some more of your flesh and blood there. You must be the most ruthless man in the world!"

"Ruthlessness is the offspring of necessity," Yanagisawa said.

"I don't suppose it matters whether the new secret weapon likes following in the previous one's footsteps."

"Not at all." Even though Yoritomo had never complained, and always professed himself eager to do whatever Yanagisawa wanted, Yanagisawa had hated to make Yoritomo sacrifice himself for his father's political goal. Because he'd loved Yoritomo. But love wasn't an issue with his other sons. "He should be glad to cooperate. He'll have a brilliant future."

As brilliant as Yoritomo's? The question was written on Kato's face. Yanagisawa pretended not to notice. Kato asked, "When do you decide which son gets to do the honors?"

"I'm going to look them over today," Yanagisawa said.

His heartbeat quickened with anticipation that had little to do with the prospect of advancing his political aims, thwarting Ienobu, or punishing Sano. He was surprised to find himself wishing that one of his other sons could fill the emptiness in him. The strength of his desire was alarming.

10

"KEEP ME COMPANY while I eat." Reiko invited the maid at the Hosokawa estate.

The maid eagerly scrambled closer. "Thank you, mistress."

"I sensed that Lady Hosokawa and Tama aren't on very good terms," Reiko hinted.

That was all it took to open the floodgates. "They hate each other," the maid said with relish. "When Lord Hosokawa brought Tama in as his concubine, Lady Hosokawa was so jealous. He gave Tama her own servants and her own rooms. When he's here, he spends his nights with her. He only went to Lady Hosokawa's bed to get children. After he had enough, he stopped going."

A *daimyo* needed one legitimate son to be his heir, others in case the first didn't survive, and daughters to use as political pawns in the marriage market, Reiko knew.

"Tama put on airs. She acted as if she were the lady of the house." The maid grimaced in distaste. "Lady Hosokawa was furious. But Lord Hosokawa made her be nice to Tama."

It was a story Reiko had heard often. How cruel the custom of taking concubines could be to wives! Again, Reiko felt lucky to be married to Sano.

"Lady Hosokawa got back at Tama," the maid said gleefully. "She put mouse dung and dead flies in Tama's food. Tama got sick and didn't know why."

Another spell of queasiness lapped at Reiko as she thought of the poisoned incense. Had Lady Hosokawa done worse than contaminate food to make her rival sick? Reiko drank more tea, combating the nausea that came with her knowledge that there were even better suspects than Lady Hosokawa within the clan.

"How did Myobu and Kumoi get along?" Reiko asked, duty-bound to bring Sano the truth even if it wasn't what he liked to hear.

The maid shook her head regretfully. "They were the sweetest little babies, and I loved them both. But the rivalry between Lady Hosokawa and Tama increased after they were born. Myobu had nicer clothes and more toys than Kumoi. She had teachers to teach her how to read and write and arrange flowers and play the *koto* and sing. Kumoi didn't. Because Myobu was Lord Hosokawa's legitimate daughter."

Whereas Kumoi was only his bastard, even though he'd recognized her as his own and professed to Sano that he'd loved her. The custom was cruel to children, too.

"It didn't help that Kumoi was prettier than Myobu," the maid went on. "Myobu was jealous. Their mothers were always comparing them. Kumoi was their father's favorite. They were born to hate each other. They fought all the time."

Had their hatred been great enough for one to have poisoned the other and, by accident, herself? Reiko's suspicion tended even more strongly toward the Hosokawa family.

"Things got even worse when they grew up," the maid said. "Myobu was the elder, so Lord Hosokawa looked to marry her off first. She got a proposal from the *daimyo* clan that has the estate across the street. They're allies of Lord Hosokawa. The *daimyo's* second son needed a wife. He was young and handsome and rich. A perfect match for Myobu.

"The trouble started at the *miai*." That was the first formal meeting between a prospective bride and groom and their families. "Kumoi was there. The young lord couldn't take his eyes off her. He barely looked at Myobu. And Kumoi couldn't take her eyes off him. They fell in love."

That was trouble indeed. "Did the marriage go through?" Reiko asked.

"Oh, yes. Both families wanted it. And Myobu liked the young lord."

There was a sound of small feet padding down the hall. The maid looked toward the door and smiled. Reiko turned to see a toddler with fat, rosy cheeks. The maid held out her arms. He ran to her, and she sat him on her lap. He sucked his thumb while he soberly studied Reiko.

"This is Myobu's son." The maid's eyes welled.

Pitying this child who'd lost his mother, Reiko said a quick, silent prayer for her own unborn baby. "What did Kumoi do after Myobu became engaged?"

"She accepted it. Or so we thought." The maid peeked out the door and continued in a whisper: "A few months later—the day before the wedding—we found out that Kumoi was with child. The father was her sister's fiancé."

Reiko's mouth opened in shock.

"Kumoi confessed that she and the young lord had been secretly meeting. Oh, you should have heard the uproar! Lord Hosokawa scolded Kumoi. Lady Hosokawa called her a whore and blamed Tama for not raising her properly. Tama had a fit because Kumoi had ruined herself. Myobu cried because Kumoi had seduced her fiancé. And Kumoi begged Lord Hosokawa to let her marry the young lord. She said he wanted her for his wife, not Myobu."

"I never heard this," Reiko said, amazed because something this big, involving two such important clans, should have created a scandal.

"It was hushed up," the maid whispered. "The young lord's parents forced him to marry Myobu, even though he didn't want to. Lord Hosokawa sent Kumoi to the countryside to wait for her baby to be born."

At least her family hadn't disowned her, as often happened in cases when a woman became pregnant out of wedlock. Reiko said, "So Kumoi was allowed to come back home to live afterward."

The maid nodded. "Tama couldn't bear to be parted from her. And Lord Hosokawa loved her too much to cast her off." She added, "Lady Hosokawa didn't like it, though."

Reiko could imagine. "Why didn't they find a husband for Kumoi?" That was the common, practical solution.

"They tried. A lot of people want to marry into the Hosokawa clan. They didn't know she was spoiled goods. And she was beautiful. She got lots of proposals. But whenever she had a *miai*, she acted rude and ugly. She chased all the men away. She didn't want to marry anyone except the young lord."

"But she knew she couldn't have him."

"Well, she did have him, in a way. She was his concubine. She lived with him and Myobu, in their house in town. He still loved her. He barely paid any attention to Myobu."

"I see," Reiko said. The contentious relationship between Lady Hosokawa and Tama had been reenacted by their daughters.

"Where is Myobu's husband?" Reiko asked. Sano would want to talk to him.

"In Higo Province. He helps take care of things there while Lord Hosokawa is in Edo. He'd been there four months. A message was sent to tell him that Myobu and Kumoi were missing. I don't know if it got through." The maid blinked away fresh tears and hugged the little boy. "He'll have to be told they're dead."

His absence cleared him of any role in the crime except furnishing a possible reason for it. Reiko remembered Sano telling her that the sisters had sneaked out of the Hosokawa estate to go to their fatal incense lesson. "What were Myobu and Kumoi doing here on the day of the earthquake? Why weren't they at their own home?"

"They lived here when Myobu's husband was away. They couldn't be alone together—without him to keep them under control, they'd have torn out each other's throats."

"What became of Kumoi's baby?" Reiko expected to hear that it had been given to a family retainer to raise.

"He's right here." The maid bounced the little boy on her lap. He chortled. "Myobu adopted him. She got back at Kumoi for taking her husband, you see. She became the baby's mother. When he got older, he would have been told that Kumoi was his aunt."

What a cruel revenge! Reiko was appalled.

"Myobu didn't do it just to be mean, though," the maid went on. "She couldn't have a child of her own, because her husband never touched her after their wedding night." He'd have had relations with her then, to consummate the marriage and make it legal. "He needed an heir, the boy was his, and she wanted a baby. Adopting the boy was the best thing for everybody."

Reiko tried to imagine a rival stealing her child. She felt a stabbing sensation in her womb. She felt antipathy toward Myobu but also pity for the wife, forced to witness the love between her husband and sister, doomed to barrenness. She also felt repugnance toward Kumoi for selfishly sabotaging her sister's marriage. Reiko couldn't imagine a scenario more likely to lead to murder.

A shadow darkened the threshold. There stood Lady Hosokawa, her expression disapproving. She must have guessed that the maid was giving Reiko a whiff of the family's dirty linens. "There are other guests for you to attend to," she told the maid. "Escort Lady Reiko out."

Reiko soon found herself standing on the veranda in the cold. As she crossed the courtyard to her palanquin, she was elated to have gleaned so much information but troubled. Everything she'd heard placed the blame for the murders within the Hosokawa clan, and the logical culprit was either Myobu or Kumoi. She hoped Sano or Hirata would turn up evidence that implicated someone else.

11

FOUL SMOKE FROM the crematoriums still lingered in the Asakusa Temple district when Sano and his troops arrived there. Once, pilgrims from all over Japan had flocked to Asakusa to worship and to patronize the shops, teahouses, and restaurants, but now people came to gawk at the ruined temples. Monks and priests guarded salvaged religious treasures from looters and lived in a tent camp that occupied the onetime marketplace inside the broken red torii gate.

Sano easily located Mizutani's neighborhood, an enclave of houses that still stood. Throughout Edo, such enclaves poked up from the flattened ruins around them like anthills. Often there seemed no explicable reason why they'd survived when similar structures had collapsed. Here, two rows of houses faced each other across a narrow road. Their ground floors contained shops in which Sano saw empty bins and shelves. People in the living quarters on the upper stories peeked suspiciously at Sano's party. Sano had heard that gangs had forced residents out of intact homes and taken them over. The police and army were spread too thin to stop it. In the new Edo, crime flourished.

A gaunt woman beseeched a man who stood outside a house at the center of one row. "Please, just a few coppers." She held out a child wrapped in a torn quilt. "For my baby."

The man was about sixty years of age, with the well-fed aspect of a rich merchant. His padded brown coat was made of cotton but looked new and warm. "Sorry, I can't help you."

"My baby is sick. He needs medicine." The woman's voice quavered. "Or he'll die."

Sano dismounted. He saw that the baby was emaciated, too weak to cry, its eyes bright with fever.

"If I give you my money, how am I going to live?" the merchant said. "Sorry."

"But I'm your neighbor!" The woman burst into tears. "I took care of your wife when she was sick. Doesn't that mean anything to you?"

The man shrugged. "Things are different now. It's everybody for himself."

Sano had witnessed similar scenes too many times. Although the earthquake had brought out the best in some people, who generously shared whatever they had with those less fortunate, others hoarded their goods. Perhaps the crisis only served to reinforce one's natural character.

Weeping, the woman stumbled away. Sano sent his attendant to give her a few coins. She cried, "A thousand thanks, master! May the gods bless you!"

"That was a nice thing to do," the merchant said. His face and hands had a soft, droopy texture that reminded Sano of a melting candle. A whiff of incense hovered around him. His shrewd eyes noted the Tokugawa crests on Sano's garments. He seemed to realize he'd made a poor impression on a high government official and hurried to justify himself. "These people would take everything from me if I let them, and then where would I be? They already looted my shop."

"I won't criticize you." Sano didn't feel in a position to do so. No matter that he tried to help people in need; he, like this man, must look out for his own interests. He wasn't only investigating the murders to serve justice or prevent a war; he had his family to protect. Sano introduced himself, then said, "I'm looking for Mizutani. Is that you?"

"None other." The incense master's smeared features arranged themselves in an expression of wariness combined with eagerness to please. "How may I be of service?"

"Tell me about you and Madam Usugumo."

"What about her?" That Mizutani didn't want to talk about her was obvious from the dismay in his eyes. "She's dead."

"How do you know?"

"I haven't seen her since before the earthquake. Her house fell into a crack in the ground." The concern in Mizutani's voice didn't hide his glee. "I assumed she was buried and crushed inside."

Maybe he knew because he'd poisoned her incense and spied on her while she and her pupils breathed the smoke and died, Sano thought.

Mizutani regarded Sano with sudden apprehension. "She *is* dead, isn't she?"

"Yes," Sano said, "but it wasn't the earthquake that killed her."

"What are you talking about?"

"Let's have this conversation indoors." Sano wanted a look around Mizutani's house.

Although leeriness molded his forehead into a frown, Mizutani ushered Sano inside the shop, which was empty but still smelled strongly of incense. "The looters took my stock and my equipment, you see," Mizutani complained, leading Sano up the stairs. "Heaven knows what they thought they could do with it. Sell it, I guess. You can't eat incense or mortars and pestles." They entered the living quarters. "Please forgive me, it's a little crowded. I'm storing the things I managed to save. Nobody wants incense lessons these days, but I've been lucky to sell incense for funerals."

The room was jammed with iron trunks, ceramic urns and jars, and a workbench cluttered with tools, dishware, and scales. Small drawers in a cabinet overflowed with pellets and sticks of incense, barks, roots, and granules, pieces of deer antler and rhinoceros horn, and vials of liquid ingredients. The air was so saturated with their sweet, sour, bitter, and animal aromas that Sano could taste them. A crucible on a brazier contained black goo and emitted tarry smoke.

Mizutani cleared a space on the floor for him and Sano to sit. "May I offer you some refreshments?"

"No, thank you, I've already eaten." Everything Mizutani had must be permeated with incense, and Sano thought it wise not to accept food from a suspect in a poisoning.

"How did Usugumo die?" Mizutani asked.

"She was murdered, with poisoned incense. She was playing an incense game with two ladies, her pupils. They died, too."

Mizutani's droopy mouth gaped. His teeth were yellow and the gums red, as if from an internal heat that had given his skin its melted-wax appearance. "Do you think I did it? Is that why you're here?"

"Did you do it?" Sano asked.

"Me? No! Of course not!"

Sano counted too many denials. "Tell me about the arguments you had with Usugumo."

"Who—" Mizutani pulled a face. "The neighborhood headman must have told you. That busybody."

"What were the arguments about?"

Mizutani looked around, as if seeking an excuse for not answering. Failing to find one that he thought Sano would accept, he sighed. "She was stealing my pupils. The ungrateful wretch! Everything she had, I gave her!" Mizutani thumped his chest with his loose-fleshed hand. "Do you know what she was before she became an incense teacher?" He didn't wait for Sano to say no. "She was a courtesan in Yoshiwara, that's what!"

Yoshiwara was the pleasure quarter, the one place in Edo where prostitution was legal. The prostitutes, called courtesans, plied their trade in pleasure houses owned by merchants and regulated by the government. Samurai were officially banned from Yoshiwara but flocked there nonetheless. So did other men, from all classes, who could afford the high prices of the women, the drink, and the festivities. But the earthquake had wrecked the brothels and teahouses and put at least a temporary end to the glittering, glamorous world of Yoshiwara.

"I started going to Yoshiwara after my wife died. That was eight years ago," Mizutani said. "I was lonely, I wanted female company, you see. It was fun for a while." He smiled reminiscently, then sobered. "But it cost too much. Buying the right clothes to wear, the trips there and back in a boat. And the women are so expensive. Not just to sleep with—I had to throw parties for three nights in a row beforehand. Afterward, I had to buy presents for them if I wanted to have them again."

Yoshiwara had many rituals that customers were required to observe, which added to the mystique of Yoshiwara and made money for the proprietors of brothels, teahouses, and other businesses associated with the trade.

"I had decided to give it up, when I met Usugumo." Nostalgia softened Mizutani's tone. "She was beautiful and charming and clever. And in bed—" He gave a lascivious shudder. "I got to thinking, why not buy her freedom? Take her home and have her all to myself, all the time? And never have to spend another copper in Yoshiwara."

Some courtesans in Yoshiwara were sent to work there as punishment for petty crimes. They could leave when their sentences were finished. Others were sold into prostitution as children by their parents. They could leave after they'd repaid their purchase price to the brothel owner, but even the most popular, highest-priced courtesans could rarely afford to buy their own freedom. The brothels charged them for their clothes, room, and board. Every day they lived in Yoshiwara they went deeper into debt. They depended on patrons to set them free.

"So that's what I did," Mizutani said. "Usugumo was a bargain because she was thirty-five, you see. Way past her prime. I figured she would be grateful to me for rescuing her before the brothel threw her out on the street. I thought she would be faithful, not like those young girls, who'll use a fellow just to get away from Yoshiwara and then run off as soon as they're out the gate. At first, everything was fine. She looked after me and my house. I taught her about incense. She was good for business. The ladies admired her because she was fashionable and glamorous and could tell them stories about Yoshiwara. The men liked taking lessons from a beautiful woman. This went on until two years ago. Then—"

Mizutani's face flushed with anger. He looked as if his wick had burned down through his head, glowing red-hot from within. "I went on a trip to buy new incense materials. I was away for three months. When I got back, Usugumo was gone. She didn't even say good-bye! Just packed her things and moved. I had to ask the neighbors where she'd gone. It turned out she'd saved the allowance I'd been giving her and rented that house in Nihonbashi. She'd also taken my best incense with her. I went there and confronted her and said, 'How could you treat me like this?' She said she'd done her duty by staying with me for six years. She said I was an ugly, bossy old miser, and she was setting up her own business so she wouldn't have to depend on any man ever again."

Sano had to admire Usugumo's initiative. "Did you report her to the police?"

"I was too embarrassed. She insulted me and robbed me. And later, took my pupils. They liked her better than me." Mizutani's expression went from shame and rancor to fear as he realized how bad he was making himself look. "But I didn't poison her incense. How could I have? She wouldn't have let me. I'm innocent."

"If you're innocent, then you won't mind if I search your house." Sano began opening drawers, digging through the contents.

"Hey!" Mizutani leaped to his feet. "Be careful with those! They're valuable!"

"I'll just take them with me, as evidence." Sano found a cloth sack, dumped in incense sticks and raw ingredients.

"No! Please don't! That's my livelihood!"

Sano held up the sack. "Hand over the arsenic, and I'll leave you this."

"I don't have any."

"Suit yourself." Sano resumed stuffing the sack.

"All right, all right!" Mizutani scuttled into the adjacent room and returned with a small brown ceramic jar. "Here!"

Sano took the jar, removed the lid, and saw grayish white powder inside.

"But I never put it in incense!" Mizutani said. "I only use it to kill rats!"

Maybe he'd thought Usugumo was one. He'd possessed the means, if not the opportunity, by which to poison the women at the incense game. Sano handed over the sack.

"If you want to find out who did it, you should talk to Korin," Mizutani said.

It was the classic, obvious way to cast off suspicion—direct it toward someone else. Sano took the bait anyway, because he needed all the leads he could get, especially leads that didn't point to the Hosokawa clan.

"Who's Korin?" Sano asked.

"Usugumo's apprentice," Mizutani said, relieved that his ploy had succeeded. "He helped her blend her incense. It would have been easier for him to put poison in it than me. Besides, I'm a respectable, law-abiding businessman, whereas Korin is a shady character. He used to work as a tout for the pleasure houses in Yoshiwara. That's where he and Usugumo met. He also had a side business pimping for nighthawks." Nighthawks were illegal prostitutes who operated outside the licensed pleasure quarter.

Skeptical, Sano said, "But Usugumo was Korin's employer. His livelihood depended on her. Why kill her? Wouldn't she have been worth more to him alive?"

"I once had an apprentice who hated me because I hit him with a stick when he ruined a batch of incense," Mizutani said. It was common knowledge that apprentices were often worked like slaves and harshly punished by their masters. "That could have happened with Usugumo and Korin. Maybe he wanted to do to her what she did to me: Rob her and run." Mizutani grinned. "That would have been easier if she was dead."

"Where is Korin?"

"I asked around. He hasn't been seen since before the earthquake."

"He may have died during it," Sano pointed out.

"He may have." Mizutani's grin broadened, showing his red gums and yellow teeth. "But if he murdered those women, wouldn't that be a good reason for disappearing?"

12

THE SHOGUN STOOD in his chamber, wearing his loincloth and a pair of quilted brown trousers fastened with drawstrings. He held his arms out to his sides while the twins dressed him in layers of quilted underrobes. "I think I'll wear my, ahh, green brocade kimono today."

Masahiro watched the shogun's other pages search for the green kimono on stands that sagged under the weight of draped garments. Robes strewn on the floor almost covered the tatami. Cabinets and drawers spilled toiletries and other personal articles. Shoes fallen from their cubbyholes lay in heaps; underclothes were crumpled haphazardly into shelves. The monthlong shortage of servants had resulted in a mess that worsened every day.

When the pages located the kimono and the twins tried to put it on the shogun, he wrinkled his nose. "It smells! Why hasn't it been washed? Bring me my burgundy satin instead." The pages found the burgundy robe wadded up on the floor. The shogun frowned and rubbed at the creases as the twins dressed him. "My black sash with the gold dragons would look well with this."

The hunt began again. Masahiro saw the shogun growing impatient, the pages worried and frantic. The twins and the shogun's bodyguard rushed to help. The shogun's expression darkened into a scowl. Masahiro joined the search because he knew what that scowl portended. They had to find that sash.

"I've had enough! I can't stand this any longer!" The shogun hopped from side to side; his hands waved. "I'm surrounded by, ahh, disorder, incompetence, and stupidity! You oafs are driving me mad!"

He picked up an ivory fan from the mess and struck one of the twins on the head with it. The boy yelped in pain. Masahiro had never seen the shogun hit anyone before, but since the earthquake his temper was even quicker than usual, and violence had seemed inevitable. The shogun beat the boy about the shoulders. The boy fell on the floor and moaned, but he didn't defend himself or protest, lest he be put to death. Everyone else stood by, helpless. The other concubines, the pages, and the guard didn't want the shogun to turn his wrath on them. The shogun shrieked as he wielded the fan against the boy's face, splitting his lip, bloodying his nose. The boy sobbed.

Even though the shogun had the right to do whatever he wanted, Masahiro couldn't let an innocent person be hurt. He lunged at the shogun, grabbed his arm, and shouted, "Stop, Your Excellency!"

The other people in the room gasped, shocked because he dared to lay a hand on their lord. The shogun emitted a startled grunt. Masahiro hauled him away from the fallen boy. He spun the shogun around to face him. Fury twisted the shogun's mouth. He raised the fan to strike Masahiro.

Masahiro seized him by the wrist. He was aghast at his own audacity, terrified because the shogun could have him killed, but he said, "Let go of that fan!" in the stern tone that his sword-fighting teacher used when he made a mistake during a lesson.

The shogun gaped. His hand opened. He let the fan fall. The room was silent except for the injured boy's weeping. Masahiro released the shogun. As they stared eye to eye, he was astonished to realize that they were of equal height. The shogun's mouth trembled as if he were about to cry. Suddenly Masahiro was the powerful adult and the shogun the child at his mercy. Suddenly Masahiro pitied the supreme dictator of Japan.

"It's all right." Masahiro spoke in the gentle voice he used toward his sister Akiko when she was upset. "There's no need to hit anybody. I'll make things all better."

"You will?" The shogun's eyes shone with hopeful trust.

"Yes." Masahiro heard the others sigh in relief because the danger had passed. He remembered when a horse in his father's stable had gone wild, kicking and bucking, and the groom had seized its reins and talked to it until it calmed down. This was just like that. "I'll find your sash."

"But how?" The shogun gazed despairingly around the room.

Masahiro took the shogun by the hand. "We'll sort everything. Your sash will turn up."

That was what his nurse had taught him when he was little, when he'd cried because he'd lost his favorite toy soldier. Now he and the shogun picked up clothes, folded them, cleared out cabinets and drawers and shelves, then refilled them with neatly arranged items. Pages, boys, and the guard helped. The shogun seemed captivated by the novelty of it. When they were almost finished, he exclaimed, "Look!" He held up the black and gold sash.

Everyone cheered. The shogun beamed at Masahiro. "From now on, you shall be in charge of my private chambers."

Masahiro felt the pride of every samurai who'd ever won a battle for his lord and been rewarded with riches. Then he realized that he'd done the very thing his father had warned him against doing. He'd attracted the shogun's notice, and there was no going back.

YANAGISAWA LOOKED AROUND in amazement as he rode through Edo with his four bodyguards. He'd not realized how bad the earthquake damage was, because he'd never gone out to see. He'd heard his retainers and servants talking about it, but the devastation was beyond belief. Along with his horror came an unexpected thrill. The politician in him, which was coming back to life, recognized opportunity in this crisis.

When they reached the Sumida River, he and his men dismounted at the lone dock that the earthquake hadn't shaken loose. They climbed into two little wooden ferryboats, the only means of crossing the river now that the Ryōgoku Bridge was gone. The boatmen rowed the ferries through the debris that clogged the shallows. As he crossed the clean middle of the river, Yanagisawa felt like a survivor of a stormy voyage, heading toward a new shore. In spite of his grief over Yoritomo, he felt hopeful, euphoric.

After the ferry docked, he and his guards trudged through the Honjo district. Its lumberyards, which had once supplied Edo with wood brought from forests in the provinces, looked as if a giant had picked up all the logs and flung them down like a fortune-teller casting yarrow sticks. Peasants labored to pull out the logs that jammed the canals, which had flooded the collapsed neighborhoods. A few houses had survived—the well-built estates of rich lumber merchants. Yanagisawa's party arrived at one of these. It consisted of four houses grouped around a square courtyard, connected by covered corridors and surrounded by a bamboo fence. Guards stationed outside the gate recognized Yanagisawa and bowed.

Yanagisawa didn't like to put all his eggs in one basket, but the earthquake had destroyed the separate villas where his four sons had lived with their mothers. His retainers had managed to commandeer this estate for them during the rush when so many people were seeking housing. Yanagisawa gazed up at the plank walls of the houses' upper stories, the wooden shutters and bars over the windows, and the drab brown tiles on the roofs. Sumptuary laws forbade commoners to flaunt their wealth. Inside, the estate was luxurious. Yanagisawa felt apprehension mount in him as he walked through the gate. He didn't know if what he found here would be good enough for his purposes. His heart bounded with the hope that one of these sons had Yoritomo's looks, intelligence, and sweet, tractable personality. If only one of them could be to him what Yoritomo had been!

Yanagisawa banished the wish from his mind. Sentimentality had no place in politics.

As he approached the nearest wing of the mansion, the guard captain came out on the veranda. Yanagisawa said, "I'm here to see my sons."

The guard captain looked surprised. Yanagisawa hadn't seen his sons up close since they were born, when he'd examined the infants to make sure they were normal before he acknowledged them as his and provided for their support. He routinely sent his aides to check on the boys and report back to him. When he'd needed one to place close to the shogun, he'd set out to evaluate his sons and choose the best. He'd met Yoritomo—the eldest—and stopped there. Now, here on the same quest, Yanagisawa found himself jittery with nerves.

"How are they?" he asked, prolonging the suspense, avoiding disappointment.

"Tokichika, the youngest, has a fever. He's often sick with one thing or another."

"I don't need to see him, then." A sickly boy wouldn't suit Yanagisawa's purposes. "What about the other three?"

"They're fine. Shall I tell them you're here?"

"No." Yanagisawa strode into the mansion. Walking down the corridor, he came upon a woman. She froze in her tracks. He barely recognized her as his former concubine; he didn't remember her name. She'd gotten old; she'd gained weight. "Where's our son?"

She gazed at him for a moment, fearful and mute, then called, "Rokuro! Come quickly! Your father is here!"

A young samurai came running. He tripped, stumbled, and almost fell. Scarlet with embarrassment, he bowed and stammered, "Greetings, Honorable Father."

Yanagisawa winced. That a child of his could be so awkward! He could see himself in Rokuro, but the resemblance was distorted, as if his son's features had been shaped by a sculptor using him as a model and working in the dark.

"Are you doing well in your studies?" Yanagisawa asked.

Rokuro looked at the floor. His mother answered, "He needs to work harder."

Yanagisawa understood that Rokuro was dull-witted. "Can you sing and play music?"

"A little," the boy muttered.

"I see." Yanagisawa saw that Rokuro could never attract the shogun, who liked only handsome, clever, charming boys. He left the room without a backward look.

As he walked through the passage to the adjoining house, a boy ran smack into him. Yanagisawa grabbed the youth's arms to steady them both. They stared at each other in mutual astonishment. Yanagisawa saw a face that was a young version of his own, the image of Yoritomo's minus some ten years. His breath stopped as if he'd been punched in the chest. Here was Yoritomo, miraculously reborn!

In the next instant, Yanagisawa realized his mistake. Grief resurged with such force that he pushed the boy away from him, turned, and ran outside, where he leaned on the veranda railing and panted. No matter that the boy looked exactly like Yoritomo and might have the same talents; Yanagisawa couldn't bear to see him again. Every time he looked at the boy, he would be reminded of Yoritomo, confronted with the fact that the boy wasn't, and could never be, Yoritomo.

Yanagisawa forced himself to walk down the steps and around the corner toward the next house, to enter another door despite his fear of what else he would find. A woman met him in the entryway.

"So it's true," she said in a tone that mixed dismay with curiosity. "You're really here."

"Someko." Yanagisawa was amazed because she'd hardly changed in eighteen years. Her deep red kimono clothed a figure that was still small and compact. Upswept hair studded with ornaments gleamed richly black. Her wide face with its delicate, rounded chin was unlined; her tilted eyes sparkled. Someko was as beautiful as the day Yanagisawa had first bedded her. Were he in the mood for sex, he would think her hard to resist even though he usually preferred his lovers—female or male—to be under thirty, and she was at least a decade older.

"I want to see our son," he said.

"I understand. Your favorite son died, so you need one of your others."

Her nerve startled Yanagisawa. "Your tongue is still as sharp as a fox's teeth."

She smiled, bitter as well as amused. "If my tongue is sharp, it's because of you."

She'd been married to a Tokugawa army officer, and he'd stolen her from her husband, whom she'd loved, and made her his concubine. He'd tolerated her anger and her vicious remarks because they'd added piquancy to the sex. After she became pregnant, he'd provided generously for her and, later, the child; but she'd obviously never forgiven him for eighteen years of forced, lonely seclusion. She'd spent them nursing her grudge.

Now Someko took a closer look at him and smirked. "You've changed, though. Still handsome as a devil, but you're an old man." Compassion altered her manner. "Yoritomo's death must have been hard for you. I'm sorry."

Yanagisawa fought tears. "Why should you be?"

The eyebrows painted high on her forehead rose. "I'm a mother. I couldn't wish losing a child on anyone." Her bitter smile returned. "But if I could, it would be you."

Tired of sparring with her, Yanagisawa said, "Where is he?"

"Who?" Someko pretended confusion. "Do you mean Yoshisato? He has a name." She spoke with rancor because Yanagisawa had ignored her child while lavishing attention on his favorite. "He's having a martial arts lesson with his tutor."

She led Yanagisawa to the courtyard at the center of the estate. On the wide, paved square stood a middle-aged samurai dressed in white martial arts practice clothes, sword in hand.

"Where is Yoshisato?" Someko asked.

"He was here a moment ago," the tutor said. "One of the maids came and told us that his father was here. He just left."

Yanagisawa realized that Yoshisato had run away to avoid him. "What a nerve he has."

"He takes after his father." Someko gave a mean, satisfied smile. "I guess he doesn't want to see you as much as you want to see him. You may as well go."

Yanagisawa had come here intending to pick and choose, and he himself had been rejected. He felt an unexpected pang of hurt. He missed Yoritomo so terribly that he wanted to go home and crawl back into bed. But he couldn't let Yoshisato get away with his insolence, and he still needed a political pawn.

"I'm going, but you can tell Yoshisato I'll be back," Yanagisawa said.

13

HIRATA PEERED DOWN at the incense teacher's house. Incense bowls and tools, the cushions, and even the tatami mats were gone. Since yesterday the room had been picked clean by people desperate for anything they could use or sell. Hirata would have left someone to guard the scene, had he known he would be investigating the crime.

Large white flakes sifted from the sky. It was snowing. That would certainly help the suffering folks of Edo, and if there were any clues left in the house, Hirata had better find them before the snow ruined them. He lowered himself through the hole and dropped into the room. There he discovered something he hadn't noticed yesterday. The rest of the house tilted at a steep angle farther down into the crack. Fallen rafters and massive rocks blocked off the other rooms. Hirata put his shoulder against a rock and exerted his mental concentration and physical strength against it. The rock wouldn't budge. No one else was around to help.

A cheery voice called, "Hello down there!"

Hirata looked up to see three faces around the rim of the hole. Tahara, Kitano, and Deguchi peered at him. He cursed under his breath. "What do you want?"

"You know," Tahara said with a winning smile.

"Forget it." Hirata crouched, raised his arms, and sprang.

He caught the earth at the edge of the hole. Deguchi pulled him up as if he were as light as the snowflakes that melted against his face. Kitano asked, "What were you looking for?"

"Nothing," Hirata said.

Tahara's high eyebrow lowered in displeasure at Hirata's curtness. "You must be on an investigation." He glanced at the sunken house. "Looks like a big job. Want some help?"

The last thing Hirata wanted was to put himself in their debt, but he needed to get into those rooms, and he couldn't fail Sano. "Sure," he said. "Make yourselves useful for a change."

"First, let's make a deal," Kitano said. "We excavate the house. You do the ritual."

"I should have known there would be a catch." Hirata decided that the ritual was a small price to pay. "All right."

Tahara, Kitano, and Deguchi lined up along the chasm. Hands held out from their sides, their feet planted wide, they gazed down. "Stand back," Tahara said.

Hirata complied. Their aura pulsed, slow and faint, then with a force that strengthened tremendously with each throb. The humor disappeared from Tahara's face. Kitano's jaw tightened under the scarred skin. Deguchi's eyes shone so brightly that Hirata almost expected their sockets to burn black. The air around the chasm shimmered, as if from rising heat waves. Hirata heard movement inside the buried part of the house. A broken rafter suddenly flew up from the chasm and landed at his feet. Hirata gaped at it, then at his companions.

"I didn't know you could—"

Their attention was concentrated on the chasm. Timbers, roof tiles, wall panels, and rocks propelled themselves upward, onto a pile that accumulated on the ground. The men's bodies were rigid, their fists clenched. Sweat dripped down their contorted, straining faces. Within moments the debris was emptied out of the house.

"Why didn't you tell me—?"

Groans burst from Tahara and Kitano. Deguchi's throat jerked. The chasm opened wider, its edges pried apart like lips separated by massive jaws. The house began to rise up from the depths. Splintered beams and boards emerged above ground level, accompanied by the noise of wood scraping against rock. Stunned, Hirata watched the house levitate, its broken plank walls and window frames and torn paper panes coming into view, then its base and stone foundation pillars. It hovered above the chasm like a corpse resurrected.

Kitano and Tahara bellowed. A visible energy wave emanated from Deguchi's speechless mouth. The men stepped backward. The roofless house wafted through the air toward them and gently landed on the space they'd vacated. Their aura turned off abruptly. The house crumbled into a heap of ruins. The three men bent over, hands on their knees, shaking and gasping.

Hirata regarded them with disbelief, admiration, and envy. "I want to learn to do that. Show me how."

"No." Tahara spat froth onto the ground. "You're not ready."

"What do you mean? I'm one of you. Whatever knowledge you have, we should share equally."

Kitano chortled between gasps. "It doesn't work that way."

"I'm tired of hearing that. And I'm tired of your keeping secrets from me. I want to learn how to do what you just did, and I won't take no for an answer!" Hirata put his hand on Tahara's bent head and shoved.

Tahara stumbled sideways and bumped into Kitano, who bumped Deguchi. They fell down, one after another, and sat on the ground, too exhausted to get up. For once Hirata was stronger than they were. If he wanted to defeat them, so that he need never fear them or take orders from them anymore, now was the time. He saw dismay in their eyes as they read his thought. Then Tahara and Deguchi smiled; Kitano's eyes crinkled with sardonic humor.

"I wouldn't if I were you," Tahara said. "We're the only people in the world who can do it. If we die, the knowledge dies with us."

"If you won't teach it to me, why are you worth more to me alive than dead?" Hirata countered.

A tense moment passed while he stared down Tahara, Kitano, and Deguchi. At last Tahara said, "All right. We'll teach you. After the ritual."

Hirata felt a thrill of triumph. The men struggled to their feet. Tahara clapped Hirata's shoulder. "We'll call for you tomorrow night."

Watching them saunter away, Hirata cursed. They had him where they wanted him. But they'd fulfilled their part of the bargain. He owed them a ritual.

The snow was falling harder, the air white with feathery flakes that frosted the remains of the house. Sano would be expecting results. Hirata got to work. Lifting and throwing aside beams and planks, he smelled the smoke from the poisoned incense. He tied a cloth over his nose and mouth, then uncovered cabinets, tables, and lacquered screens that had been crushed during the earthquake. Shattered dishware lay among pots and utensils in what had once been the kitchen. Rain had seeped into the chasm, ruining clothes, mattress, and bed linens. In Usugumo's workroom, fallen shelves had smashed valuable incense bowls into porcelain fragments. He found a broken scale, mortars and pestles, oddly shaped vessels, and measuring spoons. Fragrant roots, dried leaves, spices, and powders had spilled from broken ceramic urns. Hirata began to wonder if the favor done him by Tahara, Kitano, and Deguchi had served no purpose but to enmesh him more tightly with them. He excavated the entire floor of the house and found nothing that seemed to bear upon the murders. He kept working because he couldn't return to Sano emptyhanded.

He was making a final survey when the tatami gave way slightly under his foot, in what had been the bedchamber. Crouching, he pressed his hands against the mat and felt a square hole, about two paces wide, underneath. He flipped the mat and saw a compartment built into the floorboards. Inside was a small black iron trunk. The boards that had covered it had fallen inside the compartment, twisted loose by the earthquake.

Excited, Hirata lifted out the trunk and opened the lid. Gold and silver glittered. He blew out his breath as he picked up the heavy coins strung on thick twine. This was a fortune, many times more than Usugumo could have earned by giving incense lessons. Hirata dug through the coins. Under them he found a rectangular book the size of a woman's hand, made of cheap, off-white paper, covered with rough black cloth, and tied with black ribbon. Hirata opened the book and saw black characters written in neat but inexpert calligraphy, like a clever child's. He read formulas for different blends of incense, the secrets of Usugumo's trade. The last two pages contained names and dates—a list of pupils and the schedule of their lessons. Hirata replaced the book in the trunk, closed the lid, and put the trunk in his horse's saddlebag. Maybe this clue would help repair his relationship with Sano.

Riding away from the house, Hirata paused to look in the direction that Tahara, Kitano, and Deguchi had gone, across debris piles, falling snow, toward the distant hills. What else hadn't they told him? Hirata vowed to do what he should have done before he'd joined the society—

find out more about them. Since he didn't trust them to tell him, he must look elsewhere for information.

"WE NEED TO find the incense teacher's apprentice," Sano told Detective Marume as they rode with their troops along the highway toward the city. "As soon as we get back to the castle, you'll organize a manhunt."

"All right," Marume said.

Sano wished Marume would show some interest in the case, some sign of his old self, but Marume rode like a sleepwalker propped in the saddle.

Snow filled the gray air. It covered the empty streets by the time Sano and his party reached the city. Sano blinked flakes out of his eyes as he watched nature obscure the ruins. He pictured seasons passing, the trees, grasses, and vines shooting forth during springs and summers to cover stone foundations, the rains rotting wood and dissolving plaster, until there remained no evidence that humans had ever lived here. Sano felt guilty because he'd spent the morning investigating the murders when he should have been rebuilding Edo.

In the *daimyo* district, he heard the muffled cadence of horses' hooves. Through a veil of falling snow he saw an army of mounted samurai approaching. The leaders wore helmets with curved horns. Their troops flew banners from poles on their backs. The army bristled with swords, spears, bows, and quivers of arrows.

Sano's heart began to race with the dread and excitement that preceded a battle. His samurai blood rose up as if in the memory of other battles before he was born, those his ancestors had fought. He and his troops reined in their mounts. The army halted some twenty paces away. Sano spied the symbol on the nearest banner, a large dot circled by eight smaller dots—the Hosokawa clan crest. Lord Hosokawa lifted his hand in greeting. He left his comrades and rode toward Sano. He looked different in his horned helmet—sterner and stronger. Sano rode out and met Lord Hosokawa in the middle of the space between their parties.

"I was on my way to see you," Lord Hosokawa said. "To ask whether you've made any progress."

Sano glanced beyond Lord Hosokawa. He recognized the three other men wearing horned helmets. They were Lords Mori, Maeda, and Date. They acknowledged him with stiff, formal bows. Sano realized they were the *daimyo* who wanted to overthrow the Tokugawa regime, who were courting Lord Hosokawa's support. They numbered among the wealthiest lords with the largest domains and armies.

"Do they know?" he asked Lord Hosokawa.

"About our bargain?" A humorless smile thinned Lord Hosokawa's mouth. "No. Your finding out who killed my daughters isn't in their interest. I haven't told them, and I won't."

"If they knew, they would sabotage my investigation so that I'll fail and you'll support their revolt," Sano deduced.

Lord Hosokawa shrugged, impatient. "Well? Is there any progress?"

"I've found some potential suspects."

Lord Hosokawa pounced on the words like a starving man seizes food. "Who are they?"

"I can't tell you yet."

"Why not?"

"Because I don't want you chasing after people to take revenge on them before I've ascertained whether they're really guilty," Sano said. "I won't let you hurt someone who turns out to be innocent."

"Why do you think I would take such a rash, foolish action?" Lord Hosokawa said, offended as well as incredulous.

"I didn't think you would blackmail me into solving your daughters' murders or consider revolting against the Tokugawa regime," Sano said.

"If you don't tell me, I'll—"

"What? Tell your friends to count you in on their revolt? And start it now?" Sano's temper flared. "Who's going to hunt for your daughters' murderer during a civil war?"

"Don't you mock me!" Lord Hosokawa glanced over his shoulder at the other *daimyo* waiting in the snow with their troops.

"Are you going to ask them to kill me?" Sano said. "Do you have that much control over them?"

"Yes, fortunately for you." Lord Hosokawa laughed, an ugly sound of disgust directed at himself as well as Sano. Sano could see that he didn't like the man he'd become since he'd learned of his daughters' murders, but he was powerless to change. "Because I'm all that stands between them and the shogun."

He galloped back to the other *daimyo*. Sano sat alone, astride his horse, watching them and their troops ride off. He expelled his breath against snowflakes that smote his face. As he returned to his own troops, he happened to glance at a street that intersected the avenue. There, between crumbled walls, stood a small party of mounted samurai, watching him. Hoods and wicker hats obscured their identities, but Sano recognized the hunched figure of one man.

It was Ienobu.

14

REIKO CLIMBED OUT of her palanquin in the courtyard at home. The estate looked even bleaker than usual, with the snow coating the debris piles and the damaged mansion. Sano rode up with his troops, and she was reluctant to tell him what she'd learned.

"I didn't expect you back this soon," she said.

"There's been a development," Sano said as he leaped off his horse.

Reiko could tell from his manner that the development wasn't as good as he would have liked. "Is it about the incense master? Didn't you find him?"

"I did." As they went into the house and hung their outdoor garments in the entryway, Sano described his meeting with Mizutani. "He had plenty of reason to hate Usugumo, and possibly enough to kill her, although I'm not certain he's guilty. There's still Korin, the missing apprentice. Except for him, I haven't any other leads."

"I have, but I'm afraid you won't like them."

"Mama! Papa!" Akiko met them in the corridor. "Come see my new house!"

Delighted to have both parents home in the daytime for once, she seized their hands and towed them into their chamber. There she'd created a house under a table that rested atop two stacks of iron trunks. Four dolls sat on the floor in the space, miniature dishes arranged in front of them. Akiko scrambled inside and knelt by the dolls. "We're having a party."

Reiko and Sano smiled. "That's very clever," Sano said.

Children were better than adults at enduring the conditions caused by the earthquake, Reiko thought. They could make a game of it. Reiko described her visit to the Hosokawa estate and the animosity between Lord Hosokawa's wife and concubine. She related the maid's story about the rivalry between the two sisters.

"I'm afraid that if I had to guess how the murders happened, I would say that either Kumoi or Myobu put the poison in the incense, in an attempt to kill the other," Reiko said. "And she ended up killing herself and Madam Usugumo."

"It doesn't matter whether I like that scenario. The problem is Lord Hosokawa. I met him on my way home. He was with the *daimyo* who want to start a rebellion." Sano gave Reiko the gist of their conversation.

Reiko sensed that Sano hadn't told her everything. "What else?"

"Ienobu saw me with Lord Hosokawa."

Dismay chimed in Reiko because she knew Ienobu had wedged himself into the shogun's inner circle and that Sano didn't trust him. "Did he hear what you and Lord Hosokawa said?"

"I don't think so. He wasn't close enough. But I think he knows something is going on between Lord Hosokawa and me."

Ienobu was the last complication she and Sano needed. "Was he following you?"

"No. With the streets so empty, I'd have noticed. He came upon me by accident. But if I run into him again, I'll know it's no accident." Humor brightened Sano up. "If I can't evade a spy who looks like him, I should just give up."

"This isn't a joke!" Reiko protested. "Ienobu could send someone else to spy on you, that you won't see. If he learns that you're conducting an investigation instead of rebuilding Edo, he might also find out why you're doing it. Other people besides us know that Lord Hosokawa's daughters were murdered. Other people must know that the *daimyo* are considering a revolt—their retainers, their servants. Somebody might talk."

Sano nodded, acknowledging the possibility yet clearly determined not to let their troubles get the better of them. "That gives us all the more incentive to solve the crime quickly—to prevent Ienobu from catching on and telling the shogun."

Hirata entered the room, his face flushed from the cold. He held up a small trunk filled with coins, and a book. "I've found something."

WHEN YANAGISAWA ARRIVED home, he was shivering from the cold and so exhausted he felt ready to faint. Dismounting from his horse, he almost fell. Two of his bodyguards ran to help him. Yanagisawa waved them off, shamed by his weakness. "Go back to my sons' house. Wait for Yoshisato to come back. Then bring him to me."

He glanced around the ruins of his mansion and the small building that contained the private quarters where he lived crowded together with his guards and servants. The snow didn't render the scene more impressive.

"On second thought, don't bring him." Yanagisawa believed in putting on his best show of strength when facing an adversary—even if the adversary was only a seventeen-year-old boy. "Hold him at his house. Notify me that he's there, and I'll come over."

Yanagisawa staggered into his chamber without bothering to remove his shoes or snow-frosted outdoor garments. He flung himself on the bed. Dreading another trip across the river and back, he whispered, "That boy had better be worth the trouble."

"THIS IS MADAM Usugumo's notebook," Hirata said. "It was in her house, the part that was crushed underground."

Sano took the small black book and riffled the pages, skimming the incense formulas, while Reiko peered over his shoulder. "How did you find it?"

Hirata didn't answer at once. Sano looked up at him. Hirata averted his gaze before he said, "I managed to get in and dig it out."

More evasion, more secrets. Disturbed, Sano again recognized the necessity of confronting Hirata, but again it would have to wait.

"Look at the last two pages," Hirata said, too quick to change the subject.

Sano turned to them and found the list of names. "These are Usugumo's pupils."

"Besides Myobu and Kumoi, only two other names are on the list," Reiko said.

As Sano read the names, a hollow formed in the pit of his stomach. "Look at who the others are. Priest Ryuko and Minister Ogyu."

"Priest Ryuko is companion and spiritual advisor to the shogun's mother," Hirata said.

"He's also her lover," Reiko said.

"Since Lady Keisho-in has so much influence over her son, Priest Ryuko is the highest-ranking cleric in Japan, as well as indirect advisor to the shogun," Sano thought aloud.

"I've never heard of Minister Ogyu," Reiko said. "Who is he?"

"He's the administrator of the shogun's Confucian school," Sano said.

The shogun was an enthusiast of Confucius, the ancient Chinese philosopher. Confucianism was a tradition of moral, cultural, and political teaching, a supreme guide to life and government, that had come to Japan some thirteen centuries ago. Confucian teachings emphasized filial piety, a strict social hierarchy, administrative responsibility, and loyalty, which accorded well with Bushido. A fad that had waxed and waned throughout history, it was currently enjoying a bout of popularity. It was considered necessary knowledge for cultured men in the Tokugawa regime. Sano had attended classes and lectures at the school, a prestigious center of education and culture. So had the shogun, who gave generous patronage to the Confucian scholars who taught there.

"Is Minister Ogyu alive?" Hirata asked. Since the earthquake, that question invariably came up when someone's name was mentioned. "And Priest Ryuko?"

"Both are. I've seen them," Sano said.

Reiko took the book from Sano. She ran her finger down the list of names, perusing the dates and notes written after them. "Priest Ryuko and Minister Ogyu had their last lessons the month before the earthquake. On some dates Usugumo taught Priest Ryuko and Minister Ogyu at their houses, but on other dates, at hers."

"They had the opportunity to sneak the poisoned incense into her supplies," Sano concluded.

"So now we have two new suspects." Hirata glanced at Sano, seeking a sign that Sano approved and he'd made up for his absences.

On the one hand, Sano was glad that Hirata had done his assigned task. On the other, he felt as if Hirata had unearthed a bomb from the incense teacher's house. "I wish the suspects were anyone except these particular men."

Concern appeared on Reiko's face. "They won't take kindly to being under investigation for the murders. And they could get you in trouble with the shogun."

"Nonetheless, we have to investigate them," Sano said, "because Lord Hosokawa will cause even worse trouble if we don't solve the crime." His spirits lifted a little. "If I have to tell him the killer is Priest Ryuko or Minister Ogyu, he'll probably react more favorably than if I tell him it was one of his daughters. I'll talk to them today. Hirata-*san,* you investigate their backgrounds and see if there's anything incriminating."

"I'll get it done right away," Hirata said, too promptly.

"I know Lady Keisho-in," Reiko said. "I can ask her about Priest Ryuko and the incense teacher. But I haven't any connection to Minister Ogyu. Is he married?"

"I expect so," Sano said. Most men of Ogyu's status were.

"I'll find a way into his household," Reiko said.

"We have to be careful about how we handle Priest Ryuko and Minister Ogyu," Sano reminded her.

"We mustn't offend them," Reiko agreed.

"We also mustn't let them know we're investigating them," Sano said. "They're intelligent men with plenty of connections. We don't want them wondering why I'm interested in the murders, making their own inquiries, and finding out about Lord Hosokawa and the *daimyo* who are plotting against the Tokugawa regime."

15

FROM A DISTANCE Zōjō Temple appeared unchanged, its hilly terrain and pine forests serenely beautiful under the fresh snow. Sano could almost believe that all was well at the Tokugawa family temple, home to three thousand priests, nuns, novices, and their attendants— until he and his troops drew nearer.

The two-story main gate lay in fragments by the road. Sano's party trod carefully on shifted, crumbled stone stairs that led to the temple's main precinct. Inside the precinct, people crowded the space around the temple buildings. Some sheltered under tents; others sat in the falling snow with nothing to protect them except the clothes on their backs. Children snuggled against mothers who held crying infants. The pagoda leaned as if in a fierce wind. Walls had peeled off the abbot's residence and the novices' dormitories, exposing empty rooms. Heat waves rose from the crematorium, where the fires that would burn more dead bodies during the night had already been lit. Rhythmic chanting emanated from the main hall, whose massive structure, carved columns and doors, wooden bracketry, and undulating roofs were miraculously intact. Sano and his men entered its cavernous realm of flame-light and shadow. The smoke was so thick that Sano could hardly breathe, the smell of incense overpowering. Kneeling people packed the floor, facing the altar. Their lips moved as they chanted. They were praying to the Buddha to deliver them from evil. Sano hoped the Buddha was listening.

On the altar, hundreds of candles burned before a giant golden Buddha statue. Its many arms seemed to wave in the flickering light that reflected off thousands of golden lotus flowers that surrounded it. Priests in saffron robes knelt on the raised floor before the altar, their backs to the crowd. Their shaved heads gleamed. The tallest man, at their center, wore a glittering stole of red and gold brocade that seemed made of fire. It was Priest Ryuko. His chanting boomed above the others, deep and resonant. The earthquake seemed to have added luster to his image as Japan's leading cleric.

Sano edged around the crowd to the side of the altar. From there he had a good view of Priest Ryuko. Appearance had certainly played a part in Ryuko's good fortune. His profile was comely, with a high brow, long nose, heavy-lidded eyes, and lips as full and curved as the Buddha statue's. He must have sensed Sano's attention; he turned his head slightly. His gaze grew hooded. He rose in a motion that was smooth and quick for a man in his fifties. He beckoned Sano. They went to a side chapel, where a smaller altar held gilded statues of the spirits of prosperity, relief to the poor, and the exorcism of evil. The sound of chanting was muted here. Incense sticks gave off bittersweet smoke tendrils. In the dim light of a few candles, Sano and Ryuko bowed to each other. Sano could see that leading the faithful through this crisis had taken its toll on Ryuko. Purplish shadows smudged the skin under his eyes, and his vibrant golden skin had turned ashen with fatigue.

"I presume this is not a social call." Ryuko's voice rasped from so much chanting. "None of us has time for those nowadays."

"Indeed," Sano said. "I came to see how the temple is faring."

Ryuko studied Sano intently, as if trying to glean the significance behind the pretext. They were political allies by default rather than because of mutual trust. Ryuko detested Yanagisawa, whose power had threatened the authority of the clergy, and had backed Sano during his clashes with Yanagisawa. But Ryuko and Sano were leery of each other's power.

"Your officials were here two days ago," Ryuko said. "I've made a full report."

His suave manner had a splintery edge. The earthquake had revealed wellsprings of patience and compassion in some people; in others, their natural bad tempers. Ryuko was among the latter, goaded by frustration to turn a simple chat into a quarrel, the last thing Sano needed while conducting a murder investigation that he wasn't supposed to be conducting and questioning a suspect who wasn't supposed to know he was a suspect.

"It's good to see things with one's own eyes," Sano said in a placating tone.

"True." Yet Ryuko clearly chafed at Sano's authority. "As you've probably noticed, we haven't been able to repair our buildings that were damaged. May I ask when we can expect help from the government?"

Although religion was important to the shogun, and he'd proclaimed that fixing the temples was a top priority, he'd left Sano to allocate scarce resources. Sano had put the temples behind urgent needs such as feeding and supplying clean water to the population and repairing the castle, roads, and bridges. Ryuko had protested the decision. So had other officials who thought their homes, offices, and businesses deserved a bigger share.

"You can expect help soon." As soon as he solved the case and Lord Hosokawa handed over the money, Sano thought. If he didn't solve the case, the civil war would start and Priest Ryuko would have more serious problems to worry about than fixing the temple.

"That's good news." Ryuko's smile didn't reach his eyes.

"By the way," Sano said, "I understand that someone you're acquainted with was found yesterday, during the search for victims of the earthquake."

"Oh? Who is it?"

"An incense teacher named Madam Usugumo. Didn't you take lessons from her?"

"Usugumo is dead?" Ryuko's heavy eyelids lifted so high that the entire pupils showed, dark brown rimmed with black, shining in the candlelight.

"I'm sorry. I thought you knew."

"This is the first I've heard of it. What a pity." There was a strange note in Ryuko's voice; it sounded closer to pleasure than surprise or sorrow. Something in him had relaxed, a tension that Sano only became aware of now, in its absence. "How do you know about Usugumo's death?"

"Hirata-*san* told me. He found her while he was searching and rescuing." Sano omitted the fact of his own involvement.

"I didn't know her very well, but she was a good teacher, a fine woman." Ryuko's manner grew cautious, as if he realized that there had been something wrong with his initial reaction, which he hoped Sano hadn't noticed. "The earthquake has cost so many people their lives."

"The earthquake didn't kill Usugumo," Sano said. "She was poisoned."

Ryuko's expression stiffened; he resembled a Buddha statue more than ever. Sano felt the tension in him return, drawing his muscles tight. "Poisoned, how?" His lips barely moved.

"At an incense game with two of her pupils." Sano didn't mention that the other victims were Lord Hosokawa's daughters. "There was arsenic in the incense. All three women were found dead together, in the remains of Usugumo's house."

Ryuko swallowed visibly. "It couldn't have been an accident?" His eyes betrayed the hope that his flat tone tried to conceal.

"Anything's possible, but it looks like murder," Sano said.

"That's why you're here." Ryuko couldn't hide the fear that turned his complexion grayer. "You're not checking on the temple; you're investigating Usugumo's murder. And you think I killed her!"

"I'm not investigating any murder. How would I have time?" Sano hoped the lie sounded more believable than it felt. "Her murder will be a matter for the police, when they get around to it. But since you raised the possibility that you killed her, I might as well ask: Did you put the arsenic in the incense?"

Offense revived the color in Ryuko's face. "I shouldn't dignify that question with a reply, but I will." He said forcefully, "No."

Sano couldn't tell if he was lying. Ryuko, like all successful courtiers, was an expert actor, even when under pressure. "You've been in Usugumo's house, haven't you? You could have mixed in the arsenic while you were blending incense. Or you could have prepared the poisoned incense pellets ahead of time and brought them with you to your lessons."

"Why would I do that?" Ryuko sounded a shade more tentative now, as if he were afraid that Sano had the answer. He hurried to counterattack. "I think you are investigating the murder. If you aren't, why bother bringing it up?"

"Just curious," Sano fibbed. "I'm sorry to upset you."

"I am not upset," Ryuko said in the haughty tone that often accompanies this lie. Perspiration gleamed on his shaved scalp. "I am merely annoyed, because you have the temerity to suggest that I could be involved in such a sordid matter. And because I think you"—he pointed a finger at Sano—"are up to some kind of dirty business, and the murder investigation is a ruse."

"No dirty business, no ruse," Sano said in the artless tone in which a false denial is often spoken. "Pardon me. Forget I mentioned Usugumo. I'll be leaving now."

Ryuko thrust his finger into Sano's face. Its nail was long, curved, and sharp. "I warn you," he said, the rasp in his voice like a jagged knife. His angry eyes glittered as brightly as his stole. "Leave me alone, or I'll have a word with Lady Keisho-in. She won't like you making insinuations about her favorite priest." But his fear that he would be blamed for the murder, and lose her patronage, showed in the trembling edges of his fierce smile. "She'll turn against you. And after a word from her, so will the shogun."

He swept past Sano, his robes lashing against Sano's legs as he stalked toward the main hall where the prayers droned on and on. Sano wondered what he could have done differently, to avoid antagonizing Ryuko. He also wondered what Ryuko was hiding about his relations with the incense teacher.

"YOU DON'T WANT to go in there," said one of the ladies-in-waiting huddled on the veranda outside the Large Interior.

The Large Interior contained the women's quarters of the palace, where the shogun's mother, wife, female concubines, and their attendants lived. They still lived there, although most of their building had collapsed during the earthquake; no better accommodations were available. A bamboo fence screened the intact wing from the ruins, the workers clearing them away, and the noise.

"Why not?" Reiko noticed more women occupying the pavilion in the snowy garden. These most privileged, pampered women in Japan were living like housewives in the slums. The earthquake had equalized the social classes. They looked cold and dour.

"You'll see," the lady-in-waiting said ominously.

Carrying a small lacquer lunch box she'd brought, Reiko entered the low, half-timbered building. A din of women's shrill voices sounded like quarrelsome birds. She left her shoes by a pile of other shoes and draped her cloak on other garments that hung in the entryway. Heading down the corridor, she winced at the stale odor of too many people shut up in too little space. Chambers contained women bathing, brushing their hair, putting on makeup, eating, or playing cards. Acrimony tinged their conversations. Two girls squabbled about a broken comb. They were all like caged animals, venting their frustrations on one another. The loudest voice emanated from the largest room. Reiko stood at the threshold because so many women knelt on the floor, taking up all the space. Young and old, they wore brightly painted kimonos, their hair spiked with expensive ornaments. They sat in frightened silence. Amid them lay Lady Keisho-in, the shogun's mother.

She drummed her heels and fists on the floor and yelled, "How dare he?" in her croaky old voice. "Who the hell does he think he is?"

Small and plump, she wore a brilliant magenta silk kimono. She loved girlish clothes, which she'd never given up even though she was seventy-six years old. Thick white rice-powder on her round, double-chinned face hid its wrinkles. Red rouge on her lips and cheeks, and black hair dye, lent her a semblance of youth. As she ranted, the gaps between her teeth hardly showed; the ones that remained were painted black in the fashionable style for married women. She'd never married the shogun's father, Reiko knew; she'd been his peasant concubine. The fact that she'd given birth to the shogun gave her every privilege of fashion and rank she wanted. Reiko understood why the women were outside in the cold: They didn't like to be around while Lady Keisho-in had a tantrum.

A gray-haired attendant spied Reiko and exclaimed brightly, "Look, my lady! You have a visitor!"

The other women cleared a path for Reiko. As she walked into the room, they bowed, smiled, and backed out, leaving her to cope with Lady Keisho-in, who shouted curses. Reiko knelt. Lady Keisho-in sat up and went silent, surprised to see Reiko, puzzled because she'd lost her audience.

"Good afternoon, Lady Keisho-in," Reiko said. "May I ask what has upset you so much?"

An angry scowl creased the makeup on Lady Keisho-in's face. "It's that damned astronomer. Have you heard about his pronouncement?"

"Yes, my husband mentioned it," Reiko said.

"His constellations say the cosmos is displeased with the government in general, and an important personage in particular. He had the nerve to hint that it's me, because I was promoted to the highest rank in court, which is too far above my station." Lady Keisho-in exclaimed, "Can you believe it?"

Reiko hadn't heard that part of the story. "No, indeed, I can't." It was dangerous for anyone to criticize the shogun's mother.

"As if that weren't bad enough, he suggested that the earthquake is my fault!"

The astronomer had put Lady Keisho-in in danger, too, Reiko realized. People wanted someone to blame for the earthquake. If it was Lady Keisho-in, not even her status as the shogun's mother would protect her from harsh punishment. Reiko reflected that no matter how bad one's own earthquake-related problems seemed, others had theirs that were even worse.

"He doesn't know his anus from a hole in his head," Lady Keisho-in declared. "I deserve that rank even though I was born a peasant. I'm the mother of the shogun! Besides, my son has the right to promote anyone he wants!" She cursed, then asked Reiko, "What do you think?"

Reiko thought giving birth to a shogun was a matter of sex and luck rather than accomplishment, and it shouldn't entitle Lady Keisho-in to such high honors. But she also thought it was far-fetched to blame the earthquake on Keisho-in. Even if the gods didn't like Keisho-in's promotion, it seemed too trivial a matter for them to make millions of people suffer through an earthquake. But Reiko didn't dare say any of this.

"I think you're right," she said.

"Of course I am," Lady Keisho-in said stoutly. "That astronomer has a grudge against me because I don't invite him to my moon-viewing parties. He's jealous and vindictive, and he's out to get me. I'll have him run out of town!"

The astronomer had better prepare for a battle unless he changed his tune, Reiko thought. She steered the conversation to the topic she'd come to discuss. "What does Priest Ryuko think of this business?"

Disgruntlement soured Keisho-in's face. "That man! How should I know what he thinks? He never comes near me! I'm furious! After all I've done for him! I introduced him to my son. I even got him his own temple. If not for me, Ryuko wouldn't have a pot to make water in. But it's always, 'I'm busy helping the poor earthquake victims, my dear.'" She snidely imitated the priest's booming voice.

"I suppose Priest Ryuko is too busy for incense lessons," Reiko said.

"Incense lessons?" Keisho-in looked baffled by this new, unexpected topic.

"Somebody told me he was taking them," Reiko said. "Before the earthquake. I was thinking of studying incense myself, when things get back to normal. Now what was his teacher's name?" She frowned, as if trying to recall. "Oh, yes. Madam Usugumo."

"That bitch!" Lady Keisho-in exclaimed.

Startled, Reiko said, "Did you know her?" Then she wanted to bite her tongue because she'd spoken in the past tense. She didn't want to let on that Usugumo was dead and invite unwelcome questions.

Lady Keisho-in didn't seem to notice. "I never met her, but Ryuko-*san* mentioned her. I don't like anybody who offends my dearest."

"What did he say about her?" Reiko spoke casually, but excitement quickened her heartbeat.

"That she had taken him in. That if he had known what she was really like, he never would have associated with her."

"It sounds as if something happened between them." Containing her excitement, Reiko asked, "What was it?"

"I don't know." Keisho-in's face bunched up like a sulky child's. "He wouldn't tell me. All I know is that when he came home from his lesson, he was terribly angry and upset. After that, he quit the lessons. He never went back to Usugumo again."

"Have you any idea why?" Reiko probed. "Do you remember anything else?"

Keisho-in turned her irritation on Reiko. "No, I don't. All I remember is that my dearest Ryuko-*san* was grumpy for a long time."

Reiko didn't dare press the issue and risk irritating Keisho-in, who had a history of extreme wrath toward people who crossed her. She'd had maids, ladies-in-waiting, and even the shogun's concubines beaten, sent to the Yoshiwara pleasure quarter to work as prostitutes, or exiled to islands in the middle of the ocean for infractions as minor as not flattering her enough. The women in the Large Interior walked on tiptoe around her. Reiko changed the subject.

"I heard that Lord Hosokawa's daughters were taking incense lessons, too," she said. She had to explore the possibility that if the priest had indeed committed murder, the teacher hadn't been his intended target. "Is Priest Ryuko acquainted with them?"

"He's not acquainted with any women except me." Lady Keisho-in was renowned for her jealousy. She treated Ryuko as if he were her husband, even though he'd taken a religious vow of celibacy. It was no secret that he visited her in her bedchamber. The irritation in her eyes took on a suspicious glint. "Do you know something I don't?"

"No, no," Reiko said. "I just thought that maybe Priest Ryuko met Lord Hosokawa's daughters when he took incense lessons at Usugumo's house." She was wondering whether he'd seen anything to indicate whether they were guilty, when a new and dismaying idea occurred to her. Had Priest Ryuko been involved with Usugumo? Had their quarrel been a lover's spat? If so, then here was another suspect—Lady Keisho-in. Reiko had thought that nothing could be more dangerous than implicating Lord Hosokawa's daughters in the murders.

"Ryuko-*san* never met anyone at Usugumo's house. His lessons were private." Lady Keisho-in leaned toward Reiko, suddenly hostile. "Why are you asking me all these questions?"

The risk of making Priest Ryuko a suspect in the crime was also hazardous. Even if Lady Keisho-in believed her lover was guilty, she would be just as angry at those who exposed him as at Ryuko himself. Reiko felt danger suffuse the air, like poisoned incense smoke. The shogun loved his mother. Accusing or displeasing her was tantamount to treason.

"I almost forgot," Reiko said. "Please excuse my poor manners. I brought you a gift." She offered the lacquer box to Lady Keisho-in. Polite custom dictated that she should have given the gift as soon as she'd arrived, but Reiko had waited, in case she needed it to smooth over a difficult moment.

"Oh, wonderful!" Lady Keisho-in pounced on the box, as eager as a child for a treat. She opened it, saw the pale green cakes colored with tea, filled with sweet lotus paste, and dusted with cinnamon. Reiko's cooks had made them with the last of the spice. "My favorite!"

She crammed a cake into her mouth, chewed, and smacked her lips. The danger dissipated. Reiko relaxed.

"I just remembered something else Ryuko-*san* said when he came home from his last incense lesson," Lady Keisho-in said as she munched another soft, gooey cake. "He said that if Usugumo tried to get him in trouble, he would make her sorry." Lady Keisho-in licked her fingers.

16

SANO MADE A few inquiries and learned that Minister Ogyu
had vacated his mansion in town, which had been totally destroyed by
the earthquake, and moved to the Academy of Confucian Studies, known
as the Yushima Seido—Sacred Hall in the Yushima district, located
north of Edo Castle.

Snow lay ankle-deep in the streets as Sano and his troops rode to
Yushima. It caked the horses' hooves and manes, covered strewn debris.
Smoke from fires in the camps disappeared into the veil of white flakes.
When Sano looked back at the castle, he could barely see its shape on
the hill. It felt as if he, his men, and the few wanderers they passed were
the only people left in the world. When he reached Yushima, nostalgia
worsened the sorrow that had lodged in his heart since the earthquake.

Yushima had once been a popular recreation spot. When he was a
boy, his father and mother had brought him to the market, where crowds
were so thick that parents often lost track of their children, and to the
spring festival when the plum trees bloomed. They'd enjoyed walking
along the Kanda River, watching the boats. Now the retaining walls,
the teahouses, and the restaurants that had lined the banks had slid into
the river. Snow frosted the plum trees. Yushima was deserted except for
small groups of people roaming around, viewing the destruction. That
was the most popular pastime nowadays. Sano's father had been dead
thirteen years; his mother was remarried and living in a distant village.
He missed them and their happy times.

He came upon the ruins of the town. Here had once stood the *kagemajaya*—"teahouses in the shadows," brothels inhabited by boy prostitutes. Sano ascended the road up the hill occupied by the Yushima Seido and the Kanda Myojin Shrine. The shrine was home to the great festival held on the anniversary of the Battle of Sekigahara, at which Tokugawa Ieyasu had defeated his rival warlords to become the supreme dictator of Japan. Sano remembered the portable shrines carried by near-naked bearers, the musicians banging drums and gongs, the models of human figures, pine trees, turtles, cranes, and roosters riding on floats drawn by oxen. He could almost taste the famous sweet sake, laced with ginger, once sold in the famous shops that now lay wrecked along the road. He'd brought his family to the last festival. They'd had a wonderful time, especially Akiko, who couldn't take her eyes off the floats. He wondered if they would ever see the festival again.

The Seido evoked more decorous memories. Sano had been there for the grand opening ceremony twelve years ago. The shogun, government officials, and *daimyo* had gathered inside the academy, which resembled an opulent temple. They'd listened to speeches, readings from Confucius, and poetry composed for the occasion. The place had become an elite educational institution, the first of its kind, where the sons of Tokugawa retainers and feudal lords studied the Confucian classics. But there wouldn't be any more ceremonies, lessons, or lectures for the foreseeable future. Sano and his men had to dismount and clamber through the gaps in the broken tile walls that enclosed the Seido; the roof over the main gate had collapsed, blocking the portal. Sections of the wall around the inner precinct had fallen off the slope on which it stood; rocks littered the outer precinct.

"Hello!" Sano called. "Is anybody here!"

His voice echoed up and down the hill. A cry from above answered. He and his troops climbed the steep steps to the innermost precinct. The going was treacherous, the steps slippery with snow and riddled with cracks. At the top, Sano and his men climbed over the crumbled wall. A spacious garden of shrubs, pine trees, and boulders still existed, but the buildings once arranged in a square were long piles of ruins topped with their roof ornaments—snarling stone beasts with roosters' bodies and dragons' heads. A narrow path had been cleared through the rubble. Sano walked through this into the stone-flagged courtyard.

Where once pupils had strolled and debated Confucian theory, now stood five square tents made of bamboo and oiled muslin. Sano heard children's voices within. The main hall still had its roof, but its walls and foundations had given way. It brought to Sano's mind a prone man wearing his hat on his slanted back. Fire had charred the walls, blistered the vermilion paint. Five or six women were sorting tiles that had slid off the roof, tossing the whole ones into wheeled barrows. Some twenty men lugged pillars and statues from the ruins of the side buildings. Clad in leather gloves, thick coats, and broad-brimmed wicker hats, the people seemed oblivious to the snow. A heavy woman trundled a full barrow of tiles across the courtyard and dumped them onto a heap of others. She noticed Sano.

"Honorable Chamberlain?"

It wasn't a woman. It was Minister Ogyu. He removed his hat and used his sleeve to wipe sweat off his shaved crown as he moved toward Sano. His topknot protruded above a round-cheeked face. With his prominent paunch, he reminded Sano of sumo wrestlers. He walked with their heavy trudge. But he was shorter than average, and in his forties, he was too old to be a wrestler.

"Greetings, Minister Ogyu," Sano said. They exchanged bows while Sano's troops waited in the distance. "I'm here to inspect the academy."

"A thousand thanks for coming. I wish I could show you something better." Ogyu's voice was deep, as if it emanated from his belly rather than his throat. Maybe he wanted to compensate for his small stature. His face was as smooth as a child's, but a patch of fuzzy mustache, like black moss, shaded his upper lip, as if his valet didn't shave him closely enough. Sano had noticed this before, when they'd met at ceremonies and lectures.

"I wish I could send you more help." Sano regretted that the country's only center for higher learning was gone.

"Well, there are more important things to fix. Even though His Excellency has said that the Seido is a top priority." Ogyu smiled wryly. His lips were full, his teeth stubby but even. His pleasant manner didn't show in his gaze, which had a cool opaqueness that Sano had also previously noticed.

"I see you've started the work on the academy yourself," Sano said.

"Yes, well, my staff and servants and I haven't much else to do," Ogyu said, "with the lessons and lectures suspended."

Sano thought Ogyu's attitude was a big improvement over Priest Ryuko's. He felt sorry for Ogyu, who had lost his life's work, perhaps permanently.

"Eventually we'll get help with clearing away the ruins," Ogyu said. "In the meantime, we're salvaging everything that's usable. Wood and roof tiles will be hard to come by when the rebuilding boom starts."

He spoke with confidence that the universe would conspire in his favor. Sano reflected that in the past the universe had done so. Ogyu's family were hereditary Tokugawa vassals of low rank. His father had been a mere secretary at the castle, but was ambitious. Sano had heard that the man had gone deeply into debt to hire an acclaimed tutor to teach his only child. The tutor also gave lessons to the shogun. Ogyu had proved himself to be a genius at interpreting and writing about the Confucian classics. The shogun liked to surround himself with learned young men, and the tutor had recommended Ogyu, who became one of the shogun's favorite scholars. Rumor said Ogyu had helped the shogun with his lessons and even written his lectures for him. When the Seido had been built, and the shogun needed someone to run it, he'd picked Ogyu.

Realizing that the tour of inspection, his pretext for coming, was finished, Sano sought to keep the conversation going and lead into the investigation. "I understand you're living here because you lost your house. It must be hard."

"I'm fortunate nonetheless," Ogyu said. "So many people have lost much more than I have. Including their lives."

These words gave Sano the opening he needed. "I'm sorry to say that I've heard of another death. An incense teacher named Usugumo was found yesterday."

"Gods be merciful. I didn't know. I'm sorry." Ogyu seemed genuinely surprised and grieved.

Sano wondered if he already knew Usugumo was dead because he'd killed her. Maybe he was surprised because after a month had passed since the earthquake and she hadn't been found, he'd believed she never would be. Maybe he was grieved because he'd thought he was safe and now feared he wasn't.

"Did you know her?" Sano asked.

"Yes. I used to take lessons from her." Ogyu admitted it readily, but maybe he thought Sano could find out that he'd been Usugumo's student and realized that if he tried to hide it, he would look suspicious. But he appeared more chagrined than guilty. "I feel bad because I didn't check on Madam Usugumo after the earthquake. But there were so many other things to do. She slipped my mind." Again, he seemed sincere, but Sano noticed that the emotions his words professed showed only in the flexing of his facial muscles. His eyes held their cool reserve.

"This may ease your mind," Sano said. "The earthquake didn't kill Usugumo. She died before it happened."

"Oh?" Ogyu sounded surprised, curious. "How?"

"She and two of her pupils were poisoned during an incense game." Sano didn't mention the identities of the other women. As he explained that Hirata had found the bodies in the sunken house, he watched Ogyu closely. Ogyu didn't panic the way Priest Ryuko had. Maybe he'd prepared himself for the possibility that the crime would come to light and he would be accused.

"Have you any idea who did it?" Ogyu asked. "Is Hirata-*san* investigating the murders?"

"No." Sano had thought of putting Hirata in charge of an official investigation instead of trying to keep it secret. After all, solving crimes was Hirata's job. But Sano had decided not to risk having Lord Hosokawa think he wasn't handling it personally or to make the investigation public and risk the secret behind it coming out. "The police will investigate the murder eventually. Since we're on the subject, though, I may as well take a statement from you and save you the trouble of talking to the police later."

"Of course." Ogyu spoke as if glad to cooperate.

Sano felt a prickling sensation on his nape. He turned and looked across the courtyard. A flap had been raised on one of the tents. A woman stood in the opening, watching him. With one hand she held the flap up. Her other arm hugged a little girl and boy. Her face was narrow, sharp-chinned, and somber. She realized that Sano had seen her, and her eyes widened like those of a cornered animal. She dropped the flap, hiding herself and the children.

"That's my family," Ogyu said.

Sano turned to see that for once there was emotion in Ogyu's eyes— affection. Ogyu said, "I tried to send them to stay with relatives. But my wife wanted to be with me."

"Tell her she can join us if she likes." Sano wondered if Lady Ogyu knew anything about the murders.

"Thank you, but she would prefer not to," Ogyu said. "She's very shy." His gaze turned opaque again. "I can give you my statement now, if you like."

"Thank you." Sano asked, "How long had you known Usugumo?"

"Not long. I only had six or seven lessons."

"What were your relations with her?"

"Strictly business." Ogyu glanced toward the tents.

Sano wondered if he didn't want his wife to hear the conversation. But he didn't have the sly, guilty, or lascivious look of a man discussing a paramour. "What did you talk about with Madam Usugumo?"

"Besides incense? Nothing that I can recall. The art of incense is a form of meditation. It deserves one's full attention. We observed the rule against small talk during lessons."

Sano remembered as much from the lessons he and Reiko had taken from another teacher. Incense games were social, but not parties for chatting. "When was the last time you saw Madam Usugumo?"

"At my last lesson. During the eleventh month of this year, I believe."

That jibed with the notes in her book. "Was there anything unusual about it?"

"Unusual, how?"

"Did she seem worried? Or upset?"

"No. But if she was worried or upset about something, she wouldn't have told me. I was a pupil. She was the teacher."

For a teacher to confide in a pupil went against custom. For a commoner to impose her problems on a high-ranking samurai employer did, too. "Do you know if she had any enemies?"

Ogyu shook his head. "I would assume that if she did, they were people I don't know. We didn't move in the same circles."

"What about her other pupils? Did you meet them?"

"No. I took private lessons. Nobody else was there."

Sano thought of Priest Ryuko. Ogyu certainly knew him. Sano had seen the two talking at ceremonies. Maybe Ogyu didn't know that the priest had numbered among Usugumo's pupils. Sano wondered what, if anything, the connection between the two men signified. But it didn't appear that Ogyu would have met Lord Hosokawa's daughters.

"Wait." Ogyu raised his gloved finger, which was short and thick like his body. "There was someone else there. I just remembered. Usugumo's apprentice. He helped her prepare for the lessons. A young man named Korin."

This was the second time the apprentice had cropped up. Sano hoped Detective Marume would find him. He could be a good witness, if not a suspect. Right now Sano could do with either. It appeared that he wouldn't get much of worth from Minister Ogyu—at least not as long as he maintained the pretense that Ogyu was just assisting with a future police inquiry and not under suspicion.

"Thank you for your time," Sano said. "I'll send some workers and funds your way as soon as they're available."

"Thank you. I hope the police can find out who killed Usugumo. She was a fine woman who didn't deserve to die." Again, Ogyu spoke with sincerity.

Sano wondered if those opaque eyes saw straight through him. Leaving the courtyard, he glanced at Lady Ogyu's tent. She must have overheard his whole conversation with Minister Ogyu. Did her interest in it extend beyond a wife's nosiness about her husband's affairs? Although tempted to question her, Sano didn't want to risk seeming too eager for information and causing the wrong people—namely Ienobu and the shogun—to get wind of it and ask why. Sano would have to wait to satisfy his curiosity until after Reiko talked with Lady Ogyu.

17

WHEN HIRATA LEFT Sano's estate, he knew he should begin
questioning people who were associated with Priest Ryuko and Minister
Ogyu, eliciting information that would indicate whether one of them was
the murderer. He knew that with so many people displaced, it would
take a while to locate witnesses, and he would lose time tracing people
who turned out to have died in the earthquake. But he couldn't get out of
the ritual. If he reneged on his promise, Tahara, Kitano, and Deguchi
would force him to participate. Recalling the moment they'd levitated the
house out of the ground, he feared them more than ever, and he needed to
arm himself with knowledge before he saw them again.

Hirata rode through the falling snow along desolate, rubble-strewn
streets to the huge camp in Nihonbashi. He paused on its edge, gazing
at the tents, concentrating on the auras given off by the people. They
conveyed so much pain, fear, and grief that he wanted to suppress his
perception, but he was looking for someone, and this was the quickest
method.

He visited three other camps before he found the men at one near
the Sumida River. In the twilight, bonfires colored the falling snowflakes orange. The men had pitched their tent at the edge of the camp.
Their tent was made of two lattice partitions leaned together and covered with tatami mats. Blankets hung over its ends. Smoke tendrils rose
from an opening on top. It radiated a powerful, calm aura spangled with
cheer, which was familiar to Hirata. He also perceived another aura he'd

never encountered before, equally powerful, humorous. Hirata cautiously approached.

"Greetings, Hirata-*san*," called a male voice from within.

There was no use sneaking up on his fellow mystic martial artists. Hirata lifted the blanket. Warmth heated his face. He smelled the sour tang of pickled cabbage and radish and the reek of salted fish. "Hello, Iseki-*san*."

An oil lamp illuminated two kneeling men. One held a bowl and chopsticks. The other lifted a teapot off a brazier. He was in his seventies, his face wrinkled like crumpled paper. He had only one arm.

"Join us," he said

Hirata squeezed himself into the tent's small space, amid various cloth-wrapped bundles. He accepted a bowl of tea that Iseki deftly poured with his single hand. "I'm glad to see you're alive. I went to your barbershop, but it was in ruins."

The barbershop had been a favorite haunt of mystic martial artists, located north of the Nihonbashi Bridge near the center of the national messenger system, from which the government dispatched runners to carry documents between cities. Iseki the barber had gleaned the latest news from the messengers and given it to his customers. The earthquake had halted the messenger system, which had only just resumed with limited service, and the mystic martial artists had lost their gathering place.

Iseki grinned and raised his tea bowl to Hirata. "I'm tough. An earthquake wrecked my barbershop. An earthquake crushed my arm and ended my fighting days. Neither of them managed to kill me, though."

"Are you going to introduce me to your friend?" Hirata asked.

"Oh, pardon my bad manners. This is Onodera."

Hirata exchanged polite bows and greetings with the man, who was in his forties but fit and muscular. Onodera wore a round black skullcap, a thigh-length kimono and loose breeches printed with arcane symbols, cloth leggings, and straw sandals. A short sword hung from the sash around his waist. Beside him was a wooden chest, its shoulder harness decorated with orange bobbles. Costume and equipment marked him as a *yamabushi*—an itinerant priest from a sect that blended Buddhism, Shinto religion, and Chinese magic.

"I've heard of you," he told Hirata. He had a round face with eyes that disappeared into slits as he smiled. "The best fighter in Edo."

Modestly declining the praise, Hirata knew who the best fighters in Edo really were, although he'd yet to see them strike a single blow. "I've heard of you, too. You protect villages from bandit gangs."

"None other," Onodera said cheerfully.

"What brings you here?"

"I was passing through Edo when the earthquake hit," Onodera said. "I figured I would stay and see if I could help."

"Well, I'm glad to find you and Iseki-*san*," Hirata said, "because I need your help." He spoke reluctantly because it felt weak and shameful. But he didn't know what else to do.

"Who do you want me to fight?" Onodera put down his bowl, ready to dash into battle.

"No one." At least not yet. "It's information I need."

"Information about what?"

Hirata hesitated, recalling his oath of silence to the secret society. But asking about the other members didn't equal telling on them. "Three mystic martial artists. Their names are Tahara, Kitano, and Deguchi."

Onodera's eyes opened up as the smile left his face.

"You asked me about them, when was it, last year?" Iseki said. "Didn't I tell you to stay away from them?"

"I should have listened," Hirata said.

Iseki frowned, refilling Hirata's tea bowl, adding a splash from a jar of sake.

Hirata drank. The tea was spicy and robust, the liquor eye-wateringly potent. "Do you know them?" he asked Onodera.

"I've never laid eyes on them, let alone seen them in action. But I've heard that they were Ozuno's favorite disciples. Which means they have to be among the best martial artists who ever lived."

Hirata felt a pang of jealousy. He'd thought he was Ozuno's favorite. But he should have known better as soon as he'd met the three and learned Ozuno had been their mentor. "Is there anybody you know of who could tell me more?"

"A monk named Fuwa," Onodera said. "He used to go around with them."

"Where can I find him?" Hirata asked eagerly.

"Last I heard, he was living in Chiba."

Hirata's heart sank. The town of Chiba was a day's journey from Edo. He could never make it there and back before the ritual.

LIKE EVERY OTHER neighborhood in town, the Hibiya administrative district, south of Edo Castle, had been severely damaged by the earthquake. Barriers made of logs, scrap wood, and piled stones enclosed the sites of the mansions where the city's high officials had once lived and worked. Above the barriers Reiko could see the tops of tents that housed residents who had nowhere else to stay. Reiko called to her bearers to stop by a gate with shiny copper crests that looked incongruous remounted on beams made of cut logs. The sentries recognized her and let her in the gate. Walking toward the tents, Reiko heard muffled voices but saw no one.

"Grandmother?" she called.

A flap on one tent opened. A tiny old woman peered out. Bundled up from neck to toe, her body resembled a fat pile of quilts, but her head was as precisely modeled as that of a porcelain doll. Her silver hair was tied in a sleek knot, every hair oiled in place. Although she was past seventy, her skin was unlined; only her sagging jowls betrayed her age. She had the same delicate features and large, almond-shaped eyes as Reiko. Whenever Reiko saw her, she saw how she herself would look in the future, if she lived that long.

"What are you doing here?" her grandmother demanded. Her voice was hoarsened by the years but had nary a quaver.

"I came to see you, Grandmother," Reiko said, bowing. She needed the old woman's help with the investigation, but she was loath to ask.

"Dear me, is it New Year's Day again?"

"Not yet."

"And here I thought I was getting senile. New Year's Day is the only time you ever come—when you bring your husband and children for your annual visit."

Reiko felt the sting of rebuke, followed by the flare of temper that her grandmother never failed to provoke. "You've always made it clear that I'm not welcome."

"Why would you be?" Disapproval crossed the old woman's face.

"You're the most impertinent, unladylike creature I've had the misfortune to know."

Their exchanges always went like this. Even when Reiko was a child, her grandmother never had a kind word for her, only criticism, scolding, and slaps, often for no apparent reason. At first Reiko had wept because her feelings were hurt and tried harder to please her grandmother. When she discovered that nothing she did was good enough, she'd decided to hate the mean old woman. Not until she was ten did she learn why her grandmother didn't like her. She'd overheard a conversation between her grandmother and a visitor. Standing outside the room where they chatted, Reiko had listened to her grandmother say, "That brat killed her mother! I wish she'd never been born! If she hadn't, my daughter would still be alive."

Reiko had realized that her grandmother blamed her for her mother's death during childbirth. How unfair that she would be hated for something that wasn't her fault! The experience was one reason she was passionate about justice. She couldn't bear to see innocent people wrongly condemned, or those guilty of harming others escape without punishment. She'd exercised her passion while observing the trials her father conducted and discussing them with him afterward, and while helping Sano with his investigations. But it seemed she could never set things right with the person who'd taught her the pain of injustice.

"Won't you ever forgive me?" she asked.

"Forgive you for what?" Her grandmother feigned puzzlement. The hostility in her eyes said she knew exactly what Reiko meant. "For running wild when you were young, as if you were a boy instead of a girl? Riding horses and sword-fighting in the streets?" She snorted. "I can't imagine what your father was thinking."

He'd never held her mother's death against her, Reiko knew. Magistrate Ueda had given her, his only child, so much love that she'd never missed having a mother. He'd rewarded her intelligence, strength, and courage with the education usually reserved for sons. Of course, her unconventional upbringing had worsened her relationship with her grandmother.

"That was a long time ago," Reiko said.

"Oh, well, then. Should I forgive you for defying me when I tried to arrange a match for you?"

When Reiko had reached a marriageable age, her grandmother had obtained proposals from rich, important men. Reiko had refused them. Not only had she thought them too old, unattractive, and stuffy; she'd dreaded being trapped in the circumscribed existence of married women of her class. She'd held out until her father had insisted she attend the *miai* where she'd met Sano. She'd accepted Sano because he was young and handsome, and she'd heard of his exciting exploits. She'd gambled that he would be less conventional and more amenable to letting her do as she pleased than her other suitors, and she'd won.

"My husband is the shogun's chamberlain," Reiko said. "You couldn't have asked for anyone higher than that."

"I couldn't have asked for anyone who gets in more trouble," her grandmother retorted. Little that happened in the regime escaped her; she had sons, grandsons, and other relatives in high places, whom she badgered into telling her everything.

"We have two beautiful children," Reiko said, because she hadn't quite lost the habit of trying to show herself to her grandmother in a positive light. *And another on the way.*

"A pity, the way you're raising them," the old woman grumbled. "You're too easy on them. I worry that they'll go bad."

Another reason that Reiko didn't come more often was that her grandmother treated Masahiro and Akiko the same way she treated Reiko. Her temper ready to boil over, Reiko changed the subject. "Why are you still living in this tent, Grandmother?"

"Where else would I live?"

"I invited you to come and stay with me." Although Reiko's house was crowded, she could fit in one more person.

Her grandmother huffed. "I'm too old-fashioned for your modern home." That was a dig at Reiko's habit of leaving domesticity behind to do detective work for Sano. Her grandmother didn't approve of women who meddled in men's business. "I'd rather stay here. This is my home. Besides, who will keep an eye on things if I leave?"

Reiko watched the snow sift from the sky. She was freezing. "Can I come in?"

"Oh, all right."

The tent was crammed with lacquer chests and iron trunks. Grandmother seated herself on a futon in the center. Reiko knelt on the tatami that covered the earth. A brazier filled the tent with smoky heat. While her grandmother made tea, Reiko noticed a pile of unfurled scrolls covered with black calligraphy and red government seals, and a portable writing desk, its open lid revealing papers scribbled with notes.

"What is that?" Reiko asked.

Her grandmother slammed the desk shut and pushed the scrolls behind a trunk. "Just some things I'm doing for your uncles."

Reiko's uncles worked for the government. "It seems I'm not the only woman in our family who meddles in men's business," Reiko murmured.

"What did you say?" her grandmother said sharply.

"Nothing." Reiko couldn't afford to antagonize the old woman any further.

"What's the real reason you came?" She handed Reiko a bowl of tea. "Did you want to see if I was still alive? Well, too bad for you."

Reiko sipped tea, warmed her hands, and braced herself for another fight. "I need an introduction to the wife of Minister Ogyu who runs the shogun's Confucian academy." Social custom prohibited calling on a stranger without an introduction from a mutual acquaintance, and Reiko didn't want to barge in on Lady Ogyu and make her suspicious. She didn't have the excuse of a funeral and a political connection, as she'd had with the Hosokawa women.

"Who does your husband think she killed?"

"No one," Reiko said, taken aback. "This isn't for an investigation."

"Spare me." Her grandmother flicked a slender, elegant hand at Reiko. "Why else would you want to meet such a dull little woman? Why would you be interested in anyone except those murderers that you like to hobnob with?"

"This is important. I can't tell you why." Reiko put on her most humble, conciliatory manner. "Please. I need your help."

The old woman smiled, gratified. "Lady Ogyu is my sister-in-law's great-niece. But I won't introduce you to her unless you tell me what this is all about."

"Very well. But you must promise me that you won't pass it on."

"I'll take it to my grave, which probably won't happen soon enough for your liking."

"There has been a murder," Reiko admitted. "Lady Ogyu is a potential witness. She can't be allowed to know that I'm investigating her for my husband."

"Who was murdered?" The old woman leaned forward, rapacious in her curiosity.

"A woman named Usugumo. She was an incense teacher."

Her grandmother uttered a scornful sound. "You're holding out on me, child. Your husband wouldn't bother investigating the death of one commoner, not when he's got his hands full with earthquake problems and keeping the shogun happy. Now let's have it!"

Reiko had no choice but to part with more information. "The other victims were Lord Hosokawa's daughters."

Shock wiped the crankiness off the old woman's face. "Great Buddha! Now I understand. Lord Hosokawa is a very powerful *daimyo*. He could make trouble for the Tokugawa regime. I can imagine how badly he wants his children avenged. If your husband doesn't find out who killed them, Lord Hosokawa could even decide to start a war."

Her view of the situation was so astute that Reiko blinked.

"I'll write a letter to Lady Ogyu, saying that I'm sending you to see how she fared during the earthquake, so that you can report back to me. That should do." The old woman ground ink, dipped her brush, and wrote on thick white rice paper, stamped the finished letter with her signature seal, and rolled it into a lacquer scroll container. When Reiko put out her hand for it, she held it out of reach. "If I give you this, you must tell me how the investigation turns out."

Reiko hoped that when the investigation was finished, she would have such a good story to tell that she could withhold any dangerous parts and her grandmother wouldn't notice. "Yes, Grandmother," she said, taking the letter.

18

AFTER FINISHING HIS inquiries, Sano worked late in his office at home. He went over the day's events with his aides. Hearing the urgent messages from officials who'd come to see him, he felt guilty and disturbed because his absence had enraged many of them. In the volatile, post-earthquake climate, hostilities bred like flies. Sano hoped he could solve the crime before he made too many new enemies. He left orders with his aides and authorized them to field requests and act as his deputies until the investigation was finished.

By that time, most of his household had retired. A maid asked if he wanted dinner. Sano said yes; he was starving. He tiptoed past rooms crowded with his sleeping retainers. The house seemed to expand and contract with their snores. He went to the small room that served as a bath chamber, stripped, scrubbed, and rinsed. He longed for a warm soak, but there was no space for a tub. The room was so cold that while he dried himself and put on his night robe, he shivered uncontrollably. Charcoal was becoming scarce; everyone conserved it at night. He ate his miso soup and noodles and drank his tea at his desk. Afterward he hurried to the family's chamber.

Reiko, Masahiro, and Akiko were asleep in the bed, quilts piled on them, only their nightcaps showing. Sano climbed in between his wife and son. Reiko said drowsily, "Good, you're home. How late is it?"

"Very late." Sano basked in the body heat under the quilts. He pictured other families all over Edo bedded down together. The earthquake had fostered extra closeness, one of its few blessings.

"Did you see Priest Ryuko and Minister Ogyu?" Reiko whispered, trying not to waken the children.

"Yes." Sano summarized the conversations, then said, "Priest Ryuko was as upset as any cornered criminal I've ever seen. Minister Ogyu, on the other hand, was pleasant and cooperative." He described the man's physical appearance. "Which made me suspicious."

"So either of them could have poisoned the women?"

"Or neither. Have you discovered anything that might help determine whether they're guilty or innocent?"

Reiko described her visit with Lady Keisho-in. Sano frowned as he listened to her news that Priest Ryuko and Madam Usugumo had quarreled.

"No matter the reason for the quarrel, it does sound like Priest Ryuko had a reason to want her dead," Sano said.

"It sounds like Minister Ogyu didn't."

"What's certain is that I brought my interest in the crime to the attention of two powerful men and I antagonized at least one of them," Sano said ruefully. "And the investigation is no further ahead than before."

Reiko murmured in concurrence and sympathy. "Has Hirata-*san* found out anything about Priest Ryuko or Minister Ogyu?"

"I don't know. I haven't seen him since he brought us Madam Usugumo's book. He's missing. Again."

Reiko was silent. Sano knew she shared his worries about Hirata's behavior. She didn't want to punish Hirata any more than Sano did, especially since Hirata's wife Midori was her friend. But they both knew that the situation was coming to a head. The earthquake seemed to have that effect on many situations.

"I'm sure he'll be back by tomorrow with news." Reiko snuggled closer to Sano.

"I'm not counting on it." Sano yearned for the old days when a master could always trust his chief retainer to act in his best interests. Perhaps those days were just a fantasy. In reality, samurai were human and their personal interests often conflicted with duty. Sano couldn't deny his own struggle between duty toward the shogun and his code of justice and honor. "I'd better start looking into Priest Ryuko's and Minister Ogyu's backgrounds myself."

"I obtained a letter of introduction to Minister Ogyu's wife," Reiko said, "from my grandmother."

"Your grandmother? You went to her?" Sano was surprised; he'd seen how badly the old woman treated Reiko.

"If I can learn something that helps us identify the killer, it will be worth a lifetime of her scolding and insults," Reiko said.

"I saw Priest Ryuko today at the palace," Masahiro said.

"Oh?" Sano had thought Masahiro was asleep, but of course he'd been listening to the conversation. "He's been at Zōjō Temple leading prayers since the earthquake."

"He has a room in the shogun's guesthouse. He came back this evening." Since he'd become a page, Masahiro was a font of information. "How about if I spy on him for you?"

"Only if you can do it without neglecting the shogun," Sano said.

"Um . . ." Masahiro said.

Reiko raised herself on one elbow to look across Sano at their son. "What is it?"

"I have to tell you and Father something." Pride and apprehension resonated in Masahiro's voice. "Today the shogun put me in charge of his chambers."

"How—" Sano began so loudly that Akiko whimpered and Reiko shushed him. He was pleased that Masahiro had gained such favor, yet concerned about the ramifications. "How did that happen?" he whispered.

"I didn't do it on purpose." Masahiro sounded guilty now. As he described how he'd grabbed the shogun to stop him from beating his concubine, Reiko and Sano groaned. To lay a hand on the supreme dictator was a capital offense. When Masahiro revealed that the shogun had meekly surrendered and rewarded Masahiro for teaching him how to care for his possessions, Sano and Reiko sighed in relief.

"You don't know how lucky you are to be alive!" Reiko said.

"Yes, I do." Masahiro said anxiously, "Are you going to punish me?"

"Of course not. You did what you thought was right." Sano was distressed because that was how he'd lived his own life, often to his detriment, and his son was following his example. He silently cursed the earthquake, which had created the circumstances for Masahiro to distinguish himself. "But you're in a dangerous position. The shogun will expect more of you. Whenever you do something, he'll expect more again. Sometimes your best won't be good enough."

"Spoken from experience," Reiko murmured.

"What should I do?" Oddly, Masahiro sounded eager for the challenge as well as daunted by Sano's prediction.

"Be more careful than ever. And watch out for the people around you. There's always someone who wants to knock the high chestnut out of the tree." It was the best political advice Sano had to offer. He'd just never dreamed his son would need it this soon.

The sound of footsteps preceded light from the corridor that shone through the lattice-and-paper wall. Sano sat up as Detective Marume appeared in the doorway, holding a lantern.

"I just found Madam Usugumo's missing apprentice," Marume said.

AFTER A HOT bath, a hearty meal, and sleeping all day, Yanagisawa spent the evening with his chief retainer, going over his finances. They were in worse shape than he'd thought. After his demotion, his stipend had been reduced by thirty percent. Some lands the shogun had granted him had been confiscated, and he'd lost the income from the rice grown on them. During his eleven months of seclusion, his staff had worsened the situation by keeping all his retainers on his payroll and borrowing money at high interest to cover the shortfall. Yanagisawa was furious.

"Dismiss half my army, retainers, and servants." He hated to lose the soldiers, but he could no longer feed them. If war became necessary before he regained the shogun's favor, he would have to rely on his allies' support. "After that, dismiss yourself. I don't need a chief retainer who runs me into bankruptcy."

Horrified that he and his comrades were to become *rōnin*, deprived of their income and their honor, the man said, "But where will we go?"

"I don't care. And don't look at me like that. I counted on you to watch out for my interests, and you let me down. You're lucky I don't put every one of you to death."

The man blanched and scurried out of the room. Yanagisawa slumped behind his desk, his head in his hands, and gazed at the ledgers with their columns of debts and losses. He was as angry at himself as at his retainers. This was his punishment for indulging his grief.

One of his bodyguards came to the door with the news Yanagisawa had been waiting for all day. "He's there."

Yanagisawa's second trip was even more arduous than the first. The sky had cleared, but an icy wind blew, whipping up snow, hurling it against Yanagisawa and his bodyguards as they rode through the ruined, frozen city. Without the lights that normally burned at neighborhood gates, the stars were so brilliant that looking at them hurt Yanagisawa's eyes. The moon resembled a white skull-face. During the ferry ride across the river, waves rocked the boat; cold spray lashed Yanagisawa. Wet and chilled, he arrived at the house where his sons lived.

Inside, his bodyguards accompanied him along dim corridors to a room where the lattice-and-paper wall glowed from a lantern within. His other guard, who'd stayed to keep watch over Yoshisato, opened the door. Yanagisawa motioned to all of his men to wait outside the house. His heart thudded with apprehension as he entered the room.

A young man sat against the wall, his legs drawn up and his arms folded. When he saw Yanagisawa, he sprang to his feet. He didn't bow. It was the height of rudeness. He stood with his hands on his hips. Yanagisawa put his anger aside while he and his son studied each other. Yoshisato was shorter, with a compact, wiry build. He had Someko's wide face, rounded chin, and tilted eyes that sparkled fiercely. Yanagisawa saw nothing of himself in Yoshisato, but he felt a surge of elation, for Yoshisato was undeniably handsome; he didn't look stupid or awkward. He might do very well.

"Hello, son," Yanagisawa said. "At last we meet."

" 'At last?' " Yoshisato's voice was deeper and rougher than Yanagisawa's. He combined a frown with a scornful grimace. "We've met before. Or so my mother tells me. But you've forgotten. And excuse me if I don't remember, either. I was a newborn baby."

His impertinence shocked Yanagisawa, who couldn't help being pleased to see that his son had inherited something from him—his nerve. "You'd better file the edges off that sharp tongue," he said with amusement.

Yoshisato seemed puzzled because Yanagisawa didn't reprimand him, suspicious of Yanagisawa's motives.

Yanagisawa said, "Why did you run away when I came to see you this morning?"

"Why do you want to see me after ignoring me for seventeen years?" Yoshisato folded his arms.

Yanagisawa realized that Yoshisato was angry and hurt because he'd been ignored. That was why he'd run away—to spite his neglectful father. Yanagisawa was surprised; he'd not thought about whether his sons minded his absence. He did think he could use Yoshisato's feelings to his own advantage.

"I want to apologize." The words tasted strange in Yanagisawa's mouth; he rarely apologized to anybody. "A lot of things have happened since you were born. I've been responsible for running the government. I fought a war and lost. I was exiled. I managed to come back, but I've had a struggle on my hands."

"In other words, you were too busy for me. But not too busy for Yoritomo."

Hearing Yoritomo's name spoken in such a hateful tone made Yanagisawa so furious that he wanted to punch Yoshisato. He controlled his temper, with difficulty. "I've given you everything you need."

"Food, clothes, schooling, martial arts lessons, a nice house, yes." Rancor pervaded Yoshisato's voice. "Good enough for a bastard. But some bastards get more than others, don't they?"

Yanagisawa clenched his fists. The desire to grab Yoshisato and beat him until he begged for mercy was almost irresistible. "You're jealous of Yoritomo."

"Me? Jealous of my dead half brother?" Yoshisato spoke with disdain. "He followed you around like a dog, begging for your attention. Hah! Don't make me laugh."

He turned away from Yanagisawa, who followed him across the room. It was outfitted with the usual tatami floor and built-in cabinets whose closed doors hid garments and bedding. Yoshisato stood by the raised study niche at the end. This contained a desk with writing supplies and paper covered with elegant calligraphy on its black lacquer surface, shelves of books, long trunks that held swords, a koto and a music stand, a globe. A constellation chart sat near a spyglass for viewing the heavens. This was the domain of an intelligent, cultured man with many interests. Yoshisato evidently wasn't among the legion of young samurai who lived to strut, drink, brawl, and fornicate. Yanagisawa took pride in him even though he was growing angrier by the moment.

"Yoritomo had a place at court," Yanagisawa said, "whereas you were shunted off to the side. Of course you were jealous."

"Yoritomo's place was in the shogun's bed," Yoshisato retorted. "That couldn't have been much fun. And look." Yoshisato raised his hands, waggled his fingers. "I'm the one who's still alive."

Yanagisawa fumed. If strangling this rascal could bring Yoritomo back, he would do it in a heartbeat. "I see that we started off on the wrong footing. Let's try again," he forced himself to say. "I'm sorry I ignored you while you were growing up. I'm here to make it up to you. I want to be your father and your friend." He was disconcerted to realize how much he truly wanted it. He extended his hand to Yoshisato. "Will you let me?"

The anger fell away from Yoshisato like an armor tunic dropped on the floor. The naked longing in his eyes stunned Yanagisawa. His son wanted a reconciliation as much as he did. His heart, shriveled by grief into a cold, hard lump, started to expand in the warmth of hope for the father-son relationship he craved. It occurred to him that his son was a person whose friendship and respect was a prize worth winning. The politician in him saw his ambitions within reach. Yanagisawa smiled.

The expression on Yoshisato's face turned to pure loathing. He sucked in his cheeks, then spat on Yanagisawa's hand.

Startled, Yanagisawa exclaimed in offense. He shook the hot, wet saliva off his hand as he glared at Yoshisato. "Why did you do that?"

"Because you insulted me." Yoshisato fairly blazed. He stood with his knees bent and hands twitching, as if ready to reach for his swords, although he wore none. "You treat me like you think I'm stupid enough to believe you want to be my father. Well, I'm not. I know you're just pretending." The pain of disappointment showed through the anger in his eyes. "You just want another whore to put in the shogun's bed!"

Such rage exploded in Yanagisawa that he saw Yoshisato through a veil of red and black flames. He lashed out his dripping hand and smote Yoshisato on the face.

Yoshisato didn't try to dodge. The impact of the blow shuddered through Yanagisawa, as if he'd struck an oak tree. Pain crippled his hand. Yoshisato's cheek turned crimson. Tears of humiliation welled in his eyes, but he stood his ground.

"If you want a new whore, get one of my half brothers," he said.

If he stayed a moment longer, Yanagisawa would kill his son. He turned and strode out the door.

"Don't come back!" Yoshisato shouted, his voice ragged. "I never want to see you again!"

19

"I STARTED OUT searching the camps," Marume said. "I couldn't find anybody who knew Korin. Then I had a thought: Mizutani called him a shady character, and shady characters tend to get in trouble with the law, so maybe I'd better check the jail. That's what I did. And that's where he is."

"Excellent work," Sano said.

Marume only nodded; he didn't take his usual, joking pride in his cleverness.

Night was a mixed blessing, Sano thought as they and his other troops rode through frigid darkness and windblown snow crystals. It hid the earthquake's devastation, but thousands of people were suffering in cold tents and damaged buildings. The makeshift jail occupied the former site of a marketplace in Nihonbashi. Lanterns and jagged roof tiles topped a wall, built from the vendors' broken stalls and debris from fallen buildings, which encircled tents packed closely together. Because crime had proliferated since the earthquake, this prison contained many more criminals than had been transferred from Edo Jail. Guards patrolled outside.

"Did you tell Korin that I was coming and why?" Sano asked.

"No," Marume said.

"Good."

Conditions in the jail were even more squalid than in the regular camps. Men lay crammed four or five to each small tent. Sewage from cesspools mixed with the muddy snow on the ground. Sanitation required too much effort to waste on criminals. Marume stopped at a tent. Four dirty, sullen faces peered out at him and Sano.

"You three, go," Marume said, pointing. "Korin, you stay."

The apprentice's tent mates reluctantly crawled out of the tent. Marume and Sano squeezed into the vacated space that smelled of urine, body odor, and fetid breath. Marume said to Korin, "This is Chamberlain Sano. Sit up."

Korin obeyed. Light from the lanterns on the walls outside reached his face. It was bruised and swollen, his lips split, both eyes blackened.

"What happened to you?" Sano asked.

"A little misunderstanding." Korin smiled, then winced. Sano could see that he was young, perhaps twenty-five, with wavy black hair tied back in a short tail. He would be handsome when not beaten to a pulp.

"He was cheating at cards in the camps," Marume said. "The people didn't take kindly to it. They beat him up before they handed him over to the police."

"You deserved it," Sano said. "That's pretty low, cheating earthquake victims." He'd heard of many similar instances of unscrupulous folks trying to profit from the earthquake. Some offered to rebuild homes for a cheap price, then absconded with the money.

"But I'm a victim, too, aren't I? I did what I had to do to survive." Korin had a certain charm despite his lack of morals. "The earthquake took my work away." Sano could imagine him luring men to the brothels for which he'd worked as a tout. It was harder to imagine him engaged in the contemplative art of incense. "I gave back the money and said I was sorry."

"That's not good enough." Rage suddenly animated Marume. "I should cut your hands off so you can never play cards again."

"Hey!" Korin recoiled in fright.

Sano shared Marume's sentiment, but he needed the apprentice in good enough shape to help with his investigation. He was surprised at Marume, who'd often threatened suspects before but never really meant it. Marume clearly meant it now. Grief had robbed him of his good nature.

"Don't worry; he won't hurt you." Sano turned to Marume, who glowered but subsided. "I want to talk to you about the incense teacher you used to work for. Madam Usugumo."

"What about her?" Korin shifted to a more comfortable position. It didn't quite hide the flinch that jerked his body when he'd heard his employer's name.

That slight reaction told Sano that Korin knew something about the murders. "When was the last time you saw Madam Usugumo?"

"The afternoon before the earthquake," Korin replied, too quickly.

"What happened that day?"

"Nothing special. I helped Madam Usugumo in her workshop. She had some new cassia, nutmeg, and ambergris that needed to be ground up and cooked. Then we chose different kinds of incense for a game she was going to play that night, with some pupils." He bobbed his head and smiled, encouraging Sano to believe him, hoping this wealth of detail would head off more questions.

"Were you at the incense game that night?" Sano asked.

"No!" Korin crossed his arms and scratched under them. "Madam Usugumo gave me the night off. So I went out."

"Did you live with her?" Marume interjected.

Korin edged as far away from Marume as the small space allowed. "Yes, I did. It's the custom."

Employers usually housed their apprentices, but Sano detected a note in Korin's voice that said his arrangement with Madam Usugumo hadn't been the usual kind. "Were you lovers?"

Sheepish pride showed on Korin's bruised face. "You could say that was one of the services I did for her." As if he thought that sounded ungallant, he added, "Or one of the benefits of the job."

Marume grimaced in disgust. "When did you get home?"

"I didn't." Korin scratched his head, rumpling his wavy hair. Sano thought it was nervousness rather than fleas that made him itch. "I met some friends, and when we were drinking at a teahouse, the earthquake started. I never made it back."

"You never checked on Madam Usugumo?" Sano asked. "Weren't you concerned about her?"

"Of course I was!"

"The neighborhood headman says you haven't been seen there since before the earthquake," Sano said.

Korin's hands scrabbled over his body. The worry bugs were biting harder. "I meant to go. But one thing happened after another, and I ended up in here."

Sano noticed that he sounded most reasonable when justifying a bad deed. "You know why I'm asking you these questions, don't you?"

"No." Korin smiled as if he hoped his charm could ward off danger.

"It's because Madam Usugumo died during that incense game," Sano said. "And you're under suspicion for murder."

Korin abruptly stopped scratching. His hands plopped onto his knees. "All right, I knew." He had the look of a man who'd been trying to outrun an avalanche and failed—woeful yet relieved to give up running. "But I didn't kill her."

"If you think we're stupid enough to believe that, then you're the one who's stupid," Marume jeered. "What happened? Was she too strict? Did she whip you for ruining a batch of incense? Or wasn't she satisfied with your lovemaking? Did you get angry and poison her?"

"No! I didn't poison her!" Panic filled Korin's blackened eyes.

"You knew she was poisoned, didn't you?" Sano accused. "You just said you chose the incense for the game. You put the poison in it. And you left her and her pupils to burn it and die."

"That's not what happened!"

Sano realized that his instincts were telling him to believe Korin even though he'd had at least the means to commit the murder. "Then tell me what did happen."

Korin swiveled his head from side to side, vacillating between the benefits of telling the truth and the danger of lying. Marume made a sudden move, as if to grab him. Korin flinched, then said, "I did go home, late that night. There was a lantern still lit in the parlor. And the house was full of incense smoke. That was strange—the game should have been over hours ago. So I went into the parlor, and I saw—"

A shudder passed through him. "Madam Usugumo was lying on the floor with two ladies. They'd thrown up and soiled themselves. The incense bowl had fallen out of her hand. The ash was still smoking. I called to her. She didn't answer. At first I thought they'd all fainted. But their eyes were open. I shook Madam Usugumo and asked what had happened. But she didn't move. She was dead. So were the two ladies." His eyes brimmed with recollected horror. He swallowed, his throat convulsing.

"What did you do then?" Sano prompted.

Korin breathed hard. "I packed up my things and some incense samples, and I ran."

"Why didn't you report their deaths to the headman?" Sano asked. "Or fetch the police?"

"I was scared, all right? I thought I would be blamed." Korin explained, "I've been in trouble with the law. There are a few policemen who'd love to arrest me for murder and see my head stuck on a post by the Nihonbashi Bridge."

That was a credible reason. Sano realized something else: If Korin really had found the women dead, and if he'd reported it immediately, before the earthquake, the murders would have been the police's problem. Sano resisted the temptation to pin them on Korin. He must discover the truth about the murders, no matter how inconvenient the search or dangerous the consequences. But Korin didn't need to know that.

"You're coming with us." Sano started to rise. "Let's go."

"Where?" Korin goggled at Sano. "Why?"

"To get an executioner to put you to death. Because I've had enough of your lies."

"But I'm not lying!" Korin cried as Marume grabbed his arm. "I told you the truth, I swear!"

"I don't believe you." Sano sensed that Korin had told the truth but not all of it.

"What about my trial?" Korin tried to jerk free of Marume. "Don't I get one? Shouldn't a magistrate decide whether I'm guilty?"

"Things are different since the earthquake," Marume said. "The Courts of Justice are closed. There'll be enough delayed trials to fill them for a year after they reopen. So we'll cross your name off the list tonight. And when you're dead, that'll be one fewer scumbag taking up space in jail."

"But I'm innocent!" Korin sobbed as he struggled. "I would never have hurt Usugumo or her pupils. I depended on them for my livelihood. You've got the wrong man!"

Marume's deliberate cruelty disturbed Sano, but he let Marume drag Korin from the tent and followed them. Korin kicked and screamed while other prisoners peeked out of their tents. Sano began to wonder if Korin would force him to give up his bluff.

"I can tell you who killed Madam Usugumo, if you'll just stop!" Korin shouted.

"He's trying to trick us," Marume said to Sano. "Don't listen."

Sano raised his hand.

Marume reluctantly stopped. He lifted Korin and plunked him on his feet. "Talk."

Korin shivered from cold and terror. His wounded mouth puffed out white vapors of breath. "It was one of Madam Usugumo's other pupils. Minister Ogyu or Priest Ryuko."

A chord of dismay rang in Sano. "How do you know?"

"It had to be." Korin regained his sly smile, although his eyes glinted with desperation. "She knew secrets that they didn't want anybody to know. They were paying her not to tell."

"How did she know these secrets?" Sano said, skeptical. Blackmail seemed the kind of story that a character like Korin would dream up.

"Ogyu and Ryuko told her during their lessons," Korin said.

"You're not making sense," Marume said. "If they didn't want anybody to know, then why would they have told her?"

"They didn't mean to," Korin said hastily. "She had a special incense blend she used during private games with them. When they breathed the smoke, it made them talk."

"That's pretty far-fetched." But Sano's friend Dr. Ito had told him about potions that crumbled inhibitions and loosened tongues. "Were you at these games?"

"Not in the same room. She sent me out during them," Korin said. "But I was curious, so I spied through the window. They weren't like regular incense games. Nobody was guessing the types of incense or writing them down. She asked questions, and Ryuko and Ogyu answered."

It sounded as if Madam Usugumo had perverted the art of incense for her own nefarious purposes. Again, Sano sensed that Korin was telling the truth, but he resisted belief. "Supposing it's true, what did they confess?"

"I don't know. I couldn't hear what they were saying." Seeing Sano frown, Korin said, "But I saw the money they paid her after those rituals.

It was a lot more than she usually charged. And you know what else?" His split lips grinned triumphantly. "They both stopped taking lessons, but they kept on paying. Doesn't that sound like blackmail?"

THE BELL AT Zōjō Temple tolled the hour of the boar. Hirata heard it while eating a late dinner at home, which was a storehouse once used for keeping money and other valuables. Roughly half of the mansion, barracks, and outbuildings of his estate inside Edo Castle had burned to the ground during the earthquake. The portions still standing were too damaged for habitation. While his detectives and servants camped in tents on the grounds, Hirata, Midori, and their three children had moved into the storehouse. Its sturdy structure had withstood the earthquake; its tile roof and plaster-coated walls had protected it from the fire. Hirata had cut windows to let in sunshine and fresh air, but the interior was damp, smoky from the charcoal brazier, and crowded with his family and their possessions. The bell's tolling was loud, clear, and ominous in the absence of buildings to absorb or deflect the sound. Hirata set his soup bowl on the table at which he and Midori sat with quilts draped over them to keep them warm.

"I have to go."

"Now?" Midori whispered, so as not to wake their children—nine-year-old Taeko, six-year-old Tatsuo, and the baby Tadanobu—who were asleep in beds laid on stacked trunks. "Why must you go out this late?"

Hirata donned his coat and fastened his swords at his waist. Outside, Tahara's cheerful voice called, "Hirata-*san*, are you ready?"

Midori spoke with annoyance. "Oh. Of course. It's your friends again."

A blast of icy wind ushered Tahara, Kitano, and Deguchi into the storehouse. Tahara smiled and bowed to Midori. "Good evening. How lovely to see you."

Her plump, pretty face froze into a polite mask. Hirata knew she didn't like Tahara's mocking gallantry. Kitano's scars and Deguchi's eerie silence made her nervous. Nor did she like the fact that Hirata allowed them free access to her home. She didn't know it was because if he tried to keep them out, they might force their way in and hurt someone. He'd never told her about their mystical powers or the society. He feared that if he broke his vow of secrecy, the men would kill her and the children.

"Let's go," Hirata said, stepping into his shoes by the door.

"In a hurry, are you?" Kitano said. "Your attitude has changed."

"Where are you going?" Midori's voice was sharp. She resented Hirata spending so much time with these men and refusing to tell her what they did together. He knew she feared he was going to leave her, as he'd done for some five years while studying the mystic martial arts. "When will you be back?"

"Before you know it," Tahara said in a teasing voice.

Hirata moved through the door, forcing Tahara, Deguchi, and Kitano to step outside. Tahara waved to Midori and called, "Tell your husband good-bye!"

20

HIRATA AND HIS three companions walked up a steep, snow-covered trail into the hills. Far below them, Edo Castle's misshapen bulk hunched, the lights from the guards' lanterns moving along its corridors like fireflies. The city was a spread of black wasteland. Above, forests mounted to the heavens.

"This had better be worth it," Hirata grumbled.

Tahara's smile flashed white in the darkness. "Have a little faith, why don't you?"

They stopped in a clearing in the forest, where the ground leveled into a plateau surrounded by tall, ancient evergreen cedars whose tops fringed a circle of sky with the full moon at the center. The moon's light bleached the snow a ghostly silver. A wide, flat rock stood in the middle of the clearing. Deguchi brushed snow off the rock. Kitano emptied his knapsack onto it. He set out a ceramic flask and a metal incense burner. Deguchi lit the burner and the oil lamps around the perimeter of the clearing. The four men gathered around the rock.

Smoke billowed from the burner, purplish flecked with golden sparks. Tahara had told Hirata that the substance they burned at rituals was a mixture of herbs from China, a recipe from the magic spell book. As Hirata and the others leaned over the burner and let the smoke fill their lungs, the air didn't seem as cold, and he felt the fatigue of a long day lift like a rising fog. The foliage of the trees glowed green and the snow scintillated with turquoise and pink lights despite the darkness.

Tahara, Deguchi, and Kitano began to chant in a language, full of hisses and singsong intonations, that Hirata couldn't understand. They'd told him it was ancient Chinese. He recited the syllables he'd memorized with no idea of their meaning. Tahara took a swig from the flask, then passed it around. When his turn came, Hirata drank. The potion tasted like exotic flowers mixed with sewage, fruit, and spices, and distilled into powerful liquor. It burned down his throat and hit his stomach as if he'd swallowed a red-hot cannonball. He gagged and coughed.

Unaffected, Tahara, Deguchi, and Kitano chanted louder, faster. Heat spread through Hirata. His muscles, nerves, and bones were on fire. He held up his hands, expecting to see them blacken and wither. His fingers distorted into white, branching, rootlike shapes. Gasping, he glanced around the circle. Tahara's, Deguchi's, and Kitano's images swam, fragmented, and recoalesced.

"What's happening to me?" he cried.

"The spell is working." The chanting continued. "You're going into a trance."

The words seemed to come from all of the men. The echo ricocheted off the trees. Strange colors swirled, orange and mauve and iridescent blue. Out of the corner of his eye Hirata saw movement in the forest.

"Who's there?" he demanded.

As his eyes chased the movement, a figure reappeared and disappeared, a shadow with a horned helmet, a flared armor tunic, and jutting swords. It was larger than any man, a giant. Power radiated from it in waves that boomed and pulsed.

"It's the spirit. He's come for you."

Terror filled Hirata. He didn't care that the spirit could give him the powers he craved. He only wanted to run away. But his legs were numb as stone; they wouldn't move. He clawed the air with his hands. They turned numb and useless, too. He spun as he toppled. He sprawled on his back across the altar stone.

The trees above him leaned inward, their trunks like the sides of a funnel, the sky at the far, narrow end. Tahara, Deguchi, and Kitano extended their arms around the altar, hands touching. They stared down at Hirata, their lips moving as they chanted. Their voices sent pressure waves crashing against his ears. Veins of fiery light crossed, linked, and dissolved around him. His heart thumped so hard that he thought it would explode.

"Stop or I'll die!" he screamed.

The men's faces, bent over him, shone with exultation. The moon expanded and contracted in rhythm with their chanting. With each expansion it grew larger, exerting a force that sucked Hirata toward the sky. He felt himself rising through the funnel of trees. As he reached the treetops, his point of view suddenly inverted. He was looking down at the clearing. He saw himself lying on the altar, enmeshed in fire-veins, his face a mask of panic, surrounded by Tahara, Deguchi, and Kitano. He tried to call to them, but they didn't look up. They didn't know that his spirit had left his body.

The universe upended in another disorienting shift. The moon filled Hirata's vision. Black clouds streamed across it like ink on water. They gathered into the shape of a samurai in full armor on horseback. It was the warrior from the forest. His image enlarged as Hirata rose into the sky and the moon expanded. Now the warrior charged his mount toward Hirata. His form took on definition. Hirata could see the plates of his helmet and armor tunic, his eyes glowing above the iron face shield. He drew his sword, which shone as if forged from lightning.

Hirata screamed again. He heard the faint, feeble sound from his earthbound body. The men's chanting followed him as he rose faster and faster. Another deep, garbled voice joined theirs, speaking unintelligible words. It was the warrior's. The noises mixed into a cacophony that grew louder as he accelerated. The earth fell away beneath him. He saw Edo, the castle, and the hills shrink in a landscape of mountains and rivers and lights from distant cities, then the islands of Japan floating in the sea, dwarfed by foreign continents. The men's chanting pursued him as he whirled through the vacuum of space.

Celestial bodies appeared—a gigantic ball of red, swirling gas; an orange-and-black-striped orb encircled by a sparkling ring. Stars magnified into white suns with molten, turbulent centers. Hirata's acceleration suddenly reversed. Now he was falling. Planets and stars streaked by him in columns of light. The chanting rose to an inaudible pitch. Below, the earth soared up to meet him. Mountains raised jagged peaks. Wind shrieked in his ears. Friction burned him as the round gap in the trees around the clearing in the forest swallowed him. He landed with a crash that shattered perception, extinguished thought in silent, empty blackness.

EXCRUCIATING PAIN BURNED down Hirata's left arm. A tiger with teeth made of fire was gnawing on it. He moaned and writhed. Hands restrained him. Voices called his name. He awakened to find himself lying on the cold, hard altar stone. The circle of sky above the treetops was pale blue with morning. Tahara, Deguchi, and Kitano pinned him down, their anxious faces bent over him. Hirata raised his head. He was back in his body, alive. When he tried to wiggle his feet and fingers, they obeyed. He gasped with relief.

"What happened?" he said, wondering if his experience had been a hallucination.

"Nothing." Tahara sounded disappointed. "You just screamed all night."

"Didn't you see the warrior?" Hirata demanded as he sat up. His arm still hurt terribly.

"No. You mean you did? This is the first time we've managed to evoke him in months, and he appeared only to you." Vexation tinged Kitano's voice.

"What happened? Did he tell you anything?" Tahara asked eagerly.

Hirata described how he'd been transported out of his body, into the cosmos. "Something's wrong with my arm." The rest of his body was stiff with cold, but the pain burned and throbbed from the tiger's fiery fangs. He pushed up his sleeve.

The skin on his arm glowed as if from flames underneath. The other men exclaimed. Tiny bright lines appeared within the glow. The pain went from excruciating to unbearable. Hirata rolled off the altar stone onto the ground. He frantically scraped snow against his arm. The snow melted and steamed. As the cold penetrated his skin, the glow faded; the pain eased.

Deguchi crouched, pointing at Hirata's arm. Tahara said, "Look!"

A line of precisely written characters adorned his skin from bicep to wrist. Hirata stared in amazement. They were bloodred, but when he touched them, they were smooth, dry, and painless, like a tattoo. "Did you do this to me while I was in the trance?" he demanded.

"No. It's a message from the spirit," Kitano said.

Hirata saw that Kitano was speaking the truth. All three men beheld the message with genuine awe. Repulsed and horrified, Hirata tried to rub the characters off. Tahara restrained him and read the message: "'Bring Lord Tokugawa Ienobu to the shogun's garden at the hour of the cock, the day after tomorrow.'"

In the moment of stunned silence that ensued, a breeze disturbed the forest.

"This is the first time the spirit has sent a written message," Tahara said.

"How did he communicate with you other times?" Hirata was so distraught that he could barely get the words out.

"He spoke to us," Kitano said.

Hirata remembered the voice he'd heard. The characters wavered before his eyes. He felt nauseated.

"Ienobu is the first person he's mentioned by name," Kitano said, "except for—"

Tahara silenced him with a glance.

"Except for me? The spirit mentioned me?" Nobody answered Hirata, but he knew he was right. Fresh shock hit him. "What did it say? When was this?"

"Three years ago," Tahara admitted. "He asked us who our fellow disciples were. He told us to invite you to join our society."

Now Hirata knew why they'd invited him even though they were reluctant to share their secrets. The message branded on his arm gave him a clue to what the spirit wanted with him. "He needs someone who moves in the inner circle of power. The three of you don't. You can't do things for him there. But I can."

"More or less." Tahara's casual tone sounded forced. Hirata could tell that he and the others resented the fact that although they'd learned how to work the magic spells, Hirata was the one for whom the spirit had special plans.

"Well, I won't meddle with Lord Ienobu," Hirata said. "We can't know what will happen as a result. I won't be responsible for bringing harm to the shogun's nephew."

He rolled down his sleeve, covering the message, and started to walk away. Deguchi stepped in front of him. The men's aura began to pulse threateningly.

"You have to do it," Tahara said. "The spirit commands us."

"Why can't he do things for himself?"

"He's disembodied energy," Kitano said. "He knows everything because he can go everywhere and spy on everyone, but he has no physical form, and he can't act on humans or communicate with them except during rituals."

"Who is he, anyway?"

Tahara parted with more information as stingily as if he were squeezing blood from a vein. "He's the ghost of a soldier who died on the battlefield at Sekigahara."

That was the battle at which Tokugawa Ieyasu had defeated his rival warlords; later, he'd become the first Tokugawa shogun. Hirata remembered that the spirit's armor had looked bulky and old-fashioned. "How does that qualify him to decide what destiny is and how it should be fulfilled?"

"He's not the one who decides," Kitano said. "He's only a conduit between us and the gods of the cosmos."

"And they said I should trot Ienobu into the shogun's garden as if he were a puppet? Oh, well, then. Of course everybody has to do what the 'gods of the cosmos' say." Hirata pushed past Deguchi.

The men blocked his exit from the clearing. "You took an oath when you joined our society," Tahara reminded Hirata. "You swore to abide by all its decisions."

"I have a say in our decision about whether to follow the ghost's orders," Hirata retorted, "and I've decided I won't."

Tahara smiled with all his charm. "All you have to do is arrange for Ienobu to walk through the garden. What could it hurt?"

"Are you serious?" Hirata stared. "Have you forgotten about Yoritomo? No, I won't do it. I'm quitting the society."

"Sorry, but we can't allow that." Tahara's eyes were steely above his smile. Deguchi's blazed with anger.

"How are you going to stop me? Kill me?" Hirata laughed. "Who'll be the ghost's errand boy then?"

"No, we'll kill Chamberlain Sano," Kitano said.

Horror sent a chill through Hirata's blood. Rage enflamed him. "I won't let you near Sano!"

"The only way you can protect Sano is by doing the spirit's bidding. But how can we convince you?" Tahara felt under his coat and pulled out a small object, which he held up for Hirata to examine.

It was a flat, rectangular wooden tag with a white string looped through a hole at one end, the kind sold at Buddhist temples and Shinto shrines. Worshippers wrote prayers on them and tied them on fences or posts outside the buildings. This tag had a sword artistically drawn on it in red ink.

"Memorize this," Tahara said, and tucked the tag back under his coat. He smiled as he and his friends stepped aside and let Hirata go.

21

THE RISING SUN lightened the sky over Edo Castle from black to muddy gray. Outside the women's quarters, vapor filled the air, as if the earth had exhaled a clammy, disease-laden breath. Inside, Priest Ryuko stood at the threshold of the shogun's mother's chamber.

"You sent for me, my lady?"

"Yes! You certainly took your time getting here." Lady Keisho-in made shooing gestures at the attendants who knelt around the pillow-covered bed on which she lounged. "Go, go! My dearest priest and I have private business to discuss!"

The attendants hastily left. Priest Ryuko knelt by Lady Keisho-in and took her hand. She wore a rich red brocade robe that snarled with gilded dragons, and so many ornaments spangled her puff of dyed-black hair that it looked like a pincushion. Thick white makeup, and scarlet rouge on her cheeks and lips, hid some of the ravages of age. But Priest Ryuko noticed the food stains on the robe, the veined, loose skin on the hand he held, and her stale, old-womanish smell. He felt repugnance mixed with affection.

"Is something wrong?" Through the thin walls he could hear the chatter quiet down as news of his presence spread and the women pricked up their ears to listen.

"'Wrong?'" Lady Keisho-in snorted, in a manner more suited to the commoner she was than to the highest-ranking woman in Japan. "I would call it a disaster!"

Although he knew Lady Keisho-in had a tendency to exaggerate, her anxiety disturbed Priest Ryuko. Her mood and her well-being had such a great impact on his. Their fates had been intertwined for more than twenty years, since a series of incidents in the women's quarters had first brought him here. Minor vandalism that included broken makeup jars and torn clothes, and anonymous letters that contained insults, threats, and malicious rumors, had thrown the ladies and servants into an uproar. The shogun blamed the trouble on fox spirits masquerading as humans. He asked the abbot at Zōjō Temple to send an exorcist. The abbot sent Ryuko, a handsome, personable priest who'd enjoyed great success with women before he'd taken his vow of celibacy.

Lady Keisho-in's face had lit up with smiles the moment she saw him. She and her attendants followed him as he marched through the women's quarter, chanted prayers, and burned incense sticks. They giggled excitedly. He had been afraid the exorcism would fail and he would be punished. But when he walked down the line of women, shouting at the fox spirits to come out, and waving incense smoke over them, a young lady-in-waiting broke down in tears. She confessed that she was responsible for the incidents.

The other women fell on her. They hit, scratched, and kicked her until the palace guards came and took her away, to have her put to death. The other women cheered. Priest Ryuko backed away, shocked by the violence and his success.

"My hero!" Lady Keisho-in dimpled at him. "Don't be in such a hurry to leave."

Now she clutched his hand so hard that he winced. "I'm so afraid!" Her rheumy eyes were round, moist.

"Of what?" Priest Ryuko saw that her fear was real, not a ploy to get attention and enliven a dull day. Fearful himself, he urged, "Tell me."

"It's that damned astronomer. Have you heard about his pronouncement?"

Priest Ryuko nodded; his spirits sank. He hadn't known that Lady Keisho-in had heard, and he'd been hoping she never would. She got upset so easily, and although she was healthy for her age, a bad upset might kill her. And that would be the end of Priest Ryuko, too.

"Yes, I've heard," he said.

"Why didn't you tell me?" she demanded.

She was so much like the shogun, Priest Ryuko thought. She'd handed down to him her moods, capriciousness, and quickness to take offense. "Because I didn't think it was worth mentioning." He also didn't like to be the bearer of bad news. "Nothing will come of it."

"That's all you know! What rock have you been sleeping under? Haven't you heard the latest?"

"No." Priest Ryuko had been so preoccupied with Sano and the murders that he hadn't consulted his usual sources of gossip. "What's happened?"

"The Council of Elders had a secret meeting about the astronomer's pronouncement last night. They think the astronomer is right."

"How do you know this?" Priest Ryuko asked. Rumors had run rampant since the earthquake, few of them true.

"I had it straight from a friend who's a secretary for the Council." Lady Keisho-in had many friends who cultivated her favor because of her influence with the shogun. "He said the elders talked about which high-ranking person the gods are displeased with. Guess who most of them think it is?" Her watery eyes bulged with outrage; she jabbed her finger against her bosom. "Me!"

At first Ryuko was surprised that the elders would give the astronomer's pronouncement such a dangerous interpretation. Then he realized that they craved an explanation for the earthquake; they didn't want to believe it was an accident of nature. Blaming someone would make them feel in control, as if by punishing the culprit they could prevent more earthquakes. They probably also wanted to avoid being blamed and punished themselves. Ryuko recalled things he'd seen happen to people accused of unbalancing nature's forces. Some had been banished, others injured or killed during exorcisms. But none had been linked with a catastrophe as big as the earthquake. None had had as far to fall as Lady Keisho-in.

"What are they going to do?" he said.

"They talked about making my son send me away, in order to appease the gods." Lady Keisho-in cried wildly, "Can you believe it?"

Speechless, Priest Ryuko shook his head. The world had gone insane since the earthquake. What would happen next? Animals would talk and men fly?

"They'll stick me in some convent at the end of the earth, and I'll lose my home and my place in court, and never see my son again!" Lady Keisho-in wailed.

The elders must be so desperate to restore normalcy, order, and peace—and protect their own skins—that they would jump on the astronomer's pronouncement, dare to accuse the shogun's mother, and risk death. And perhaps they wanted to kill two birds with one stone—mend the breach with the gods and get rid of Lady Keisho-in, who had more influence over affairs of state than they liked. Priest Ryuko tasted horror and bile as he saw his own lot take a turn for the worse.

He'd feared that Sano's investigation into the murders would expose the secret he'd hidden from Lady Keisho-in. He'd feared losing her patronage and his influence with the shogun. But now she herself was in danger of taking a fall.

"Have you spoken to your son about this?" Ryuko asked. "Can't you persuade him to stand by you?"

"I've tried to talk to him, but he's always too busy or too ill to see me." Lady Keisho-in uttered a sound of despair. "His own mother!"

Priest Ryuko suspected that the shogun didn't know his mother was trying to see him. Someone must be keeping them apart, and Ryuko had a good idea who it was: Lord Ienobu, who wanted to secure his position as the shogun's heir and didn't trust Lady Keisho-in not to interfere.

"The earthquake isn't my fault. I'm innocent. This is wrong, wrong, wrong! What should I do?" Lady Keisho-in burst into tears; she tugged Priest Ryuko's hand. "Tell me!"

"First you must calm down," he said, stalling because he didn't know what to do. "Let me give you a massage."

She nodded, opened her robes, and flopped on her back. She loved massages. With sensuous, soothing motions, Priest Ryuko stroked the sagging flesh on her stomach. Soon she began to sigh with pleasure. As he gently kneaded the withered sacs of her breasts and rubbed their brown, droopy nipples, her sighs turned to purrs. She undulated, arching her back. He slipped his fingers between her legs. She gasped, thrust her hips, and gave excited little cries until she reached her pleasure. She moaned and relaxed.

"I can count on you to take care of me," she murmured.

As she drifted off to sleep, Priest Ryuko covered her with a quilt. He sat beside her, musing on their relationship. Everyone thought it was a matter of a greedy climber servicing a foolish old woman sexually as well as spiritually in exchange for her patronage. But Ryuko was genuinely fond of Lady Keisho-in, never mind that she was flighty and stupid and too old to be attractive to him. They had a strong, human bond. She was the grocer's daughter who'd given birth to a shogun; he was a village peasant boy who'd made his fortune as a Buddhist cleric. They would always be two commoners against the aristocrats.

"We'll always stand by each other," Priest Ryuko said.

"Yes," Lady Keisho-in whispered in her sleep.

He wished he could believe her, but he knew she was as fickle as her son. Resisting the panic that clawed at his mind, Ryuko began to plot. He would have to bury his secrets deeper. That was his top priority. He reassured himself that Sano wouldn't bring him down. He had at least one good weapon in his arsenal.

"MAMA, CAN I go with you?" Akiko asked.

"No, I'm sorry." Reiko inserted the last comb into her hair and put on her coat. "It's too dangerous in the city."

Akiko tugged at Reiko's skirts. "But I'm tired of staying home. I want to go out."

"This is where you're safe. When I get back, we'll play dolls."

"No! Please?"

In the crowded chamber, Sano smiled as he fastened his swords at his waist. Akiko was so much like her mother. Reiko would have her hands full, trying to protect, discipline, and teach the adventurous Akiko. And so would he, with two such strong-willed, contrary womenfolk.

Akiko pleaded; Reiko refused to relent; their tempers flared. Sano said, "Akiko, you can come with me." He told Reiko, "I'm going to Hirata-san's house on my way to see Priest Ryuko and Minister Ogyu." It was time to confront Hirata about his absences, his secrecy. "She can play with the children."

"Good!" All smiles and sweetness, Akiko hugged Sano.

"Come put on your coat." Stuffing her daughter into the little pink garment, Reiko gave Sano a glance that thanked him for resolving the argument.

Sano took Akiko's hand. She skipped beside him out of the estate. He realized he'd never gone anywhere alone with her; Reiko and the servants usually accompanied them. The walls of the passage that led to the official quarter were broken, full of gaps. Akiko broke away from Sano and started to climb a rock pile. Before Sano could catch her, she slid down it and fell on her knee.

"Akiko! Are you all right?" Sano examined Akiko's knee. It was scraped raw, but she didn't cry. She was brave like her mother.

Two patrol guards sauntered by. They hid smiles as they bowed to Sano, the great chamberlain playing nursemaid. Sano got a firmer grip on Akiko's hand. They arrived at Hirata's home without further incident.

Midori hurried out of the storehouse, the baby in her arms, her other children following. The expectancy on her face turned to disappointment as she recognized Sano and Akiko.

"I brought you a visitor," Sano said.

Akiko ran to Taeko and Tatsuo. Midori said, "I thought you were my husband coming home." She looked worried. "Have you seen him?"

"No," Sano said. "I was hoping to find him here."

Midori brushed her disheveled hair off her face. "He didn't come home last night."

Sano was disturbed. His irritation at Hirata for his absence during the investigation gave way to fear that something bad had happened to him. Sano didn't trust those friends with whom Hirata had become so close. But he didn't want to voice these thoughts and upset Midori.

"He'll probably be home soon," Sano said. "I'll stop by again later."

"Yes, you're right," Midori said, reassured.

"Can I leave Akiko with you?"

"Of course." Midori turned, saw the three children climbing a rock pile, and shouted, "Get down from there!"

Sano left in search of Priest Ryuko.

22

A MESSENGER BOY from Edo Castle called into the courtyard of the Yushima Seidō: "Honorable Minister Ogyu! His Excellency
the shogun wants you. You're to come at once!"

The summons awakened Minister Ogyu, who lay in bed with his wife
and children in their tent. Groggy consciousness gave way to an agonizing headache that felt as if a spike had pierced his right eye, stabbed
through his brain, and pinned him to the bed. His body's response to
mental strain, the headache had come on yesterday after Chamberlain
Sano's visit. Ogyu wished he could go back to sleep, but he couldn't
ignore the shogun's order. He rolled over and stifled a groan.

His wife roused immediately. She searched his face, read the pain
that he hid from everyone except her. "Is the headache bad today?"

"Not very," Ogyu lied, not wanting to worry her.

The mental strain had been his constant companion for as long as
he could remember. Even when he was a child, fear and anxiety would
pump through him and turn into pain in his head. "Make it go away!"
he'd sobbed to his mother.

She had shaken him and scolded, "Never cry! Don't be a sissy!"

"Obey your mother," his father had said. "It's for the good of us all."

Even though they withheld comfort, Ogyu had never doubted that
they loved and cherished him. He'd known their story ever since he'd
been old enough to understand. His father had been a court physician,
his mother from a minor noble family. They were desperate for a son to

carry on the family name, until at last Ogyu was born, the precious only child. They expressed their love through ever-vigilant discipline.

His wife clambered out of bed, wrapped herself in her heavy coat, and said, "I'll brew you some opium tea."

She was more sympathetic than his parents had ever been. Ogyu loved her dearly for it. Most other men would think her plain and worthless, but he wasn't like most other men. He appreciated her as the luckiest thing that ever happened to him.

He said, "I'll have just a little." Opium was the only thing that took the pain away, but he rationed his doses; he didn't want to become a slave to it or impair his wits. "Because of Chamberlain Sano and his investigation. I need a clear mind."

They hadn't spoken about Madam Usugumo or the murders. They had a tacit agreement that they wouldn't, except indirectly.

"But you dealt with Chamberlain Sano," his wife said. "He went away."

"He's not finished with me," Ogyu said. "We have to be on our guard."

"We always are." She smiled, proud of their unity against a world they'd both found cruel.

But Ogyu could see how tired she was, how dark the shadows under her eyes. Life after the earthquake was wearing her down, and she'd shared the burden of his problems for the nine years they'd been married. He himself badly needed a rest from the pressure to dissimulate, achieve, and impress. But it never let up.

Dragging himself upright, he remembered mealtimes at his parents' house during his childhood. "Eat!" his mother commanded, holding a bowl under his chin and spooning rich meat stew into his mouth. "Get bigger!" He ate until he was bloated. "Take your medicine!" He swallowed the bitter herb potion. Before he went out in public, his father coached him. "Walk like this, with bigger steps. Don't mince! Shoulders back. Head high. If someone speaks to you, speak up; don't whisper. Talk deeper in your throat."

His parents were gone now, but his wife had taken over for them. She put more coals on the brazier and heated gruel, thick with fish and vegetables and lard. As she mixed his medicine, he said, "I don't think I can eat."

"You must."

She urged him with kindness, but it was still a regimen he wished he could escape. Knowing he never could, he dutifully ate and drank. Afterward, she shaved him, oiled his hair, tied his topknot, and neatly trimmed the end. Unlike other men of his status, he didn't have a valet. She helped him dress in his loincloth, white silk under-kimono, his formal black satin robe ornamented with gold family crests, his black trousers, and black padded coat. On his feet she put socks she'd laundered herself, and high-soled sandals. She checked every detail of his appearance so thoroughly that he didn't need a mirror.

"There," she said with a satisfied smile. "You're ready for the shogun."

Ogyu took small comfort in knowing that he looked the perfect scholar. His headache stabbed, each thrust deeper. Involuntary tears stung his right eye. The pain was as bad as during the most stressful occasions of his life.

One of those was the day he'd had his first lesson with his tutor, at age six. Up until then, the only people he knew were his parents and their servants. They'd kept him at home, not allowing him to mix with other children; they had no friends or visitors. But they wanted him to have a good education, necessary for their family's advancement. At great expense they'd hired the tutor—a strict, humorless scholar from the shogun's court. The tutor was the first stranger that Ogyu had had to impress. For years he toiled to learn math, literature, history, and Confucian philosophy while practicing everything his parents had taught him. He excelled at his studies, but that only created a new challenge.

When Ogyu was twenty, his tutor took him to Zōjō Temple. It was his first venture into public without his parents. The magnificent buildings, the crowds, and the noise terrified him. In front of the main hall, Confucian scholars gathered to show off their talents. They took turns lecturing to each other and whoever happened by. As Ogyu waited for his turn, his head ached so badly that he could hardly hold it upright. His vision speckled the scene around him with black spots one moment, dazzling lights the next. When he mounted the stairs, he was almost blind with pain, almost too weak to stand. But his days of writing, rewriting, and rehearsing his lecture paid off. He delivered it perfectly and received enthusiastic cheers.

Soon afterward, he was invited to visit the shogun at Edo Castle. Determined to make the most of this opportunity, his parents drilled him on his speech, manners, and comportment. They made him study for extra hours, preparing to discuss Confucianism with the shogun. Such excruciating strain and headache did the pressure bring upon Ogyu! But his suffering was worthwhile. He became the shogun's favorite scholar. Important people began courting his favor. He managed to overcome his nervousness enough to enjoy his new position.

Then his parents decided he must marry. A man in his position needed a wife, an heir. High-ranking families offered their daughters to Ogyu. The very thought of marriage made him sick with dread. His mother and his nurse were the only women he knew. Unlike other young men, he'd never patronized brothels. The idea of sexual relations was terrifying. So was the idea of meeting prospective brides and their families. Ogyu feared being accepted as much as he feared rejection. But his parents told him to trust them; they would find him the perfect wife.

Now his wife fretted over him, smoothing his clothes, adjusting the swords at his waist. "You'll come back soon?" Even before the earth- quake and the murder investigation, she'd hated any separation.

When they'd met at their *miai*, he'd immediately seen that his parents had chosen well. His own personal torment made him sensitive to it in other people, as if it were a smell they gave off. She'd reeked of it. Her lavish kimono had only emphasized her plainness. She'd been rejected by other clans and her parents were eager to get rid of her—facts that Ogyu's parents knew. And her shame was obvious. She'd stood with her head ducked, shoulders hunched, hands fidgeting. After the *miai*, Ogyu agreed to marry her. She would be in no position to complain when she found out that he wasn't the powerful, confident man he seemed.

The wedding ceremony had been an ordeal for both of them. Despite the pain in his head, he felt sorry for her because she was as terrified as he. She trembled so hard that when they took the ritual sips of sake that bound them together as husband and wife, she almost spilled the cup. Tears glistened on the white powder on her face. After the banquet, af- ter the guests had left and Ogyu was alone with her for the first time, there came the part of the ordeal he'd dreaded the most. They'd knelt in the bedchamber, the bed between them, not looking at each other. Ogyu could hear her breathing, fast and ragged with panic. He'd forced himself to go to her, take her cold, damp, trembling hand in his, and speak. He was the husband. It was his duty to prepare her for the realities of their marriage.

And he discovered that she had her own troubles, which their marriage forced her to confess. They talked, and by morning they were united in a special way that other couples weren't. To their amazement and gratitude, their marriage brought them the love and happiness they'd never dared to hope for because it seemed so impossible.

Now Ogyu tenderly caressed her cheek. "Of course I'll come back soon. Nothing can separate us."

But fear, like a chisel made of ice, drilled the pain deeper into his head. The murders, and the consequences, had the potential to destroy them both, and their beloved children.

He vowed that he would die before he would let that happen.

23

WALKING UPHILL THROUGH the passages inside Edo Castle, Sano sidestepped fallen stones from the walls. He came upon a tall samurai with a roguish expression and one eyebrow higher than the other, who jostled him. The samurai apologized, bowed, and passed. Sano went on to the guesthouse, where a servant told him that Priest Ryuko was visiting the shogun's mother. On his way there, Sano met Lord Ienobu outside the palace construction site. They exchanged polite, wary greetings.

"How is the earthquake recovery progressing?" Ienobu asked.

"As well as can be expected," Sano said.

"Didn't I see you with Lords Hosokawa, Mori, Date, and Maeda yesterday?"

It cost Sano an effort to keep his expression placid. "Yes. Lord Hosokawa is a good friend of mine. What were you doing out in such bad weather?"

"I needed a little change of scene. And I'm glad I went. Sometimes one sees interesting things when one steps out of one's usual routine." Ienobu's smile was sly, private. "As I'm sure you are aware."

"Indeed," Sano said.

A whole, unspoken world of thoughts accompanied their exchange. Sano could see that Ienobu wondered what that meeting with Lord Hosokawa was about but didn't dare to come out and ask. He could also see that Ienobu knew he would rather not say, and Ienobu didn't want to offend him. Although Ienobu resented the fact that the shogun relied on Sano, Ienobu needed Sano's support for a bid for the succession.

"Well, I won't keep you from your work," Ienobu said.

He shuffled off. Sano watched him for a moment, then went to the women's quarters. He arrived just as Priest Ryuko was coming out. Ryuko's expression was a smooth skin stretched over turbulent emotions. He paused, bowed, said, "Good morning," then started to walk past Sano.

Sano could tell he wanted to pretend that yesterday's clash had never happened. Falling into step beside him, Sano said, "I'll walk with you."

"Your company does me an honor." Priest Ryuko's courtesy sounded forced.

They walked in silence along the path through the snow-frosted grounds. Sano didn't broach the subject of Madam Usugumo's murder. He sensed that all he had to do was wait. Priest Ryuko had the air of a man with a scab he wanted to pick even though he knew better.

"You're not going to ask me about my former incense teacher again, are you?" Priest Ryuko sounded vexed that his impulse had won out over wisdom.

"I wasn't," Sano said, "but since you brought her up, is there anything else you can tell me?"

"No." Ryuko's air vibrated with his need to know if Sano had any new information.

"I did wonder if you've heard the rumor about her that I heard."

"What rumor?" Ryuko said too quickly.

"That she had learned secrets about her pupils, and she was blackmailing them."

"No, I hadn't heard." Priest Ryuko walked faster, as if to escape Sano. "Who told you that?" He blurted the question out as if unable to hold it back, then frowned at his mistake.

Sano fabricated a story. "It was Hirata-*san*. I sent him to check on conditions at the jail. Madam Usugumo's apprentice is a prisoner. Korin has evidently been telling tales on her, in an attempt to get himself pardoned for cheating earthquake victims."

Priest Ryuko looked straight ahead, his profile taut, his face moist. "Detestable."

"Whom do you mean? The apprentice? Or Madam Usugumo?" When Priest Ryuko didn't answer, Sano asked, "Was she blackmailing you?"

Priest Ryuko plodded to a stop and faced Sano. He had the look of a man who'd buried a cesspool that had fermented underground and just exploded onto him—appalled, furious, and eager to push the mess off onto someone else. "You told me you weren't investigating the murder, but I know otherwise. I also know why you're interested in it. After we spoke yesterday, I made a few inquiries myself. I sent my assistant to Madam Usugumo's house. He talked to the neighborhood headman and found out that she wasn't the only person who was poisoned. Two of her pupils died with her. They belonged to the Hosokawa clan, which you knew because you were there when the bodies were found." Priest Ryuko finished with a triumphant glare. "My assistant also discovered that Lord Hosokawa's two daughters are dead. You are investigating the murders on behalf of Lord Hosokawa."

Sano was dismayed that his secret investigation wasn't a secret any longer. "It's none of your business whether I'm conducting an investigation or not."

Priest Ryuko smiled a thin, sardonic smile. "It is if I'm a suspect, which you obviously think I am. But why the secrecy? Why not make the investigation official?"

"All right—let's make it official," Sano said. "I'll tell the shogun that you're under suspicion for killing Lord Hosokawa's daughters. I'll tell Lord Hosokawa, too. He'll be interested to know. He's out for blood revenge."

Priest Ryuko's face was dripping now, and sickly pale. "You wouldn't."

"I will, unless you answer my questions truthfully," Sano said.

"Very well." *And if I ever get an opportunity to retaliate, then woe betide you!* said Ryuko's expression.

Sano regretted sealing their enmity, but it was better than failing at the investigation and bringing down the consequences. "Did Madam Usugumo blackmail you?"

"No," Priest Ryuko said, adamant. "I haven't any secrets for her or anybody else to use against me. My life is as transparent as water."

Sano thought of the Sumida River, polluted with debris from the earthquake. "Then why were you so upset that you quit your incense lessons?"

Priest Ryuko flinched at this mention of a fact he hadn't expected Sano to have learned. He admitted through clenched teeth, "Because she tried to blackmail me. During my last lesson. It didn't work. I washed my hands of her after that."

At last Sano was getting somewhere. "Tell me what happened."

Priest Ryuko sighed, venting the emotion from his body. He spoke in a leaden voice. "I went to Madam Usugumo's house. She served me tea before the lesson, which was typical. The tea tasted odd, though, and I asked what was in it. She said it was a new blend from China. I drank it, and while she set out the things for the lesson, I started feeling dizzy and drowsy. She lit different samples of incense, and she talked to me about the ingredients and where they came from, and the special aspects of the odors. She held the burner under my nose, and she told me to breathe deeply and concentrate on the voice of the incense.

"After the first three or four samples, I actually started *hearing* it, which was strange because 'the voice of incense' is just a figure of speech; smells don't really produce sounds. It was like a whispering in my ears. I started to get nervous. I said I thought I might be ill and we should stop. But Madam Usugumo said it was a breakthrough—I had reached a new level of my education. So I kept going.

"Her voice began to blend with the whisper of the incense. I couldn't tell who was speaking. She, or it, told me to raise and lower my arm. I obeyed without intending to." Priest Ryuko demonstrated. "It just floated up and down, as if it were attached to a string that someone had pulled. Then the whisper told me to say my name, and my mother's name, and where I'd been born. The words just flowed out of me. I wanted to ask Madam Usugumo what kind of ritual this was, but my tongue was paralyzed except when the incense allowed me to speak.

"Then it asked me questions and commanded me to answer each one truthfully: Did I gamble? Did I bed the courtesans at the Yoshiwara pleasure quarter? Or boy prostitutes? I said no. I started getting angry. What right had anyone to ask me such personal questions? I was shaking and fuming, but I couldn't resist. Then it asked me if there was something that I didn't want anyone to know. Had I done something I was ashamed of, that I was afraid could get me in trouble? It said, 'The secret is a stone you carry on your back. It's getting heavier and heavier.'

"I swear, I could feel the stone. My back started to hurt. My shoulders bent over. I could hardly breathe. I saw Madam Usugumo gazing into my eyes as she held the incense burner under my nose. I began to realize that she must have put something, a drug, in the incense and the tea. I was in some sort of trance. Her lips moved as the incense voice whispered, 'Just tell me your secret, and you'll be free.'"

Sano listened, amazed. What Korin had said was true: Madam Usugumo had perverted the incense ritual to extract shameful confessions from her pupils.

"I gathered all my strength of will," Priest Ryuko went on. "I reached out and knocked the incense burner out of her hand. The hot ash spilled. She hurried to sweep it up before it could start a fire. I stuck my finger down my throat, and I vomited up the tea that was still in my stomach. When I stopped retching, the dizziness and drowsiness went away. I couldn't hear the incense whispering anymore.

"I shouted at her, 'What were you trying to do to me, you witch? Put a spell on me?' She tried to pretend she was confused. She said 'Nothing.' I slapped her face, then stalked out of her house. I never went back. I never saw her or heard from her again."

Sano gazed askance at Ryuko. "Is that all?"

Ryuko looked Sano in the eye. "Yes." His sincerity seemed a manifestation of will rather than innocence.

"You didn't tell her your secrets?" Sano asked.

"I told you, I haven't any."

"Did you take any action against Madam Usugumo?"

"No."

Sano knew that Ryuko was quick to punish anyone who crossed him. He remembered a case when some priests who disliked Ryuko's influence at court had started evil rumors about him. "You could have told Lady Keisho-in." She'd gotten the shogun to send the priests to work in the government's silver mines. The priests had died there within a few months.

"I didn't want to bother her," Priest Ryuko claimed. "She's getting on in years; she's frail. It seemed better to let the whole thing go."

But Sano thought he knew the real reason the priest hadn't told Lady Keisho-in. "Or is it because you didn't want her to wonder whether you had any secrets and demand to hear what they were?" By taking action against Madam Usugumo, he'd have risked his private business becoming public. And if he had indeed confessed secrets to her during the ritual, she could have exposed him before he managed to do away with her.

"For the last time, Madam Usugumo wasn't blackmailing me. If you want to catch whoever killed Lord Hosokawa's daughters—which I know you do, whether you'll admit it or not—you'd better bait someone else." Priest Ryuko said with the air of a gambler playing his best card, "Such as Minister Ogyu. He was also her pupil."

Priest Ryuko beat a hasty escape. Sano went home and fetched his horse and troops. They rode downhill through the passages inside the castle. As they neared the castle's main gate, a samurai came riding toward them. It was Minister Ogyu. He'd saved Sano the trip. Sano raised his hand in greeting. "Minister Ogyu. May I have a word?"

24

AS OGYU AND Sano faced each other from astride their horses, Ogyu's head felt as if the right side of his brain had turned into a fist that clenched and unclenched, crushing itself. How he wished he could go back to the academy and sort rubble! The earthquake had given him a welcome respite from interaction with people, the pressure. He must be the only person in Edo who'd found life better after the earthquake than before.

"I'd be glad to speak with you, but the shogun has summoned me." The pain was agonizing, but Ogyu hid it. He never let his true emotions or his physical discomfort show in public. "I must go to him first."

"I'll go with you." Sano turned his horse and rode uphill through the passage alongside Ogyu.

Yesterday's talk had been bad enough. Now Ogyu dreaded having Sano present while he dealt with the shogun. "That would be my pleasure."

Ogyu and Sano found the shogun in the sunken bathtub in his chamber. Most of Edo's bath chambers, private and public, had been destroyed by the earthquake; the shogun was among the few people who still had one. His head and neck stuck up from the steaming water. His valet dressed his hair while he soaked. Charcoal braziers heated the moist air. Ogyu felt as if he would suffocate.

He and Sano knelt and bowed. The shogun barely nodded to Sano. He exclaimed, "Ogyu-*san*, I'm so glad you're here!"

Ogyu relaxed a little; the headache didn't stab quite so painfully. He felt more at ease with the shogun than with anyone except his wife and children. Most people feared the shogun's power of life and death over them, but Ogyu hadn't been afraid of the shogun since they'd first met almost twenty years ago. On that fateful day he'd crept into the shogun's chamber, trembling with nerves, drenched in cold sweat. His aching head echoed with his parents' orders to make the best of this onetime opportunity. Ogyu had expected the shogun to be a physical and intellectual giant, harshly critical. To his surprise, the great dictator was a slight, frail man with a meek manner. He'd invited Ogyu to read aloud a passage from Confucius, in Chinese, then translate it into Japanese. As Ogyu obeyed, his headache and anxiety faded because he was on familiar ground. The shogun was impressed. He said, "I'm having a banquet for my scholars tonight. Would you, ahh, do me the honor of attending?"

That was the beginning of Ogyu's rise to glory. Instead of studying alone, he studied with the shogun. Instead of lecturing outside Zōjō Temple, he debated with the court's most renowned Confucians. He even wrote the shogun's Confucian lectures. Best of all, the shogun had to be the least observant person in the world. Ogyu never had to worry about lapses of appearance or behavior in his presence.

"How may I serve you, Your Excellency?" Ogyu said.

"A terrible problem has come up," the shogun fretted. "I am in, ahh, desperate need of your advice."

The shogun often consulted Ogyu about affairs of state and how to apply Confucian principles to them. Ogyu had always managed to give advice that satisfied the shogun and didn't create hindrances for the men who really ran the government, but this was the first time the shogun had asked for his advice since the earthquake. Many political careers were foundering as officials failed to meet the shogun's demands to solve the problems. Ogyu's could be next.

He tried to ignore Sano while maintaining his smoothest composure. "I'll advise you to the best of my ability. What is the problem?"

"Have you heard what my astronomer said, about the bad constellations?" the shogun said. "That they mean the cosmos is displeased with a high-ranking person within my regime and sent the earthquake as a message?"

"Yes." Ogyu would rather not get involved in the dangerous controversy. His head pounded like a blacksmith's hammer on an anvil.

"My spies say there's much speculation about which high-ranking person has, ahh, offended the gods. Many people think it's me!" the shogun cried.

Ogyu exchanged astonished glances with Sano; they shared the thought that the madness in the air was inducing men to commit treason by blaming the shogun for the earthquake and risking death. Ogyu quickly broke eye contact, afraid that Sano would read his other thoughts.

"They say I'm not a good ruler. And that the gods will——" The shogun sobbed.

"What is it, Your Excellency?" Sano said with concern.

Ogyu felt his own concern to be magnitudes greater than Sano's. He, unlike most people, was truly fond of the shogun. "You can tell me, Your Excellency."

"The gods will send other disasters unless I, ahh, step down!"

This shocked Ogyu, even though it was no secret that the shogun had serious shortcomings as a ruler and that many people would like to see the government in more capable hands. The office of dictator was hereditary; Japan was stuck with the shogun until he died. But now it seemed that some men would take advantage of the earthquake to force him out.

"You don't have to listen to the opinions of people who are so cowardly that they talk behind your back instead of coming forward and saying their say in person," Sano said in a reasonable tone.

"But what if they're right?" the shogun asked anxiously. "What if I am such a terrible ruler that I caused the earthquake? If so, and I don't step down, the world could end!"

Ogyu watched Sano try not to roll his eyes. Sano was skeptical about the idea that the shogun had such a degree of control over nature, but Ogyu believed in the mystical interplay between humans and the cosmos, and what mattered was that the shogun also believed in it.

"That's why I summoned you," the shogun told Ogyu. "You're the expert on Confucius. Confucius was the expert on, ahh, how to keep government in harmony with the cosmos. Tell me, please, what would Confucius have me do?"

This was the most important service the shogun had ever asked of Ogyu. This moment could make or destroy him, could preserve the status quo or shatter the regime. If only it hadn't come while Sano was watching, while the threat of a murder investigation loomed over Ogyu's throbbing head!

"According to Confucius, it is not for your people to decide whether the government is in harmony with the cosmos," Ogyu said carefully. "The decision belongs to you, their leader. You and your advisors must analyze your policies and determine whether you are doing right."

The shogun puckered his brow. "But what if I discover I'm doing wrong?" Steam from the bathwater condensed on his face and dripped down his cheeks. "Must I abdicate?"

Ogyu stole a glance at Sano, whose expression was grave, cautious. They were both dismayed that the shogun was so afraid of the gods, he might be willing to relinquish the dictatorship and let a war over the succession begin.

"No, you must identify the errors of your ways and change them," Ogyu said.

"Are you sure?" Hope brightened the shogun's perspiring face. "I really wouldn't want to abdicate. I like being a great dictator."

"Yes, I'm sure," Ogyu said, confident in his knowledge.

Sighing in relief, the shogun slid deeper into the tub until his chin touched the water; he leaned his head back against the rim. "Ahh, your advice has done me good, Ogyu-*san*. As a token of my gratitude, I'll send you a present as soon as I finish my bath."

He waved his hand, dismissing Ogyu and Sano. As they walked outside together, Ogyu felt his heart pounding in time with the fist that clenched and unclenched in his head.

"I commend you for preventing His Excellency from stepping down and throwing the country into chaos," Sano said.

Ogyu heard genuine respect and gratitude in Sano's voice, but he knew better than to think he was safe. He also knew he should wait for Sano to say why he wanted to talk again; he mustn't reveal his interest in the murders or the fact that he knew things about them that he was hiding. But Sano didn't speak. The suspense cranked up the pain in Ogyu's head, which was almost unbearable.

"Is there any news about the murders?" Ogyu finally said.

"As a matter of fact, yes." Sano sounded strangely glad that Ogyu had spared him the need to broach the topic. Ogyu wondered if he wasn't the only one of them with something to hide. "Madam Usugumo's apprentice has been arrested."

Tentative relief infused balm into Ogyu's headache. "Because he's the killer?"

"No." Sano regarded Ogyu with a speculative expression.

Did he guess that Ogyu wished for someone else to take the blame for the murders so that he would be safe? Did he know that Ogyu feared he was getting close to the truth? Probably yes on both counts, Ogyu decided. The pain in his head increased. He would cut into his skull with his sword if that would end the agony.

"He was arrested for an unrelated crime," Sano went on. "But he has an interesting story. He says Madam Usugumo drugged her pupils, put them in a trance, and extracted compromising information from them. Afterward, she forced them to pay blackmail money in exchange for her keeping their secrets."

"How shocking." Ogyu forced his body to express the emotion he'd verbalized—voice hushed, eyes wide, mouth hanging open for an instant before he said, "Is it true?" All the while his mind blared, *He knows about the rituals! He knows about the blackmail!*

Sano watched him closely, as if wondering if Ogyu was putting on an act. "You tell me. You were Madam Usugumo's pupil. Did she try it with you?"

"Never." Ogyu made himself sound incredulous at the very idea. "Her behavior toward me was always entirely proper."

"You never felt strange after you drank tea? She didn't tell you to do things, such as to raise or lower your arm? Or ask you questions about yourself?"

Ogyu felt sicker as he remembered his arm lifting then dropping of its own will, and the voice of the incense whispering. A lifetime of dissembling came to his rescue. "No . . ." He let his voice trail off; he pasted a look of revelation on his face. "But if Madame Usugumo did perform rituals, I may have accidentally managed to avoid being drawn into one. I had to cancel my last lesson because some scholars from Miyako were coming to visit the academy and I needed to prepare." If Sano checked with his colleagues from the academy, they would confirm that the scholars had come. "Then the earthquake happened. I never resumed my lessons." Ogyu put on the expression of a man who'd crossed the street an instant before a runaway horse trampled the next person to cross. "Perhaps I was lucky."

He saw Sano wonder if perhaps he was lying. A seasoned detective like Sano would automatically distrust convenient explanations from murder suspects.

"Supposing Madam Usugumo had drugged you and put you in a trance," Sano said. "What secrets about you would she have learned?"

This was dangerous territory that Ogyu had successfully skirted his whole life. He'd built a mental wall around the private things he could never let come to light. The wall had never failed him. Confident that not a hint of his secrets showed on his face, Ogyu chuckled as if Sano had made a joke.

"Madam Usugumo wouldn't have learned anything worth my paying blackmail for, I'm afraid," Ogyu said. "I might have confessed to telling fibs to my parents when I was a child. My life is quite dull." He saw Sano narrow his eyes: Sano knew he was hiding something important, and Ogyu knew Sano was hunting the killer whether he would admit it or not. To deflect Sano's suspicion, Ogyu said, "But it appears that someone else's peccadilloes aren't as innocent. When the police begin looking for the murderer, I would suggest that they investigate Madam Usugumo's other pupils. I believe one of them was Priest Ryuko."

INSIDE THE GUESTHOUSE, Masahiro carried a bundle of dirty laundry down the corridor. Suddenly Priest Ryuko rounded a corner and came striding toward him. Ryuko's face was grim, his eyes focused straight ahead. To avoid being run down, Masahiro flattened himself against the wall. The priest rushed by. Opportunity beckoned. Clutching the laundry, Masahiro tiptoed after Ryuko.

Ryuko headed to the section of the house in which the shogun had installed people whom he wanted near him who'd lost their homes. Masahiro tiptoed a safe distance behind the priest, but he needn't have worried about being caught. Ryuko was so preoccupied that he never glanced backward. He slipped through a doorway. His voice, low and urgent, spoke to someone inside the chamber.

Masahiro stopped by the door, which was slightly open. He peeked inside at a small space crammed with furniture and bundles. He had a clear view of the monk who served as Priest Ryuko's aide, but all he could see of Ryuko was his backside. Ryuko was bent over, apparently rummaging inside a cabinet.

"But the roads are blocked," the monk said. "The bridges are down. I'm afraid you wouldn't be able to get very far."

"I'll have to take a chance." Priest Ryuko's voice was muffled.

Masahiro deduced that Ryuko was planning a trip. He waited, hoping to hear the reason for what seemed like a sudden, reckless departure.

"Can't you wait a month or so?" the monk asked. "The roads should be clear by then, and ferries should be available at the river crossings."

"I can't wait."

Masahiro heard desperation in his tone. Was it because of the murders?

"If you go now, there won't be any place to stay at night," the monk said. "I've heard there's not an inn open within a two-or three-day journey from Edo."

"Stop bringing up problems! Help me!" Priest Ryuko said, his voice louder and clearer as his posture straightened. "I need porters and a palanquin and bearers."

The monk looked worried. "They'll be hard to find. All the able-bodied men have been put on rebuilding the castle and city."

"Get them taken off! Bribe someone!" Priest Ryuko turned. Now Masahiro could see his angry profile. He held out a cloth pouch that jingled as he shook it at the monk. "This should be enough money."

Masahiro silently willed the priest to say where he was going and why.

The monk took the pouch and said, "All right."

"We have to be ready to go by tomorrow." Priest Ryuko's tone was threatening as well as fretful. "Or it's over for all of us."

Although Masahiro had failed to learn the destination or the reason for the trip, he knew that people who were innocent didn't need to leave town in a hurry. Guilty people did.

Priest Ryuko moved toward the door. Masahiro bolted, clutching the laundry to his heart, which beat fast with excitement. He couldn't wait to tell his father what he'd heard.

25

AFTER LEAVING MINISTER Ogyu, Sano went to the headquarters of the *metsuke,* the Tokugawa intelligence service. After the earthquake had flattened its offices inside the palace, it had moved to a watchtower on the castle wall halfway up the hill. The tower's upper story had fallen off, but the lower level was solid enough for occupation. Sano pushed open the door and entered. Lanterns supplemented the light from the barred windows. Smoke from charcoal braziers turned the air gray and noxious. The room was crowded with trunks and cabinets moved from the palace. A lone agent hunched over a desk. He bowed to Sano and said, "Welcome, Honorable Chamberlain."

The left sides of his face and neck, and both his hands, were bandaged with white cloth. He'd been burned when his house had caught fire during the earthquake, Sano knew. He wore a brown-and-black-striped kerchief tied around his head. The visible, unscathed half of his face was so ordinary, its features so unmemorable, that Sano had always had difficulty recognizing him. His appearance had once served him well in his profession as a spy.

"I'm glad to see you alive, Toda-*san,*" Sano said.

Toda smiled wryly with the half of his mouth that showed. "Thanks to the earthquake, I won't be doing any more secret surveillance." He lifted his hands to Sano, then touched the bandages on his face. "These would attract the attention of anybody I tried to spy on. The scars will be just as noticeable."

Sano smiled, too, pitying Toda and admiring his philosophical attitude. "I'm glad you've kept your sense of humor."

"My sense of humor is about all I did get to keep. The fire destroyed all my worldly goods. But sometimes in this life you just have to be glad that things aren't worse."

"True," Sano said. "I came by to inspect the state of the *metsuke*." His other purpose, he couldn't allow Toda to guess.

"Half of our agents died during the earthquake, I regret to say. Twelve are still missing. As for our informants, we're still trying to track them down." The *metsuke* had employed hundreds of informants. "But we've located most of the people we like to watch, those that survived." He gestured toward the walls, which were covered with charts that listed the names and whereabouts of high government officials, the *daimyo,* the wealthiest merchants, the most powerful gangsters, and the clergy at the important temples. "If we notice any unusual activity, I'll let you know."

Sano felt guilty because he knew about a threat to the regime and he couldn't alert the *metsuke*. "By the way, I just spoke with Minister Ogyu from the Confucian academy. Do you know him?"

"We've met a few times." Toda's visible eye gleamed with curiosity. "Do I smell an investigation?"

"No, I just wondered what you think of him." Sano recalled the conversation he'd witnessed, Ogyu giving the shogun advice. "Is he trustworthy enough to be around the shogun?"

"As trustworthy as anyone else." Toda studied Sano as if wondering whether to trust him. "But he's hard to get to know. His manner is too smooth. One slips off him before one can penetrate beneath the surface. Even when he drinks at banquets, he never loses his self-control and starts blabbing like other men do."

"Have you investigated him?"

"Of course. His reputation is clean. There's never been a hint of scandal associated with him or his family. We officially pronounced him harmless, although I can't guarantee that he's as pure as the Buddha."

"Why not?" Sano asked.

"No one is." Toda exuded cynicism. "The problem with investigating Ogyu was a lack of sources."

"What about his parents?"

"Both dead. And he hasn't any brothers or sisters or close relatives. Or any friends who know him very well."

"How about the scholars and teachers at the Yushima Seidō?"

"They said he never talked to them about anything except Confucianism or business concerning the school."

"Have you cultivated informers inside his household? His retainers and servants?"

"We've tried. They're remarkably closemouthed. They won't betray him for money, or sex, either." Toda sounded amazed by such loyalty, which he must have found to be rare.

"Such extreme privacy suggests that Ogyu has something to hide," Sano said.

"Good luck finding out what it is."

"I also ran into Priest Ryuko," Sano said. "He's very bad-tempered these days. Could he be a security problem?"

"He's running scared," Toda said. "Lady Keisho-in is a target of rumors about the astronomer's pronouncement. Ryuko knows that if she goes down, so will he."

That fear, plus the trauma caused by the earthquake, could drive any man to distraction, but Sano thought something more was afoot with Priest Ryuko. "But he has a close relationship with the shogun. Wouldn't that continue even after Lady Keisho-in dies?"

"Doubtful. He hasn't made himself very popular with government officials. Many of them blame him for the dog protection laws."

The dog protection laws had been instituted when the shogun had first become concerned about his inability to father an heir. Priest Ryuko had advised Lady Keisho-in that an heir would be born only after the shogun made a law proclaiming that dogs should be protected, and killing or hurting one was a crime punishable by death. Lady Keisho-in had helped Priest Ryuko convince the shogun. So far no heir had appeared, and dogs bred unchecked, running rampant through Edo, fouling the streets, attacking citizens. People who'd defended themselves and hurt a dog in the process had been executed. The government shelter for stray dogs cost a fortune to maintain. It had been destroyed by the earthquake, and rebuilding it and feeding the dogs was a drain on scarce resources.

"No one is allowed to complain about the law, but they're free to dislike Priest Ryuko." Toda gave Sano a speculative look, trying to gauge the state of relations between Sano and the priest. Sano kept quiet. "If Lady Keisho-in dies, Ryuko will lose his temple and his stipend. He could end up an itinerant priest, begging alms along the highway." Toda smiled with sly relish. "No wonder he's scared."

"Could there be another reason?" Sano asked.

Toda looked alert. "Do you know something I don't?"

"No, I'm just conjecturing. What's Ryuko's financial situation?"

"We've heard he's been spending more than usual." Toda's eye watched Sano, bright and curious. "He's recently taken out big loans from several moneylenders. We haven't been able to figure out why—he hasn't built new houses, he doesn't gamble or go to Yoshiwara or any of the usual things—but he's deeply in debt."

Here was evidence that Priest Ryuko, despite his denials, had been paying blackmail to Madam Usugumo. Sano was glad to think he was getting closer to solving the crime, yet he felt disturbed. Ryuko was still a formidable adversary. "How about Minister Ogyu? Has he recently increased his spending?"

"Not that we're aware of. He hasn't any debts. But his wife comes from a very wealthy clan, and her dowry was huge." Toda added, "That's another reason Ogyu is hard to know: Wealth buys privacy. His retainers handle his finances. He doesn't employ merchant bankers, who give us the occasional tip."

Sano felt as if Ogyu were a locked door that he was pounding on. "If you hear anything about him or Priest Ryuko, will you let me know?"

"My pleasure." Toda sounded sincere, but Sano knew better than to trust him entirely. Toda served everyone and didn't play favorites. That was how he survived political upheavals. In the past he'd withheld important information from Sano and helped Sano's enemies. The only reason Sano consulted him was that Toda gave him more dirt than anyone else could.

"And don't mention this conversation to them," Sano said. "That's an order."

"I'm a paragon of discretion." Toda smiled and put a finger to his lips.

Sano also knew that Toda wasn't above defying an order from him or any other government official. Toda was duty-bound only to the shogun, whose regime he was employed to preserve. Betrayal was a risk Sano took every time he consulted Toda.

172

"I must say it seems odd that you mention Priest Ryuko and Minister Ogyu in the same breath. They move in different circles." Toda's one-eyed gaze probed Sano. "One would guess that they're both suspects in a crime you're investigating. But, of course, you don't investigate crimes anymore."

"Of course," Sano said evenly. That Toda would see through his subterfuge was another risk he'd taken.

"If you were investigating them, I would offer you some friendly advice," Toda said. "Beware of Priest Ryuko. When you corner a frightened dog, it bites."

HAVING LEFT TAHARA, Deguchi, and Kitano behind in the forest clearing, Hirata rode at breakneck speed to the edge of town. There he slowed down and looked backward. He didn't see them following him, but he felt the faint pulse of their aura. They were too close no matter how much distance he put between them and himself. Riding, he felt light-headed from the trance and the potion. He had an obsessive desire to roll up his sleeve and see if the words on his arm had faded. He checked ten times before he reached the main gate of Edo Castle. Each time, the words were still there.

He decided to go home first, because he dreaded seeing Sano. Tahara's threat accompanied him like a cold shadow licking his heart. When he dismounted from his horse inside his ruined estate, Midori peeked out of the storehouse.

"Thank the gods you're back! I was so worried about you! Are you all right?" Without waiting for an answer, she said, "Sano-san is here."

Now Hirata would have to face Sano before he'd had time to think of what to say. "Could you and the children go somewhere, so we can talk in private?"

Midori looked as if she had more questions, but she took the children away. Sano's daughter Akiko was with them. Entering his cluttered room, Hirata found Sano kneeling on the floor. Sano's expression was a mixture of anger, worry, and distrust. He said, "Where have you been?"

Hirata knelt opposite Sano. He owed Sano an honest explanation even if it had to be incomplete. "With my friends Tahara, Kitano, and Deguchi."

"That's what I thought." Sano spoke with displeasure. "I don't suppose you did any investigation on Priest Ryuko or Minister Ogyu."

"I can do it now," Hirata said, eager to make up for his absence.

"Never mind," Sano said coldly. "I've already taken care of it myself. What were you and your friends doing?"

A lifetime of following the samurai code of obedience compelled Hirata to answer. Fourteen years' friendship with Sano required him to tell the truth. Tahara's threat bound him to silence. "I can't tell you."

A frown deepened all the emotions on Sano's face. "Can't or won't?"

Hirata was mute. He'd never felt so at odds with himself, so helpless, or so miserable.

After a long, tense pause, Sano said, "You've changed since you met those men." He shifted position as if he were physically uncomfortable. "There's something wrong, and it has to do with them. Have they gotten you in some kind of trouble?"

You can't imagine, Hirata thought glumly.

Sano leaned forward, his coldness warming to apprehension. "If you are in trouble, I wish you would tell me what it is so that I can help you."

That Sano could be so generous after Hirata had let him down! He thought yearningly of the times he and Sano had faced danger together and prevailed despite odds that had seemed insurmountable. But he must not pit Sano against Tahara, Kitano, and Deguchi.

"I can handle it," Hirata said.

A sigh of exasperation gusted from Sano. He raised his empty hands, then let them fall onto his thighs with a loud clap. "If that's the way you want it, then we need to come to an understanding." His manner turned so ominous that Hirata felt the air between them crackle, as if lightning were about to strike. Yet he could also see that Sano hated the words he spoke next.

"I've been patient with your absences and your secrecy. I've made allowances for you that I wouldn't make for any of my other retainers." Sano moved again; his upper body twitched inside his clothes. "But you've been taking unfair advantage, and I've let you get away with it for too long. It has to stop. I'm ordering you to tell me what's going on. And if you refuse, then we won't be able to work together anymore."

This was the moment Hirata had feared since he joined the secret society. His commitment to them had collided with his loyalty to Sano; he'd compromised the sacred bond between samurai and master, and there was only one way to mend it. The knowledge brought terror but also relief. Hirata must confess and hope that he could avert the consequences.

Before he could speak, Sano frowned, glanced down at his waist, and felt under his sash. He pulled out a small object whose edges had apparently been irritating him and causing his restless movements. It was a wooden prayer tag on a string. Hirata inhaled a sharp breath. He recognized the red sword drawn on the tag. Cold, nauseating horror gripped his stomach.

Sano looked up. Puzzled by the alarm he saw on Hirata's face, he said, "It's just a prayer tag. My daughter must have found it and slipped it under my sash, as a joke."

But Hirata knew that Tahara had planted the tag on Sano, to demonstrate that he could get close enough to kill Sano whenever he wanted. Tahara had somehow arranged for Sano to discover the tag when Hirata was present, as a warning.

Sano tossed the tag on the floor. It landed with the picture of the red sword facing up. "Which will it be? Are you going to tell me, or do we part company?"

Hirata felt an anguish as painful as if his innards were being torn, by Sano in one direction, by the secret society in the other. "I can't tell you." He forced the words past the tears swelling in his throat.

Resignation settled over Sano; his eyes darkened with disappointment through which a spark of anger glinted. "Very well, then."

"Does this mean you're——?" Hirata couldn't bear to ask whether Sano was casting him out to become a *rōnin*, a masterless samurai. The thought of the disgrace, the loss of everything that mattered, was too terrible.

"Not yet," Sano said. Hirata could see that he was reluctant to impose such a harsh punishment, even though he had every right as well as the responsibility to uphold the samurai code of honor. "I'm giving you one last chance to settle whatever business you have with these men. Take a leave of absence for as long as you need. If you can't settle it and return your full attention to your duties . . ." Sano paused, then spoke with resolve as well as misgivings. "Your leave of absence will have to become permanent."

26

REIKO CLIMBED THE steep, crumbling steps to the Yushima Seidō while her palanquin, bearers, and guards waited below. She carried a gift-wrapped package and a lacquer scroll container. Reaching the portals, she heard children's tinkling laughter. In a courtyard surrounded by fallen buildings, a woman, a boy, and a girl held hands, dancing in a circle on the snow, as the children laughed and the woman chanted a song. The children looked to be seven or eight years old. The woman, Lady Ogyu, was in her twenties, thin and tall and sinewy in her padded, steel-blue silk coat. Long, lank black hair spilled from the scarf wrapped around her head. Her face was too rawboned for prettiness, but smiles carved dimples into her cheeks as she swung her children's hands. Reiko smiled too.

Lady Ogyu saw Reiko. She stopped chanting and dancing; she gathered her children close. Her face had a naturally sad cast—eyes, brows, and mouth downturned.

"Good day, Lady Ogyu." Reiko walked toward the family.

"Who are you?" Lady Ogyu looked as scared as if Reiko were a bandit. She pushed the boy and girl behind her. They clung to her skirts and peered out at Reiko, solemn and silent.

"I'm sorry for frightening you," Reiko said. "I've come to visit. My name is Reiko."

Lady Ogyu backed away, drawing the children with her. "Have we ever met?"

"No, but we have a relative in common. My grandmother is your great-aunt by marriage."

Suspicion deepened the fear on Lady Ogyu's face. She reminded Reiko of a deer, to whom all humans were hunters. The children's eyes were huge; their lips trembled. Reiko wished she could leave them in peace, but she had to help Sano solve the crime, prevent a war, and protect her own family.

"Grandmother asked me to come and see you because she's concerned about you. I have a letter from her." Reiko proffered the scroll container to Lady Ogyu, who made no move to accept it. Reiko took out the letter and held it out to Lady Ogyu.

Lady Ogyu snatched the letter from Reiko's hand, leery of even the briefest contact. As she read, her eyes darted back and forth between the letter and Reiko. Finished, she hesitated.

Reiko smiled at the children, said, "I've brought you something," and offered them the package.

Tempted by the pretty red wrapping, they looked at their mother. She reluctantly nodded. The boy opened the package. When he and his sister saw the sweet-bean cakes inside, their eyes lit up. They began stuffing cakes in their mouths. They probably hadn't eaten sweets since the earthquake. Reiko felt lucky that her cooks had saved some.

"Come inside," Lady Ogyu said grudgingly. She sidled toward one of three tents pitched in the courtyard and held up the flap for Reiko to enter. "Play outside," she told the children. "Don't go too far."

Daylight shining through the tent illuminated the small interior. Two layers of tatami padded the ground. Despite the burning charcoal brazier, it was so cold that Reiko hated to remove her shoes. Toys were jumbled in a corner—dolls, miniature swords, balls, and wooden soldiers. Folded clothes and bedding piled along the walls provided extra insulation. Lady Ogyu picked two cushions from a stack and tossed them on the floor. She handed Reiko a quilt and wrapped another around her shoulders. They knelt on the cushions. Lady Ogyu offered refreshments. Reiko demurred, was pressed, and finally accepted. Lady Ogyu lifted a water jug that sat on the brazier, sloshed water into a teapot, and threw in some loose tea from a jar. She kept her gaze averted from Reiko. They sat in silence as the tea steeped. Lady Ogyu poured two bowls, handed one to Reiko. Reiko sipped weak, lukewarm tea. Lady Ogyu made no attempt at conversation. Rarely had Reiko seen a less gracious hostess; but she was no friend to this woman.

"I heard that your house was destroyed. I'm sorry," Reiko said.

"Yes, well," Lady Ogyu murmured, her gaze fixed on the tea bowl she clutched.

"How about if I look for someplace more comfortable for you and your children to stay?" Reiko felt sorry for Lady Ogyu, guilty for deceiving her, and eager to atone.

Lady Ogyu stared at Reiko in horror. "I don't want to go! Please don't make me!"

Reiko was surprised by her distress. "Of course you needn't go if you don't want to."

"My husband wants to stay here," Lady Ogyu whispered. "I want to be near him."

Reiko seized the chance to talk about Minister Ogyu. "You must love your husband."

Lady Ogyu nodded, cringing.

"I love mine, too," Reiko said. "I wouldn't want to leave him even if we had to live on the street to be together."

Lady Ogyu didn't take the opportunity to exchange confidences. Gulping her tea, she retreated into her shell. Reiko tried to keep the conversation going. "How long have you been married?"

"Nine years." Lady Ogyu glanced at the flap of the tent, as if she wished someone would come and take Reiko away.

"How old are your children?"

Reiko hoped that her interest in them would thaw Lady Ogyu's reserve, but Lady Ogyu squirmed as if Reiko had poked her. "They're both eight. They're twins."

"How nice. I have a boy who's twelve and a girl who's five." She thought of the new baby inside her and smiled. "Where is your husband?"

"He went into town." Lady Ogyu pressed her lips together as if afraid of leaking too much information.

"When will he be back?" Reiko wanted to know how much uninterrupted time she would have with Lady Ogyu before Minister Ogyu returned. He was a possible murderer, she'd promised Sano she would be careful, and she was more concerned than usual about her safety because she was pregnant.

"Soon, I think." Lady Ogyu glanced at the tent flap again, obviously hoping her husband would rescue her from Reiko.

"He's the director of the academy, isn't he? A very important man?"

Lady Ogyu nodded. She set down her empty cup. She didn't offer to refill Reiko's.

"He must be busy. I know my husband is. I hardly ever see him. Tell me—is your husband the kind of man who works all the time? Or does he take time for pleasure?"

"He works hard," Lady Ogyu blurted out, "but he likes to be with me and the children as much as possible."

Reiko saw that here was a love-marriage as strong as hers with Sano. She didn't want to discover that Minister Ogyu was the killer and end this couple's happiness, but she forged ahead with her inquiries. "Is there anything special that you do together?" When Lady Ogyu didn't answer, Reiko prompted, "How about incense lessons? They're very popular, or at least they were before the earthquake."

Lady Ogyu regarded Reiko with renewed suspicion. "Why are you asking me all these questions? Why do you care whether we take incense lessons?" Her eyes widened in dismay. "Wait—I know who you are." She pointed at Reiko. "You're the wife of Chamberlain Sano. I thought you looked familiar. I've seen you at the castle. The chamberlain was here yesterday, asking my husband about his incense teacher who was murdered. I think you want to trick me into saying something the chamberlain can use against my husband."

"No," Reiko protested, but Lady Ogyu cut her off.

"Don't bother to lie." Anger at Reiko's deceit made Lady Ogyu bold. "I'm not telling you anything else." She stood, lifted the tent flap, and said, "Go home. Leave us alone."

Reiko shamefacedly exited the tent. Descending the steps, she saw four samurai on horseback join her guards and bearers in the lower, outer precinct. The four dismounted. Reiko recognized one of them, from Sano's description, as Minister Ogyu. He was stout, pudgy, and shorter than his attendants. He glanced curiously at Reiko's escorts, who bowed to him. His attendants led the horses away. Minister Ogyu climbed the steps while Reiko continued down them. She was afraid to look directly at him, lest he ask who she was and what she was doing there. A covert glance showed her a round, youthful face with a faint mustache. When they passed, she bobbed a quick bow and cast her gaze modestly downward. She felt him turn to look at her. Reaching her palanquin, she looked over her shoulder and saw him disappear through the portals. She knew Lady Ogyu would tell him about their talk. How she wished she could hear his reaction and what it might reveal!

She looked around the precinct. The attendants were nowhere in sight. "Wait," she told her bearers, and hurried up the steps. At the top she peeked into the courtyard. It was empty. From within the tent she heard Lady Ogyu's voice, loud and agitated, and a lower, calmer voice. She stole into the courtyard and crouched outside the tent.

"—Chamberlain Sano's wife," Reiko heard Lady Ogyu say.

"What did she want?" asked the other voice, Minister Ogyu's. It was deep for such a small man, with an oddly resonant quality.

"She asked me questions about you." Lady Ogyu sounded on the verge of tears. "Oh, I wish you'd been here to chase her away before I had to talk to her. I was so afraid!"

"It's all right. I'm here now. Nobody's going to hurt you. What questions about me?"

Reiko heard a note of worry in his soothing tone. Lady Ogyu said, "She asked if you took incense lessons. That's when I figured out who she was. Then I knew she was fishing for information that her husband can use to prove that you killed Madam Usugumo." Lady Ogyu sobbed. "They're out to get us!"

Minister Ogyu let out a short sigh as eloquent as a curse.

"What is it?" Fright hushed Lady Ogyu's voice.

"I just saw Chamberlain Sano at the castle. He asked whether Madam Usugumo had been blackmailing me, and if I had any secrets. I said no, but I don't think he believed me."

Lady Ogyu moaned. "What if he finds out?"

Excitement filled Reiko. This was as good as an admission that Madam Usugumo had blackmailed Minister Ogyu, who did have a dangerous secret.

"He won't." Minister Ogyu sounded too adamant, as if he were trying to convince himself as well as his wife. "Madam Usugumo is dead. She can't tell."

But it wasn't proof that Minister Ogyu had killed her. Maybe Priest Ryuko had, and Minister Ogyu had innocently benefited from the crime.

"Someone else might," Lady Ogyu said.

"There's no one else who knows," Minister Ogyu said. "Except us."

A long silence ensued. Reiko willed them to say what the secret was. She wished she could see through the opaque fabric of the tent and read it in their eyes.

"What about Kasane?" Lady Ogyu said.

"She must be a hundred years old. She's probably forgotten."

"She might remember." Lady Ogyu sounded as if she wanted to believe her husband, but couldn't.

"If she does, then she'll also remember that she was sworn to secrecy," Minister Ogyu said with a touch of impatience. "Besides, if she hasn't told anyone yet, why would she ever?"

"If Chamberlain Sano should get hold of her—"

"Don't worry. He doesn't even know she exists."

He soon would, Reiko thought.

"But what if he somehow finds out?" Lady Ogyu said, still fearful.

Another, longer silence fell. Reiko wordlessly exhorted the couple to say something that further identified the old woman and explained what bearing, if any, she had on the murders.

Light footsteps ran toward Reiko, then skidded to a halt. She turned and saw the Ogyus' little boy, who stood a few paces from her. They beheld each other in alarm. Reiko put her finger to her lips.

"Mama! Papa!" the boy cried.

Reiko fled.

27

AFTER LEAVING HIRATA's estate, Sano met General Isogai, chief of the Tokugawa Army, in the street in the official quarter. General Isogai was a stout, middle-aged samurai with a thick neck and pugnacious expression. His belly strained the lacings of his armor tunic. The rim of his metal helmet indented his fleshy head.

"Folks have been looking high and low for you," General Isogai said. His voice was hoarse from barking orders; his piggish eyes were bloodshot. He'd been working day and night, deploying his troops across the city and creating a semblance of order. "The shogun has called an emergency meeting."

Countless emergency meetings had been called since the earthquake. "What's this one about?" Sano asked.

"I guess we're going to find out," General Isogai said.

At the guesthouse Sano and General Isogai found the shogun and Ienobu seated on the dais with the four aged men of the Council of Elders. The floor below them was crowded with the council's aides, the shogun's guards, and palace officials. The audience overflowed out the open door; on the veranda, men stood three deep. The crowd buzzed with low, speculative conversation. The shogun beckoned Sano and General Isogai. As Sano knelt in his place at the shogun's right, he saw Toda Ikkyu's bandaged face in the front row of the audience. He noticed Masahiro kneeling in a corner. He remembered that Masahiro was now in charge of the shogun's chambers, but this was the first time he'd seen

Masahiro in an official role at such an important gathering. His son had a man's job, at twelve years old. The earthquake had created strange circumstances indeed.

The shogun raised his hand; the crowd quieted. "I, ahh, called you together because I, ahh, have just, ahh, received, ahh, disturbing news. Toda-*san*, tell them what you told me."

Toda rose on his knees and turned around to face the crowd. "I've discovered some activity among the Mori, Maeda, and Date *daimyo* clans." Sano felt an internal drumbeat of foreboding. "I've done a rough count of their troops, based on what my agents have reported. The number is much higher than normal. It appears that the troops have been sneaking into town since the earthquake. They've been parading through the streets, all decked out for battle."

Murmurs rumbled. Men exchanged alarmed glances. Everyone knew what this massing of troops could mean—a revolt brewing. The shogun cringed inside his quilts. Masahiro looked worriedly at Sano, who fought to keep his composure. It sounded as if the *daimyo* who wanted to overthrow the Tokugawa regime were so bent on revolt—and so certain they would come out on top—that they didn't care who knew about their plans.

"Why have you only just discovered this?" General Isogai demanded.

"Because the intelligence service has been as impaired by the earthquake as every other section of the government," Toda said.

Sano looked at Toda. Toda returned his gaze, inscrutable.

"How have those troops managed to get from the provinces to Edo?" asked Kato Kinhide, on the Council of Elders, a crony of Yanagisawa. "Aren't the highways impassable?"

"The troops apparently got through somehow," Toda said.

"Why haven't the officials at the checkpoints let us know they were coming?" Ienobu asked. Distress knotted his ugly features. Sano supposed he was worried about inheriting a civil war along with the Tokugawa regime.

"The checkpoints have been closed since the earthquake," Toda said. "The messenger service is virtually shut down. There's nobody to bring us news from afar."

Edo was a sitting target, blindly unaware of danger. Sano felt guilty because he'd been aware but hadn't told.

"Are the *daimyo* going to attack me?" The shogun clutched Sano's sleeve. "What should we do?"

All eyes turned to Sano. Sano still couldn't tell what he knew because that would force the government to respond to the threat and the *daimyo* to proceed with their insurrection regardless of whether Sano solved the crime and Lord Hosokawa joined them. "We shouldn't leap to the conclusion that the *daimyo* are preparing for war," Sano said. "There could be other reasons why they would bring in extra troops. To fix their damaged estates, for example."

"Ahh." The shogun looked relieved.

Skepticism appeared on faces in the assembly, including Masahiro's. Toda studied Sano with curiosity, Kato with veiled suspicion.

"All due respect, Honorable Chamberlain, this would be a perfect time for those *daimyo* to strike at us—while we're down," General Isogai said. "I should take our army and go order them to send their extra troops home or they'll be sorry."

Sano saw the disaster he dreaded shaping up. "That could provoke them into attacking even if they never intended to. Everyone's temper has been on edge since the earthquake. Do you want to risk starting a war?"

"No, oh, no!" Eyes wide with fright, the shogun clapped his hands over his mouth.

"Then we mustn't take military action until we're sure it's necessary," Sano said.

General Isogai scowled at Sano. "Your Excellency, if the *daimyo* are intending to attack, we can't just sit and wait for it." Rumbles of agreement came from the audience, including Kato.

"Yes, we have to show them who's in charge," Ienobu said.

Encouraged by the support, General Isogai said, "We can't afford to look like we're blind to what they're doing, or too weak to protect ourselves."

The rumbles faded into an uncomfortable silence.

The shogun looked around in confusion. "What's the matter? Someone say something. You." He pointed at Toda.

Toda reluctantly voiced the assembly's shared thoughts. "We've been severely weakened by the earthquake. Our army has only about ten thousand soldiers left in town. They're too exhausted to stand against fresh troops from the provinces. The castle's defenses are in no shape to withstand an invasion. I think Chamberlain Sano is right: We shouldn't show aggression toward the *daimyo* when there may not be good reason and since we won't be able to handle the consequences."

Horror and shame filled the chamber, like the reek from an infected wound. Men bowed their heads. It was a terrible moment. That the Tokugawa regime was no longer invincible! That its disintegration could come during their lifetime! Sano felt the blow to the assembly's collective samurai pride. His own spirit contracted painfully. Ienobu stretched his lips over his protruding teeth and brooded. The shogun was a picture of woe. Even he understood his predicament.

"All right, then, what should we do?" General Isogai demanded, red-faced, his eyes bulging with impotent anger.

"Yes, Chamberlain Sano, what?" the shogun echoed anxiously.

"We'll watch the *daimyo*," Sano said; it was the only thing he could say. "Toda-*san,* keep us informed about their business." He could only hope Toda's agents wouldn't see anything that would provoke the regime into taking action it would regret or expose his own duplicity. "We'll fortify the castle as best we can and prepare our troops for battle."

THE ASSEMBLY FILED from the room as quietly as mourners exiting a funeral. General Isogai aimed a derisive snort, disguised as a cough, in Sano's direction. Sano followed Toda, caught up with him in the garden, drew him away from the other men, and said, "Did you know about the *daimyos'* troops when we spoke earlier?"

Unfazed by Sano's accusing tone, Toda said, "Yes."

"Then why didn't you tell me?" Sano demanded.

"I don't tell you everything." Toda smiled wryly. "Need I keep reminding you?"

"Something as important as that, you shouldn't have withheld from me," Sano said, infuriated by the spy's attitude.

Toda shook his head, his expression pitying. "It looks as if I need to remind you that I report information to you only when it doesn't conflict with my duty to the Tokugawa regime, of which you are a part but not the ruler."

That Toda was correct made Sano all the more furious. "You're evading the question. Why did you bypass me and take your news straight to the shogun?"

"Because he deserved to know." Toda matched Sano's belligerence. "And I didn't trust you to deliver it to him or to anyone else who should have been informed."

"Why not?" Sano said, feeling insulted even as his heart beat faster with apprehension.

"Forty years as a spy. While we were talking earlier, I sensed that something wasn't right. I wondered if you already knew about the *daimyo*." Toda fixed his unblinking eye on Sano, who found it hard not to flinch. "Well?"

Your spy instincts be damned, Sano thought. "That's ridiculous." He tried to speak with just enough conviction; too much or too little would alert Toda that he was lying. "You're so immersed in deceit that you smell it even when it's not on anybody but yourself."

Canny mirth creased the skin around Toda's eye. "My nose hasn't been wrong very many times, and I don't think it is now. But listen." His expression turned sober; he lowered his voice. "You and I have always gotten along. I consider you a friend. May I offer you some friendly advice? Whatever you're doing, think hard about whether it's good for you. And if it isn't, then quit while you can."

He glanced across the garden to the gate, where the crowd of officials had gathered. "Well, well, look who's risen from the dead."

Amid the officials, exchanging bows and greetings with them, stood Yanagisawa. Shocked to see him after all these months, Sano stared. He forgot Toda and moved toward Yanagisawa, compelled by the forces that had drawn them together, pushed them apart, and pitted them against each other for fourteen years.

The crowd melted away. Alone, Sano and Yanagisawa stood at arm's length. Sano saw how gaunt Yanagisawa was, how he'd still managed to retain his looks. The air thickened with bitter memories of the wounds they'd dealt each other. But Yanagisawa's mood seemed indifferent as he examined Sano. He looked like he'd walked through fire and had all the emotion seared out of him. But Sano never trusted appearances when it came to Yanagisawa. His mind teemed with questions that he couldn't ask outright. For almost a year he'd planned for this moment, but now that it had come, he was speechless.

"It's been a long time," Yanagisawa said. His suave voice had the tired quality of a convalescent's.

"Yes," Sano said, "it has."

The banal words were incongruous with the fact that they'd once rolled in the dirt trying to kill each other. Sano pitied Yanagisawa terribly: He'd undergone the worst experience a parent could—the death of a child. Sano felt guilty because his investigation had created the circumstances that had been fatal for Yoritomo. He couldn't blame Yanagisawa for blaming him. But he couldn't forget that Yanagisawa had tried to kill Masahiro and almost succeeded. Anger and hatred adulterated his compassion. He couldn't be sorry that Yanagisawa had been disgraced and demoted by the shogun, whereas Sano had been promoted and acclaimed.

"What brings you here?" Sano needed to know why Yanagisawa had finally reemerged and what it meant for himself.

"I'm getting back into circulation," Yanagisawa said. "It's time."

Time for what? Sano wondered. To end his mourning for Yoritomo? To take up his quest for power again? Or to avenge Yoritomo's death? Whatever the reason, the time couldn't have been worse for Sano. He had a murder investigation to conduct in secret, a clandestine deal with Lord Hosokawa, and a possible revolt on his hands. The last thing he needed was Yanagisawa complicating matters.

"Have you seen the shogun yet?" Sano asked.

"Not yet. I was just about to go in and pay him my respects."

Sano stepped aside, clearing Yanagisawa's way to the door. Yanagisawa circled around Sano, who turned to keep him in sight. The specter of Yoritomo lying with his throat cut in a pool of blood loomed between them, as palpable as if made flesh. Sano didn't want to mention Yoritomo; nothing could ease the pain of such a loss. But certain words must be said. Courtesy demanded them. So did Sano's own need to express the thoughts that had weighed on his mind for almost a year.

"I never had a chance to tell you how sorry I am about Yoritomo," Sano said. "May I offer my condolences?"

A breath inflated Yanagisawa's chest. Although his mild expression didn't change, Sano sensed a swell of emotions within him. Sano braced himself, aware that if a man he blamed for his child's death should dare to express sympathy, he would explode into violent rage.

"You may." Not a sign of rancor did Yanagisawa display. "I gratefully accept."

Sano was so unbalanced by Yanagisawa's reaction that he had to grope for something else to say. "Yoritomo was a good man. His death was a tragedy."

"Yes," Yanagisawa said. "Thank you."

Perhaps grief had reformed Yanagisawa from an evil schemer into a decent human being. Sano had seen stranger things happen. He came out with a speech that his conscience needled him to make.

"I'm sorry for my part in the trouble that cost Yoritomo his life." But Sano couldn't help thinking that it had been Yoritomo's own actions that had ultimately gotten him killed. He'd gone over and over the events leading up to the scene, and he always concluded that if he had it to do again, given the same facts that had been available to him then, he would have done everything the same. "I never meant for Yoritomo to be harmed. If I could change the past and bring him back, I would." But Sano wasn't sorry not to have Yoritomo plotting against him. Even though he meant every word of his speech, it felt false.

Yanagisawa nodded as if he accepted Sano's words at face value. "Why don't we just let bygones be bygones. You have more important things to think about. And so have I."

He smiled. His eyes flashed with the old cunning and menace.

Sano's hackles rose.

28

"WHAT DID SANO-*SAN* say?" Midori asked, entering the storehouse where Hirata sat.

Hirata looked up at his wife. Sick with shame about what had happened between him and Sano, he didn't want to worry her. She had enough problems, caring for the family under post-earthquake conditions. "Nothing serious. He's giving me a leave of absence."

Midori's eyes flared with alarm; she understood that the leave was a punishment, not a holiday. "Why? What did you do?"

"Why are you always in such a hurry to assume I did something bad?" Hirata vented his anger at himself on her.

"Why do you always criticize me when I'm right and we both know it?" Midori put her hands on her hips. She was no traditional wife who would bow to her husband's authority or let him divert her from a topic he didn't want to discuss. "Tell me what you did!"

Hirata didn't like giving in to her, but it wasn't fair to keep her in the dark. If things kept going the way they were, she would share the consequences. "Sano-*san* gave me a job to do. I let him down." It made Hirata feel as low and dirty as a worm. Samurai had committed ritual suicide for similar offenses. Perhaps he should, too. That would get him out of the secret society, but it would create other, disastrous problems.

Midori opened her mouth. She looked from side to side, caught between anger and confusion and unable to decide which to express. "Why didn't you do what he told you to?" She studied Hirata's face.

"Don't tell me—I can guess. It was those friends of yours, wasn't it? Yes! I knew it!"

"You carry on our conversations so well by yourself, why do you need me to say anything?" Hirata snapped.

"I knew they were trouble the first time I laid eyes on them. Where did you go last night? What happened?"

"I can't tell you," Hirata said between clenched teeth. "You know that."

"I know that you've changed since you met those three. You're secretive and cross all the time. I don't like it. And neither does Sano-*san*, obviously." Fear quenched her anger. Her hand went to her throat, and she said in a hushed voice, "What happens next? Sano-*san* throws you out and you become a *rōnin*?"

"No. He wouldn't," Hirata lied.

Midori bent and clutched his arm. "Whatever you're up to with those men, you have to stop it! Before you ruin us!"

Their hold over him shackled Hirata like iron chains. "I can't."

"Why not? Are you so infatuated with them that you'll let them make you lose everything?" Midori's anger resurged. "Maybe you don't care about yourself, but what about me and our children? How are we supposed to live when we're thrown out in the streets? Don't you care about us anymore?"

"That's not it," Hirata protested.

"Then what is it? Why must you continue going along with those men?"

The secrets he'd been keeping filled Hirata like pus in a boil. Their volume had swelled to the bursting point. Hirata had to let something out. "Unless I do, they'll kill Sano-*san*."

Midori crumpled as if he'd struck her behind the knees. "Oh." She understood that his master's murder was a calamity that a samurai must do everything in his power to avert. "Well, can't you protect Sano-*san*?"

"No." Hirata heard the flatness of defeat in his voice. "They're stronger than I am."

Midori frowned in disbelief. "You're the best fighter in Edo."

"I'm only the one who's won the tournaments and duels. Tahara, Kitano, and Deguchi have kept their powers to themselves—so far."

"Tell Sano-*san*. Surround him with guards," Midori suggested. "Those men won't be able to get close enough to touch him."

"Yes, they will." As Hirata told her about the prayer tag that Tahara had planted on Sano, he watched horror erase her disbelief. "I can't keep him safe. Except by doing what they want me to do."

"What do they want you to do?"

"I can't tell you. I've already said too much." Hirata knew the men would kill whoever learned more about their business than they liked, including women and children. "It's too dangerous for you to know."

Midori wrung her hands. "What's going to happen to us?"

"Nothing, I promise," Hirata said with too hearty confidence. "Everything will be fine." But first he must do the ghost's bidding.

After Midori left him to look after the children, who were playing outside, Hirata glumly contemplated the message branded on his arm. He couldn't just walk up to Lord Ienobu and say, "Come to the shogun's garden with me." Ienobu would want to know why, or refuse outright. Hirata supposed he could use his mystical powers to make Ienobu follow him as mindlessly as a sleepwalker. But they might run into someone who would notice that something was odd about Ienobu and accuse Hirata of casting an evil spell over him. Hirata especially didn't want Sano to see him and wonder what he was doing. He decided against sneaking up behind Ienobu, hitting him on the head, knocking him unconscious, putting his body in a sack, and dumping him in the garden at the designated hour. In addition to the risk of being caught, he might hurt Ienobu. *Think!* he exhorted himself. *You haven't much time left!*

Hirata mulled over his store of information about Lord Ienobu, whom he didn't personally know. He'd heard the man was ambitious, sneaky, selfish, and had his eye on the dictatorship. That was all. It was enough.

Rummaging in the household clutter, Hirata found writing supplies and a blank sheet of paper. He prepared ink, dipped a brush, and wrote in square, blocky characters that disguised his calligraphy: *Go to the shogun's garden at the hour of the cock tomorrow, and you will learn something to your advantage.* Hirata rolled the letter without signing it and put it in a bamboo scroll container. Surely Ienobu wouldn't be able to ignore an anonymous tip. All Hirata had to do was get the letter into Ienobu's hands.

Then he would continue his investigation into Tahara, Kitano, and Deguchi.

"YOU'RE BACK ALREADY?" Reiko's grandmother said, standing outside her tent. "Did you have a nice visit with Lady Ogyu?"

Reiko climbed out of her palanquin. "Not especially."

"I want to hear all about it." Grandmother's eyes sparkled with eagerness. "Come inside."

They sat in the tent, where the old woman served murky soup that reeked of onions, fermented fish, and vinegar. Reiko said, "None for me, thank you," and described her attempt to pump Lady Ogyu about her husband and the murders.

"Well, you really flubbed your chance," her grandmother said. "You should have been more subtle."

"Like you?" Reiko couldn't resist saying.

Her grandmother waggled a finger at Reiko. "Now, now, don't be sarcastic, my girl. Was my letter of reference completely wasted?"

"Not completely." Reiko described how she'd eavesdropped on Minister Ogyu and his wife.

"That's exactly what I'd have done. Maybe you did inherit a few of my wits. So what did you hear?"

Reiko related the Ogyus' conversation. "I think the old woman named Kasane may be able to supply the proof that Minister Ogyu is the murderer."

"And you want my help finding out who she is and where she is." Grandmother shook her head. "Can't you do anything without me?"

"I would be very grateful for your assistance," Reiko said humbly.

Grandmother pondered. "Kasane, Kasane. Give me a moment." Reiko imagined the old woman sorting through pages of history stored in her capacious memory, the paper yellowed but the writing still black and clear. "The Ogyu family had a nursemaid named Kasane."

Reiko wasn't surprised that her grandmother knew the servants employed by high-society families. She poached them whenever she fired her own unsatisfactory servants.

"There was something odd," Grandmother went on. "Kasane was

given a yearly income and went to live near relatives in Mitake. It must have been more than fifteen years ago."

"That is odd," Reiko said. Usually, longtime servants either were allowed to stay on with the family, which supported them in their old age, or were cast off to fend for themselves. It was a rare, benevolent employer who let a servant go her own way on his payroll.

"So." Grandmother gave Reiko a smug look that proclaimed her own superiority and Reiko's indebtedness to her. "Hadn't you better go home and prepare for the trip?"

AFTER HE FINISHED exchanging respects with the officials who'd welcomed him back to court, whether they were glad to see him or not, Yanagisawa entered the guesthouse and headed toward the shogun's chambers. He'd been away too long. How superfluous he'd made himself, how vulnerable! But he'd needed to let his grief have its way with him so that he could rise again, stronger than ever, when the time came. That time was now. He must fight to reclaim the place that was rightfully his, and here was the first obstacle to surmount.

Ienobu stood in the corridor. His small, hunched figure blocked Yanagisawa's path. His ugly face was twisted with displeasure.

"Greetings, Lord Ienobu." Yanagisawa stopped and bowed.

Ienobu demanded, "What do you think you're doing?"

"I'm going to call on His Excellency." Yanagisawa thought it was too bad he hadn't arranged a fatal "accident" for Ienobu a long time ago. He'd wrongly assumed Ienobu would never crawl out from under his rock.

"But you haven't left your house in almost a year." Ienobu had apparently thought that grief had done Yanagisawa in and he needn't worry about competition from the shogun's old friend. "You've taken no interest in *my uncle*." He emphasized his relationship to the shogun. "Or in government business."

"That's all changed." Yanagisawa smiled at Ienobu's vexation. He advanced down the corridor, forcing Ienobu to shuffle backward. "You have only yourself to blame." If not for Ienobu's order to leave the capital, Yanagisawa might still be lying in bed, a threat to no one.

"You mustn't bother my uncle," Ienobu protested. "He doesn't want to see anybody."

"He'll see me." Yanagisawa kept going, with feigned confidence. How would the shogun take his sudden reappearance?

"You had better get your affairs in order for your trip to your new post in Tosa Province," Ienobu said, shuffling faster. "You're supposed to leave in a few days."

Yanagisawa snorted. That this grotesque insect thought to dispense with him so easily! "I'm not going."

"My uncle ordered you to go. You have to obey."

"We both know who those orders really came from." Yanagisawa jabbed his finger at Ienobu as he bore down on him. "I don't obey *you*."

Ienobu stopped with his back against the closed door to the shogun's chambers. "You can't go in there." His eyes bulged with his fear that Yanagisawa would undo his efforts to secure his place as heir to the dictatorship.

"Who's to stop me?" Yanagisawa said.

"Guards!" Ienobu called. Two soldiers came. "Take this trespasser outside."

Yanagisawa gave the guards a look that concentrated the power of his personality, that bespoke his reputation as a man to be feared. "You're dismissed. Leave."

The guards went. Yanagisawa said to Ienobu, "Step aside."

Furious yet impotent, Ienobu obeyed.

A victory always energized Yanagisawa, and this first one over Ienobu reassured him that he hadn't lost his touch. But his heart raced as he entered the room, shut the door behind him, and approached the shogun, who lay on cushions on the dais with his eyes closed. Two pages hovered. Yanagisawa shot them a glance; they tiptoed from the room. This might be the most important conversation he'd ever had. He waited, tense with nerves.

"Who's there?" the shogun said.

"It's I," Yanagisawa said.

Surprise fluttered the shogun's eyes open. "Yanagisawa-*san*?" He sat up, squinting in disbelief, then smiled. "You're back!" He held out his hand to Yanagisawa. "Ahh, it's good to see you again!"

He'd obviously forgotten that he'd ever been upset with Yanagisawa, ever demoted him. Yanagisawa breathed easier. He mounted the steps to the dais, knelt, and took the shogun's soft, moist hand. That quickly he was back where he belonged.

"Where have you been?" the shogun asked. "Why did you leave me for so long?"

"I was in mourning for Yoritomo." Yanagisawa's voice cracked.

"Who?" The shogun frowned in confusion, then said, "Ahh, yes, your son."

Yanagisawa felt hot outrage roil inside him. Yoritomo had been the shogun's lover for nine years. He'd died trying to save the shogun's life, and the shogun barely remembered who he was! Yanagisawa compressed his lips in a tight, false smile. He reminded himself that he'd always known how selfish and callous the shogun was and that he'd often taken advantage of it. He warned himself that losing his temper would get him in trouble, which Ienobu would love.

"I'm here now," he said. "Ready to serve Your Excellency."

He hated having to suck up to the shogun. Someday he wouldn't have to anymore. When that day came, he would be safe at the top of the regime.

"Well, ahh, I'm glad. So many, ahh, terrible things have happened. The earthquake, and all the problems. I'm at my, ahh, wit's end." The shogun clung to Yanagisawa's hand. "But now that you're here, I feel better. You'll tell me what to do, won't you?"

Yanagisawa's smile turned genuine. "Oh, I certainly will."

The door scraped open. Ienobu poked his head into the room. Trust him to intrude when things were going so well, Yanagisawa thought with annoyance.

"Nephew, I don't need you now," the shogun said. "My old friend Yanagisawa is back."

An angry flush worsened Ienobu's looks. He started to withdraw, but Yanagisawa said, "Wait a moment." Ienobu froze, suspicious. "Your nephew sent me an order stamped with your signature seal," Yanagisawa told the shogun. "It said I'm supposed to leave Edo and take up a new post in Tosa Province. Is that what you want?"

"What? For you to leave?" The shogun shook his head, bewildered and dismayed. "No." He clung harder to Yanagisawa.

"Then you rescind the order?" Yanagisawa asked.

"Yes, of course!" The shogun waggled his finger at Ienobu. "Never again take the liberty of acting on my behalf without asking me! Now leave us in peace."

"Yes, Honorable Uncle." Ienobu cast a venomous glance at Yanagisawa.

Yanagisawa smiled. Ienobu shut the door harder than necessary. Yanagisawa said to the shogun, "I have good news for you."

"Really?" the shogun said eagerly. "I could use some good news, to make up for all the, ahh, bad things that have been happening."

"There's a very handsome, charming young man that I think you would like," Yanagisawa said. "His name is Yoshisato. I'll introduce you to him, if I may."

Interest brightened the shogun's eyes. "Indeed you may. Bring him soon." He hauled himself to his feet, using Yanagisawa's hand as a support. "I have to go to the Place of Relief. Masahiro, come help me."

Yanagisawa was startled to see the boy step out of the shadows in the corner. It was Sano's son. He was taller than when Yanagisawa had seen him—almost a man. He'd been there all along, heard the entire conversation. Yanagisawa inwardly cursed his own obliviousness. He would have to be more alert.

The shogun leaned on Masahiro's arm. Masahiro accompanied him toward the door that led to his inner chamber. Yanagisawa studied the boy through narrowed eyes. Sano was responsible for Yoritomo's death. Sano's own son was still alive. Yanagisawa seethed with envy and hatred.

Masahiro looked over his shoulder at Yanagisawa. His gaze was sharp, intelligent. He was so much like Sano! Yanagisawa had to exert all his self-control to keep himself from killing Masahiro. He rose and walked out of the chamber. Ienobu was waiting for him in the corridor.

"I know what you're up to." Ienobu was so agitated that he looked like a swatted fly trying to flap its smashed wings. "You're trying to put your other son in the shogun's bed. You want to make him the shogun's heir and yourself the father of the next dictator!"

"That sounds like a good plan," Yanagisawa said smoothly. "Thank you for suggesting it."

Ienobu pointed a shaking, withered finger at Yanagisawa. "Mock me if you want. Your plan won't work. It might have with Yoritomo. He had Tokugawa blood; he was eligible for the succession. This one doesn't. He can never be shogun."

Here lay the flaw in Yanagisawa's plan. Trust Ienobu to point it out.

"But I am a Tokugawa." Ienobu thumped his concave chest, triumphant. "I'm first in line for the succession. And I won't be pushed out of my rightful place by a bastard of yours who services my uncle."

"'Bastard?'" Yanagisawa laughed. "It takes one to know one." He watched Ienobu turn purple with rage at this reference to his own parentage. "And if you want to inherit the dictatorship, you can't just rest on your Tokugawa blood. You'd better start servicing your uncle. How hard can you suck?"

Ienobu gaped so wide in astonishment that Yanagisawa could see every big tooth in his mouth. He sputtered, "Nobody has ever spoken to me that way!"

"Now somebody has." Yanagisawa strode off.

He regretted his words the moment he was outside the guesthouse. During his time away from court he'd lost too much self-control. He shouldn't have fanned the fire of his enmity with Ienobu. The man wouldn't give up after one failed attempt to get rid of him. Yanagisawa thought of Masahiro and what the boy's closeness to the shogun signified. Sano was undoubtedly using his own son as a spy, and to gain power. Yanagisawa would have to deal with them soon. Striding through the wintry garden, he thought of Yoshisato and cursed under his breath.

His plan to replace Yoritomo with another son who could gain influence with the shogun was all he had. He really needed Yoshisato as a weapon against Ienobu, as a toehold in the future. But what if Yoshisato would never cooperate?

29

HAVING REACHED A dead end in his investigation of Priest Ryuko and Minister Ogyu, Sano worked with General Isogai to prepare the regime for an attack. They organized troop deployments, concentrating soldiers at the castle, leaving a scattered few to patrol the city. They inventoried the arsenal and ordered guns and ammunition placed at strategic locations. They conferred with the engineers and arranged the construction of emergency fortifications. Repair of buildings was postponed while craftsmen and laborers shored up the castle's ruined defenses. As evening fell, Sano and General Isogai stood in a watchtower and surveyed the results.

Gaps in the broken wall around the highest level of the hill had been filled in with stone-covered earth to create a barrier around the shogun, his family, his top officials, valuables, arsenal, and food supply. Lights shone on the lower levels, where army squadrons were stationed. But the castle was still far from impenetrable.

"I hate to say it, but the crumbled pavements, landslides, and debris left by the earthquake are the best deterrent to an attack," General Isogai said.

"Any rebels who invade will risk breaking their necks," Sano agreed.

On the one hand, he was glad the *metsuke* had noticed the potential threat from the *daimyo*; on the other, he hoped the regime's shaky defenses would never be put to the test. He felt more pressure than ever to solve the crime and prevent Lord Hosokawa from joining the rebels.

"Here's another thing I hate to say," General Isogai said. "It's not just the Mori, Date, and Maeda clans we have to worry about."

Or the Hosokawa clan, Sano thought. "You're right. If a civil war starts, all the other *daimyo* will take sides. How many will uphold the Tokugawa, and how many join the rebels?"

He and General Isogai exchanged wary glances as they foresaw alliances shifting, the defections that war always involved. Perhaps the next time they looked at each other it would be from different sides of a battlefield.

A guard shone his lantern into the tower. "Honorable Chamberlain, the Council of Elders needs you at an emergency meeting."

Sano was dismayed to hear of another emergency so soon, before he could resume his investigation. He rode to the Council's temporary chamber. Set on a cleared foundation where a wing of the palace had once stood, the chamber was a plank shed large enough to seat a hundred people. Light glowed through chinks in the window shutters. Inside, Sano found the Council occupying a dais improvised from low tables pushed together. Kato Kinhide sat beside Ohgami Kaoru, who was Sano's ally on the Council. Flanking them were the Council's other two members. More officials lined the walls. Sano recognized members of the junior council, judicial council, and department heads. Isolated at the center of the room were two samurai. Bundled in winter garments, they warmed their hands at a brazier. The assembly's expressions were deadly solemn.

Ohgami spoke. "The scouts we sent to inspect the provinces have returned to give their report." He gestured toward the two samurai.

Sano knelt opposite them. "What did you see?"

Soldiers in their twenties, they looked as if they'd aged ten years during the month since they'd left on their inspection tour. Their hollow eyes contained hellish memories. Sano felt dread trickle through his blood.

"It's bad," one scout, named Horibei, finally said. His route had taken him west, along the Tōkaidō, the highway that led to the imperial capital in Miyako. "In Odawara, the town and castle were almost completely destroyed by earthquake and fire. Twenty or thirty thousand people died. In Hakone, there were about four hundred casualties." He related more death tolls and the sights he'd seen in other towns—mass cremations, mass graves, survivors maimed, homeless, and suffering from disease and starvation.

Sano had hoped that the earthquake zone had been confined to Edo and its near environs.

"It's bad along the coast, too," said the other scout, Hazama, who'd surveyed the provinces that encircled Edo Bay. "A tsunami came ashore after the earthquake. It washed away entire villages in Awa, Kazusa, and Shimosa provinces. In some places all we found were bodies on the beaches. The waves moved up the rivers far inland. Hundreds of people drowned in floods."

The devastation was much bigger than Sano or anyone else had suspected. "How many dead, total?"

"It's hard to estimate," Horibei said. "Town officials were killed. Hundreds of missing people are unaccounted for. Records were burned. Huge areas haven't been searched yet."

"Maybe ninety percent of the people along the Edo Bay coast died," said Hazama.

"The death toll across the earthquake zone could be as high as a hundred thousand," Elder Ohgami said.

The number was too vast for Sano's mind to encompass. It approached the death toll from Edo's Great Fire forty-six years ago. Sano had never imagined a comparable disaster occurring during his lifetime. Everyone was silent. Wet streaks glistened on the stoic faces of the men around him, tears impossible to restrain.

"Does the shogun know about this?" Sano asked

"No," Ohgami said. "The Council has decided he shouldn't be told."

"We're afraid he couldn't stand the shock," Kato said, for once in agreement with his rival.

Here was another secret for Sano to keep from the shogun.

Kato said to the assembly, "What you've heard in this room tonight is not to be repeated outside. Is that understood?"

Everyone murmured in assent.

"Good," Ohgami said. "Now we must decide what to do about the provinces."

Men sat silent, their heads bowed, already sagging under the weight of their duties. Although half dead from exhaustion himself, Sano had to accept the responsibility for organizing a relief effort.

"We'll bring supplies to the survivors," he said. "That means sending a team of men to buy food and building materials and hire workers from areas that weren't affected by the earthquake. The team will have to include oxcart drivers, and troops to guard the money and shipments. And laborers to clear the roads along the way. And carpenters to build new bridges." With each item he added, Sano realized anew how impossible the job sounded.

"We'll have to provide food and tents and fuel for the men while they're traveling," Ohgami said. "They can't count on finding enough to eat, or places to sleep, until they're out of the earthquake zone."

"The team needs competent men, and a leader," Kato said. "Whom can we send that's not needed here?"

No one answered. Every able-bodied, intelligent person had already been pressed into service. Ohgami said, "Each of you, come up with a list of names by tomorrow morning. We'll reconvene then and start putting the team together."

Sano had to find the money to provision the team, and he saw another problem. "The situation in the provinces can't be kept a secret for much longer—not with that many other people having to be told what's happening."

"Maybe by the time the news has to come out, the shogun will be in better shape to receive it," Ohgami said with scant optimism.

WHEN SANO ARRIVED home, the sentry told him, "Lord Hosokawa is here to see you."

Sano's heart sank even though he'd thought it had already hit bottom. He went to the makeshift reception chamber, which had once been an office. Lord Hosokawa knelt there. A tray beside him held empty dishes, a cup half filled with tea, and dirty chopsticks. Sano's servants had fed him dinner. Lord Hosokawa regarded Sano with a mixture of anticipation and menace. He said, "I've been waiting for you all afternoon."

"Thank you for your patience." Sano got a firm grip on his own patience.

"Have you identified my daughters' killer yet?"

"No. I'm sorry." Sano had to remind himself once again that the man was a grieving father, single-minded in his need for vengeance.

The anticipation in Lord Hosokawa's eyes winked out like a snuffed lamp flame to be replaced by anger. "Can you at least tell me who the suspects are?"

Sano had to tell him something, and he was under too much stress to be tactful. "One is Madam Usugumo. Another is her apprentice, a young man named Korin. There are also your daughters."

"My daughters? What nonsense is this?"

"It's not nonsense, it's logic. Your daughters were at the incense game. One of them could have mixed the poison into the incense. I have to consider them suspects."

"Why would they do such a thing?"

"They hated each other, didn't they?" Sano said. "They'd been rivals all their life, just as their mothers are. Myobu married the man Kumoi loved, and adopted the child that Kumoi bore him out of wedlock. It seemed possible that one sister had tried to kill the other."

Lord Hosokawa appeared mortified as well as furious. "You investigated my family."

"My investigation wouldn't be thorough if I hadn't."

"Who told you our private business?" Lord Hosokawa demanded.

"My sources are confidential." Sano wasn't going to throw the maid—or Reiko—into the fire of Lord Hosokawa's wrath.

"You have to tell me. You're working for me."

Sano stood his ground even though it was thin ice. "You coerced me into solving the murder because I'm the expert, not you. I'm likelier to succeed if you let me do my job instead of criticizing the way I do it."

Lord Hosokawa nodded reluctantly. "What other suspects are there?"

"Their identities are still confidential." Sano wouldn't throw Mizutani, Minister Ogyu, or Priest Ryuko into the fire, either, until he was sure whether one was guilty.

"I'm warning you, Honorable Chamberlain." Anger tightened Lord Hosokawa's lips.

Sano's temper snapped. "And I'm warning you. Do you think I don't know that your friends are gathering their troops in Edo? Do you think the *metsuke*, and the army, and the shogun don't know?" He was gratified to see concern on Lord Hosokawa's face. "I managed to keep General Isogai from going on the attack, but I don't know how long I can hold him off. So make your friends be discreet. No more parading in battle formation. Or you'll find yourself fighting in a civil war whether you really want to or not."

Lord Hosokawa sagged a little, as if Sano's words had punctured him and let out the hot wind of his rage. But he said, "I will fight in a civil war unless you keep your part of our bargain. You'd better have more progress to report when I come back tomorrow."

Sano thought of everything he had to do tomorrow. "That's too soon." He wished he could tell Lord Hosokawa about the situation in the provinces and the necessity of a relief effort. "My investigation will have to be postponed for a few days."

"No. I won't allow it." Lord Hosokawa rose.

"Be reasonable!" Sano's voice was harsh with frustration.

Lord Hosokawa shook his head.

"You've forced me to compromise my honor and my duty to the shogun," Sano said, his anger turning cold and deadly. "You won't get away with it. There will come a day when you'll be at my mercy."

Lord Hosokawa gave a desolate chuckle. "So be it. But if you don't solve the murder, that day will never come."

A KNOCK ON his door woke Yanagisawa. He called through his quilt, "What is it?"

"There's a woman here to see you," his guard said.

"It's late," Yanagisawa said, groggy and vexed. "Find out who she is and what she wants and tell me in the morning."

A shrill, furious voice shouted, "Come out, damn you!"

Yanagisawa sat up in surprise. "Someko?" His sons' mothers never came to his house. They had strict orders to communicate with him only via messengers.

"Yes! I have to talk to you!"

Something was seriously wrong. She hated him so much that she would never, under ordinary circumstances, seek him out. He climbed out of bed, threw on his coat. The instant he emerged from the house, Someko flew at him like a rabid bat. Her face was stark white in the light of the lantern that his guard held, her beauty distorted by anger.

"This is all your fault!" She waved a scroll container at his face.

"Hey!" Yanagisawa ducked. "What's my fault?"

"Why couldn't you leave us alone?" She pummeled him with the scroll container. Yanagisawa grabbed her wrists. She dropped the container and broke down sobbing. "We were all right until you came. Now my son is going to die!"

Alarmed, Yanagisawa demanded, "What are you talking about? What's happened?"

Someko sagged to her knees. She pointed at the scroll container that lay on the snow-glazed ground. "That!"

Yanagisawa picked up the black lacquer container, opened it, and unfurled a scroll. The guard shone the lantern on the columns of elegant black calligraphy and the shogun's signature seal at the bottom. Yanagisawa read aloud,

Yanagisawa Yoshisato, you are accused of plotting to assassinate His Excellency the Shogun. You are hereby ordered to stand trial for treason. A special tribunal has been created, which will conduct your trial the day after tomorrow. Troops will be sent to escort you to the trial. If you attempt to flee, you will be hunted and killed on sight.

Shock stunned Yanagisawa. "When did this come?"

"This evening." Someko shot to her feet and focused her streaming, furious eyes on him. "I don't know what you did, but you must have done something. Nobody ever bothered about Yoshisato before."

Yanagisawa knew. He'd made his reappearance at court; he'd drawn attention to his sons by visiting them. There must be spies in their house. Fury boiled up in him as he realized who was responsible for everything in this document.

"Now he's going to be convicted of treason!" Someko shrilled. Virtually all trials ended in conviction. "He's going to die!" And treason was a capital offense. "Damn you to hell!"

Yanagisawa smelled Ienobu all over this. Ienobu was ruthless enough to eliminate Yoshisato before Yanagisawa could use him as a political tool. Ienobu had trumped up the treason charge, had created the tribunal, had connived for the shogun's approval. Ienobu also wanted revenge on Yanagisawa for insulting him this morning.

"Damn the bastard!" Yanagisawa crumpled the document and hurled it to the ground. He wasn't upset only on his own account. Against his will, he'd begun to care about his hostile, angry son.

"Oh, so your enemies are attacking you through Yoshisato." Always clever, Someko comprehended the situation. She let loose a spate of mocking laughter. "Look at you! Your flesh and blood is about to be condemned as a traitor, and you'll go down with him." Close associates of a traitor shared his punishment. That was the law. "And all you can do is lose your temper like a little boy!"

"Shut up!" Yanagisawa couldn't bear for her to rub his frustration in his face.

"But I'm right, aren't I?" Her mockery dissolved into more tears. "Yoshisato will be put to death, and there's nothing you can do to save him."

"No!" Yanagisawa spoke with all the force of his refusal to admit defeat. "There is."

"Merciful gods, what?" Someko said, hopeful and pleading now. "How can you save Yoshisato?"

Yanagisawa's mind never worked faster or better than when he was threatened. Inspiration struck now. "I have a plan. But it depends on Yoshisato. He would have to work with me."

Someko's face crumpled in despair. "He doesn't even want to see you. I begged him to come with me, to ask for your protection, but he refused. He says he can take care of himself."

Incredulous, Yanagisawa said, "How does he think he's going to do that?"

"He says he'll convince the tribunal that he's innocent."

Yanagisawa combined a laugh with a groan. The tribunal's verdict was already decided; nothing Yoshisato said would change it. "I'll make him see reason."

30

WIND BLEW ASH and litter through the deserted streets outside the temporary Edo Jail. Dogs scrounged in garbage piles that had accumulated along the wall. Dozing sentries crouched at the gate. The jail was quiet, except for occasional moans from prisoners.

The sound of hoofbeats startled the sentries awake. They sprang up to face two mounted samurai. One of these said, "We're here to fetch a prisoner named Korin."

"What for?" asked a sentry.

"Who are you?" asked the other.

The two samurai wore helmets with visors shading their eyes and face guards covering their noses and mouths. The Tokugawa crest was painted on the breastplates of their armor tunics. The spokesman said, "We have orders from the shogun."

The sentries looked at each other; they shrugged. One opened the gate. The other said, "I'll help you find your man."

Inside the prison, Korin lay curled up alone in his tent. He drowsed, glad to be alive. His tent mates had been taken away and executed; three other men had died of illness today. He could hear more prisoners tossing and groaning. Korin grinned, thinking that once again he'd dodged misfortune. His mother used to tell him he must have done something good in a past life, because he didn't deserve to be so lucky. As a boy, he'd been in one scrape after another and always got away unharmed. He'd shoplifted from market stalls, been chased by the police, and managed to escape. When he'd worked as a tout for the brothels, he'd overcharged the customers and pocketed the difference without his employers ever knowing. He'd cheated at cards many times before he'd gotten caught. Chances were, he would get out of his present trouble, too.

Heavy footsteps stopped outside the tent. A rough voice called his name. "Get up!"

The voice belonged to one of the guards. Korin looked outside and saw two soldiers. The guard said to them, "He's all yours."

The soldiers beckoned him. Korin knew there was only one place they could be taking him—the execution ground. Fear stabbed his heart. "No!" he cried, shrinking from them. "Please!"

They hauled him out of the tent as he struggled. "I promise I'll never cheat anybody again! I swear!" The soldiers forced him to walk through the prison yard. "Help!" he shrieked. "Don't let them take me!" Wild with terror, he thrashed. The men twisted his arms. Faces peered out of tents; patrolling guards paused to watch; no one came to Korin's aid. His undeserved good luck had run out. Now he would pay for all his sins.

He would join Madam Usugumo in the special hell reserved for criminals, where they both belonged.

As the soldiers propelled him along, one whispered in his ear: "We're rescuing you. If you want to live, then come peacefully."

Surprise choked off Korin's screams. He looked up at the soldier. "What?"

"No questions," hissed the soldier. "Just be patient."

Korin ceased resisting. His cocky grin returned. He didn't care who these men were or why they would bother to break a lowly crook like him out of jail. He couldn't afford to wonder where they were taking him or what would happen to him there. Now he wouldn't have his head cut off for cheating at cards. Now Chamberlain Sano couldn't put the blame for Madam Usugumo's murder on him. His miraculous luck was still holding!

Fairly dancing out the gate with his escorts, Korin called over his shoulder, "Good-bye, you poor fools!"

* * *

"YOSHISATO?" SOMEKO CALLED. "I've brought your father."

She and Yanagisawa stood in the corridor outside their son's room. No answer came through the paper-and-lattice wall, but Someko said, "He's there. Go in."

Braced for another rejection, Yanagisawa entered the chamber, shut the door behind him, and faced Yoshisato. The young man stood in the center of the floor. He had the awkward stance of someone who'd risen too hastily. He looked shocked.

"I didn't think you would come," he said.

Yanagisawa detected gratitude in his son's voice. That gave him hope. "Of course I came. As soon as I heard about the order you received."

"Why did you?"

"Because you're my son, and you're in trouble. And because I want to help." Yanagisawa watched the fierce independence in Yoshisato resist his need to put his troubles in the hands of a father who would protect him. Yanagisawa admired Yoshisato's strength. He realized that however much he'd loved Yoritomo, he'd never admired his favorite son; he'd always thought of Yoritomo as weak, not especially clever, and too submissive.

"Oh, I see." Scorn twisted Yoshisato's mouth. "To advance your political schemes, you need a son, and you found my half brothers lacking. So you can't have me condemned as a traitor. And if I go down for treason, so do you. You wouldn't like that."

Again, Yanagisawa realized that Yoshisato's affection wouldn't be easily won. He resisted his tendency to use charm and glib words to get what he wanted. "I'll be honest with you. I do need you to further my schemes, and I don't want to die." He saw Yoshisato's eyes narrow. "But that's not the only reason I want to save you. I think you're a man who's worth saving." He was embarrassed to say something so personal and true, afraid it would meet with derision. "As a matter of fact, you're one of the few men I've ever known who is."

Yoshisato stared, astonished by the genuine esteem in Yanagisawa's words. He took a step toward Yanagisawa, then stopped. "Then you must have more talent for making enemies than friends. Which of your enemies is attacking me to get at you? Is it Chamberlain Sano?"

"No," Yanagisawa said, surprised that Yoshisato had gleaned more information about politics than he'd expected of such a sheltered youth.

But then Yoshisato was his son. Politics ran in Yoshisato's blood. "It's Lord Ienobu."

"The shogun's nephew." Yoshisato sounded appalled. "You've gotten us into a real mess, haven't you?"

His disapproval stung, but at least he now appreciated the seriousness of his predicament. "Yes," Yanagisawa said, "Ienobu is a powerful enemy. That's why I don't want to hear you say that you don't need my help and you're going to convince the tribunal that you're innocent. That's not only foolishness; it's suicide."

Frowning at the harsh words, Yoshisato said, "Well, then, how do you think you're going to save me? Can you get the order rescinded? Or make the tribunal acquit me?"

Once the shogun had signed an accusation of treason—no matter whether he'd been manipulated into it—he couldn't rescind it without losing face. Yanagisawa hadn't yet regained enough influence to convince the shogun that losing face to save Yoshisato wasn't so bad. He also had no authority over Ienobu's judges. To think that he'd once been the most powerful man at court! Yanagisawa regretted those lost, glorious days.

"No," he said. "I can't."

"Just as I thought." Yoshisato looked disappointed, but smug because he'd correctly assessed the situation. "So I might as well defend myself in front of the tribunal. Because there's nothing else to do but go down fighting." He squared his shoulders, held his head high. Yanagisawa ached with pride in him. "When I'm convicted, I'll be ready to commit *seppuku*." He added, with a touch of sardonic humor, "You'd better be ready, too."

Nettled because he didn't want Yoshisato to think him so impotent, Yanagisawa said, "Don't sharpen your sword just yet. There's another way to get you out of this."

"How?" Yoshisato regarded him with hope tainted by suspicion.

"If you could win the shogun's favor before the trial—"

Yoshisato uttered a sound of repugnance. "I don't like sex with men. I'd rather die."

Yanagisawa admired Yoshisato for standing up for himself, as Yoritomo never had. "I'm not asking you to become the shogun's concubine. I have a plan that's far better." He beckoned Yoshisato.

Yoshisato took another step toward him, as if irresistibly drawn, then stopped.

"I don't want anyone else to hear this yet," Yanagisawa said. "Not even your mother, who I'm sure has her ear to the wall."

Reluctant, Yoshisato moved closer. Yanagisawa whispered into his ear.

As soon as Yanagisawa finished speaking, Yoshisato recoiled. Stunned wordless, he gaped at Yanagisawa.

"Well?" Yanagisawa said, gratified by his son's reaction yet uncertain about what it boded. "Are you going to cooperate?"

Yoshisato sputtered, then asked, "Do you really mean to go through with this?"

"Can you think of a better idea?"

Shaking his head, in awe as well as in reply, Yoshisato chuckled. "I underestimated you, Father."

"Many have." Yanagisawa noticed that this was the first time Yoshisato had verbally accepted their kinship. It warmed his heart even though Yoshisato had spoken with grudging respect rather than fondness. "My plan depends on you. Are you with me or not?"

Yoshisato bit his lip and frowned. Yanagisawa could feel the pressure on him: This was the first adult decision he'd had to make. "I'm with you," Yoshisato said with a smile that was half wry, half malicious. "What have I got to lose?"

WHEN SANO RETURNED home, he was so tired he thought that if he closed his eyes for too long when he blinked, he would fall asleep on his feet. If only he could keep moving, one foot after another, long enough to reach his bed before he collapsed.

The damaged mansion looked lonely and inhospitable amid the ruins of the barracks. With the crisscrossed beams that supported the veranda roof, the entrance resembled a giant cage. Shadowy forms of wild, restless animals moved behind the bars. More creatures roamed the surrounding darkness. Sano realized he was dreaming; he roused himself. While he plodded toward the building, the door opened. There stood a small figure. It was Akiko.

Sano's heart lifted as he climbed the steps. Taking her hand, he said, "What are you doing up so late?"

"I wanted to see you." Akiko hopped up and down on the veranda. Her feet were bare.

"Let's go inside before your poor toes freeze." Sano heard a clatter as something hit the floorboards near him, then running footsteps in the distance. He looked down and saw a lumpy object the size of a small melon. A yellow flame sizzled at one end.

"What's that?" Akiko stooped to pick up the object.

A danger signal blared through Sano. He yanked Akiko away from the object and gave it a swift, hard kick off the veranda. It flew through the railings and exploded in midair.

Akiko screamed. The blast hit Sano like thunderclaps against his ears. He caught Akiko up and whirled her around to shield her from the hot, orange fireball that seared his eyes. The blast hurled him and Akiko against the house. He felt sharp, piercing sensations, like arrows striking his back, and Akiko's screams vibrating through her body. The house shuddered. Blinded and dazed, Sano smelled fire, smoke, and sulfurous, acrid gunpowder; he heard creaking and rumbling noises. The supports holding up the roof were coming down. Timbers clubbed his back. Sano shielded Akiko with his body as he fell. A post struck his head with a tremendous bang, and everything went dark.

SHRILL SCREAMING AWAKENED Sano. Brutal pain throbbed on the right side of his head. His whole body ached. Moaning, he opened his eyes. Grit stung them. Warm liquid flowed onto his face, which was pressed against the hard surface where he lay. He tried to move, but heavy weights across his back and limbs pinned him down. He knew something bad had happened, but he couldn't remember what.

Underneath him, someone wriggled and screamed. Akiko. Memory resurged. The bomb. The explosion. Thank the gods she was alive!

Sano became conscious of urgent voices clamoring, Reiko frantically calling his name and their daughter's. Lanterns bathed him in light. Weights lifted off him. Sano groaned, in relief because he could move his arms and legs. Unseen hands cleared away the beams, planks, and roof tiles that covered him and Akiko. She crawled out from under him, jumped up, and cried, "Mama!"

Reiko knelt beside him, hugging Akiko. Her face was terror-stricken as she bent, touched his face, and cried, "Speak to me!"

"I'm all right." Dust caked Sano's mouth. He knew Reiko must have been in the house during the explosion. "Are you?"

"Yes." Reiko called to the guards who'd lifted the wreckage off Sano. "He's bleeding! Fetch a doctor!"

"Akiko?" His first concern was for her.

"She's fine," Reiko said. "Not even a scratch on her, that I can see."

Sano rolled onto his back. Pain stabbed him as if he lay on a bed of flints. The movement worsened the ache in his head, which pounded violently. He was so dizzy that he felt as if he were sliding sideways. Nausea assailed him. He could see the night sky: The roof over the veranda was gone. When he moved his eyes, the stars smeared white streaks across his vision. His stomach heaved. Turning his head away from Reiko and Akiko, he vomited.

Reiko made soothing noises, wiped his face. Detective Marume said, "Let's bring him inside." He carefully lifted Sano's shoulders. A guard lifted his legs. They carried Sano into the building, which had survived the explosion. They lowered him onto the bed in the family's chamber. Sano lay on his left side because his head didn't hurt there and his back was too sore. Eyes closed, he listened to people tramping around outside and speculating about the explosion. The doctor arrived, spoke to Reiko, and made clattering noises with his equipment. Sano heard Akiko protest as Reiko handed her over to the nursemaid. As the doctor cleaned the wound on Sano's shaved crown, Reiko murmured in consternation.

"This is a bad gash," the doctor said. "It will require stitches."

He held an ice pack over Sano's scalp to numb it, then began sewing. Sano clenched his teeth against the pricks of the needle and the tugging of the thread. Then the doctor set to work on Sano's back. He picked out particles that the blast had driven into the flesh and washed the cuts. Sano winced at the sting of alcohol. After the doctor applied an herb poultice to the cuts and bandaged them, the dizziness and nausea abated enough for Sano to open his eyes. The doctor held his hand in front of them and said, "How many fingers do you see?"

Sano's vision was blurry. "Two," he guessed.

"Just as I suspected," the doctor said. "You have a concussion."

"What does that mean?" Reiko asked anxiously.

"His brain was jarred inside his skull."

"Will he be all right?"

"Yes, if he rests in bed for a few days." The doctor held a cup near Sano's mouth and placed a bamboo straw between his lips. "Drink this. It will ease the pain and help you sleep."

The sweet wine, astringent herbs, and bitter opium made Sano gag, but the pain soon dulled and drowsy warmth spread through his body.

"I'll leave medicine for you to take later," the doctor said before he left.

Masahiro came running into the room. "Father, are you all right?"

"Yes." Sano felt weak and helpless. He hated to worry his family.

"Can you tell us what happened?" Reiko asked.

Sano described the events that had preceded the explosion. "It was a bomb. Someone threw it onto the veranda. I heard him running away."

"I heard a loud bang," Reiko said. "I thought it was a gun."

"So did I," Masahiro said. "I heard it in the shogun's house."

Detective Marume entered the room. "I found these in the wreckage." He held out his hand. On his palm were small, curved, sharp ceramic fragments—the remains of the bomb, the container that had been filled with gunpowder.

Another memory surfaced in Sano's mind. "I felt something lurking outside. It must have been the person who threw the bomb. But I thought I was dreaming. I was so tired."

"I have men searching the area," Marume said.

"He's probably long gone." Sano pounded the bed with his fist, angry at his negligence. "I should have investigated!"

"Never mind," Reiko said, although visibly shaken by their close call. "Let's just be glad you're going to be all right."

Sano was newly aware of how vulnerable they were without the walls that had once enclosed them. He said to Marume, "Put guards around the house day and night. And up the hill to watch from above."

"I've already done it," Marume said.

"Who threw the bomb?" Masahiro asked.

"I don't know," Sano said, "but I have an idea."

"Maybe Yanagisawa is up to his old tricks," Reiko said.

"Maybe," Sano said. "He's back. He put in an appearance at court today."

"I saw him," Masahiro said. "He's made friends with the shogun again. Ienobu didn't like it."

Sano thought of Ienobu, and Kato Kinhide, and other men he'd clashed with, who would like to see him gone. "But I don't think it's a coincidence that this happened while I'm investigating the murders."

"Could it have been one of the suspects, trying to prevent you from finding out that he's guilty?" Reiko said.

"One of the suspects or somebody associated with one of them," Sano said.

"It couldn't have been Madam Usugumo or Lord Hosokawa's daughters," Masahiro said. "They're dead."

"I'm fairly certain that it wasn't Mizutani, the incense master," Sano said. "He's a commoner. He doesn't have access to the castle."

"The same applies to Korin the apprentice," Reiko said. "Besides, he's in jail."

"That leaves Priest Ryuko and Minister Ogyu," Masahiro said.

Something good had come out of the bombing, Sano thought. It had whittled down the list of suspects.

"I bet it's Priest Ryuko," Masahiro said. "I found out something about him today. I wanted to tell you earlier, but I couldn't get away from the shogun." He described how he'd spied on Ryuko and learned that the man was planning a journey. "Maybe he decided to kill you so he wouldn't have to leave."

"I wouldn't put it past him," Sano said. "He's not feeling too friendly toward me."

"Is he bold enough to try to kill you?" Reiko wondered. "I've never heard anything about him to indicate that he would resort to violence."

"Everyone has the capacity to resort to violence." Sano considered his wife, his son, and himself. All of them had killed, albeit in self-defense or in defense of each other or someone else. Maybe Priest Ryuko had been desperate enough to forsake his Buddhist vow to protect all forms of life. "I'd better find out where he's going."

"You'd better not do anything but rest," Reiko warned.

Because of the medicine, Sano felt little pain, but he was too drowsy to argue that he couldn't postpone the investigation without angering Lord Hosokawa. "Did you learn anything about Minister Ogyu?"

"I did," Reiko said. "The whereabouts of his old nurse, who knows his secret."

Sano drifted off to sleep during her explanation.

31

DAWN FOUND HIRATA riding his horse along the coast of Edo Bay. The quiet ocean rippled with little waves, like shirred silk. Thin clouds laced the pale blue sky; sunlight gilded the sand where the tide had melted the snow. Seabirds wheeled overhead, swooped down, and flocked at the water's edge. A whale spouted offshore. But the natural beauty couldn't lighten the darkness inside Hirata. For the first time in longer than he could recall, he had no duties to perform. Sano was investigating the murders without him. The freedom was sobering, humiliating. He felt as useless as a samurai in battle without his swords.

Before leaving town yesterday, he'd planted the letter in Ienobu's room. He already regretted it. Ienobu was sure to show up in the garden at the designated hour, and Sano was safe for the time being, but Hirata dreaded the consequences of his actions.

Last night he'd camped in the woods above the beach. After securing his horse and covering it with blankets, he'd collected sticks, built a fire, and eaten pounded rice cakes, dried fish, and hot tea. Then he'd wrapped himself in a quilt and performed the breathing and meditation exercise that would warm his blood while he slept. Now, as he continued his journey, he noticed something strange.

He'd been to these parts before, but he saw nothing he recognized. The ocean had taken huge bites out of the land. The road was buried under mud and uprooted trees. Where fishing villages had stood, debris littered the beach and floated on the water. Hirata realized that the earthquake had caused a tsunami, which had washed them away. Broken dishes and furniture, planks and roof tiles covered the sand. Corpses with bones showing through rotted flesh hung in tree branches. A wave tossed up a child's sandal. The cold sea breeze carried the reek of death. Hirata wondered if the government in Edo knew about this. It seemed as if no one here had lived to tell. Hirata felt as if he were the only man on earth. Grieving for the lives lost, he despaired of finding Fuwa, the monk whose name he'd obtained from his acquaintance at the tent camp. If Fuwa hadn't left the coast before the tsunami, surely he'd drowned. But Hirata kept going, past the wreckage of more villages, until he reached the site where Chiba had been. There he perceived a lone human aura, a quiet but strong pulse emanating from above the beach.

On a high, wooded bluff stood a tent made of fabric patterned in green and brown shades. Beside it a man crouched perfectly still. He rose and lifted his hand in greeting. Lean and tall, he had a shaved head and wore the hemp robes of a monk.

"Who goes there?" he called, neither friendly nor hostile.

"My name is Hirata. Are you Fuwa?"

Caution edged Fuwa's aura. "I am. How did you guess?"

"A friend told me you might be here. I came from Edo to talk to you."

"I'll come down."

Hirata dismounted. By the time his feet touched the sand, Fuwa had descended the bluff, stepping on exposed roots and rocks, as easily as if they were stairs, to stand before Hirata. "I've heard of you." His face reminded Hirata of an axe blade. Cheekbones and nose curved outward; forehead and chin receded. It was wider and sharper in profile than from the front. "The best fighter in Edo."

Hirata shrugged off the admiration in Fuwa's glance. "Were you here when the tsunami came?"

Fuwa nodded somberly.

"How did you survive?"

"I hung onto a tree."

"Are you the only person in Chiba who wasn't swept away?"

"There were a few others. They left. Everything they had is gone."

"Why did you stay here?"

216

"Why not?" Amusement twitched the corners of Fuwa's firm mouth. "I'm doing what I would be doing anywhere else."

Itinerant mystic martial artists camped in the wilderness and liked solitude. "Well, I'm glad I found you." Hirata offered up a silent prayer of thanks to the gods.

"Is Edo very badly damaged?" Fuwa asked.

"Very." Hirata described the conditions in the city.

Fuwa looked grave, but all he said was, "What did you come all this way to talk to me about?"

"Some mutual friends. Tahara, Kitano, and Deguchi."

Fuwa turned abruptly away. His axe-blade profile, backlit by the sun on the sea, was sharp and dark. "I don't talk about them."

Enlightenment startled Hirata. "You were in their secret society. They swore you to secrecy."

Fuwa's head snapped around. "You, too?"

"Yes." Hirata had never imagined that the secret society had had another member. "So you can talk to me. We're comrades."

"I'm not in the society anymore." Fuwa strode down the beach, as if he wanted to escape not only Hirata but his past.

Hirata followed. "Did they throw you out?"

"No. I quit."

"I didn't think they let anybody quit." Maybe there was a chance for Hirata to get out alive, too. "How did you?"

"I walked away," Fuwa said. "They weren't in a position to stop me."

"Why not?" Hirata couldn't imagine Tahara, Kitano, and Deguchi being that powerless.

Fuwa halted and faced him. "Why don't you ask them?"

"Because I don't trust them to tell me the truth."

"You don't trust them, but you joined their society anyway?" Fuwa laughed good-naturedly. "Well, I guess we are comrades. We both made the same mistake."

Hirata laughed, too, in relief. "How did you meet them?"

"Why do you want to know?" Fuwa asked, still not ready to share his secrets.

"Because I'm in trouble." Hirata poured out the whole story of his dealings with the men. He described the ritual, showed Fuwa the ghost's orders branded on his arm, and said that Tahara, Deguchi, and Kitano had threatened to kill his master unless he obeyed the ghost.

"Why do you think that anything I say could help?"

"I don't know," Hirata admitted. "I'm just desperate."

Fuwa gave him a long, thoughtful look. "They've left me alone all these years. I doubt if they'll bother me even if I do tell tales on them. They'd probably rather never see me again. But they won't like your knowing things they've hidden from you. It's you they'll punish."

"I'll take that chance," Hirata said, even though the thought of their wrath made the wind off the bay feel colder.

"It's your funeral."

They strolled along the beach together, avoiding wreckage from the drowned village. Fuwa spoke over the slapping of the waves and the cries of the gulls. "I met Tahara, Kitano, and Deguchi ten years ago. I was living in Kamakura." That city was located southwest of Edo. "I'd recently finished my martial arts training, and I was working as a bodyguard for a merchant. I was bored with my job. I had dreams of adventure. One night I was sitting in a teahouse, when Tahara, Deguchi, and Kitano came in. We got to talking. I was impressed to learn that they were disciples of the great Ozuno. My teacher is respected but not as famous. We told stories about our training. They seemed impressed with me. I was flattered. They said they were hunting for a great treasure, and they'd learned it was in Kamakura."

Hirata felt a stir of uneasy premonition. "What was this treasure?"

"An ancient book. More than a thousand years old. From China. They said it contained magic spells for communicating with the spirit world. Whoever did the spells would learn incredible secrets and gain superhuman powers. They said the book belonged to a scholar who'd bought it from a Chinese sorcerer. They were planning to steal it. They asked me to help."

Here was a different version of the story they'd told Hirata. "And you went along?"

"Yes. It sounded like what I'd been waiting for. They said it would be dangerous, we would have to fight for the book. Then we formed a secret society. We swore that we would be loyal to one another and never tell anyone outside about our business. We would share the book and work the magic spells together, and we would become the greatest fighters in the world." Fuwa contemplated the clouds thinning over the sea. "If only I'd known."

Here was the disgraceful origin of the secret society. "What happened?" Dread almost quenched Hirata's desire for the truth.

"That night, we went to the scholar's house, a shack on the edge of town. We sneaked in and found an old man lying asleep in the room, and a knapsack on the floor beside him. Kitano crouched down to open the knapsack, when the old man suddenly sat up. He wasn't some scholar. He was Ozuno. I'd seen him before, and I recognized him. Tahara and Deguchi drew their swords. I drew mine. Ozuno said, 'What are you doing here?' Then he saw Kitano with his hand in the knapsack and he said, " 'Oh, it's the spell book you want. Didn't I forbid you to read it? Didn't I tell you it was too dangerous?'

"Tahara said, 'Yes, that's why we're stealing it.' He raised his sword and started toward Ozuno. Ozuno leaped out of the bed. He had a sword in his hand. Tahara, Kitano, and Deguchi lunged at him. After that, it was all flying blades and shouting and bodies flying, I've never seen anything like it. I didn't join the fight, I couldn't even see who was where. All I could do was lie flat with my arms over my head and pray I didn't get killed.

"It was over in an instant. When I looked up, Tahara and Kitano and Deguchi were lying on the floor. Tahara was unconscious, and blood was pouring out of cuts on his chest and stomach. Deguchi's neck was twisted, and he was clutching his throat and wheezing. Kitano's face was covered with blood, cut up like raw meat."

Hirata was horrified to learn about the men's other lies. "Kitano told me that his face had been injured in a drunken brawl. Tahara said that when Deguchi was a child, working as a prostitute, a customer strangled him and damaged his throat, and that's why he's mute."

Fuwa smiled pityingly. "Whatever else they told you, it's probably not true, either."

"What happened to Ozuno?"

"He had wounds, too, but they were minor. He was still on his feet."

"What did he do to you?" Hirata asked, amazed Fuwa had survived.

"Nothing. He said, 'Whoever you are, get out of here. Don't tell anyone what happened tonight, and don't come near me again, or this is what will happen to you.' He pointed his bloody sword at Tahara, Deguchi, and Kitano. I got up and ran away as fast as I could."

"What happened to them?" Hirata couldn't believe Ozuno had let them live after they'd betrayed him.

"At the time, I figured Ozuno had left them to die. But a few years later, I heard they'd been sighted." Fuwa explained, "I had given up my dreams of adventure. That night was enough adventure for me. I joined a monastery and took my vows. Then I went wandering. I occasionally met other martial artists on the road. One of them told me he'd seen Tahara, Kitano, and Deguchi. I don't know why, but Ozuno had let them go."

Maybe he'd had a soft spot in his heart for the men he'd trained and couldn't bear to kill them, Hirata speculated; or he'd thought they'd learned their lesson.

"One day I ran into them on the street in Miyako. Kitano's face was all scarred, and Deguchi gestured with his hands instead of speaking, but Tahara looked completely normal, and they all seemed as fit as ever." Fuwa sounded perplexed. "I don't know how they did it."

Hirata did. They'd used the same medicines and mystical healing rituals that had helped him regain his health after his injury. Perhaps Ozuno had even doctored the men.

"When they saw me," Fuwa said, "they acted as if they didn't recognize me. I figured they didn't like being reminded of that night."

Puzzlement beset Hirata as he thought of their powers, the rituals. "They managed to get hold of the book. I know they did, I've seen proof. But how?"

Fuwa looked satisfied, as if a matter he'd been wondering about had been resolved. "I had my suspicions, after what happened next. And after what you just said, I figured it out."

"What happened next?" Hirata asked anxiously.

"I was curious about what they were up to. So I secretly followed them. All the way to Nara." That was a city south of Miyako, a sacred center of Buddhism. "I spied on them from outside the inn where they stayed. The next night they rode to a temple. I followed them and waited until they came out, only a few moments. They walked right up to me where I was hiding behind a bush. They'd known all along that I was watching them. Tahara said, 'Forget you saw us. Leave us alone from now on, or you'll be sorry.' Then they rode off. I wanted to know what they'd done, so I stayed put. At dawn I heard a commotion. I went inside the temple and met a servant. I asked what had happened. He said that an old man who'd been staying in the guest cottage had died in the night. I had a bad feeling."

So did Hirata, who remembered that Ozuno had died at a temple in Nara.

"I asked the servant to let me see the dead man," Fuwa said. "I went in the cottage, and there in the bed was Ozuno's body. He was so thin and frail and old compared to the last time I'd seen him. The servant told me he'd been sick."

Ozuno had died in his sleep of natural causes—or so Hirata had heard. He hadn't known that Tahara, Deguchi, and Kitano had been there.

"Then I noticed a cushion on the bed by his head. There was a wet spot on it. I lifted up Ozuno's upper lip and looked in his mouth. The skin was broken. And I knew what had happened."

"They smothered him with the cushion," Hirata said, his voice hushed by shock.

"That's what I figured," Fuwa said. "They waited until they'd recovered from their injuries and built up their strength. By that time Ozuno was sick and weak. Stealing the magic spell book was as easy as taking a toy from a child."

"They said they inherited the book from Ozuno. But they murdered him to get it!" Even though he'd never trusted them, Hirata couldn't believe the extent of their lies. What else had they lied about?

"So now you know what I know," Fuwa said. "What are you going to do?"

32

CROWDED INTO BED with his family, Sano was glad when morning came. The opium had filled his sleep with vivid nightmares of bloody sword battles he'd fought. Masahiro's place in the bed was empty; he'd gone off to attend the shogun. Akiko said, "Mama, I'm hungry."

Reiko said, "I'll get your breakfast," then peered at Sano in the dim light and saw that he was awake. "How is your head?"

"Not as bad," Sano said, "but I could use some more of that medicine before I leave."

Reiko regarded him with concern as she pulled her coat over her night robe and called for a maid to stoke the braziers. "You're not going after Priest Ryuko?"

"I have to." Sano sat up. Dizziness washed over him. His head pounded through a wave of nausea. Reiko's worried face blurred before his eyes.

"But you aren't well enough, I can tell." Reiko urged, "Send Detective Marume. Stay home and rest."

"I'll feel better if I'm busy," Sano said. "I can't just lie here and hope the murder gets solved without me while there's a civil war brewing."

"At least lie down until I bring your medicine and your breakfast," Reiko said as she and Akiko left the room.

Shamed by his frailty, Sano obeyed.

The medicine helped. Soon after he swallowed it, Sano was able to dress and eat, although he still felt shaky. "I'd better start spying on Priest Ryuko before he slips past me."

"And I'd better begin my trip to Mitake to see Minister Ogyu's nurse," Reiko said.

"HERE HE COMES," Sano whispered to Detective Marume. From behind a grove of bamboo outside the guesthouse, they watched Priest Ryuko hurry down the steps. He wore a heavy, hooded cloak over his saffron robe. He climbed into a waiting palanquin. The bearers carried him out the gate.

Sano and Marume, dressed in garments without identifying crests and wide-brimmed wicker hats that shaded their faces, followed on horseback at a safe distance. "If Priest Ryuko is going on a journey, where's his baggage?" Marume asked.

"I don't see the porters he was trying to hire, either. Maybe he's not leaving town after all." Sano hated to think he was wasting time on this surveillance while he could be looking for other leads. "Let's see what happens."

As they rode through the passages inside the castle, his horse's every footfall aggravated his headache. He resisted the temptation to take the opium pills he'd brought, which would dull his mind along with the pain. Priest Ryuko's bearers walked briskly. Sano and Marume mingled with the soldiers and the workers who thronged the passages. Outside the castle, the crowd of beggars on the streets and the roving squadrons of troops in the *daimyo* district shielded Sano and Marume from Ryuko's view. Sano warily eyed the troops. Either Lord Hosokawa hadn't yet warned the *daimyo* not to flaunt their armies or they'd chosen to disregard the warning.

Beyond the *daimyo* district, the crowds thinned. Townspeople crawled over the wreckage of Nihonbashi, picking out wood and paper scraps to burn in their bonfires. The heaps were shrinking. Eventually, all the combustible materials would go up in smoke. Sano and Marume dropped farther behind the palanquin. Past a tent camp, the bearers carried Ryuko to an oasis of houses amid the ruins. Sano and Marume watched from a distance as the priest climbed out of the palanquin. They dismounted and hid their horses behind one of the tall debris piles that dotted the area, which had been an affluent merchant district. Sano's legs felt weak and wobbly. Taking cover behind other piles, he and Marume stole up to the houses.

There were three, flanked by the burned remains of neighboring residences. Peasants armed with spears were stationed at the gates. In many improvised forts like this, the lucky few citizens who still had their homes tried to bar trespassers seeking loot or shelter. Sano and Marume positioned themselves behind a pile some thirty paces from the houses.

Priest Ryuko walked up to the guards, who let him in the gate. Sano waited. His head throbbed. He blinked to focus his eyes on the house. After a long while, a muscular peasant man backed out the gate, carrying one end of a large wooden trunk. A second man followed, holding the other end. The porters dropped the trunk by the palanquin. Priest Ryuko emerged, shepherding a woman and a little boy. The boy was about three years old and so padded with clothing that he looked like a ball, his fat arms sticking out from his sides, a red cap with earflaps on his head. The woman was slender and young. She wore a blue coat whose hood framed a pretty, anxious face. Priest Ryuko led her and the boy to the palanquin and opened its door. He spoke to the woman. Sano couldn't hear his words, but he seemed to be reassuring her. She climbed into the palanquin. Priest Ryuko crouched before the boy. He smiled and said something that made the boy laugh. Then he lifted the boy into the palanquin and settled him beside the woman.

"Priest Ryuko isn't going on the journey," Sano said. "They are."

Sano and Marume strode toward the priest. Ryuko shut the door of the palanquin and turned. His eyes hollowed and his mouth sagged with shock. "What are you doing here?" He moved in front of the palanquin, as if to hide it from Sano's view. "Did you follow me?"

"Yes." Sano peered around Ryuko. The open window of the palanquin framed the woman's and boy's frightened faces. "Who are those people?"

Ryuko's expression darkened. "That's none of your business."

"You don't have to tell me," Sano said. "I can guess. The woman is your mistress. The boy is your son. They're your secret, aren't they?"

"Yes, damn you, and keep your voice down. I don't want the whole world to hear."

"You mean, you don't want Lady Keisho-in to hear." Sano realized the magnitude and dangerousness of the priest's secret. "Imagine what she would do if she found out that you'd not only been unfaithful to her, but that you have a child with your mistress."

"Lady Keisho-in is insanely jealous." Fear of her wrath made Ryuko's voice quiver. "She would kill me." He gestured toward his woman and son. "She would kill them, too."

"Madam Usugumo knew about them, didn't she?" Sano asked. Ryuko nodded weakly. "You confessed to her during her incense ritual. You couldn't stop yourself."

"A curse on her! She threatened to go to Lady Keisho-in unless I paid for her silence."

"Would Lady Keisho-in have believed her?" Marume said skeptically. "Would she have even been able to get an audience with Lady Keisho-in? Couldn't you have kept them apart?"

"Madam Usugumo wouldn't have had to speak with Lady Keisho-in. She could have started a rumor. Lady Keisho-in hears all the rumors, and she listens. She's always accusing me of something or other—stealing from her or making friends with people she doesn't like. I've always managed to get around her. But this—" The breath gushed out of Ryuko. "This, she would never forgive."

"So you paid Madam Usugumo," Sano said.

"Yes."

"She was bleeding you dry. You were afraid you would run out of money and she would let out your secret. So you slipped her the poisoned incense."

"No!" Ryuko swelled with the wind of his denial. "I said I didn't kill her, and I didn't."

"You said you didn't have any secrets, but you do," Sano reminded him.

"I'm telling you the truth this time. The truth is that I would have killed Usugumo if I thought I could get away with it. But it turned out that I didn't need to." Ryuko smiled, triumphant yet shamefaced. "Because somebody else did."

Sano didn't know whether to believe him. "Either you were fortunate or you're still lying."

"You can't prove I poisoned her."

"But you're still my best suspect," Sano said. Unless Reiko discovered evidence just as incriminating about Minister Ogyu. "Because now I know that you have a secret that's worth killing to hide." He pointed to the woman and child in the palanquin. "There's proof."

Priest Ryuko wiped his hand down his face, which was shiny with sweat. His ghastly expression said he'd been struck anew by the seriousness of his predicament. "I should have sent her away before our son was born, but I couldn't bear to let them go."

He gazed at his family, and Sano saw love in the eyes of this vain man who'd never appeared to care about anyone except himself. Mother and child gazed solemnly back at him with utter trust and dependence. Sano pitied them.

"I have to get them out of town to someplace where they'll be safe. Before anyone else can find out about them." Ryuko raised his clasped hands to Sano. "Please don't keep them from leaving. Please don't tell Lady Keisho-in."

Sano saw a dilemma. The mistress and son were evidence in his investigation. If he let them go, Ryuko could deny their existence. Ryuko would have no verifiable motive for the murders even if he were guilty. Without one, could Sano convince Lord Hosokawa that Ryuko was the culprit? Lord Hosokawa had already warned him against framing a scapegoat. If Ryuko were guilty and Lord Hosokawa didn't believe it, Sano would either have to frame someone else or let Lord Hosokawa join the rebel *daimyo* clans and the civil war would begin. Ryuko would surely escape justice because Lady Keisho-in and the shogun would never believe he was guilty in the absence of any reason for him to have committed the crime. They would protect him. And Sano would have let a killer go free.

"I'm begging you!" Priest Ryuko fell to his knees, heedless of the mud that soiled his cloak. He lay forward, arms extended, fingers at Sano's toes. "Have mercy!"

But Sano couldn't subject that innocent woman and child to the jealous wrath of Lady Keisho-in, even if Priest Ryuko was a murderer.

"They can go," Sano said. "I'll keep your secret for now. But if I find out that you killed Madam Usugumo and Lord Hosokawa's daughters, it will have to come out."

33

THE TRIP TO Mitake was more difficult than Reiko had anticipated. Escorted by four mounted guards, she traveled all morning. They detoured through fields, avoiding huge cracks in the road. She frequently had to get out of her palanquin so that the bearers could maneuver it through the woods. About two-thirds along the way they met a massive landslide of rocks and earth, a cliff that had fallen across the highway. Reiko had to abandon her palanquin and tell her bearers to wait for her. As she climbed over the landslide, her sandals slipped on loose dirt. She clung to Lieutenant Tanuma's hand for support. Her other escorts walked the horses up. Reiko was afraid she'd fall, afraid for the child inside her, but she'd come too far to turn back. The downward slope was gentler, and Sano needed the information she'd promised him. She wouldn't let the truth go undiscovered and have a civil war start because she was a coward.

On the other side of the landslide, Tanuma lifted Reiko onto his horse and climbed up in front of her. She clung to him and hoped the swaying and jolting wouldn't shake the baby loose.

Fewer obstacles arose the farther they traveled. By the time they turned onto the branch of the highway that led to Mitake, it seemed as if the earthquake had never happened. Dikes and canals bordered wide rice fields frosted with snow. Crows flew, black and sharp-edged as ink marks against the blue sky. Mitake consisted of a dirt road that ran past some fifty huts with mud walls and thatched roofs, surrounded by bamboo fences and small yards cluttered with farm equipment. A torii gate marked the entrance to a Shinto shrine. As Reiko and her party rode into the village, peasants lined up along the road to watch. It was probably rare for any samurai except local tax collectors to visit them, and they'd probably never seen a lady on horseback.

"We want to talk to an old woman named Kasane," Lieutenant Tanuma announced. "Who can tell us where she lives?"

The crowd shifted and murmured. A man lurched forward, pushed by his neighbors. He was short, solid, in his fifties, with a tanned, wind-burned face. Bowing hastily, he said, "She's my aunt."

Reiko and her guards followed him to a house at the edge of the village. Larger than the others, it had a stone wall with a roofed gate. The thatch was neatly trimmed, the walls coated with fresh white plaster. The nephew ushered Reiko into the house while her guards waited outside. After she removed her shoes in the entryway, he took her to a room that served as kitchen and parlor, with the hearth, cookware, hanging utensils, and cutting board at one end and a raised tatami floor at the other. He gestured for Reiko to sit on the tatami near a brazier.

"Auntie!" he called. "You have company!"

A tiny woman shuffled in through a doorway at the back of the room. Skeletally thin, bent at the waist and shoulders, her elbows sticking out at angles, she leaned on a wooden cane. She reminded Reiko of a grasshopper. Loose skin hung on her pointed face, which had caved in around her toothless mouth. Her hair was like cobwebs. She was probably closer to eighty than a hundred. She halted in front of Reiko and peered into her face. "Who are you, little girl?" Her voice was high, tremulous. Droopy lids shaded her eyes.

Reiko spoke in a loud, clear voice. "My name is Reiko. I'm the wife of Chamberlain Sano, the shogun's second-in-command."

Kasane winced. "You needn't shout. I may be almost blind, but I'm not deaf."

"I'm sorry," Reiko said, ashamed of her mistake.

Carefully lowering herself to the floor, Kasane folded her bony limbs and knelt opposite Reiko. She laid her cane at her side and called to her nephew, "Make my guest some tea."

She overrode Reiko's polite refusals. The nephew brewed and poured tea, set rice cakes on a dish, then decamped. Kasane's toothless smile brimmed with pleasure. "I never had a samurai lady come to visit me. Not even when I lived in Edo. I used to be a nursemaid in the house of a very important family there, the Ogyu clan. My young master grew up to be head of the shogun's big school."

"Yes, I know," Reiko said.

Kasane beamed proudly, then looked confused. "What was it you wanted?"

Reiko had spent much of the journey thinking about how best to approach Kasane. "I need to talk to you about Minister Ogyu."

"Well, I haven't seen him in—oh, it must be twenty years. Since I came to live here."

Ogyu had tried to cut his ties to his old nurse. Reiko was more certain than ever that Kasane had dangerous knowledge about him. Maybe he believed that if she didn't see him, she would forget it, or that any tales she told wouldn't reach the ears of anyone who mattered.

"But he still sends me letters and money," Kasane said. "Because I took care of him when he was young. He's taking care of me now that I'm old. He was always such a good, kind boy. I never married or had children, but I raised him and loved him as if he were my own."

But Reiko heard a dubious note in Kasane's wavering voice. That wasn't the real reason, and Kasane knew it. The pension Minister Ogyu had given his nurse, that must have paid for this house, was akin to the blackmail Reiko was now sure he'd paid Madam Usugumo.

"I came to see you because Minister Ogyu is a suspect in a murder that my husband is investigating," Reiko said.

"Murder?" Kasane's toothless mouth gaped. "Who was murdered?"

"A woman named Usugumo, his incense teacher. And two young ladies, her other pupils."

"I don't believe it."

"Madam Usugumo found out something about Minister Ogyu. It must be the same secret you've been keeping for him."

"Secret? I don't know any secret." Kasane's gaze wandered, belying her words.

Reiko described the bodies in the sunken house, the fatal incense game. "She blackmailed him. He poisoned her so that he wouldn't have to pay her anymore and she could never talk. I must warn you that he may kill you next."

"But I've kept quiet for twenty years!" Alarmed into forgetting to deny knowing the secret, Kasane said, "Why would he think I would tell now?"

"He's tired of paying you and waiting for you to die." Reiko was intentionally brutal. "He'd rather murder you than let nature take its course."

The nurse sat in the shambles of her illusions about the man she'd thought of as her son. She reminded Reiko of the earthquake victims sitting by their ruined homes. "I don't want to die." She clutched at Reiko. "What should I do?"

"The only way to protect yourself is to tell me the secret," Reiko said. "I'll let the whole world know. Then it won't serve any purpose for Minister Ogyu to kill you. You'll be safe."

Kasane trembled. Reiko thought of the earth quaking and splitting open the ground. The secret buried inside Kasane was erupting, shattering her as she wrestled with her conscience, her instinct for self-preservation, and her loyalty to her master. She said, "I always knew I would have to tell someday." The words shook out of her like rice on the sieves used to separate grains from husks. Resignation eased her trembling, saddened her face. "It's time." She sighed.

"My mother was a midwife in Nihonbashi. My father was a doctor. He died when I was very little." Kasane's voice took on a remote, nostalgic tone. "But my mother made a good living. She was one of the best midwives in Edo."

Reiko glanced at the window. It was past noon, and if she wanted to get home before darkness made the journey even more difficult, she must leave soon. She resisted the urge to hurry Kasane, which might change her mind about confessing.

"Very few of the babies she delivered ever died," Kasane said proudly. "Very few of the mothers, either." That was a great accomplishment, Reiko knew, considering that childbirth was fraught with hazards and many mothers and infants didn't survive. "All the rich ladies in town would call her in as soon as they knew they were expecting. She gave them potions she made from secret recipes she learned from her mother, who was also a midwife. It kept them and the babies healthy. And she learned acupuncture from my father. When the women went into labor, she used the needles to relieve the pains. The parents paid my mother very well. And they told other people about her. Samurai ladies started asking her to deliver their babies. When I was ten years old, she started taking me to the births. I'll never forget the first time I saw a child born." Awe illuminated her old face. "Out of all the blood and suffering, a miracle."

Reiko smiled. Truer words she'd never heard.

"At first I helped my mother with simple things, like boiling water and laying out her tools and cleaning up afterward. As I got older, she taught me her trade. How to make the potions. How to turn a baby that was coming out feet first. How to sew up tears. How to stop bleeding and cure fevers. She died when I was twenty." Sadness tinged Kasane's voice. "By then I was almost as good a midwife as she'd been. It was me that everybody called to deliver babies. I never got around to marrying, but I didn't mind. It was as if I was put on earth to be a midwife. And one day I was called to the Ogyu house."

At last she was getting to the meat of her story. Reiko's impatience eased.

"Lady Ogyu—my master's mother—was pregnant," Kasane said. "She'd already had four miscarriages and two stillborns. She begged me to help her bear a live child. She was desperate. I promised to do my best. But some women aren't meant to have children. When she went into labor, I prayed as hard as she did. I'd never lost a baby yet, and it was my worst fear."

Reiko imagined the scene—the pregnant woman convulsing on the bed, the midwife holding her hands and urging her to push, both hoping for the miracle that neither expected.

"The gods must have heard us," Kasane said. "The baby was born alive. It was the last one I ever delivered. It was a healthy, perfect little girl." Her expression signaled a deep, incongruous guilt. "So now you know."

"That's the secret? That Minister Ogyu has an older sister?" Reiko couldn't imagine why this fact would be worth killing to hide.

"It wasn't his sister," Kasane said. "He was his parents' only child."

"What?" Reiko was thoroughly confused. "You just said his mother gave birth to a—"

"Listen and you'll understand." The sudden sharpness of Kasane's voice silenced Reiko. "When Lady Ogyu saw that she had a daughter instead of a son, she was very upset. She cried so loud that her husband came to see what was the matter. When he saw the baby girl, he was disappointed. He told me to take her into the next room. I washed her while I listened to him trying to comfort Lady Ogyu. She said, 'I'll never be able to have another baby! This was my only chance, and I've let you down!'

"After a while, she got quiet. I wrapped up the baby and went to listen at the door." Kasane craned her neck. Her arms curved around the shape of the infant. "Lady Ogyu said, 'The baby doesn't have to be a girl. We can raise it as a boy. To be your son. Your heir.'"

Now Reiko understood. Now shock hit her so hard that she fell forward. She caught herself with her hands. Palms splayed on the floor, mouth open, she stared.

The baby wasn't Minister Ogyu's sister; it was *him*.

That was his secret: He'd been born female.

Never would Reiko have guessed. She'd thought his secret would turn out to be embezzlement, treason, or even murder, the usual vices. Instead, it was a simple fact of nature, a circumstance beyond his control.

"How could he and his parents get away with it?" Reiko exclaimed, even though they obviously had. In retrospect, she saw the signs she'd missed: Minster Ogyu's soft, pudgy figure; his voice that sounded falsely deep; his face that was unnaturally smooth except for those few whiskers—all had hinted at his true sex. But such a deception was unheard of. Minister Ogyu had not only fooled everyone into believing he was male; he'd attained a coveted position in the government.

"That's what Master Ogyu asked his wife. She said, 'We'll say I gave birth to a boy. Nobody knows differently except us.' He said, 'Very well.' Then the baby started to cry. They looked up and saw me."

The scene was vivid in Reiko's mind: The woman on the blood-stained bed, plotting with her husband; the shocked midwife standing in the doorway holding the baby. "You were the only witness to the baby's birth."

"They asked me to stay and be the baby's nursemaid. They offered me a lot of money, and something I didn't know I wanted until then." Kasane smiled, reliving the surprise she'd felt. "The chance to bring up a child instead of walking away after I'd delivered it. So I stayed."

Reiko could still hardly believe what she'd heard. "But why would they go to such lengths? Couldn't Minister Ogyu's father have just adopted a boy?" That was the custom for men who lacked male offspring. The shogun himself would follow it unless he fathered a son, or as soon as he gave up his hope that it was possible. An adopted heir had all the rights and status of a sired one. "Or had one by a concubine?"

"Lady Ogyu didn't want him to," Kasane said. "She wanted to be the mother of his heir. She couldn't stand the thought of having to treat another woman's child as the son of the family. And her will was stronger than her husband's. He did what she wanted."

"But how could they have turned a girl into a boy?" It seemed impossible. Since birth, Masahiro had been so masculine, and Akiko so feminine, that Reiko couldn't have imagined trying to switch their sexes.

"It was hard," Kasane admitted. "Especially for my poor young master. His parents gave him medicine made from goat weed and *dong quai* to make him masculine and grow whiskers. They were always after him to eat more and get bigger. To talk and act like a boy. To learn everything he would need to know as a man. He had terrible headaches." She sighed regretfully. "I nursed him as best I could, but not even my potions could take away the pain."

Reiko couldn't entirely pity Minister Ogyu. He'd reaped benefits that most women would never have—an education, financial independence, an outlet for his talents, freedom. "Didn't anyone notice he was different from other boys?"

"My young master was a good, dutiful child. He worked hard at it," Kasane said. Reiko belatedly noticed that she always referred to Ogyu with male pronouns. She had completely accepted him as a boy. Reiko herself couldn't help thinking of him as male, even now that she knew better. "He was smart, too. Good at his lessons. And his parents kept him away from people who might find him out. Like other children. No martial arts practice. And they hired tutors who had their heads up in the clouds, who didn't notice they were teaching a girl."

Minister Ogyu would have made a good actor, Reiko thought. Although fooling the shogun was no great feat, Ogyu had tricked countless smarter, more observant men, including Sano. But there was one person he had taken into his confidence.

"His wife knows," Reiko said, remembering the conversation she'd overheard between Minister and Lady Ogyu.

"I wondered what would happen when it was time for him to marry. Then I heard he picked a plain, timid girl. I suppose she didn't have the nerve to complain to somebody."

"They have two children. He couldn't have fathered them. Where did they come from?"

Kasane shook her head, as perplexed as Reiko. "Having children helped him pretend he was a man. Nobody ever guessed he wasn't."

How fortunate for him, Reiko thought. "If his secret became public, there would be serious consequences." The daughter of a magistrate, Reiko knew there weren't any laws against women posing as men; the problem had never arisen. But the government wouldn't let Minister Ogyu's deception go unpunished. "At best, he would be stripped of his position and all his rights as a man, including marriage with a woman." Lady Ogyu would lose her husband and her status as a wife, her children their legitimacy. "At worst, he would be put to death for fraud against the shogun. So would his wife, as an accomplice in the crime. And no matter what, he would be the center of a scandal, the butt of jokes."

For the proud samurai into which Minister Ogyu had fashioned himself, the humiliation would be worse than death.

Reiko knew that his was a secret imminently worth killing for. Every intuition told her that Minister Ogyu had murdered Madam Usugumo. She didn't need physical proof. She didn't need to wait for news that Priest Ryuko was innocent. She would stake her life on the fact that Minister Ogyu hadn't been willing to risk the chance that Madam Usugumo would talk after he spent his entire fortune on paying her blackmail. He had poisoned the incense that Madam Usugumo used in her last game.

"He was so desperate that he didn't care whether he killed her pupils, too." Reiko was appalled by his indifference to the side effects of his crime. "Lord Hosokawa's daughters were just accidental casualties."

"What's going to happen to him?" Kasane asked anxiously. It was clear that she still cared about him in spite of how he and his family had used her. Her face was woeful with her shame that she'd betrayed his trust. "And his family?"

"That's for my husband to decide," Reiko said.

There came the sound of a door opening at the back of the house. A cold draft swept into the room. "Who's there?" Kasane called.

34

AFTER SANO FINISHED with Priest Ryuko, he was so shaky that he feared he would faint in the saddle as he and his troops rode through town. His head pounded like a drum, the stitches on his scalp burned, his back hurt, and dizzy spells raised cold sweat on his body. He dug in his waist pouch and removed a small black opium pill, which he swallowed dry.

"Let's go back to Madam Usugumo's house," Sano told his troops.

"Why?" asked Marume.

"Just a hunch." In truth, Sano wanted to look for clues that Hirata had missed.

By the time they arrived in Usugumo's neighborhood, the opium had taken effect. The pain had ebbed; drowsiness softened the edges of the world around Sano. He saw a big, new pile of debris by the crack that had swallowed up the house. A man was pawing through the pile.

"Where did this come from?" Marume asked.

Sano peered into the crack. A sinister chill raised bumps on his skin. The crack was empty, as clean as if it had been swept out. "From in there, apparently."

Marume shook his head, nonplussed. "How did all that get up here?"

"That's a good question," Sano said.

The scavenger said, "Greetings, Honorable Chamberlain."

It was Mizutani, the incense master. His coat was covered with dust from his digging. He smacked his loose-fleshed hands together to clean them. With his soft, droopy face perspiring, he looked more like a melting candle than ever. He smelled of incense and sweat.

"What are you doing?" Sano asked.

"Uh, just poking around." Embarrassment reddened Mizutani's cheeks. He must have been looking for something he could steal from the dead woman who'd misused him. "Isn't it strange? It's as if the house climbed out of the hole."

"It is," Sano said. "Do you know when it happened?"

"I found it like this today."

Sano felt a disturbing suspicion. "Did anyone see what happened?"

"Not that I know of."

Between now and the time when he'd first seen the house, Sano had sent Hirata back to it to search for evidence. Had Hirata somehow managed to levitate the house's remains from the hole? If so, why hadn't he told Sano? Sano recalled that when Hirata had brought Madam Usugumo's book, he'd behaved oddly. Had Hirata not wanted to confess that something wrong had happened here? Sano chewed the inside of his cheek. Eventually, he must extract the truths that Hirata seemed determined to conceal.

"Well, I guess I'll be going." Mizutani backed away.

"Wait," Sano said. "I want to talk to you some more."

"About the murders?" Mizutani halted, reluctant and morose. "I said I didn't poison Madam Usugumo and her pupils. I wish you would believe me."

"I actually do," Sano said. "But I'm hoping you can answer some new questions that have come up since we last met."

Mizutani cheered up. "Ask me anything you like."

Between the headache, the drowsiness, and the upset stomach, Sano was having difficulty thinking. He managed to recall one topic he wanted to broach with Mizutani. "You told me that Madam Usugumo stole your pupils. Was one of them Priest Ryuko?"

"Priest Ryuko? *He* was her pupil? No. I've never even met him." Mizutani looked envious of his enemy, then curious. "What does Priest Ryuko have to do with the murders? Is he a suspect?"

Sano ignored the question. "What about Minister Ogyu from the Confucian academy? Did Madam Usugumo steal him from you?"

"Yes, as a matter of fact. Him and Lady Ogyu."

Sano felt the pulse-quickening excitement that always accompanied an important clue. He frowned as his drugged mind struggled to figure out why it was important. Through the opium fog he saw a connection between the two phases of his investigation—the phase when his suspects had been limited to Mizutani, the apprentice, and the dead women, and the phase after he'd learned about Priest Ryuko, Minister Ogyu, and the blackmail.

"Lord Hosokawa's daughters," Sano said. "Were they your pupils before they were Madam Usugumo's?"

"Them, too," Mizutani said resentfully.

"Why didn't you tell me all this before?"

"With all due respect, Honorable Chamberlain, you didn't ask."

Now Sano realized that Mizutani was the connection. Mizutani had known all the victims, plus Minister and Lady Ogyu. Lady Ogyu, as a pupil of Madam Usugumo, would have had the opportunity to sneak poisoned incense into Usugumo's supplies. And Sano remembered Reiko saying that Lady Ogyu shared her husband's secret. Lady Ogyu could have committed murder on his behalf.

"Were Minister and Lady Ogyu acquainted with Lord Hosokawa's daughters?" This seemed important to ask, although Sano couldn't grasp why.

"I don't know if he was, but she was. I give group lessons for women. They usually enjoy it. Lady Ogyu took some lessons with Lord Hosokawa's daughters. But I don't think they had much fun. The daughters were always quarreling. It was so uncomfortable, I was almost glad when they switched to Madam Usugumo." Mizutani added, "Lady Ogyu never said a word. A strange woman. I could never tell what she was thinking."

Nor could Sano fathom why the connection between Lady Ogyu and Lord Hosokawa's feuding daughters was significant, although his instincts said it was.

"Sano-*san*?" Detective Marume's image blurred in front of Sano. "What's wrong?"

Sano realized that he was scowling in an effort to concentrate, and swaying on his feet. "Nothing," he lied, then told Mizutani, "Thank you for your assistance. You can go."

"I'm taking you home," Marume said as he and Sano walked toward their horses. "It's my duty to tell you that you need to follow the doctor's orders and stay in bed."

"Not yet," Sano said. "We're going to the Yushima Seidō. I have to talk to Lady Ogyu."

35

TRAVELING BACK TO Edo, Hirata set such a fast pace that his horse staggered to a halt on the outskirts of town. He jumped down, glanced up at the sky, and cursed. The sun was rapidly descending toward the western horizon. Desperate to reach the castle before the hour of the cock, he looked around. A mounted soldier trotted in his direction. Hirata ran to the soldier, pulled him off the horse, leaped on, and galloped away. He crouched low in the saddle; the horse's hooves pounded the earth; Edo's blighted landscape streamed past him. When the horse gave out in the *daimyo* district, Hirata leaped from the saddle and ran. Outside the castle, a long line of samurai waited at the gate. Hirata raced to the head of the line.

"This is an emergency," he told the sentries.

They let him in. He hurried upward through the walled passages, veering around pedestrians, detouring around crumbled pavement. Half-way up the hill, porters carrying wooden beams blocked the path. On their left, the hill rose steeply to the next level of the castle. Hirata scaled the slope, grabbing at trees and shrubs. He climbed a broken wall and jumped down into another passage. Running past mounted patrol guards, he began to tire. Not even mystical powers could keep his body moving so fast indefinitely. By the time Hirata entered the palace gate, his leg ached from the old wound. He limped around the ruins of the palace. Reaching the guesthouse, he fell to his hands and knees. Sweat poured down his face. Panting, Hirata crawled.

Temple bells began tolling the hour of the cock.

* * *

SEATED ON THE dais inside his chamber, the shogun announced, "It's time for my exercise." He held out his hand to Masahiro, who pulled him to his feet.

"Fetch His Excellency's outdoor clothes," Masahiro told the other pages.

The pages glowered at him; they didn't like him giving them orders, but they obeyed. The shogun had granted him authority to tell everyone what to do. The pages dressed the shogun in the mounds of clothes he wore when he went for the brief walk his doctor had recommended. The shogun leaned heavily on Masahiro as they strolled around the garden, where dark green pines, leafless cherry trees, and frozen flower beds circled a pond with a bridge to a little pavilion. The shogun sniffled. Masahiro turned to him. Was he catching a cold? Everyone in Edo Castle feared he would take ill and die. Then Masahiro saw tears on the shogun's cheek.

"What's the matter, Your Excellency?" Masahiro asked.

"Ahh, I'm so unhappy." The shogun sobbed.

"Why?" Masahiro was puzzled. The shogun had everything a person could want.

"Because I feel so lost," the shogun said. "Life seems like a, ahh, path through darkness and confusion and danger. I don't know which way to turn. And I'm all alone."

This was Masahiro's first inkling that power and wealth didn't guarantee happiness. "But you're not alone. You're always surrounded by people."

"That's part of my problem!" The shogun turned to Masahiro. His eyes and nose were red from weeping. "They're so smart, and so, ahh, sure of themselves. They know what to do."

"But that's good, isn't it?" Masahiro said, mystified. "They can help you figure things out. You don't have to do it by yourself."

"But I wish I could!" the shogun exclaimed. "I wish I were like my ancestor, Tokugawa Ieyasu, who defeated his enemies on the battlefield and founded the regime. He didn't need anyone to tell him what to do or think. The cosmos would never think *he* was a poor ruler and send an earthquake to warn *him*!"

Masahiro was amazed. He'd thought the shogun liked being dependent and idle. Maybe that was one of the many things the earthquake had changed.

"But I'm too weak and stupid and useless," the shogun said, wiping his tears on his sleeve. "And everybody thinks so."

"No, they don't," Masahiro hastened to lie. "They respect you."

"Only because they're afraid that if they don't, they'll be put to death! I know! I've seen them sneer and roll their eyes when they think I'm not looking."

Masahiro had thought the shogun was too dense to notice. He didn't know what to say.

"And I deserve it." Dissolving into sobs, the shogun leaned more heavily on Masahiro. "Ahh, how I wish I could be different! But it's too late. I've been a fool all my life. I'll be one until the day I die!"

Masahiro didn't know how to console the shogun. He thought about fetching help, but the shogun wouldn't want anyone else to see him in this condition. And Masahiro felt protective toward his lord. He searched his brain for words.

"It's not too late. As long as we're alive, there's a chance to do the things that are important." That was what his father had once told Masahiro when he was little, when he'd complained that he wanted to be a great sword-fighter and a great archer but he didn't have enough time to practice both martial arts. "If you really want to change, you can."

The shogun regarded Masahiro with eager hope. "Do you really think so?"

"Yes." Masahiro believed his father.

"But how do I become a great samurai like Tokugawa Ieyasu?"

That was an easy question. "You must study the Way of the Warrior." Masahiro had had its principles drilled into him, by his tutors and his parents, ever since he could remember. "You must apply it to everything you do."

"Yes! I will!" Enthusiasm cheered up the shogun. Then his brow wrinkled. "But I'm afraid that people won't like it if I start, ahh, making decisions and taking actions on my own."

They wouldn't, Masahiro thought. The shogun's men enjoyed running the government themselves. But he said, "You're the dictator. It's your right."

"But I'm afraid I'll make mistakes."

Again Masahiro quoted his father: "'Mistakes are our best teachers.'"

The shogun vacillated. "People will disapprove. They won't say so, but I'll be able to tell. I don't think I can bear it."

"If you're doing what you believe is right and honorable, then no one else's opinion matters. Don't be afraid to stand up for yourself." Masahiro had never exactly heard these things said at home, but he had watched his father—and his mother—act accordingly.

"Ahh, you are so wise so young." The shogun beamed affectionately at Masahiro, patting his arm. "I'm so glad I have you to talk to. I feel much better now."

As they circled the garden arm in arm, a dark, crooked shadow fell across their path.

USING THE LAST of his strength, Hirata crawled into the garden behind the guesthouse. Cramps shot pain through every muscle as his veins overflowed with the poisons from burning so much energy during his mad rush. He gasped as he inched along the ground. After such intense exertion, even the strongest, most adept mystic needed to rest. Hirata fought the tide of exhaustion. Pulling himself along, hand then knee, hand then knee, he cleared the trees that bordered the garden. Beyond the pavilion, through the sweat that dripped into his eyes, he saw the shogun strolling with Masahiro. He heard their entire conversation.

He had only an instant to be surprised that while he'd been gone, Masahiro had gained the trust of the shogun. Panic blasted through him. His lord and his master's son were in the scene that the ghost had ordered him to engineer. This couldn't be good. Hirata opened his mouth to call out, to warn them to leave, but he couldn't catch enough breath. Masahiro spied him and frowned, obviously wondering why Hirata was on the ground. Now Hirata saw Ienobu hobbling toward Masahiro and the shogun. Ienobu had shown up promptly at the place where Hirata's letter had lured him. Hirata could tell that Ienobu had overheard the conversation, too. He was so angry that his face was crimson.

Realization struck Hirata: The ghost wanted Ienobu to witness the scene between the shogun and Masahiro.

"Stop!" Hirata called out to Ienobu. His voice was a barely audible wheeze.

Ienobu hunched in front of Masahiro and the shogun. Startled, they paused. Ienobu demanded, "What's going on?"

The shogun shrank from his nephew's angry tone. "We were, ahh, having a little talk."

"So I see." Ienobu turned on Masahiro. "What in hell do you think you're doing?"

Hirata wanted to rush over and put himself between Masahiro and Ienobu, but cramps immobilized him. Masahiro spoke up bravely: "I'm giving His Excellency advice."

Ienobu's eyes bulged like those of a carp dunked in boiling water. "I know. I heard you." His voice trembled with rage. "How dare you presume to tell my uncle what to do? You're just a child!"

"His Excellency asked." Masahiro squared his shoulders, held his head high. "It was my duty to answer."

"Don't quote Bushido to me, you little upstart," Ienobu retorted.

"Don't speak to Masahiro that way," the shogun piped up timidly. "Yes, he's a child, but I, ahh, respect his judgment."

"Honorable Uncle, you should have consulted me before giving this boy such great responsibility." Ienobu's ominous tone said he realized how much power Masahiro had gained and he didn't intend for it to continue. He didn't want the shogun thinking for himself instead of meekly allowing Ienobu to manipulate him into naming Ienobu as his heir. "What he's telling you is nonsense. I'll find you a more suitable head of chambers." Ienobu turned to Masahiro.

"You're dismissed. Leave us."

Masahiro said to the shogun, "I'll leave if Your Excellency wants me to."

"I don't want anybody but Masahiro," the shogun said in a stronger voice. "And if you keep trying to tell me what to do, Nephew, I will dismiss *you*."

Shaking with impotent rage, Ienobu glared at Masahiro. "I won't forget this." He turned on his heel and shuffled out of the garden. Masahiro looked stunned. The shogun beamed, proud of his own nerve, as he and Masahiro went inside the guesthouse. Hirata lay on the ground, tortured by cramps, horrified by what had happened.

His master's son had just made an enemy of Ienobu, who was first in line for the succession. Hirata was to blame, no matter that he hadn't anticipated it and had never intended to jeopardize Masahiro. Ignorance didn't excuse him. He had put the secret society ahead of his duty to protect Sano and Sano's kin. Now, after learning the terrible truth about Tahara, Kitano, and Deguchi and witnessing the dangerous consequences of his actions, he finally realized what a mistake he'd made.

Hirata pushed up his sleeve and looked at his arm. The ghost's message was gone.

36

REIKO LISTENED TO the floor in the old nurse's house groan under stealthy footsteps. Uneasy, she rose and backed toward the wall, away from the passage that led further into the house's interior. "There's someone in the house," she whispered.

"Nephew, is that you?" Kasane called.

Six samurai marched into the room. The air filled with the raw, animal odor of their horses, the warmth of their bodies. Reiko put her hand over her mouth to stifle a gasp. Were these *rōnin* bandits, come to loot the village? They didn't notice her; she was outside their line of sight. They loomed over Kasane, who blinked in surprise.

Kasane smiled a toothless, uncertain smile. "Young master?"

Reiko was stunned. The man Kasane had addressed was Minister Ogyu. Reiko recognized the short, pudgy figure and smooth face she'd glimpsed at the Confucian academy. His jaws were clenched, as if with strong emotion he was trying to contain.

"I'd know you anywhere, but dear me, how long it's been since I last saw you." Kasane's voice quavered with guilt because she had just betrayed him. "What brings you here?"

His five comrades waited silently. They had the hard, brutish look of bodyguards. Reiko heard Ogyu's breath hiss in and out through his teeth. Alarm filled her as she realized what he was working up the courage to do.

He drew his sword with the clumsiness of someone unaccustomed to handling weapons. Reiko's prediction, fabricated to convince Kasane to reveal his secret, had come true. He'd come to silence the other woman who knew his secret.

He lashed at Kasane. Reiko screamed, "No!" and lunged to restrain him. She was too late. His blade sliced Kasane across the throat.

The old nurse gazed blankly up at him. The gash in her neck splattered Reiko, Minister Ogyu, and the walls. Her mouth overflowed with blood. She crumpled into a heap of bones.

Reiko fell back, horrified by the sudden violence and her failure to save Kasane. Minister Ogyu groaned; his throat muscles jerked. He turned to Reiko. His full lips were white, his complexion greenish. He looked as shocked to see her as she'd been to see him. He frowned, trying to place her. Recognition filled his eyes with dismay.

"Chamberlain Sano's wife." His voice was higher than Reiko remembered. "You came to see my wife. You eavesdropped on us. That's how you found out about Kasane."

Reiko backed toward the door. Minister Ogyu advanced on her; his men blocked her way. His hand grasped the blood-smeared sword. "What did she tell you?" he asked.

"Nothing." Reiko feigned innocence. He'd already killed four women; he wouldn't hesitate to kill her. She could easily defeat him in a battle, but not his men. Terrified because it wasn't only she who was trapped, but also the child she carried, she screamed to her guards, "Help! Help!"

"Shut up!" Minister Ogyu ordered. His voice was so shrill, and his face so lacking virility, that Reiko couldn't believe she'd ever thought him a man. "You're lying."

"No." She heard her guards muttering outside and their footsteps hurrying. "Kasane refused to tell me anything."

The footsteps arrived at the front door, then clattered in the entryway. Minister Ogyu's five men turned in that direction and drew their swords.

"Look out!" Reiko shouted to her guards. "They're going to attack you!"

Minister Ogyu swatted her face. The blow landed hard against Reiko's jaw. As she staggered, her four guards burst in, their swords drawn. Minister Ogyu's men moved with such speed and power that their blades whistled like the wind. Reiko's guards parried frantically. Lieutenant

Tanuma blocked a strike that broke his blade in two. As he groped for his short sword, one of Minister Ogyu's men ran his blade through the lacings between the armor plates of Tanuma's tunic. Tanuma shrieked, fell, and lay still.

Although she knew she shouldn't engage in combat while she was pregnant, Reiko couldn't let her loyal guardians die while she stood idle. She drew the dagger strapped to her arm under her sleeve. The battle filled the room like a caged tornado. Men sprang, pivoted, and swung. Their blades carved the air. They collided and slammed against the walls; they trampled Kasane's corpse. Reiko lashed at Minister Ogyu's guards. Her dagger glanced off armor. Through the storm of whirring blades and hurtling figures, she saw Ogyu pressed flat against the wall, his eyes squeezed shut, his lips moving in prayer.

Reiko was filled with contempt for him. Being a woman was no excuse for cowardice!

One of Minister Ogyu's men kicked Reiko's hip, as if she were a puppy he wanted out of the way. She fell on her hands and knees. Blades whistled over her. Crawling on tatami slick with blood, she slashed at the men's legs. Someone stomped on her hand until she let go of her dagger. He seized her waist and lifted her. As she struggled, he twisted her arms and pinned them behind her back. Suddenly the battle was over.

Seven men lay motionless on the floor. Reiko was aghast to see that all four of her guards, and only three of Minister Ogyu's, were dead. The man who held her spoke to Minister Ogyu, who still stood against the wall. "What should I do with her?"

Panic skewered through Reiko. Her womb tightened as if to protect the child inside. "Let me go!" The man wrenched her arms harder. Pain choked her voice as she said, "Please!"

Minister Ogyu opened glassy eyes. When he saw all the corpses, he vomited.

"Should I kill her?" the man asked.

His muscles were like iron. Reiko couldn't break his hold on her. She said, "If you let me go, I won't tell anyone what happened."

"Don't believe her," the other man said to Minister Ogyu, who was wiping his mouth. "She'll run straight to her husband. He'll come after us with his troops and kill us."

"Not if I kill her first." The man holding Reiko tightened his grip.

Minister Ogyu raised a trembling hand. It was small, the fingers delicate—obviously a woman's, now that Reiko knew the truth about him. "Be quiet." His voice was reedy; he cleared his throat, then found its masculine register. "Let me think."

"What's there to think about? If we want to live, she has to die."

"We can't kill her," Minister Ogyu said. "If she's murdered, her husband will know I'm responsible."

"He won't. She'll disappear. We'll hide her body."

"No." Regaining command, Minister Ogyu spoke sharply. "She probably told Chamberlain Sano that she was going to visit my old nursemaid. If she disappears, this is the first place he'll look. When he comes here and finds this—" Gesturing around the room, he retched. "He'll guess what happened."

"All right, then what should we do?" Reiko's captor demanded.

Minister Ogyu's glassy eyes darted. Reiko's mind raced as she tried to think of a way to save herself and her baby. She forced her muscles to relax.

"Take everything off them that could identify them," Minister Ogyu said, pointing to Reiko's dead guards. "Destroy their faces."

"Why not just burn down the house?" asked the other man. He had jagged teeth, probably broken in fights, that gave him a savage look.

"Because that would bring out the villagers, you idiot," Reiko's captor said. "Even if they don't see us before we can run away, they might put out the fire and discover the bodies before they can burn up." His grip on Reiko loosened. She yanked one arm free, but his hand locked tight around the other.

"Now who's the idiot?" Jagged Teeth said. "You almost let her get away." Walking among Reiko's guards, he relieved them of their swords, which bore their family crests.

Reiko's captor held his sword against her throat. His free hand held both her wrists. Her breath caught. The skin on her neck contracted against the cold, blood-wet blade.

Jagged Teeth went to work on the guards' faces. Reiko averted her gaze. She told herself that the men couldn't feel the pain.

"What about her?" Reiko's captor asked.

"Find some rope, and a box big enough to hold her," Minister Ogyu told Jagged Teeth. "We're taking her with us."

Reiko's terror crystallized like ice within her. He'd decided to kill her in spite of his reluctance. He would dump her in a river or bury her in the woods. The box would be her coffin, and her child's.

"This will do." Jagged Teeth opened a wicker trunk and emptied firewood out of it.

"Listen to me." Reiko strained to speak as the chill from the blade paralyzed her throat muscles. "Your master doesn't deserve your help. He's been making fools of you."

"What are you talking about?" Her captor's fingers tightened cruelly around her wrists.

Reiko gasped in pain. "He's tricked you into thinking he's a man. But he's not. He's female. That's why he killed his nursemaid. She knew. He was afraid she would tell."

A beat of silence passed as her captor and Jagged Teeth exchanged surprised glances. Minister Ogyu stared at Reiko with naked horror, as blatant as a confession. But his men burst out laughing.

"It's true!" Reiko cried. "Have you ever seen him without his clothes? Take them off and look!"

"Some people will say anything to save their necks," Jagged Teeth said.

"Tie her up." Smiling faintly, Minister Ogyu slicked sweat from his forehead with the back of his dainty hand.

Jagged Teeth found a coil of rope. While he bound her wrists and ankles, Reiko fought desperately, but the other guard held her down. He was young, with hard eyes and a falsely winsome smile. She screamed until the men tied a kerchief around her mouth as a gag. They forced her knees up to her chest and wrapped rope around her curled body. They lifted her and dumped her into the trunk. Minister Ogyu stood over her as she keened and strained against her bonds. His face was drained of his relief that his men hadn't believed her, and crazed with desperation. Reiko agonized because her gamble had backfired. If he'd ever considered sparing her life before, he wouldn't again. He knew that she knew his secret.

"Where are we taking her?" Jagged Teeth asked. "To Saru-waka-cho?"

"Yes." Minister Ogyu closed the lid of the trunk.

37

"LADY OGYU?"

Sano listened to his voice echo across the courtyard of the Confucian academy, where he and Detective Marume stood. He heard birdsong from the trees down the hill and the beat of his head throbbing. The opium had worn off, and the pain resurged like a vanquished enemy returning to attack. Dizziness and nausea persisted. No one answered his call. He lifted the flap of the tent where he'd seen Lady Ogyu and the children. The tent, crammed with household items, was unoccupied.

Marume touched Sano's arm and put his finger to his own lips.

A child's babble was quickly silenced. It had come from across the courtyard. Sano and Marume crept around the collapsed building at the back. The building's whole roof had slid onto the ground. About half of the roof had caved in. Sano and Marume peered between the beams of the other half, exposed where tiles had fallen off. Underneath, Lady Ogyu and her children cowered like animals in a cave. She held her hands over the boy's and girl's mouths to keep them quiet.

"We're not going to hurt you," Sano said gently. "We just want to talk. Come out."

Lady Ogyu buried her face against the little girl's head, as if by refusing to look at Sano she could make him vanish. She obviously knew that he was a danger to her family. Sano noticed that the boards that sealed the gable on the end of the roof had been pried loose. He squeezed through the narrow gap. The roof's sides slanted, but the peak was high enough for him to walk under. The cold space smelled of damp earth and wood. As he moved toward Lady Ogyu, she and the children scuttled backward until they reached the caved-in section of the roof. Splintered rafters heaped with loose tiles kept them from retreating farther. Lady Ogyu aimed a desperate, pleading gaze past Sano, too afraid to look directly at him. "Please don't hurt my babies," she whispered.

"I won't." Sano stopped ten paces from Lady Ogyu. He crouched so that he wouldn't loom over her. Her eyes and nose were red and swollen, her face wet.

"Please don't hurt him," Lady Ogyu whispered.

"Who? Your husband?"

Nodding, Lady Ogyu clutched her children so tightly they squealed.

"Where is he?"

"He hasn't done anything wrong!"

Sano hated to take advantage of this vulnerable woman, but his first duty was to protect the regime from war and serve justice. "I believe it was your husband who poisoned Madam Usugumo and Lord Hosokawa's daughters."

Lady Ogyu cried, "No, he didn't kill them, it wasn't him, you mustn't hurt him, it was me, I did it!"

The headache, dizziness, and nausea interfered with the extra sense that helped Sano determine whether people were lying. Maybe she was trying to protect her husband. "Then tell me how you did it. But first send your children outside while we talk."

Lady Ogyu clung to them. She didn't seem to care if they heard her confess to murder. "It was my husband's idea to poison Madam Usugumo. He bought rat poison and mixed it with incense. But he couldn't go through with it. He was afraid of getting caught. So I took it upon myself. I would do anything for him!" Devotion blazed in her eyes. She reminded Sano of a mother bird, flying between its young and a predatory hawk. "I used the poison on Madam Usugumo without going near her." Her timidity gave way to pride; her downturned mouth curved in a smile. "I used those two Hosokawa girls. They were always quarreling. They hated each other."

Sano remembered Reiko mentioning the sisters' rivalry. He'd decided it had no bearing upon the murders. Now he was surprised that it apparently had.

"I could hardly stand to listen to them hissing and snapping like cats," Lady Ogyu said. "But later I was glad I knew them. They were taking lessons from Madam Usugumo. I went to see Kumoi. I told her that I could help her get back at her sister Myobu. At first she didn't believe me. She told me to mind my own business. I said, 'Do you want your sister's husband? Do you want your son? Then you should listen to me.' And she listened while I told her that if she killed her sister, she could marry the man she loved and be a mother to her own son. She was so excited, she didn't even ask me why I would help her. She just begged me to tell her what to do."

Sano felt as dazed as if he'd swallowed all his opium pills. He was that shocked to understand how the crime had happened.

"I gave Kumoi the poisoned incense," Lady Ogyu said. "I told her to take it with her when she and Myobu went for their next lesson and sneak it in with the samples for the game."

The crime had resulted from a conspiracy between two women with different goals. Lady Ogyu had wanted a blackmailer dead; Kumoi, her hated sister. Their hidden collaboration was finally revealed. Sano shook his head in astonishment. Never had he imagined that the crime was so complicated.

"Didn't you warn Kumoi that she would be poisoning herself and Madam Usugumo as well as her sister?" he asked.

"She was worried about that," Lady Ogyu said. "But I reminded her that Myobu always took the first turn during the incense games. I said that as soon as Myobu breathed the poisonous smoke, she would drop dead. I told Kumoi to pour water on the incense burner and then accuse Madam Usugumo of poisoning Myobu. Everybody would blame Madam Usugumo because the incense was hers and she was a commoner. Nobody would believe it was Kumoi."

Kumoi's ignorance, selfishness, and gullibility had been her downfall. "But you must have known that the smoke could be lethal enough to kill all three women."

"I knew," Lady Ogyu said. "I didn't care."

Never would Sano have guessed that this timid woman was one of the most ruthless criminals he'd ever met. "What did Madam Usugumo learn about your husband that's so dangerous that you would sacrifice two innocent people in order to silence her?"

Lady Ogyu responded with bewilderment. "Isn't it enough that I confessed? Can't you just punish me and let my husband keep his business private?"

"No." Sano wanted the whole story. "If you don't tell me the secret, I'll tell Lord Hosokawa that you and your husband were accomplices and he should take revenge on you both."

Worry darkened Lady Ogyu's brow. "I promised not to tell. He promised to take care of us." Her glance wandered as if she'd lost control of it. Sano glimpsed shame in her eyes. "He promised not to tell on me. He said no one would ever know."

Sano was surprised by this first hint that Minister Ogyu wasn't the only person in this couple who had a secret. "Did Madam Usugumo know something about you?"

Lady Ogyu rocked her children from side to side. She smiled tenderly at them. "It doesn't matter that he isn't their father. He loves them as much as if he were."

"You were unfaithful to your husband? You had your children by another man?" Sano didn't understand why Minister Ogyu would have paid blackmail to hide his wife's affair. "Why didn't he just divorce you?"

"That's not how it happened," Lady Ogyu said vehemently. "It was before we met." Her gaze clouded, as if with polluted memories. When she spoke, her voice was high and tiny. "He would come into my bed at night. He would lie on top of me and push himself between my legs. He would put his hand over my mouth so I wouldn't cry out. My sisters knew what was going on. They were there in the room. They must have heard." Lady Ogyu's face took on a childishly frightened cast. She was describing a rape inflicted on her when she was a girl, Sano realized. "But they pretended to be asleep. Because they were scared of him. If it wasn't me, it would be one of them. He was our brother. Our father let him do whatever he wanted."

"You don't have to tell me this." Sano looked at her children. They watched her, their faces blank. He didn't want them listening even if they were too young to understand. He also doubted that the story had any bearing on the blackmail. Incest was common; so was sex between adults and children. Sano considered both detestable, but neither was against the law; society usually looked the other way. Had Madam Usugumo revealed this secret, the rapist wouldn't have been punished, and neither Lady Ogyu's reputation nor her husband's would have suffered. Minister Ogyu would have realized that.

Lady Ogyu said, as if she were too immersed in the past to hear Sano, "It went on for years. Until my mother noticed I was sick in the mornings. She took me to my father and told him I was with child. He was very angry. He hit me and called me a disgrace to the family. He didn't ask who the child's father was. I think he guessed. I didn't tell him. He never let anyone say anything bad about my brother. He decided that I should be married off right away."

That was the usual solution. But why would Minister Ogyu have wanted to cover up the fact that his wife had been pregnant when he married her? The children were legally his. Madam Usugumo couldn't have proved he wasn't their real father. And why would Lady Ogyu have killed Madam Usugumo? She was safely, respectably married to the man who'd accepted her and her children. An incense teacher spreading gossip about her might have embarrassed her, at the very worst.

"I went to one *miai* after another." Lady Ogyu's face twisted with revulsion. "I couldn't bear the men looking at me. I didn't want to be with any man. I prayed that they wouldn't want me. And they didn't. Time went by. My parents were worried that they wouldn't find me a husband soon enough. And then they introduced me to Ogyu-*san*. He agreed to marry me."

Lady Ogyu spoke in her regular, adult voice, but her face still belonged to the terrified girl she'd been. "When the wedding was over, and my husband and I were alone, I was so afraid that I hid my face and cried. My husband asked what was wrong. I didn't have the words to tell him, so I—I opened my robe."

Sano imagined the scene, the darkened bedchamber, the tearful bride revealing her swollen belly. He could see the shock on Minister Ogyu's face.

"I thought he would be angry at me for tricking him. But he wasn't," Lady Ogyu said. "He looked as if he were glad. He sat down beside me, and said, 'I'm sorry. Who did this to you?' He was so kind that I told him everything. And he said, 'It's all right.'" Gratitude filled Lady Ogyu's voice. "He promised to take care of me. He said no one would ever know that I was pregnant before we married.

"Then he frowned, but not because he was angry; he seemed to be thinking hard. He said, 'You never have to be afraid of me.' And he started to undress." Lady Ogyu sucked her breath in. "I thought he was going to, to—" She cringed. "I shut my eyes. I waited for him to climb on top of me and push himself between my legs. But he just said, 'Look at me.' He sounded as afraid as I was. I opened my eyes. And . . ."

Lady Ogyu blinked with remembered shock. "On top, he had . . ." Her hands cupped the air in front of her bosom. "And between his legs . . . nothing."

As her meaning sunk in, Sano's jaw dropped. Minister Ogyu had breasts where he shouldn't. He had no penis where he should have. That was why a woman who feared men need not fear him. That was his secret.

"Your husband is female?" If Sano hadn't already been kneeling, his astonishment would have knocked him to his knees. He was all the more shocked to remember that when he'd seen Minister Ogyu wheeling a barrow at the academy, he'd thought Ogyu was a woman. His senses had noticed what his mind hadn't.

Lady Ogyu nodded as if she thought her marriage with another woman were the most natural thing in the world. "He told me that when he was born, his parents were disappointed because he was a girl, so they decided to turn him into a boy."

Sano thought Madam Usugumo must have been thrilled when her incense ritual uncovered such rich ground for blackmail. Had she spread the story that Minister Ogyu was a woman, it would have aroused so much curiosity that the government would have eventually forced Minister Ogyu to reveal his sex. Then would come his humiliation and the loss of all his rights and privileges that depended on his being male.

"He said we were lucky that fate had brought us together," Lady Ogyu said. "I thought so, too." Sano saw how relieved she'd been that she need never again endure sexual relations with a man. "Because he's kept his promise. He's taken care of me. And the children. When they were born, he called them blessings." Sano could imagine how thankful Minister Ogyu had been, conveniently provided with an heir, assured that no one would ever question his virility. "He's been so good to us."

At the Confucian academy Sano had witnessed Minister Ogyu's love for his wife. Now he saw Lady Ogyu's eyes brim with love for her husband. Had their love, based at first on mutual need, later become physical? Maybe it had. Sex between women was as natural as sex between men.

"For a long time I thought we were safe. After his parents died, I was the only person who knew about him. Except for . . ." Terror reclaimed Lady Ogyu's expression. For the first time she looked directly at Sano. "Please, you must stop my husband!"

"Why?" Sano said, confused by her sudden change of mood. "Where is he?"

"He's gone to Mitake."

Sano recognized the name of the village where Reiko had gone to visit Minister Ogyu's old nursemaid. "For what?"

Lady Ogyu began to cry. "At first he thought that since she hasn't told yet, she never will. But this morning he changed his mind. He said that as long as there's someone who knows about him, we'll always be in danger. So he went to find Kasane. I begged him not to go, but he said it was for the best." Lady Ogyu whispered, "Kasane was his mother's midwife."

A chill crept through Sano as realization penetrated his throbbing head. The midwife knew Minister Ogyu's true sex. Minister Ogyu meant to eliminate her. Kasane was like a pebble in his shoe, whose existence he could no longer tolerate. Sano's investigation had driven him to murder.

"He hasn't hurt anyone yet! But if he's not stopped . . ." Lady Ogyu's speech disintegrated into babble.

If Minister Ogyu wasn't stopped, Kasane's blood would be on his hands even if Madam Usugumo's and Lord Hosokawa's daughters' blood wasn't.

"Marume-*san*!" Sano called. "Get one of my troops up here to guard Lady Ogyu. Hurry! We have to go to Mitake at once."

As he ran out from under the roof, Sano prayed that Reiko wouldn't be there when Minister Ogyu arrived.

38

SPECKS OF LIGHT pierced the darkness of the wicker trunk in which Reiko lay. Her muscles ached from being bent in the same position for so long. The ropes bit into her wrists and ankles. Her mouth hurt around the gag, which was soaked with saliva. She smelled the musty odor of the trunk, the salty-sweet metallic rawness of Kasane's blood, and the sour pungency of her own urine. Her robes were wet and cold; she shivered. Afraid that her body, in the throes of its panic, would expel the child from her womb, Reiko tried to calm herself with meditation techniques learned during her martial arts lessons. But her heart refused to slow its frantic pounding. Her harsh, rapid breaths were loud in the enclosed space. She forced herself not to strain against her bonds or try to scream. She must save her voice and strength for the time when— if—a chance to escape arose.

She listened to the rapid gait of the horses ridden by Minister Ogyu and his men. The trunk rocked atop the horse on which they'd tied it. The motion thumped her cheek against the trunk's coarsely woven bottom. Dogs barked. Rubble clattered under the horses' hooves. A gong clanged. Oxcart wheels rattled in the distance. She was entering the city, but she heard no voices or footsteps. The population in the area must be so reduced that three men with a woman in a trunk could travel openly, unnoticed. The earthquake had granted free rein to evil.

The procession stopped. Reiko heard thuds as the men dismounted and their feet hit the ground. This was the end of the journey. She tried to call for help, but she couldn't force her voice past the gag. Faint squeals were all she produced. The trunk jerked as the men untied the ropes that secured it on the horse. Reiko felt herself lifted down. She writhed while the men carried the trunk. It rocked, then slanted as they tramped up stairs. Reiko could tell from the quality of the sound that they had brought her inside a building. No one would see her and come to her aid. Hopelessness brought tears to her eyes.

A thud jarred her as the men set her down. Their footsteps were quiet on a padded surface. The light that pierced the wicker brightened. Hands fumbled with the trunk's latch. The lid came up. Wedged inside the trunk, Reiko couldn't move. She blinked in the sudden yellow glare of lanterns. Minister Ogyu loomed over her. He tore the gag out of her mouth.

Reiko screamed. She screamed until her voice rasped, her throat was sore, and she was gasping for breath.

"Scream all you want," Minister Ogyu said. "There's nobody to hear you except us." He moved out of her view and said, "Take her out of there."

Men lifted her and dumped her on a tatami floor. Curled within the tight coils of ropes, lying on her side, Reiko counted five pairs of armor-clad legs standing around her. Minister Ogyu must have had the other men waiting here. Reiko's heart sank lower. Even if she could untie herself, even if she had her dagger, she could never fight her way past all these men.

"Who is she?" one man asked. "What are you going to do with her?"

Reiko held her breath, anxious yet dreading to hear her fate.

Minister Ogyu said, "Come with me. I'll explain." The men's legs moved away. "You two, stay with her." As he left, he said, "Unwrap her, but leave her hands and feet tied."

The two men knelt in front of Reiko. They were the guards from Kasane's house. One drew his short sword. She gasped. He grinned. It was Jagged Teeth. He cut the ropes. The younger man, with the winsome smile and hard eyes, pulled them off Reiko. She straightened her body. Relief was immediately followed by painful spasms that shot through her stiff muscles as the blood rushed back into them. The men watched her struggle into a sitting position. Faintness and nausea washed through her; she'd been lying down for so long, and she hadn't eaten since breakfast. She looked around the room.

It was elegantly furnished with silk cushions, lacquered tables, and a mural of a river scene, but it was as cold as outdoors and, strangely, set on a wide wooden platform. A gangway extended across the space below, which was divided into compartments by a grid of wooden beams. Reiko realized that she was on stage in a theater. The compartments had once provided seating for the audience; the actors had once entered the stage via the gangway. The center of the theater was a pile of timbers and tiles open to the sky because a large section of the roof had collapsed. The light from the stage dimly illuminated railed galleries hanging off walls that leaned inward. Minister Ogyu had chosen the ruined theater as a place where he could do his evil business in complete, uninterrupted privacy.

Reiko seized her last chance to enlist allies. "If Minister Ogyu murders me, you'll be as guilty as he," she told the two men with her. "My husband will kill you."

They laughed.

"If you want to live, you should stop him," Reiko persisted even though she knew samurai didn't defy their masters to protect strangers. "And then take me back to the castle and tell my husband that Minister Ogyu killed Kasane and kidnapped me. My husband will be grateful. You won't be punished."

Winsome Smile said, "You saw what we did to your guards," and pinched her cheek so hard that her eyes watered. He was paying her back for calling his master a woman, Reiko supposed. "Keep quiet, or no more pretty little face."

Minister Ogyu returned without his other men. His plump face was closed like a fist, as if it were gripping his emotions. His eyes wouldn't meet Reiko's. "Go outside and watch for anyone coming," he told Jagged Teeth and Winsome Smile.

They left. Fear closed an icy hand around Reiko's heart. Minister Ogyu was going to kill her; he didn't want his men to see. All she could do was hope for a quick, painless death.

SUNSET FLAMED BRIEFLY as Sano and his troops galloped on horseback along the highway. Night brought a darkness so pervasive that it was as if a cosmic hand had painted fields, woods, and hills black. Stars glinted like ice chips in a sky like frozen lava. The troops wore lanterns on poles attached to their backs, but hazards loomed too abruptly into the small halo of light in which Sano's party traveled. A rider in the lead tumbled with his horse into a wide chasm. Branches on an uprooted tree knocked another man off his horse. Sano left behind troops to rescue their injured comrades. As he sped onward, his head pounded in rhythm with his horse's hooves, but he couldn't take more opium; he needed to stay alert. He peered into the blackness, hoping to see Reiko's palanquin coming toward him. His vision smeared the lights from the lanterns, whose erratic motions worsened his dizziness. He could barely remain upright.

"You don't look good," Detective Marume, beside him, said. "We should slow down."

"No." Sano gripped the reins. "We have to get to Kasane and Reiko."

Cliffs hunched like giants' shoulders over the road. The procession came to a stop at a mountainous pile of earth, a landslide. Four men stood at its base. They called to Sano's troops, who greeted them by name. Sano felt his spirits lift as he recognized the men. They were Reiko's bearers. Then he saw her palanquin resting on the ground, empty.

"Where's my wife?"

"She and her guards climbed over the landslide," said a bearer. "She told us to wait for her."

"When was this?" Sano asked.

"Three, four hours ago."

Dismay stabbed Sano. "Has anyone come by?"

"Six samurai on horseback. About an hour after Lady Reiko went. Going that way." The bearer gestured over the landslide.

"It must have been Minister Ogyu and his men." Certain that Reiko had met them and come to harm, Sano climbed off his horse and urged it up the landslide. His men followed suit. Clinging to the reins, he let the horse drag him. The lanterns flashed on boulders, chunks of clay, and tangled tree roots. Sano stumbled; his knees struck rocks. When he reached the top, he lay there for a moment, panting, while the earth pitched under him like the deck of a ship during a storm. On the way down the other side of the landslide, he lost his grip on the reins. He rolled side over side, bumping painfully, until the ground leveled.

"Are you all right?" Marume barreled down the landslide and knelt beside him.

Wincing, Sano held his head. "Put me back on my horse."

His men hoisted him up. As the procession galloped, he rested against his horse's neck. Fatigued, he drifted toward sleep. Dimly aware of movement, the cold wind, and the cadence of hoofbeats, he lost track of time. A shout from Marume jolted him alert. He raised his head to see the lights in the distance. As soon as he and his men rode into Mitake, he knew something was wrong.

Villages usually shut down at sunset, but lamps burned in the windows of the thatched huts, and peasants clustered outside the bamboo fences. They gazed toward the village's opposite end. As his procession thundered into their midst, Sano saw horror written on their faces. He urged his horse faster in the direction they'd been looking. He was first to arrive at a house with a stone wall. He jumped off his horse by the gate, which was open to reveal men loitering in a courtyard. Another man sat on an overturned bucket, his head between his knees.

Barging into the courtyard, Sano said, "What's happened?"

The men stared in surprise, then noticed that Sano and his troops, who'd followed him, were samurai. They hastily bowed. One said, "Murder." He gestured to the man seated on the bucket. "His aunt was killed."

The midwife, Sano thought. He was too late. Fighting dizziness and dread, he hurried to the house. Voices and light emanated from the open door through which he staggered. "Reiko!" he shouted.

The room beyond the entryway was full of people. The raw, meaty odor of blood nauseated Sano. The scene tilted. Regaining his sense of what was up and what was down, he saw only three people standing. Eight others lay in puddles of blood that gleamed wetly red on the tatami. Blood had also splashed the walls. In the kitchen section of the room, dishes had shattered. Smeared, bloody footprints on the floor charted a vicious battle fought. All the corpses were male except one, a tiny old woman so emaciated that her body was like crooked sticks inside her robes. Papery lids drooped over her blank eyes. Her toothless mouth overflowed with blood. Her throat was cut.

Hope welled up through Sano's horror like the sun rising on the morning after the earthquake. Reiko wasn't among the dead. Calling her, he ran, slipping in the blood, toward a doorway that led to the house's other rooms. One of the men stepped in front of Sano and said, "Excuse me, who are you?"

Sano was so distraught he could barely stammer his name and rank. "My wife. I have to find her. Get out of my way!"

"There's nobody else here." The man had a permanently suntanned face like a farmer's, but his crown was shaved, his hair in a topknot. He wore a *jitte*—an iron rod with a prong at the hilt for catching the blade of an attacker's sword, standard equipment for police He was a local *doshin*. The two men with him looked to be his civilian assistants.

"Then where is she?" Sano demanded.

"She must have been the lady that was seen riding through the village today," the *doshin* said in the satisfied tone of a police officer who'd fitted together facts of a crime. "Those dead samurai must be her guards. She came to see old Kasane, according to her nephew. He came in and found this." The *doshin* shook his head at the bloody scene. "There are reports of another group of mounted samurai in the area. They were probably *rōnin* bandits. They must have broken in here and killed Kasane and your wife's guards."

Sano didn't have time to correct the *doshin*'s impression. He had to look for Reiko. Maybe she'd managed to run away from Minister Ogyu and his troops.

Maybe they'd caught her, and her dead body was lying in a field.

Banishing the thought, Sano started toward the door. A gurgling noise stopped him. It sounded as if someone were calling his name under water. One of the *doshin*'s assistants said, "Hey, that one's alive!"

Sano crouched beside the fallen man who'd spoken. The man's armor tunic was drenched with blood. Sano was aghast to see what he'd not noticed before: The man's face had been mutilated. So had the faces of the dead men. Their noses had been cut off, their eyes, cheeks, and mouths crisscrossed with slashes. Minister Ogyu must have disfigured them in an attempt to obscure their identities.

"Who are you?" Sano grasped the man's hand.

Blood frothed around the hole that had been his nose as the man breathed. His hand squeezed Sano's. His cut lips moved in a whisper. "Tanuma."

He was Reiko's chief bodyguard. Sano said urgently, "Where is Reiko?"

"Ogyu." Tanuma's eyes were swollen shut, their lids covered with blood, leaking muddy fluid. "Took her." His pierced lungs gurgled as they sucked air. "Couldn't. Stop. Him."

"She's alive, then?" Caught between eagerness to believe it and fear of disappointment, Sano said, "Where did Ogyu take her?" He felt Tanuma's grip on his hand, and on life, weakening.

"Saru-waka-cho." Tanuma exhaled for the last time.

39

INSIDE THE THEATER, Minister Ogyu knelt at the end of the stage where Reiko sat. His soft features were set in lines of unhappy resignation. "I didn't mean for any of this to happen." His gaze fixed on a point above her head, as if he were unable to look directly at her. "Things just spun out of control."

He sounded as if eight people had died without any involvement from him! Angry words leaped into Reiko's mind, but she held her tongue, afraid to antagonize Minister Ogyu.

"Life is a path that one must walk, sometimes regardless of one's wishes. My path was determined the day I was born. I was the only child. They wanted an heir to carry on our family name and bring honor to our clan." Pride and tears glistened in Minister Ogyu's eyes. "They didn't let nature stand in their way."

This was the only admission of his true sex that he would ever make, Reiko thought. She listened while frantically trying to think of how to turn him away from this destructive path along which he was taking her.

"They never let down their discipline. 'Eat more! Get bigger! Talk deeper in your throat. Never cry! Don't be a sissy!' " His voice imitated an angry woman's. "I did everything they wanted. All the acting and pretending. Even when I thought it would kill me." A spasm disfigured the right side of Minister Ogyu's face. He groaned. "What choice did I have? According to Confucius, whose teachings I began studying as soon as I learned to read, duty to my parents was my highest duty."

Reiko remembered Sano telling her that Minister Ogyu's parents were dead. She risked a comment that might lead him to realize the error of his ways. "When your parents died, there was no need to pretend anymore. You could have stopped."

"When I was young, I used to think that when they were gone, I would go someplace far away, and live all by myself, and be however I wanted, and nobody would care." He spoke as if he hadn't heard Reiko, but his thoughts had followed the same course as hers. "But my duty to them didn't end with their deaths. One also has a duty to one's ancestors. And by the time my parents died, it was too late for me to change. I had my position at the academy. I was a married man. I had my wife and children to consider."

Anguish added to the suffering on his face. "I didn't do it only to protect myself. I did it to protect them, too."

"I understand. Madam Usugumo found you out—she was a threat to your wife and children," Reiko said. "She had to be silenced."

"She discovered my secret. I had to silence her." Again he echoed Reiko's words without seeming to hear them. "But I hadn't the courage. I gave my wife the poisoned incense. She did what I should have."

Reiko was astonished. Lady Ogyu, not her husband, had actually murdered the women at the incense game.

"But Madam Usugumo wasn't the only danger. There was Kasane." Pain screwed Minister Ogyu's right eye shut. "I couldn't risk her telling. And after what my wife had done, I had to be the one to take the next step, didn't I?" He seemed to be arguing with himself, not Reiko. "I had to do what a man, a samurai, would."

He was using Bushido to justify cutting the throat of a helpless old woman who'd loved him. Reiko despised him, but her life depended on currying his favor while guiding him to a different conclusion than he had planned.

"You did right," she said. "Everybody who knew about you is dead." *Also people who'd only been in the wrong place at the wrong time.* Tears stung Reiko's eyes as she thought of Lieutenant Tanuma and her other guards. "It's time to stop the killing."

Minister Ogyu glanced directly at her and whispered through gritted teeth. "There's still one more person. You."

"I don't know anything that I can prove," Reiko hurried to say. "It would be my word against yours. Nobody would believe me. Your guards didn't."

"You know I killed Kasane. You know I kidnapped you." Facial spasms punctuated Minister Ogyu's sentences. "You'll tell your husband."

"I'll say you didn't hurt me and I forgive you." Reiko couldn't keep her voice from stuttering with panic.

"Lord Hosokawa won't forgive me or my wife for his daughters' death."

"Lord Hosokawa doesn't matter," Reiko said, even though he could start or prevent a civil war. "It's my husband whose opinion counts. I'll convince him to pardon you."

Minister Ogyu raised his hand to dismiss her words, then massaged his temple. "Maybe he'll excuse me for what I did to you. But not for what I did to him and his little girl."

He was responsible for the bomb, Reiko realized. And he was right: Sano would never forgive someone who'd almost killed Akiko. Neither could she. Her anger toward Minister Ogyu grew into a wild, raging animal inside her, that wanted to claw out his throat.

"I didn't mean to hurt her," Minister Ogyu said. "It was an accident. I was waiting for Chamberlain Sano to come home. When I saw him, I was so intent on lighting the bomb and throwing it that I didn't notice her until it left my hand."

Reiko fought the urge to shriek, *Coward! You couldn't challenge my husband face-to-face. You hid in wait for him, and you tried to kill him and our daughter, and you call it an accident!*

"My husband will pardon you if I ask him to." Her voice shook with her effort to control her temper. "You can go on as if nothing had happened. Your wife and children will be safe."

His hopeless glance said he wished to believe her but knew her claims were absurd. "I've made up my mind. One last person. Then it can stop."

A mournful relief filled his voice. The spasms in his face ceased; the muscles unknotted. His decision had snapped the tension between good and evil inside him and brought him peace. Reiko thought she felt the child move in her, like a baby bird instinctively trying to escape from a cracking egg. Minister Ogyu rolled his shoulders as if a weight had fallen off them. His confessing to Reiko was akin to dumping his secret into her grave.

"Please have mercy!" Reiko fell forward, her bound hands clasped, and sobbed. "I'm pregnant. Please spare my child. Please let me go!"

Deaf to her cries, Minister Ogyu sat with his hands folded, his face calm; his eyes watched the door. He seemed to be waiting for something.

"IS THERE ANOTHER road to town?" Sano asked the village men who'd followed him out of Kasane's house into the cold night. There had to be, or Minister Ogyu and his men would have had to transport Reiko along the highway and been seen by her bearers waiting at the landslide.

"Yes. I'll show you," the *doshin* said.

The road was a narrow lane that skirted fields and climbed up and down forested hills. Sano and his men rode single file, slowly over rough terrain. Under normal conditions the highway would have been faster, but the back road was freer of obstacles created by the earthquake. Sano and his men reached Edo in half the time it had taken them to travel to Mitake. A temple bell tolled midnight as they came onto the main street through town.

Sano floated in a fog of pain and dizziness, fear and exhaustion. He dozed, then woke to see a rubble-strewn landscape lit by his men's lanterns and the stars and moon in the black sky. The procession had stopped.

"Is this the Saru-waka-cho theater district?" he asked.

"My sense of direction says so," Marume said, "but I don't see anything I recognize."

Neither did Sano. Where once great theaters had stood amid teahouses, restaurants, shops, and houses, now broken walls rose from deserted ruins. The homeless actors, musicians, directors, and stagehands had moved to the tent camps. Dogs howled. Windblown debris skittered. Riding through the district, Sano and his men came across signs of bygone gaiety. Atop rubble piles lay strings of crumpled red paper lanterns from the eaves of teahouses. Sano's horse trod on a broken samisen. A square wooden tower, from which drummers had once summoned theatergoers, lay in pieces. None of the buildings appeared whole or inhabited. Sano's party located the main street, which was blocked in both directions by collapsed theaters. Sano felt a growing desperation.

Where in this shambles had Minister Ogyu taken Reiko?
Was he already gone and she already dead?

MINISTER OGYU WAITED, still and detached and ominously calm. Reiko was bathed in sweat from the effort of straining against her bindings. The rope around her ankles loosened, but her wrists remained tightly secured. Minister Ogyu turned his head. She lifted her wrists and gnawed the rope; its coarse fibers abraded her mouth as she worked at the knot. Then she heard the footsteps and voices that had drawn his attention away from her. His men were returning.

Reiko hastily lowered her wrists. The four men marched down the gangway. They had another man with them, a young stranger with purple bruises that stained his cheeks, swelled his mouth, and circled his eyes. "What am I doing here?" he asked Minister Ogyu. He didn't notice Reiko. "Can I go now?"

"No. I'm not finished with you." Minister Ogyu beckoned his men.

They brought the stranger onto the stage. Ogyu's men surrounded him closely, and Reiko saw that he was as much a prisoner as herself. While Ogyu and the other men were occupied with him, she chewed at the rope around her wrists. The knot began to fray.

"But I already told you, Madam Usugumo didn't tell me anything about you," the stranger protested. "Thank you for breaking me out of jail, you saved my life, and I appreciate it, but what more do you expect me to say?"

Reiko froze in astonishment, her teeth clenched on the rope. The stranger was Korin, Madam Usugumo's apprentice. Minister Ogyu must have wanted to find out if Korin knew his secret and taken him from the jail to question him here. Apparently Korin didn't know. But why, then, had Ogyu kept him? Reiko deduced the answer. Ogyu wasn't convinced that Korin really didn't know his secret and therefore was unable to let Korin go free; but he hadn't killed Korin because he hadn't yet made the decision to resort to violence.

The young man spied Reiko. He smiled at her; his eyes twinkled roguishly. "Well, hello. Who are you?"

"She's Lady Reiko," Minister Ogyu said. "Chamberlain Sano's wife."

Reiko intuited that neither she nor Korin would survive this night.

"It's an honor to make your acquaintance." Korin bowed gallantly, then frowned, turning to Minister Ogyu. "Hey, why is she tied up?"

Reiko shouted, "Run, Korin!" Maybe she could save him, even if she couldn't save herself and her child.

He gaped in surprise, then bolted. He was quick, but his pause had cost him a critical moment. As he ran down the gangway, Minister Ogyu's men pounded close on his heels.

"Don't let him out!" Minister Ogyu said.

Reiko wriggled to the foot of the stage, rolled off, and fell into the nearest seating compartment with a bone-jarring crash. The dividers were long wooden beams, supported at intervals by wooden panels that were perpendicular to the floor. Wriggling between the panels, Reiko heard a thud on the gangway and a yell as the men tackled Korin.

Ogyu shouted, "She's getting away! Catch her!"

His men ran along the dividers. The lanterns they carried flashed light over Reiko. Angling through rows of compartments, she felt like a mouse she'd once seen in a maze at the Ryōgoku Bridge entertainment district.

"There she is!" Jagged Teeth called.

He jumped down and seized her. She writhed and fought, but two other men joined him. They boosted her up onto the gangway, carried her to the stage, and dumped her at Minister Ogyu's feet. While Reiko lay gasping, Ogyu merely glanced at her. He seemed devoid of emotion now that she was captured. Winsome Smile and another man held Korin by his arms.

"Why are you doing this?" Korin struggled and kicked. "What do you want with me? Or her?" He jerked his chin at Reiko.

"You lured her here," Minister Ogyu said.

"What?" Surprise halted Korin's struggles. "It wasn't me who brought her."

"It was you." Minister Ogyu spoke in a quiet monotone that was more frightening to Reiko than any angry threat. "Because she knows you poisoned Madam Usugumo and Lord Hosokawa's daughters."

"I didn't poison anybody!" Korin cried.

"You lured her here to kill her," Minister Ogyu said. "So that she can't tell her husband or Lord Hosokawa that you're guilty and you won't be put to death."

"I'm not guilty! I don't want to kill anyone! I don't know what you're talking about!"

Comprehension stunned Reiko. Minister Ogyu meant to settle the blame for the poisonings on Korin. He'd also solved the problem of how to eliminate her and avoid the consequences. He was going to frame Korin for her murder.

40

"MY HUSBAND WILL never believe Korin lured me to this theater and killed me," Reiko told Minister Ogyu.

"Yes, listen to her, she's right," Korin said, trying to break free of Ogyu's men. Anxiety shone in his swollen eyes. "Chamberlain Sano came to talk to me in jail. He doesn't think I poisoned those women. If he did, he'd have put me to death already."

"He'll believe it when he sees the letter," Minister Ogyu said in that same chilling monotone.

"What letter?" Korin shook his head, as if trying to waken himself from a nightmare.

Jagged Teeth walked across the stage and gave Minister Ogyu an old playbill and a stick of the charcoal that actors used for makeup. Minister Ogyu knelt, spread the playbill on the table, wrote with the charcoal stick, then and read aloud, " 'To Lady Reiko: I have information about Madam Usugumo's murder. If you want it, come to the Nakamura-za Theater alone. Don't tell anybody. Signed, Korin.' "

Reiko was amazed at his ability to make up a scenario as he went along. But his scenario had glaring faults. "My husband will never believe I would follow those instructions."

"When he finds the letter by your body, he'll have to believe it," Minister Ogyu said.

"How will he find me?" Reiko asked, incredulous. "Why would he think to look here?"

"An anonymous tip will do."

"He knows I was going to see your nurse," Reiko said. "I told him. Besides, I didn't go out alone. His guards saw me leave with my escorts. And my palanquin bearers are waiting for me at the landslide. They'll tell my husband where I was."

"Going to see my nurse was just a pretext," Minister Ogyu said. "You left your bearers and walked to the theater district."

"How will you explain away Kasane's murder?"

"I won't need to. He'll assume you never got to her house. He won't bother looking there."

"But he'll discover that my guards are missing." Reiko felt as if she were pushing against a stone that kept rolling in the wrong direction no matter what she did. Minister Ogyu seemed impervious to reason. "He'll figure it had something to do with what happened to me. He'll send out search parties. When their bodies are found, he'll know I was at Kasane's house. He'll know you followed me and took me."

"The bodies are unrecognizable. They'll be taken for bandits who broke into Kasane's house, murdered her, then fought over the loot and killed one another."

"If they did that, then who cut their faces?" Reiko said. "And where did their weapons go?"

Minister Ogyu's calm silence said he'd decided to ignore any inconsistencies in his scenario.

"Hey, excuse me, I couldn't have written that letter," Korin chimed in. "I don't know how to write."

"You hired a scribe," Minister Ogyu said.

Korin glared. "You have an answer for just about everything, don't you? Well, answer this: How are you going to make me kill her? Because I won't."

Minister Ogyu rose. "You laid in wait for her." He walked to the center of the stage and stood facing the door. "She arrived." His gaze tracked Reiko's imaginary progress down the gangway and onto the stage. "She said, 'What did you want to tell me?' And you attacked her."

"With this." Jagged Teeth held up a wooden club, a prop from a play, studded with iron spikes.

"I'm not doing it," Korin declared.

272

"But Lady Reiko suspected a trap," Minister Ogyu said. "She came alone but not unarmed." He extended his hand. Winsome Smile gave him Reiko's dagger. "She fought back. You killed her, but she wounded you so seriously that you died, too."

He advanced on Korin. Korin yelled, "Hey!" He scuffled his feet backward, but Minister Ogyu's men held him in place.

Reiko desperately worked her ankles against the rope. Her skin was raw. The loop widened. Minister Ogyu swiped at Korin. The dagger cut Korin's chest. "Stop!" Korin screamed while Minister Ogyu cut his torso, again and again. Blood trickled onto the stage. His clothes hung in tatters.

Gasping, Reiko tugged at the frayed rope around her wrists. It wouldn't break. The men released Korin. He flung up his hands, and Minister Ogyu slashed them. Screaming, he tried to run, but the men shoved him at Ogyu, who worked with deliberate concentration, as if he were cutting wood instead of flesh. The blade carved deep into Korin's thigh. He fell to his knees, clutching at the wound, from which blood spurted. His screams faded to mewling.

"Help," he whispered, collapsing on his side. He stretched a blood-drenched hand out to Reiko. His expression went slack.

Minister Ogyu carefully laid the dagger on the stage. Moving toward Reiko, he took the spiked club from Winsome Smile. His eyes were empty sockets drained of humanity. There was no use pleading with him. Reiko wriggled backward. He raised the club over his head. He swung it down.

Reiko rolled. The club bashed the stage with a resounding thud. He hauled it back for another swing. Reiko kicked at him. Her feet hit his knee. He stumbled backward. Reiko yanked her right foot out of the rope. Rising, she staggered; her muscles were stiff. One of Ogyu's men hurried to block the gangway. The others gathered behind her. Ogyu raised the club and advanced on her. His face was like a wax mask, soft but unanimated by emotion.

Caught between him and his men, Reiko ran at Minister Ogyu. He hadn't expected that; he faltered. Before he could hit her, she clasped her tied hands into a tight lump of knuckles. She lowered them to thrust them upward at his groin, but in a split instant corrected her error and swung at his chest. Her knuckles connected with soft flesh flattened by wrappings under his clothes. Minister Ogyu screamed. It was a woman's scream, shrill and piercing. He dropped the club and clutched his wounded breast.

Reiko ran past him. His men yelled and chased her. She jumped off the edge of the stage, onto the nearest divider. It was narrower than her foot. She'd seen refreshment sellers scamper nimbly along the dividers, carrying baskets of snacks, but she teetered as she ran. With her hands tied, she could hardly keep her balance. Ogyu's men ran onto the dividers, which shook under their steps. Reiko almost fell off before she reached the mounded debris in the center of the theater. As she loped over it, jutting boards tore off her shoes. Sharp roof tiles pierced her feet through her socks. The men were close behind her. Clear of the debris pile, she teetered down a divider. The back wall of the theater loomed. Her heart juddered. Where was the door?

She jumped off the divider, into a passage that extended along the back of the theater. She spied a narrow crack in the wall, at the bottom, where two panels had buckled apart. She dropped to the floor and squeezed into the crack just as the men landed in the passage. On the other side was darkness. While she wriggled through the crack, a hand grabbed her ankle. Reiko kicked and pulled. Her sock slid off in the man's hand. She was free.

Inside the theater, Minister Ogyu shouted, "Bring her back here!" Reiko heard the men racing for the door. Rising, she found herself in an alley between the theater and a row of teahouses whose walls leaned together like cards stood on end. She ran.

"WAIT." SANO HALTED his troops in the street where they were riding between houses whose shattered roofs rested atop flattened walls. "Did you hear that?"

Faint screams drifted across the night. They struck hope and dread into Sano. Here at last was a sign of life, a clue to Reiko's whereabouts but also evidence of violence in progress.

"It's coming from over there." Marume pointed in the direction of the main street.

As Sano and his men galloped through the theater district, ruins forced them to detour farther from the noise instead of closer. Sano leaped off his horse. His troops followed suit, detaching the poles from their backs, flinging the poles aside. They carried the lanterns as they and Sano and Marume ran. Vertigo tilted the street under Sano's feet. His head pounded with every step. The light from the lanterns glanced off walls that seemed to undulate. He reeled. Marume caught his arm, kept him running. The screams were louder now; they had a masculine harshness. They abruptly stopped. Sano and his men raced up an alley, lined with collapsed buildings, that joined the main street. One building had fallen across the exit. Ready to backtrack and find a clear path, Sano heard another, different scream.

It was high-pitched, a woman's.

Terror spiked through Sano like a vein of lightning. The breath rushed from his lungs in a whisper: "Reiko."

He flung himself at the wreckage and climbed. His hands gripped splintered beams; slivers pierced his fingers. He crawled over broken planks and jagged tiles that cut his knees. He and his men slid down the other side on a spill of plaster fragments. Clambering to his feet, he swayed. His men moved their lanterns in arcs, illuminating what remained of Saru-waka-cho, Edo's great dramatic arts center. All the theaters had collapsed except one, some fifty paces down the street.

"They must be in there." Clinging to the hope that Reiko was still alive, Sano signaled his men to be quiet as they all hurried toward the theater.

Six horses were tied to poles outside that supported vertical banners advertising the last play performed. But there was no sign of Minister Ogyu or his troops. The building leaned toward the street, its sides inward. Posters fallen off the upper stories lay on the ground with the lattice partitions that had once enclosed the entryway. Sano heard shouts coming from beyond the building. The doorway gaped. Flame-light glimmered from within. Drawing their swords, Sano and his men cautiously entered.

The middle of the theater's roof had fallen in. Debris covered most of the seating area. The space appeared deserted. The light came from a lantern on a stand on the stage, which was furnished like a room in a mansion. There lay a crumpled figure. Sano's heart seized. He climbed onto the gangway, ran to the figure, and knelt. A steaming red puddle of blood surrounded it. Sano touched wavy hair. He saw a familiar, bruised male face.

"That's Korin." Marume crouched beside Sano. "What's he doing here?"

Sano had no time to think about that. He felt only a fleeting relief at discovering that the corpse wasn't his wife. "Where is Reiko?"

Shouts came from outside the theater. The night echoed with the sound of running footsteps.

AS REIKO RAN, her lungs heaved rapid breaths. Her bound hands swung from side to side. It was so dark she couldn't see where she was going. Ruins hemmed her in like mountain ranges whose valleys the moonlight barely penetrated. Reflected glimmers in puddles were all she could discern of the ground.

Jagged Teeth shouted, "I hear something over there!"

Light flared at the end of the alley. Reiko dove sideways onto a debris pile. She burrowed under boards and lay, holding her breath, while Ogyu's men stampeded past her. She crawled out and ran, veering around corners. Her lungs couldn't draw enough air. Her feet were sore, frozen lumps that tripped on themselves; her knees knocked. She paused to rest and get her bearings. Which way was Edo Castle? The familiar landmarks were gone. Panting, Reiko looked up at the sky. She didn't recognize any constellations.

Footsteps pelted. Shouts came from everywhere. A man raced toward her, waving a lantern, calling, "There she is!"

Turning to flee, Reiko heard someone else yell, "We've got her!" and saw two men charging at her from the opposite direction. She ran to the next block and turned the corner. A crushed gate blocked an alley. Reiko crawled through the narrow space between the gate's portals and roof. She hobbled along the alley, which was strewn with soggy paper lanterns from fallen teahouses.

"Go around! Head her off!" Minister Ogyu's men shouted.

Reiko emerged onto the main street. Her heart was pounding so hard it felt ready to burst. Fatigue dragged her toward the ground. To her right and left, theaters had collapsed. Directly across the street was one that hadn't. In front stood six horses and Minister Ogyu. She'd ended up back where she'd started.

41

PALE SUNLIGHT FILLED the reception room in the guesthouse. The shogun sat on the dais, Masahiro behind him. Sano knelt on the shogun's left, Ienobu on his right. Sliding doors to the veranda stood open. Two days after Sano's investigation ended, the weather had turned unseasonably warm. Trees in the garden bristled with buds. Below the dais, the Council of Elders sat along one wall; along the opposite wall were General Isogai and his top army officials. Lord Hosokawa and three other *daimyo* knelt before the dais and bowed to the shogun.

"Your Excellency, please allow us to present you with a small gift," Lord Hosokawa said.

Servants carried in fifty black lacquer chests and stacked them against the back wall. They staggered under the weight of the gold coins in the chests. Sano wondered if the floor would hold it. Everyone except the shogun looked impressed by such a huge sum of cash.

"This is our contribution to repairing the damage caused by the earthquake, and a token of our loyalty to you," Lord Hosokawa said with solemn reverence.

Sano could tell that the other *daimyo* weren't pleased about bowing down to the shogun and handing over their wealth. That must have been some scene when Lord Hosokawa told them he wouldn't join their rebellion and they must help him supply the funds to shore up the Tokugawa regime.

"A million thanks." The shogun spoke casually, taking the tribute for granted. "You have, ahh, done a great service to me. Much better than some people." He shot an unfriendly glance at Sano, for being absent too often, for not catering to him enough.

Ienobu scowled at Masahiro. The elders exchanged glances of relief: They knew that paying this tribute had depleted the *daimyos'* coffers so much that they couldn't afford an insurrection. Sano sensed the elders wondering why the *daimyo* had suddenly fallen into line. General Isogai scratched his bald head. Neither they nor the shogun knew what Sano had done to earn the money the *daimyo* had donated and avert a civil war. Sano and Reiko didn't intend to tell, and only Sano and Lord Hosokawa had been present at the scene that decided the outcome of the events set in motion by a fatal incense game.

The morning after the debacle in the theater district, Sano returned to Lord Hosokawa's estate with an oxcart whose cargo was covered with a blanket. When Lord Hosokawa met him at the gate, his troops and driver waited down the street while he said, "Would you like to see who killed your daughters?" Sano dismounted and threw back the blanket. Underneath were the dead bodies of Minister and Lady Ogyu.

"There were two murderers?" Lord Hosokawa said, gazing at them with surprise and concern. "Isn't that the administrator of the Confucian academy?"

"Yes."

"Who is the woman?"

"His wife."

"You killed them?"

Sano nodded, accepting responsibility for both deaths.

"I can see what happened to Minister Ogyu." Lord Hosokawa contemplated the separation between Ogyu's bloody neck and body, then turned to Lady Ogyu. Her homely face was pale, distorted. "But what about his wife?"

"She swallowed some of the poison that she and Minister Ogyu used to kill your daughters and Madam Usugumo," Sano said.

That morning Sano had returned to the academy to find Lady Ogyu dead with her children clinging to her body. *I didn't know she was going to do it!* his distraught guard had cried. Lady Ogyu must have had a premonition that her husband wouldn't survive the night. She'd decided to die before she could be forced to reveal his secret to anyone else.

"But why did they poison my daughters?" Lord Hosokawa exclaimed.

"They didn't mean to," Sano said. "Madam Usugumo was their intended victim. She was blackmailing Minister Ogyu. I wasn't able to find out what dirt she had on him." Sano couldn't reveal the secret. Having examined Ogyu's body and confirmed that it was female, he was taking the bodies to Zōjō Temple for immediate, private cremation. If Ogyu's deception became known, the shogun would lose face and his government would become an object of ridicule. That could weaken it enough that the *daimyo* might be tempted to revive their plan to overthrow it. "But Minister and Lady Ogyu did confess to the murders." Sano couldn't let Lord Hosokawa know that the Ogyus had made unwitting tools of his daughters. That would only cause the man more pain.

Lord Hosokawa contemplated the bodies. "I should feel triumph, or at least satisfaction, knowing my daughters have been avenged." He lifted a bewildered gaze to Sano. "But I don't feel any better. How can that be?"

"Revenge brings justice," Sano said, "but it can't bring back the dead."

Lord Hosokawa nodded in sad resignation. "Still, I appreciate what you've done for me. I will keep my part of our bargain."

Now Lord Hosokawa and the other *daimyo* bowed to the shogun and the assembly. As they somberly filed out of the room, Lord Hosokawa met Sano's gaze. His expression said their business was finished. But Sano knew better. He couldn't trust Lord Hosokawa or let him get away with his extortion. He would have to do something about Lord Hosokawa sooner or later.

"Well, ahh." The shogun brushed his hands together, as if dispensing with a trivial affair. "Now I have a surprise for all of you." His eyes twinkled with mischief; he clapped his hands.

Into the room strode Yanagisawa and a young samurai. Yanagisawa surveyed the company with as much aplomb as if he'd never left it. The handsome young samurai, with his athletic build, wide face, and tilted eyes, looked vaguely familiar to Sano. A woman dressed in deep red followed the two men. She was some forty years old, still attractive. She and the young samurai carried themselves with dignity and caution. The trio mounted the dais. Yanagisawa knelt nonchalantly beside Sano. The woman knelt near them. The shogun drew the young samurai down to kneel at his right side.

"It is my pleasure to introduce my son." The shogun smiled fondly at the young samurai. "My flesh-and-blood son and heir, that I always wanted."

The assembly gasped in shock. Sano felt a wave of vertigo that wasn't from his head injury. He'd not had any dizziness, nausea, or much pain today. Elders and army officers whispered furiously among themselves. The shogun preened. Ienobu looked horrified by the youth seated between him and the shogun. In an instant he'd lost his position as heir apparent. Yanagisawa gloated.

"My son's name is Yoshisato," the shogun said.

Yoshisato kept his head high and his expression serene while the assembly stared at him. He had considerable poise for someone so young. His name reminded Sano of who he was.

"Forgive me, Your Excellency," Sano said, "but there must be some mistake. Yoshisato isn't your son. He's Yanagisawa's."

The other men murmured, disbelieving and amazed. Yanagisawa was passing his son off as the shogun's! He had plopped Yoshisato into first place in line for the succession, to guarantee that he would be the power behind the next dictator.

The shogun regarded Sano with condescension. "Yoshisato has been raised as Yanagisawa's son, but it was a, ahh, subterfuge." He looked to Yanagisawa.

Yanagisawa smiled at the stir that he and his son had created. He indicated the woman, who sat rigidly. "This is Lady Someko. She was once His Excellency's concubine. Eighteen years ago, she conceived a child. But she didn't tell His Excellency, because it would have put him in grave peril. The court astronomer had predicted that a son would be born to His Excellency, but the stars said that unless the son was hidden away right after his birth, His Excellency would be killed by an earthquake that would strike Edo in eighteen years."

Sano leaned forward as astonishment caved in his chest.

"The astronomer brought me the prediction," Yanagisawa continued. "I gave orders that any pregnancies in the palace women's quarters were to be reported to me and no one else. When Lady Someko found herself with child, I took her into my home, and when her son was born, I gave him my name. We kept Yoshisato's real parentage a secret, even from him, for seventeen years. But now the earthquake has come and gone. The danger to His Excellency has passed. Now the truth can be told."

Never in his life had Sano heard such utter tripe!

Yanagisawa swept a grand gesture toward the young samurai. "Behold Tokugawa Yoshisato, His Excellency's one true son and heir."

The shogun stroked Yoshisato's arm. "The gods have granted my dearest wish at last!"

The elders and General Isogai looked as outraged as Sano was. Even Kato, Yanagisawa's crony, shook his head. Ienobu looked ready to explode. "But, Honorable Uncle," he began.

"But what?" The shogun fixed Ienobu with such a baleful stare that Ienobu subsided. The other men didn't dare object, even though they suspected Yanagisawa was Yoshisato's real father. The shogun accepted Yoshisato as his son. That was that.

WHEN SANO LEFT the guesthouse, Yanagisawa caught up with him and said, "What do you think of the shogun's new son?"

"He's astonishing," Sano said, "but not nearly as much so as his father."

Yanagisawa chuckled; he knew Sano wasn't talking about the shogun. His humor turned to menace. "My adopted son will inherit the dictatorship, which will make me as good as the father of the next shogun. But I won't wait that long to deal with you." His eyes blazed through tears. Today's coup hadn't assuaged his grief for Yoritomo or his rage at Sano. "Your days are numbered." He looked past Sano. "And so are your son's."

Sano turned and saw Masahiro in the garden with Ienobu. Ienobu was jabbing his finger at Masahiro, scolding him in a loud, raspy whisper. Yanagisawa strode back into the guesthouse. Before Sano could join Masahiro and Ienobu and find out what was going on, he saw Priest Ryuko and the shogun's mother walking toward him.

"Chamberlain Sano!" Lady Keisho-in was all dimples. "Have you met my new grandson? Isn't he wonderful?"

"Yes, Your Highness," Sano said, bowing.

"I'm so excited. All these years I've prayed for a grandson, and this is a dream come true!" She turned to Priest Ryuko. "My dearest love, you can be his step-grandfather."

Priest Ryuko smiled down at her, nodded, and said, "Suppose you go inside and give Yoshisato my regards while I speak to Chamberlain Sano." After Lady Keisho-in left, he said, "My sources tell me that you discovered it was Minister Ogyu and his wife who poisoned those women, and they're both dead."

"Your sources are well informed," Sano said.

Ryuko spoke in a lowered voice. "Regarding what you discovered about me—don't try to use it against me. I've told Lady Keisho-in that there's a rumor that I fathered a child on another woman. I've assured her that the rumor is false, and she believes me." He added, "You just saw how high in her favor I am. And she's high in His Excellency's. All is well within the upper stratus of the Tokugawa court."

"What about the astronomer's proclamation that the cosmos is displeased with an important person in his regime who's to blame for the earthquake?" Sano asked.

Ryuko waved his hand, as if brushing away a fly. "That's old news. All the shogun cares about is the astronomer's latest proclamation, the one about Yoshisato."

Yanagisawa must have bribed the court astronomer to back his hoax, Sano thought.

"Lady Keisho-in is safe, and so am I." Ryuko added with a sly smile, "Probably safer than you, Chamberlain Sano."

YANAGISAWA MET YOSHISATO inside the guesthouse. "We need to talk," Yanagisawa said, glancing up and down the corridor to make sure no one was listening.

"I don't think so." Yoshisato tried to brush past Yanagisawa.

Yanagisawa caught his son's arm. "I have to coach you on how to prevent the shogun from being manipulated by our enemies."

"You've already drummed that into my head," Yoshisato retorted. "How could I forget? Do you think I'm stupid?"

"What's the matter?" Yanagisawa asked, surprised by his son's anger.

"Nothing. Your scheme worked. You've positioned me to rule Japan after the shogun dies. Everything is fine."

"I also saved your life," Yanagisawa reminded him. "Now that the shogun has accepted you as his son, the order for you to be convicted of treason has been canceled. Ienobu can't touch you. You should be grateful."

"Oh, I'm grateful." Yoshisato said the last word as if it tasted bad.

"Grateful to you for disowning me, for foisting me off on the shogun. Grateful because you don't have to pretend to be my father."

Astonishment struck Yanagisawa. He'd never dreamed that Yoshisato would mind. "But it was necessary." Now he saw that Yoshisato hated him for denying their kinship. "We agreed."

"Not that I had much choice."

"You should be happy about the way things worked out," Yanagisawa said. "You'll get to be the next shogun without sleeping with the current one." The shogun drew the line at sex with the fruit of his own loins.

"Oh, yes, I'm happy." Yoshisato gave a bitter laugh. "Because now that I'm the shogun's son, I don't need you anymore." He smiled.

For the first time Yanagisawa saw himself in Yoshisato. It chilled him to the core.

SANO SPENT THE rest of the day organizing the relief mission for the provinces. By evening, the team members had been designated and provisioned, the carts and oxen assembled. The mission would leave at dawn tomorrow, accompanied by troops to guard the cash contributed by the *daimyo*. For the first time since the earthquake, Sano felt as if he'd actually accomplished something, even though so much remained to be done.

When he got home, he found Reiko propped up in bed. She was watching Akiko play with her dolls. Sano smiled at the cozy scene and greeted his family. A maid brought them a dinner of rice, soup made from dried bonito and seaweed, and pickled radish.

"Aren't you going to eat?" Sano asked Reiko as he wolfed down the food.

She sipped a cup of mint tea. "No, I feel sick to my stomach. But that's a good sign that I'm not going to lose the baby. The doctor says it should be fine."

Sano was glad but still a little angry with her. "You should have told me about the baby before I let you help me with the investigation."

"But if I had told you, then you wouldn't have let me help. We might be in the middle of a civil war now."

"I can't argue with that." Sano never could argue with his wife when she was right. Things had worked out better than he'd expected, although he regretted the deaths of Minister Ogyu's nurse and Madam Usugumo's apprentice, which Reiko had told him about. If he hadn't told Ogyu where Korin was, Ogyu couldn't have taken Korin out of jail and brought him to the theater where he'd died. Then again, if Ogyu hadn't, perhaps he'd have killed Reiko at the nurse's house and Sano couldn't have saved her. The events of that night were far from simple or clean. Sano knew that Reiko mourned for her guards, especially Lieutenant Tanuma, whose dying words had saved her life. Sano also pitied the Ogyu children, now orphans, adopted by relatives. Their parents' deaths would surely haunt them all their lives.

Akiko stacked wooden blocks, building a house. She put her dolls inside, shouted, "Boom!" then knocked down the blocks. She clapped her hands and laughed.

"I wish she wouldn't keep doing that," Reiko said.

"Maybe it comforts her to make a game of it." Sano hoped the bombing wouldn't have any permanent ill effects on Akiko. Some scars were invisible. As Reiko sipped her tea, he told her about the shogun's dramatic announcement. She sputtered tea and choked.

"The shogun has a new heir, and it's Yanagisawa's son, but he thinks Yoshisato is his!" she exclaimed. "I can't believe it!"

"Neither could I, but in retrospect, passing his son off as the shogun's seems just like Yanagisawa. This could be the biggest political upheaval of the shogun's reign."

"It's disgusting how Yanagisawa took advantage of the earthquake."

Sano thought back over the past month. "He's not the only person who has, or has tried to. There's Ienobu, who ingratiated himself with the shogun while the shogun's usual companions were either too busy or dead. There's Lord Hosokawa, who used the regime's financial problems to blackmail me into investigating the murders, and the *daimyo* who wanted to overthrow the Tokugawa regime while it was vulnerable. There's Korin, who cheated earthquake victims, not to mention the scores of merchants who are making fortunes off them. Don't forget the people who tried to get rid of Lady Keisho-in and the shogun by blaming them for the earthquake. And then there's Masahiro and his promotion."

"Masahiro deserved that promotion," Reiko protested, loath to include him in such dubious company. "He's very capable, even though he's only twelve."

"But there's no denying that he benefited from the disaster," Sano said. "There's no denying that the disaster has created opportunity."

"That's a different point of view." Reiko didn't sound convinced.

"Look around, and you'll see other examples of opportunity arising from disaster. I'm chamberlain because Yanagisawa's son Yoritomo died. Going further back, I got into the Tokugawa regime fourteen years ago because someone tried to assassinate the shogun and I saved his life."

Reiko warmed to Sano's theory. "Hirata is the top fighter in Edo because he was crippled and he studied the mystic martial arts." Suddenly stricken by revelation, she said in a hushed voice, "I'm who I am because my mother died giving birth to me."

"Does everything good have origins in something bad?" Sano mused. "Perhaps. One thing I'm sure of is that when it comes to taking advantage of the earthquake, Yanagisawa has everyone else beaten."

Apprehension clouded Reiko's eyes. "What does his coup mean for you?"

"Yanagisawa has gained a big advantage over me. If that were all, I'd predict that the two of us would continue our feud as always, with one's fortunes rising when the other's falls. But Yoshisato changes the equation. He's an unknown quantity."

"Does this mean Ienobu is out of the picture?" Reiko said.

"I wouldn't count on it," Sano said. "He has allies who are enemies of Yanagisawa and won't want Yoshisato inheriting the dictatorship. And Ienobu isn't the kind of man to accept defeat without a fight."

Masahiro came into the room, greeted his parents, and said, "Is there any food left?"

"Yes. You're in luck," Reiko said.

Sano remembered something. "What did Ienobu say to you this morning?"

Masahiro ducked his head over his rice bowl. "He said I was overstepping my station. He told me to stop giving advice to the shogun, or he would make me sorry."

"What kind of advice?" Reiko said, sounding as puzzled as Sano was.

"Just some things you and Father taught me."

"How did Ienobu know you were advising the shogun?" Sano said.

"He heard us," Masahiro said.

"Didn't I tell you to be careful?"

"I try to be. But the shogun was upset, and he asked me what to do. I had to say something. And it was during his exercise in the garden. I'd never seen Ienobu there. He doesn't like the cold. But he was there that day."

"What an unfortunate coincidence," Reiko said sympathetically.

But Sano's instincts tingled in warning. "Somehow I don't think it was a coincidence. Why did Ienobu choose that particular time to brave the cold in the garden?"

"Maybe Hirata-*san* knows," Masahiro said. "He was there, too. I saw him."

A bad feeling rippled through Sano as he thought of the house that had mysteriously risen from the chasm. He wondered if Hirata's presence at the scene wasn't a coincidence either. "Yoshisato isn't the only unknown quantity. There's something else going on."

THAT NIGHT HIRATA climbed the hills to the clearing in the forest. There he found a ritual in progress. Tahara, Kitano, and Deguchi stood chanting inside the circle of flaming oil lamps, their hands touching, around the altar. They didn't notice Hirata watching nearby. A figure hovered in the gold-flecked purple smoke from the incense burner. It was the giant warrior in the horned helmet and the old-fashioned armor, his face hidden by his helmet's visor. Fiery veins of light connected him to the men. Hirata was surprised that he could see the ghost even though he hadn't drunk the potion or breathed the smoke. Perhaps after seeing it once, he didn't need to be in a trance to see it again. Its terrifying power boomed and pulsed. He resisted the urge to run.

"Why are you troubled, my lord?" Tahara asked the ghost. "Ienobu has witnessed Masahiro's influence on the shogun. He can counteract it. Everything went just as we planned."

Fury beset Hirata. The secret society had known all along, and not deigned to tell him, that his action would put Masahiro in jeopardy!

The ghost spoke in its alien language that Hirata could now understand. "The boy is a minor threat compared to the bastard who purports to be the shogun's son." Hirata frowned, confused. Something must have happened while he'd been away from court. "The bastard must be eliminated. Nothing must stand in the way of Ienobu's becoming the next shogun."

"How will Ienobu's becoming the shogun destroy the Tokugawa regime?" Kitano asked.

"Ienobu and his allies are plotting changes in the regime," the ghost replied. "Within a generation the Tokugawa will crumble under pressure from inside and outside. And I will have my revenge for my defeat at Sekigahara."

Hirata burst into the circle of light. Tahara, Kitano, and Deguchi started. They turned toward him, their hands still touching. "What are you doing here?" Tahara said without his usual humor.

"Joining the ritual," Hirata said. "Why didn't you invite me?"

"We never told you that you would be part of every ritual." Kitano's eyes were cold.

"There's a lot you never told me," Hirata retorted. "Such as, that the spirit was an enemy of the Tokugawa. Or that its idea of 'destiny' is to destroy the regime that I serve!"

"If we'd told you, you wouldn't have joined us," Tahara pointed out. Deguchi nodded.

Their callousness fueled Hirata's rage. "I was a fool to trust you, or it." He flung out his hand toward the ghost, whose image wavered because he'd interrupted the three men's concentration. "But I won't trust you anymore..Because I've uncovered your lies.

"Ozuno wouldn't give you his magic spell book, so you tried to steal it. He fought you. That's how your face got cut up." Hirata glared at Kitano, then Deguchi. "That's why you're mute." He said to Tahara, "You didn't inherit the book. You stole it from Ozuno on your second try, after you killed him. When you lured me into your secret society, you made me a party to our teacher's murder!"

The men's dismayed faces were taut and perspiring with their effort to maintain their trance. The veins of light dimmed. The ghost's image faded.

"Then you forced me to endanger my master's son." Hirata was so angry that he could hardly speak. "All the while you were intentionally involving me in treason against the Tokugawa regime!"

"So the detective has found us out," Tahara said. "Congratulations."

Infuriated by his sarcasm, Hirata said, "Did you ever stop to wonder if I'm not the only one who's been deceived? What did the spirit promise you in exchange for meddling with politics? Mystical powers such as have never been seen? A chance to train and lead a legion of superhuman martial artists that will rule the world someday?" It was a wild guess, but the men's cagy expressions told Hirata it was correct. "How do you know that the spirit won't dump you after he's given you nothing more than a few magic tricks? Maybe you'll have sold your honor for nothing but a selfish, petty man's revenge on his dead enemy."

For the first time Tahara, Kitano, and Deguchi looked worried. The ghost's image shrank as their energy faded. "We're going through with it." Tahara sounded as though his fear of betrayal had only solidified his conviction. He looked to Kitano and Deguchi, who nodded. The ghost's image enlarged, grew clearer. "And so are you. Or Sano will die."

"No," Hirata said. "I'm ending this now." He drew his sword despite the fact that he was outnumbered by these men whose individual skills exceeded his own.

Alarm, then aggression, flared in their eyes. They must defend themselves, even if they didn't want to fight Hirata, because someone was bound to be killed, which would ruin their plans. But they didn't reach for their swords. Their outstretched hands seemed stuck together as if by magnets on their fingertips. Their jaws clenched with their effort to break free.

Sword raised, Hirata lunged at them. The veins of light crackled. He stalled in midair. The ghostly warrior glowed bright, brighter, orange-hot, then white, leaching energy out of Tahara, Deguchi, and Kitano. Blinded, Hirata had the sensation he'd experienced during his trance, of being sucked up toward the sky, then falling, accelerating, and cartwheeling. He thought, *The ghost prevented a battle because it needs us all alive.*

Consciousness briefly fled him, then returned. Hirata found himself lying on cold ground by the altar, in the gray dawn. Tahara, Kitano, Deguchi, and the ghost were gone. All that remained was Hirata's conviction that he must make a clean breast to Sano, shut down the secret society, and consign the ghost to the netherworld from which it came.

If only he knew how.

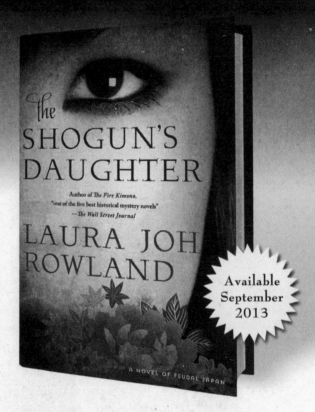

Available
September
2013

Don't miss these Laura Joh Rowland titles:

MINOTAUR
BOOKS